Praise for *The Irregular* and Gerald Seymour

'Jonas Merrick has been among the best thriller creations of the past decade . . . [Seymour's] insights into the world of crime and intelligence remain as compelling as ever, as do the staccato stabs of his prose'

The Times

'You don't read Gerald Seymour, you commit to it totally. His stories have amazing detail, yet you still fly through them'

Sun

'There are strong echoes of George Smiley in Merrick's mild and unprepossessing manner, which disguises a razor-sharp brain and considerable courage when necessary'

Financial Times

'Seymour's finger is always on the current socio-political pulse'

i News

'[Charles] Cumming is perhaps matched only by Gerald Seymour now when it comes to recounting field operations'

Sunday Times

Gerald Seymour spent fifteen years as an international television news reporter with ITN, covering Vietnam and the Middle East, and specialising in the subject of terrorism across the world. Seymour was on the streets of Londonderry on the afternoon of Bloody Sunday, and was a witness to the massacre of Israeli athletes at the Munich Olympics.

Gerald Seymour exploded onto the literary scene with the massive bestseller *Harry's Game*, which has since been picked by the *Sunday Times* as one of the 100 best thrillers written since 1945. He has been a full-time writer since 1978, and six of his novels have been filmed for television in the UK and US. *The Irregular* is his forty-first novel.

Also by Gerald Seymour

Harry's Game	The Unknown Soldier
The Glory Boys	Rat Run
Kingfisher	The Walking Dead
Red Fox	Timebomb
The Contract	The Collaborator
Archangel	The Dealer and the Dead
In Honour Bound	A Deniable Death
Field of Blood	The Outsiders
A Song in the Morning	The Corporal's Wife
At Close Quarters	Vagabond
Home Run	No Mortal Thing
Condition Black	Jericho's War
The Journeyman Tailor	A Damned Serious Business
The Fighting Man	Battle Sight Zero
The Heart of Danger	Beyond Recall
Killing Ground	The Crocodile Hunter
The Waiting Time	The Foot Soldiers
A Line in the Sand	In at the Kill
Holding the Zero	The Best Revenge
The Untouchable	A Duty of Care
Traitor's Kiss	

THE
IRREGULAR

Gerald Seymour

HODDER &
STOUGHTON

First published in Great Britain in 2026 by Hodder & Stoughton Limited
An Hachette UK company

This paperback edition published in 2026

The authorised representative in the EEA is Hachette Ireland, 8
Castlecourt Centre, Dublin 15, D15 XTP3, Ireland (email: info@hbgi.ie)

1

A CIP catalogue record for this title is available from the British Library

Paperback ISBN 978 1 399 74376 1
ebook ISBN 978 1 399 74377 8

Typeset in Plantin Light by Hewer Text UK Ltd, Edinburgh
Printed and bound in Great Britain by Clays Ltd, Elcograf S.p.A.

Hodder & Stoughton policy is to use papers that are natural, renewable
and recyclable products and made from wood grown in sustainable
forests. The logging and manufacturing processes are expected to
conform to the environmental regulations of the country of origin.

Hodder & Stoughton Limited
Carmelite House
50 Victoria Embankment
London EC4Y 0DZ

www.hodder.co.uk

PROLOGUE

The road was dry. It would have had a stone foundation, put down years ago, but it was now covered with a layer of dust, sand, crushed dirt. Under the weight he carried, his boots moved through it heavily, kicking up clouds of the bloody stuff, same as the boots of all the others in the patrol. It found its way into his eyes, ears, mouth, and up his nostrils and the only sound he made was a rasping cough as he tried to clear it from his throat. What he had swallowed seemed to taste of a mix of donkey shit and old engine oil and the stench of the caked mud in the ditch at the side of the road.

He tried to stay alert. Not easy, not in the heat. The sun had been up for long enough to burn the soles of their boots and the fabric of their uniforms, crumpled and stained, and seemed to cling to their armoured vests, roasting their chins and cheeks. Where the camouflage cream had been smeared in the half light of dawn while they were scoffing food and listening to the briefing, there were now rivers of sweat running haphazardly down their necks. They had been told by their lieutenant that the need was for aggression, 'so none of these fucking Talibs gets the mistaken idea that we are in anyway backing off from getting stuck into their territory'. The lieutenant wasn't with them now, but the sergeant was, a miserable sod, but he knew what was what in that sector of Helmand. 'Just stop thinking of fucking women, getting your end away. Just concentrate on the road, where it's been disturbed, where there's loose soil, where there is anything, fucking anything, that is not normal. Look at it, think about it fast, hit the fucking deck, and shout it to me.' The sergeant was not a man to love but was probably the best chance they had of staying alive, of getting home in one piece.

The sergeant was in front of him. "Keep fucking watching, Chopper, don't stop. Keep at it."

Which Chopper did, raking his eyes to right and left, straining into the haze to see what was ahead of him, swivelling to look behind him. He was in the middle of the patrol, where he liked to be. His general-purpose machine gun was loaded, ready to go, a belt on board and the bullets bouncing against his knee. He had, he reckoned, the best place in the patrol that stretched out on either side of the road. He had never been in an ambush, did not know how it would be, but was familiar with the thudding impact of the beast against his shoulder, and was thought to be a marksman with it, an expert.

They were heading towards a village. They had a medic with them whose rucksack was stuffed with medicines and they'd hang around while he did a bit of a surgery stint, what was called Hearts and Minds, then scarper and leave sullen and hostile faces behind them. Being in the centre of the patrol was a good place. The worst two were point man up at the front, or back marker who had to walk for three-quarters of the time with his arse facing the rest of them, like a punishment posting. Across the road, level with him, was Lofty, all five feet and four inches of him – and that might have been when he stood on tiptoe. Lofty carried his own gear, and also three extra mortar shells for the 81mm, and had four loaded belts draped over his shoulders. Chopper did the shooting and Lofty did the feeding. He also carried spare barrels in case they fired so much and so often that the bloody thing over-heated and needed replacing. Lofty was Chopper's best friend, maybe his only friend.

The name Chopper had stuck with him since he had joined the regiment as a recruit. He had been selected for the company's football team to play against the Bravo side. One of the opposition had gone off on a stretcher and another had limped to the touch-line as proof of the force of his contact, and he had been picked for the battalion side and they had played a commando squad and his tackles had been ferocious and had caused casualties. He was Kenny Harris, and he had received the Commanding Officer's personal congratulations as a lightweight silver cup was raised, and there were marines who'd have beaten the hell out of him if they'd found him. There was a guy called Ron Harris who played for Chelsea, was a hero at their ground, and he was lauded as 'Chopper' Harris for the quality of his tackling. So Delta Company of the 2nd Battalion of the Parachute Regiment created their own 'Chopper' and the name had stuck. He had done the business in Helmand against a REME team and a Logistics unit. His football marked him out and he had been given the machine gun to carry and had chosen Lofty as his feeder.

All of them in the patrol looked for signs of the bloody horrible IEDs. Improvised Explosive Devices were what sent guys home in boxes or without a limb and mutilated. There might be loose earth where a pressure plate had been inserted above an explosive charge or a buried mine. Or there might be a mass of dynamite for an anti-tank job dug in at the side of the road, linked by a command cable that was paid out a couple of hundred yards to cover where the plunger was, and there might be a gang to ambush them and put down fire once it was detonated, and they were in bad order. The patrol needed to scour both the road surface and the shit and the dust and the dirt and the ditches and – hopefully – spot what they'd put in place before the fucking thing was fired . . . They had the medical boy with them and, if they were lucky, they'd get to the village and he would do his good works. None of the men gathered would show any gratitude. And the patrol would not know which of those men was the star turn at disguising the little excavation of the dust covering the road surface, and the overgrown earth at the side and the command cable leading away, nor which was the one with keen enough eyesight to use the soldering iron on the circuit board, and who packed the explosives in a parcel of nails and screws and goat shit.

Chopper was beginning to think . . . where the fuck were they? Where were the kids? Where were the women? Where were the boys who ought to have been out in the fields, clearing out the weeds between the crop lines?

Nothing was down the road, not even a donkey. No kids, no women, no ragheads.

Chopper saw the sergeant's head as he walked from side to side, heard the hissed instruction that they keep their fucking eyes open. To his left the ground dipped away and there was no ambush cover for a couple of hundred yards and it would have been a long run for a wire. To his right the crops were close to the road – wheat or maize or lines of planted poppies, the blooms not yet sprouting. Chopper could remember their first briefings on the deployment, back in Colchester, when an enthusiastic woman had lectured the battalion on the evils of the heroin trade and how one of their tasks would be to 'win over' the locals and get them to plant crops of potatoes and healthy greens and have cattle and sheep and goats, and become real farmers – perhaps with a market once a week . . . but here it was dangerous to dream. His concentration slipped.

"You all right, Lofty?"

"Nowhere I'd prefer to be, loving every minute."

"Keep your eyes open."

They kept going, footstep following footstep, safe in the knowl-edge that if it were a pressure plate they would know they had made a bad decision about where to tread about a quarter of a second later.

Lofty and Chopper had been good muckers since the para-chute regiment induction, and the first jump. They stayed close, watched each other's backs . . . the shared bit was nothing to do with football and Chopper's awful record for tackling. Lofty turned out for every game, and carried the bucket and the sponge, and sliced oranges for half-time. They were close because of the arse-pucker factor, greater for some than others, when recruits were winched up in the basket hanging underneath a balloon. It rose painfully slowly, and creaked because the drum was insuffi-ciently oiled, and shook as the wind grew. It would rise to 800 feet, and the instructors said it would 'sort the men from the boys'. Chopper was fine with heights . . . had seen that Lofty was terri-fied, more so every time the balloon's basket lifted a few more feet. The climb had stabilised, and they were suspended, the swaying of the basket increasing: the bar across the gap had been opened by a corporal in charge who grinned like the old Cheshire cat and showed no sympathy. Three went out, arms and legs gyrating. Chopper saw that Lofty was pressed against the side of the basket, furthest from the gap . . . Chopper knew that the one thing this shrivelled little kid wanted more than anything was to get the red beret, be a paratrooper – and he was frozen rigid and the corporal wasn't going to help. He would count to ten, gesture for Chopper to go for his first time and then signal for the balloon to be hauled down, and Lofty would be transferred into a van as soon as they touched down, given three minutes to clear his locker and then dumped at the railway station. Anyone contaminated with fear was not wanted, and the humiliation would be felt for years. So, Chopper had taken the boy's shoulder, checked that the guide wire was attached and, near as dammit, dragged Lofty forward . . . Absolutely forbidden, and the kid couldn't move. So Chopper gave him a push and heaved him into freefall. The chute had opened, Chopper had jumped and seen Lofty go smoothly down below him, clumsily hitting the grass, then rising to his knees and punching the air in triumph, and wave . . . Never stopped bloody talking all night, but passed the test. The reason for a friendship, and Lofty was the feeder to one of the best machine gunners in the unit.

Across the road from him, Lofty was struggling, like they all were, and there was another hiss from the sergeant for them to stay awake, be alert. Some of the sweat on Chopper's forehead seeped through the khaki bandana he wore – in Delta company their boss was 'relaxed' about dress code and appearance, not a bloody Guards officer. The camouflage cream seeped into his eyes and he felt near blinded and was blinking and trying to lose the incessant irritation. Chopper thought, was not sure, that the sergeant shouted, to get down, down flat, just get down, and his eyes cleared and there was a Talib in a field beyond Lofty, and he seemed to make a gesture with his hands like a contact was joined and there was a yell, similar to the 'God is great' cry that it was said the martyrs made, and . . .

Lofty was flying. The sergeant was rocking on his feet like a drunk outside the Colchester barracks when the pub closed, and the medic they were taking to the village had a smaller face than before, and it was red, blood-red. Then the light came . . . brilliant, pure white, illuminating the road so that he could see the raised dirt clouds with a greater clarity than before. He was hit on the back of the head and thought it looked like an arm when it fell in front of him. After the light came a darker glow and then the shock wave of the blast which flattened him, and he realised that none of the others in the section was standing. He might have been the last of them to have crumpled. It was like a great wind, more violent than anything he had known, which put him face down on the scoured road surface, and the dirt blew around him and he couldn't see. He did not hear the noise of the detonation. The sergeant's mouth was perhaps a foot from Chopper's right ear and he could see the contorted mouth and flapping tongue and feel the sergeant gasping for air, but it was hard to make out the words . . . 'Get the fucking gun going, got to keep the rags back. They'll be all round us and cutting us up. Keep them back, Chopper . . .' And the sergeant's head sagged.

They were his family: 3 Platoon, Delta Company, 2nd Battalion. The extended family was the Company, and the wider family, including distant cousins, was the Battalion. He smeared a hand across his face and realised that the film on it was not sweat and camouflage cream but blood. He had lost hold of the machine gun when he had been knocked down but old disciplines from training on the Brecons kicked in. He had it up and the bi-pod down and scanned fast and saw puffs of dirt away to the right where there was a gap in the crop. A mistake by the rags because his sergeant had always taught them to put water on the ground under a barrel tip, or a mug of piss, so that the sand or earth did not make the little giveaway clouds. He started to give them something back. Around him, the last of the soil and tufts of grass and stones from the detonation point had settled.

Other guys took a cue from Chopper and started to shoot, and the boy with the mortar tube was able to get some heavy gear in the air. The effect of the bursts from Chopper's machine gun and the thud of the mortar shells exploding lifted them. But not Lofty, and not the sergeant, nor the medic. Someone had the radio transmitting and was bawling, 'Contact . . . Contact.' Guys dragged what remained of Lofty close to Chopper and he wrenched the body over and was able to free two of the belts which gave him plenty . . . and he noticed that Lofty was short of an arm, and that some of his guts were hanging free, the rest held in by his belt and his armoured vest: but at that time it did not seem to matter to Chopper. The volume of the incoming was heavier: if the rags had a feeling that resistance was collapsing then they would close in for the kill and the favoured weapon would be a knife. Seemed an age and probably was not, and one of them from the far ditch let off a brilliant yellow flare and Chopper did not hear it but saw the first of the Apaches come over and the team up there would have seen the fire positions at which the machine gun bullets were aimed, and onto which the mortars were landing.

The ground around them was plastered by the Apaches, and then Chopper sensed a sort of quiet. Would have been one of the last shots the rags fired and it seemed to cut a scar in the road surface, enough to jolt his left ankle but he felt no pain and his leg was already drenched with blood from when he had been up against Lofty . . . His finger eased off the trigger and he took it clear of the guard and had to massage it to get his finger to straighten again. He let off three belts . . . the Apaches were making circles around what was left of the patrol, like ill-tempered dogs who'd decided they needed protection. More dust rose, would have been the last that could be shifted, and that was the twin rotors of a 'chuck chuck', which was what they called the Chinook heavy lifter, and it came down in the centre of the road, and the team spilled out from the back ramp with more guns to provide a close protection perimeter.

Chopper stood. Felt so damn tired; thought he might collapse but since he rated nothing was wrong with him, reckoned that would have been out of order. The triage team from the Chinook decided who needed to be handled first, where the initial morphine jabs should go. They didn't bother with Lofty, just put a bodybag beside him, and another bodybag was dropped over the sergeant, and another for the medic. There were stomach wounds and limb damage, and someone had a head wound which was always top of the list for attention. A Chinook would not hang about, not in bad lands . . . he could hear better now and a doctor reported to a colleague that the gunships thought 'about fifteen of Tommy Taliban are winging it to Paradise right now'. Chopper was on his feet but unsteady and there was smoke over where the mortars had landed and a nearby field was smouldering. He was surprised that his balance was screwed, and more surprised when the nurses came to him, prised the gun from his hands and took him to the Chinook ramp. He was trying to protest that he was, fine, unharmed. They took no notice. He was eased onto a gurney and a nurse started to snip at his right trouser leg with a pair of heavy scissors, and went through hardening blood, and called a doctor to join her – and they were airborne, and it was all action inside the big bird.

And heard someone say, "They did well, but won't get medals for it. Best will be a Mention. Getting bloody routine, and getting bloody pointless. What we got?"

"Took one in the ankle, clean entry and clean exit. What will need looking at is what shit got carried in with it, trouser fibres, socks – God, he stinks. Won't kill him but it'll be a life changer."

"He'll last. Get him jabbed please."

A syringe of morphine went into his leg, and he felt the resistance slacken. A decision was made to get him on to a Globemaster rather than keep him in an already overcrowded base camp medical centre. He did not know that a squat little cluster from his family, Headquarters Company, came to see him off and that he would be flown back to RAF Brize Norton overnight along with the three boxes. Nor did he know that up by the bulkhead was a bin liner with his personal stuff, nor how close he would be on the journey to what was left of Lofty.

An in-flight nurse checked him over and said to her supervisor, "Sleeping like a little lamb. Good-looking boy isn't he? Quite shaggable, I'd say. Sorry, shouldn't have said that, ma'am."

"Say what you like, I'm not disagreeing. The paras won't want him, not with that hole. A soldier's career gone down the plug – yes, more's the pity – but a pretty lad . . . You'd better strip him off, wash him down and get him into something cleaner before we land – don't want to frighten them. Poor sod, always a doubtful outlook for a winged paratrooper, they get a quick boot, an uncertain future – probably left with a load of resentment. But a pretty lad."

I

He was not supposed to be there.

Jonas Merrick – Queen's Gallantry Medal and Bar, Thames House analyst, fêted and offered undiluted praise by the CIA in Langley and the DEA in DC, and rather feared by his own people – was, on that Monday morning, walking into the teeth of the wind as he crossed Lambeth Bridge. He should not have been on the pavement, his old briefcase chained to his wrist and his free hand clinging to his trilby, the flaps of his coat splayed out behind him, and his flannel trousers flattened against his legs. He should have been on a week's leave, and the dates would be logged by Human Resources in the Security Service's computer system.

The river – polluted, it was said, to the point of being poisoned – ran dark and threatening far below him. He did not pause at that stretch of balustrade where once he had been dragged over and had plummeted down, and gone under, and had by a combination of circumstances survived. Past history and pushed aside. What should have been on his mind at the start of that week was what he and Vera would be doing after he had shut Olaf in his cage, left the caravan in the field on the Isle of Purbeck, near to the ruins of Corfe Castle – gone for a bracing walk on the coastal path, taken in a museum in Swanage . . . Going to work had been a decision taken out of frustration.

In the briefcase, marked with a faded EIIR imprint, was his flask of coffee and his plastic sandwich box, chicken and cucumber that day with a trace of mustard, and an apple and a small bar of chocolate. No papers. He carried nothing that referred to an operation instigated by Jonas that teetered on the edge of success – or failure. Jonas feared failure, and barely acknowledged success. He had left behind him when he walked out of Thames House the previous Friday afternoon the sitreps and biographies of the principals concerned because he had seen no need of them when clambering up and down rural paths in Dorset. But a degree of disaster had struck on the forecourt of his modest home in Raynes Park. In front of the semi-detached, pebbledash, and mock-Tudor house, his and Vera's home all their married life, stood the caravan. 'Don't worry, dear,' he'd said from the doorstep about to head for his train, 'I'll sort everything out when I'm back this evening.' And that evening, February and vilely cold, he had gone to the caravan, key in hand, to get it ready to load that night, and a bit more on the Saturday morning before a 10.00 am departure, and a good run to the south-west down the A31, and had opened the door to start the little jobs he ought to have completed the week before, even the month before … But his mind had been focused on work. It had been a complicated operation to put in place, more so than most, hellishly complicated. And Vera had had bronchial problems and not taken over.

So now, as he headed for work, the concrete forecourt was empty. On Saturday afternoon the caravan had been towed away for repair. On Saturday evening their bags had been unpacked and the food they would have taken returned to the fridge, and Olaf's fiendishly expensive cat food was back in the cupboard, and rather than mope around and be continuously reminded of his failure to ensure a functional caravan he had decided to go back to work.

Years before, in the hours before the warm prosecco and the handing to him of an envelope with a John Lewis voucher, and the start of his unwelcome retirement, Jonas Merrick had surprised himself, and many others. Sitting by the river, contemplating the awfulness of being a past employee of the Service, he had found himself sharing a bench in the darkness with Ivanhoe Gunn, a wannabe suicide bomber who was about to stretch his legs and head in the direction of the Mother of Parliaments, and Jonas had disarmed the vest bomb, and taken the lad back to Security. And it had dropped, like a heavenly bolt, into the mind of the Assistant

Deputy Director General at Thames House that Merrick might indeed be a man with talents worth hanging on to. Each job that came his way seemed to need more fleshing, have more consequences, be more pregnant with risk – and danger. This one, he thought, had the potential of marking his finest hour – well, something like that. The pieces were in place, and there remained little for him to influence.

It had its stamp on it, Jonas Merrick's, which meant preparation, methodical planning, and a taste of something bizarrely outside the loops of convention. Four months before, a booze-laden lunch between a man ranked far above him in Thames House and a senior from another agency had meant a proposition was dumped on his lap – and implicit was 'don't mind how you manage it, don't terribly want to know, so just get on with it.' A fallow time over and boredom banished. Three months before he had been taken to a mansion for a police search, the officers believing he was a photographer's assistant, and had seen a girl – and the pace quickening. Two months back he had scrounged an invitation to a bonding binge at a north London pub, where the detectives as a common trait carried a desiccated periwinkle shell in their pocket as a mark of who they were and their expertise, and had noted a guy who seemed a loner and outside the team. One month earlier he had manufactured a moment when the two young people met, that girl and that police officer, total strangers, and pretty much all bets would be off and the business moving beyond the reach of his intervention . . . he was confident. Had to be, it was the best he could manage.

He dealt with matters reflecting three different aspects of the Security Service's work. There was the perpetual hazard of *terrorism*, the regular scourge of *espionage*, and the one that least interested his masters but the one that he enjoyed confronting the most, *crime*. He had his teeth into this one . . . He had come to the end of the bridge and the traffic ahead of him was, as ever, inching forward and the road was jammed. On the far side, in front of the Fivers building, Thames House, he saw the armed police officers Kev and Leroy, scanning traffic but not looking out for him because he was not supposed to be there. He had told them himself that he was off the whole of the next week with his caravan and his wife and his Norwegian Forest cat, and they had wished him well and hoped 'nothing daft' would happen to him . . . They did not see him, did not come forward to escort him through the cars and vans and cyclists. He plunged forward, blustering his way through the traffic and into the fog of exhaust fumes, and the blast of horns and abuse from angry drivers. Jonas was a man of tight schedules, as was the DepDG, Brian, sitting in his chauffeur-driven car, as his driver braked sharply, and Jonas saw the lowering dislike pressed up against the privacy window. He felt the usual exhilaration as he arrived at the other ride of the road and headed for the side of the building.

"Hello, Mr Merrick, thought you were on holiday," said Kev.

"Good to see you, Mr Merrick. Has there been a bit of a cock-up?" asked Leroy.

He grimaced. Fact was he loved these two men, might have owed his life to them, certainly trusted that life with them. He made a sheepish grimace, and went to buy his cappuccino and his Danish from the café. He would take them, as he did every weekday morning, sunshine or rain – he had no truck with Working From Home – to St John's Gardens where he watched the gardener sweeping and hoeing as he ate and drank.

He went down to the basement of Thames House to the Post Room, to which he had been banished by a kangaroo court for 'flagrant breach of regulations'. His working space was behind a barricade of filing cabinets. To the staff, he was known as the Guv'nor, the cuckoo who had been planted into their territory. Surprise and puzzlement greeted him, but he did not acknowledge his colleagues' confusion and headed for his den where his assistant was on her hands and knees with a pan and brush and a wet cloth cleaning around his chair.

"Hello, Mr Merrick. Holiday gone pear-shaped?" Effie asked him. "Anyway, it all seems to be tripping along nicely here – so far."

A month earlier (January '26)

"You good then, Chopper, ready and able?" Effie asked.

"Good and ready."

"And able. Remember who you are, and that you're used to getting what you want. Go for it. Try and pace it. Don't need to do a hamstring, and an ACL would be disaster time. Good luck, Chopper."

They had been sitting on a bench, both of them with fags lit, and the wind came lightly off the sea and wafted the smoke into his face. He could see the girl jogging towards them. They were in Dubai, that exorbitant little corner of the United Arab Emirates, on the Palm Jumeirah resort area where the serious wealth hung out, looking out at the Persian Gulf. Effie was with her boyfriend who had been in Special Recce Regiment and been co-opted . . . He'd had little to say and was getting on with developing his tan. She did the talking, was in charge; she had been there at the start when they had roped him in . . . Chopper had come willingly enough, didn't have a whole host of options.

He had told them, when it was spelled out to him, that it was the dumbest plan he had heard of. She had said, 'Well, that's your opinion, and the old boy who worked it out will not be shifting because of it. Do it, or fuck off and go back where you came from . . . I hear he usually gets things right. He comes with a reputation.' It was the dumbest and most ridiculous plan ever put to him, and to see if he was right, or the 'old boy' was, he had been flown from Heathrow to Dubai, more than seven hours in the air. The previous day they had done the sniff round the location together and had seen the girl on the same track alongside the built up rocks on which the resort had its foundations. She had jogged past them – decent legs and a decent waist, and all of her quite decent – and their little group had pretended to be in deep conversation, heads averted, and she'd not seemed to notice them. The word was that the girl would have been well aware of anti-surveillance procedures, but she had seemed relaxed, and in spite of the heat was running comfortably.

And that morning she was back again, and far behind her was an older man with too much weight on him, labouring on a bicycle and about to pack it in, like he had the previous day.

Effie said, "That's a snogging face. Not beautiful, nothing classic, but a nice face. She'd think she's way out of your reach, Chopper. Not for the likes of you."

He reached into his pocket and pulled out his loose change and a small seashell and gave them to Effie to mind for him.

Simon said, "Get a squeeze and a cuddle, so she remembers you."

He could see her backside wobbling. He knew her name was Julie. Knew also that her father was Lachlan Wilson. Knew from photographs the house that was her home, and about her two older brothers, and about two more boys, teenagers. Knew what her father did and why he was of interest. He started to run.

Chopper rarely gave chapter and verse on the scar that he had brought home from a shitty road in a shitty place. He had limped his way to Lofty's funeral which was quiet and sad and short of pomp, and had also hobbled along behind the coffin of his sergeant, leaning on a stick, and that had been a full military job. He had moved on, had tried to find another 'family' that might foster him. Had played football but not often and the recovery time had grown longer after each game. Might have been that the surgeons had seen their job as just getting him mobile, but not to athlete level. Might have been that the ankle wound was more complex than first thought. His present 'family' was likely soon to move him on because each year, and certainly each month, the pain was harder to absorb when he pushed himself . . . he hid it well, had to.

"Going to be a bit of a struggle catching her. Wish me luck, Lofty . . . it's the stupidest thing I ever heard of but . . ." Chopper often talked to Lofty.

There had been times when the wound had puckered and then healed, reduced to a small hole, an indentation that was redder than the skin around it, and then he had been able to cover ground fast, almost forgetting that a Talib had been lined up on him at the time that the bomb was detonated and probably would have killed him if the blast had not dropped him. In his own language the guy would have cursed because a marksman always knew whether he had a kill or only a flesh wound and it was not more than that because the machine gun had put down sufficient fire to prevent them creeping close with their knives out, and then the attack birds had come.

It hurt more now. Pain laced up his shin and with each step thudding on the hard walkway it hurt some more. The extent of the pain was his secret and shared only with Lofty, not talked about at the building on the edge of London where he was clinging to a place in the Flying Squad Team 3, Barking, and swallowing half a pack of paracetamol each day to mask it. He had warmed up that morning, jogged a quarter of a mile and done some of the old football exercises for loosening up; if he ruptured something that would be on a catastrophe scale, banging at the top.

He ran after her . . . He did not understand why the girl chose to go running with the sun climbing and the temperature rising, and only a slight breeze coming off the water and not a square handkerchief of shade in sight. He ran and the pain came, as he expected it to. It would not have been Chopper's style to say, when propositioned, 'Of course I'd like to, but I got this little wound in Afghan, not much to look at but it gives me grief, so I'll have to pass.' She wore little floppy shorts, functional navy-blue, and a Pepsi T-shirt. He rehearsed what he would say. Before he had been to Helmand he would have easily caught her. But he *had* been there and what he had thought of as his family had turned their backs on him. His breathing came harder and the ache was sharper and climbed up his leg, and he was sweating. He was awkward in female company, and defensive. He came level with her and could smell the faint scent of her body.

"Your trainer lace is loose . . . you'll trip . . ."

She stopped, dragged air down into her lungs. Looked down at her laces, and they were both secure – and frowned and looked at him, and frowned some more and clicked on her phone to stop the timing of her run, and gazed hard at him. It was the moment he was supposed to offer an explanation.

He knelt. His fingers were stiff at the knuckles, and made him clumsy. She peered down at him and the frown deepened on her forehead and her eyes flashed. She could have clouted him. He took the tightly knotted laces on her right foot, and made a poor fist of untying them, then succeeded and freed them. He looked up, and she was scowling, and he sensed that he only had a few seconds. Another runner passed them, and from the other direction came someone pushing a buggy and neither spared them a glance. He had already gauged that Dubai was a private place and staring was unwelcome. He tightened the laces, then made a decent knot.

He used the smile that he was famous for, what everyone said Chopper did well. "There you are, no chance of you spilling over now."

"Am I supposed to thank you?" She had what he thought a regionless accent, something from the Home Counties perhaps but lacking in clues as to location or heritage.

Chopper smiled and shrugged. "Don't have to . . ."

Her jaw jutted and her lips thinned, and he fancied that her fists had tightened, and she looked sharply around her.

She said, "The lace was never loose. So what was that about?"

A wider smile from Chopper and a flick of the shoulders – all done the way they had practised it in the hotel bedroom the previous evening. "You are the prettiest girl out running this morning, far and away the prettiest. I was with my pals back there on the bench, and it's what I said about you. They bet me."

Something of the defensiveness left her. "What was the bet?"

Maybe she would just laugh at him. "A dumb bet, don't know that I should . . ."

"What was it?"

The sun seemed fiercer and the glare off the walkway was brighter and the ripple of the water on the stones was sharper, and she might kick his head in. "I am not sure I ought . . ."

What he knew of her she was unlikely to be familiar with being stalled. Said what she wanted and expected it done, what the briefing paper had said. What he was supposed to do seemed even more ridiculous.

"Cough it up or I'm gone . . . is the bet worth winning?"

He thought she might kick him, punch him, or just gaze at him for a moment like he was some pitiful little pervert, and resume her jog. "Definitely worth winning."

"What was it?"

"I get a kiss off you. Sorry, bloody rude. Prettiest girl out running, and they bet I couldn't get a kiss off you. I said I could. I . . ."

She came down on one knee. Didn't seem to think about it. Put a hand on his shoulder to steady herself. Looked into his face, and he could see every rivulet of sweat on her skin, and her eyes were a soft blue, and she grinned.

She kissed him. She was Julie, third child of Lachy and Victoria Wilson.

He kissed her. He was Kenny Harris, or Chopper.

He didn't close his eyes, nor did she. Just a daft moment. Two strangers who had met by chance, and he thought she believed that. But she surprised him, and drove her tongue into his mouth, probing almost to the back of his throat. She moved away, wiped her tongue round her lips, and she was chuckling as she straightened. The hand that had been on his shoulder tapped Chopper's forehead . . . The Company Commander when he had been with Delta in Colchester had owned a spaniel, a Welsh Springer, and if it did what it was told to, rare, it was rewarded with a treat and the same sort of tap on the top of its head, and the pleasure of it would send its tail into overdrive . . . She pulled him up, grinned some more, wiped a hand over her mouth.

The photo he had been shown, surveillance stock, or the sight the previous day of her jogging past: ice-cold eyes, granite eyes, steeled eyes, eyes that slotted in with who she was, what she did, the eyes of a person of importance in her trade, brutal eyes – not now, and they had softened. Like they had been exchanged for eyes that were fresher, warmer, softer, and belonged to a girl with a normal way of life that did not involve mass poisoning with the chemicals of trafficking. Lovely eyes that told him he had tapped into places in her personality that stayed hidden, covert, were not on public view. Because what had happened was so outrageous? He'd be remembered, did not doubt it, and she would, which had

a certainty in his mind. And himself . . . a winter month, and no
sun tan on his cheeks, and a working day spent in an office and
peering at a screen, or in a car and with an anorak keeping his
body warm. Parchment-toned skin that would show he was fresh
out from the cold and fog and frost of the far north, yet there was
colour spreading over his face – was blushing and could not
contain it, and blood pulsing in him, running riot. If he had then
punched a fist in the air, what a para did when a successful waste
of Talibs had been achieved, and what his present crowd did when
a good snatch was done, it would not have been because the aim
of a mission was fulfilled – but because of who she was and what
she had done with her eyes, blue and with a trace of the sea's
colour beyond the surf. Was special to him and dared to think that
it might have been the same for her, special . . . and over.

A kiss on his cheek, a deep breath, then she fiddled with the
phone on her arm to restart her stopwatch.

Chopper said, "I'll see you round."

Julie said, "Don't bank on it."

He said, "Paths can often cross."

She said, "If you say so."

She was gone, running into the heat. He thought he had done
well, but that would be for Effie to say. His ankle hurt and it had
been an effort to chase after her. He went back to the bench at a
little faster than a walk.

Effie spoke. "You did well. Bit far away but didn't I see her
French kiss you? Tongue down your throat? Won't do that every
day. Too right you'll be remembered. Most boys, her age, would
run a mile if they knew who she was, and anything about her. She
won't forget you."

Simon went to buy him an ice cream, vanilla because he'd no
wish to contaminate her salt taste, and Effie used her phone and
would have had a secure link to call London and the guy who had
thought it up: described by the few inside the loop as rubbish,
ridiculous, idiotic, but was – in fact – a little bit of genius. It would
be remembered by the girl, and would not be forgotten by him.

The lorry edged forward the last few metres until the cab was level with the uniformed customs official. The frontier check had advance knowledge that the heavyweight Mercedes vehicle was coming through. There was a wave towards the administration building and within moments a senior man had emerged and was sauntering towards the cab. Considerable planning was needed to ensure that this particular officer from the IRGC was present at the border post on that day and at that time, in this no man's land between the authority of Afghanistan and that of the Islamic Republic of Iran. He was dressed not in the uniform of his organisation, the power in the country, but in that of a customs official. The lorry was known to him, as were the driver and his colleague beside him, and the near side door was opened and they acknowledged each other. A bulging manila envelope handed down. No name was scrawled on it, only a number – 2. The envelope was slid into a wide tunic pocket. In exchange, a slip of paper with two lines of Farsi script and an official stamp was passed up, taken by the passenger and placed carefully in his wallet. A transaction was completed . . . it was business, not a matter of friendship or trust, but business. A similar procedure had been followed a kilometre back at the Afghan point of Islam Qala, and on that envelope the number displayed had been 1, the start of the journey. The officer turned his back on the cab and went back into the building and would wait there a few more hours until the next lorry came through. The customs check was astride the historic Asian Highway, AH1, that ran, in theory, between the city of Tokyo in the far east and Istanbul, the gateway to continental Europe. For centuries 'arrangements' had been in use that smoothed the traffic of goods coming from producers in the east and consumers in the west.

The driver waited while the barrier was raised then eased the lorry forward. He was Mehmet, a Turkish Kurd, small and wiry, and he needed two cushions to get him high enough to see through the windscreen. Beside him was Dragan, ethnically something of a mongrel, but listed as of Serbian nationality. In the cab, in the event of business understandings collapsing, was a leather bag that held flash and bang grenades and incapacitating gas, and a Makharov PM 9mm pistol with eight bullets in the magazine. Hidden in a false panel behind the passenger were an elderly AK47 assault rifle, loaded, and two magazines strapped together.

They hit the road. The listed load they were transporting was 32,500 kg of pine nuts, raisins and pistachio nuts. 'Listed', but with licence. The contents of envelopes 1 and 2 on either side of the frontier line drawn in a flat, monotonous, desert region ensured that the load was not taken off, laboriously weighed, every last nut and raisin, and damaged in the process. Had such measures been taken then a discrepancy would have been found. Secreted against the bulkhead were 1,000 carefully weighed kilos of dramatically greater value than the nuts and raisins. On the Afghan side of the border, without an arrangement in place, the pair of them – Mehmet and Dragan – would have faced a bad end, perhaps a fatal stoning, while on the Iranian side they might well have had a noose placed around their necks before being hoisted up from a crane's raised beam . . . But it was in place. The money was allocated, the arrangements were made. The lorry surged forward and was soon lost in the heat haze.

Out on the open road, driver and passenger touched fists, turned up the music as they headed west. They were both mercenaries of a sort, available for hire, and knew as well as any how to transit some of the more 'challenging' territories of the region. Their services and skills were known to a select few employers and they were kept in constant work and had been for close to nine years, but it was not forever. A time would come when Mehmet would return to Dogubeyezit in north-eastern Turkey, in Anatolia, and Dragan would slip back to Vojvodina among the rivers and lakes of northern Serbia, and one of them might take tourists out onto the slopes of Ararat and sell them genuine pieces of timber from the Ark that had been Noah's after being marooned high on that mountain when the flood waters subsided, and the other would grow some tomatoes and cucumbers and make goat's cheese . . . but not this year. They were selective in the employment they took, and wary, and wanted the future to feature tourists and food markets, not a maximum-security gaol in Turkey or the Balkans or Germany or Belgium.

This assignment had surprised them: they had dealt with the man before when he was rising in his world, and dealt with him often when he was astride the plateau of his power. Then the lines of communication had broken, until recently. Perhaps retirement had been as hard for him as it would be for them, perhaps the itch had afflicted him and so one more shipment had been set up. They would not have worked for anyone, not for a man or a cartel in whose preparations they did not have total faith. Not their job to decide whether boredom had captured him, or whether an investment opportunity had seemed too good to be ignored.

One bit into an apple, one smoked a cigarette.

If they had not had faith in the man who had hired them then they would not have taken this contract, driven into Afghanistan and loaded the lorry with product and supervised where it was secreted and then had the sacks of nuts and raisins brought into the space behind them. He was a man to be relied on, their opinion.

The potential rewards were considerable – had to be because of the territory they crossed – which the man understood.

Up early and heading to the shed where the grain was kept, and sniffing at the cold and damp of the morning, Lachy Wilson had his dogs at his heels, and walked with a spring in his step.

A week before he had celebrated his 53rd birthday. With his wealth he could have, and not noticed it, taken over a substantial wing of a Marbella hotel, filled an airliner with those whom he might have wished to impress, treated his guests to a long weekend of luxury, cabaret, gluttony. Instead he had sent Softboy to the fish and chip takeaway in Dorking, eleven miles away, with an order big enough for himself and his wife and his daughter and the two boys, and the Prof and Mrs Plumb, and Softboy, to eat round the kitchen table. And that had been the limit of it. He was not interested in good, bad, or indifferent wines, neither smoked nor drank, only spent money when he had cleared the expenditure with Vic. The home he left behind him as he went out into a cold and damp dawn, with a threat of sleet in the air, and walked towards the chicken run where he kept his birds and where Softboy shot rats and enjoyed their death throes, would have been priced at around five million. Had it been in Wentworth or Weybridge, its value would have been closer to ten million. But eleven years before, Lachy Wilson had moved his family from the edge of Epping Forest to the rolling hills of that part of Surrey notable for the Tillingbourne chalk stream, properties with land and privacy, and had purchased a home of eight bedrooms, five bathrooms, set in thirteen acres on the edge of the parish boundary of Abinger Hammer. Vic, his partner and wife of thirty-four of those fifty-three years, had decided where there would be gold taps and where there would be chrome, but had matched her man's moods, and The Gables was furnished as if it were a lived-in home, not an interior designer's brochure model. Strange to all those who maintained an interest in his affairs that Lachy seemed so uninterested in the trappings of wealth. But he spent most of his waking hours in making a supreme effort to augment it. He did not read anything other than the *Financial Times*, no books other than those dealing with wealth creation, did not go to nightclubs, of which he owned four. A seeming hobby was a weekly round of golf, and the small regular team who played with him, all of whom were on his payroll, were always able to manufacture defeat, and he inevitably won. But the reason he played was his need to be distanced from the possibility of bugs, trackers, mikes, recorders, transmitters – anything that could be used against him – when discussing his business dealings. He thought the chickens looked well . . . Softboy was a fine shot with a .22 air rifle but sometimes aimed for the rats' back legs so that they would be rendered crippled, defenceless, but still alive and squealing and they would then be hung up on a wall of the coop, which did not seem to bother the chickens. It was a job that he had taken for himself. Lachy went each morning to collect the eggs and was likely to have one poached by Mrs Plumb for his breakfast.

Five chickens, all Rhode Island Red, all with names given them by the children. Doris looked peaky which disturbed him.

In his time Lachy had shot men, had sliced men with a box cutter blade deep enough for the skin to fold away and hang loose, had kicked men's heads hard enough to fracture their skulls, had stamped on men's legs with a force that ensured they would not walk again without crutches. Yet he possessed a deep love for each of the chickens, and would be irritated by Doris' failure to recover fully from whatever malignancy affected her. Beyond the chickens was an open paddock. Once Julie had had a pony there but the lazy kid refused to clear out its nightly mess, refused to brush the creature's coat – just wanted to join a pony club and mix in that set. The pony had been sold and that had hurt because it went for less than he had paid for it. The paddocks were empty of livestock but they had a small tractor with gang mowers to trail after it which kept the grass neat, and the land ran up the hill towards the North Downs and down the hill on the far side and towards a line of trees and then the main road linking Gomshall to Shere. The open ground was covered by sensors and beams that, if broken, would set off alarms, and at boundaries of the property was high fencing reinforced by generous lengths of barbed wire coils. It was where he lived and where he felt as secure as he was ever likely to. His home and that of his wife, and of his daughter, and of his two sons, a garden hut close to the chicken run where the Prof had his workshop, and another near to it that was used by Softboy as a gym. At night, Softboy was in the lodge by The Gables' drive gates on to the main road monitoring the screens.

There were areas of ignorance in his life, and he worked hard to preserve them.

Lachy Wilson had never heard the words uttered by the robed judge with a wig on his head. '*You are, Wilson, a menace to society, a man of overweening arrogance – and one of supreme brutality. Your behaviour, marked by inhuman cruelty and greed, is a disgrace. For what you have done, to remove the poison you peddle, you shall go to prison for a minimum term of twenty-five years.*'

Lachy Wilson had never felt, in the immediate aftermath of the sentence, the court officials gripping his arms, spinning him round

                                    Gerald Seymour

and thrusting him towards the steps leading from the dock. '*This way, lad, and let's not have any bother off you.*'

Lachy Wilson had never known the isolation in the moments after the cell door closed on the back of his barrister who had shrugged, turned away, and muttered over his shoulder, '*Can't for the life of me, Mr Wilson, say where we go from here, not after that summing up from the bench. Fell over himself to prevent grounds of appeal.' 'Fraid you'll just have to make the best of it – a hazard of the lifestyle.*'

The sleet was pricking on his cheeks, but the cold that February morning bothered him not at all. The dogs stayed close to him, both German Shepherds – Ulrich and Gustav. He felt good that morning because he knew of the progress of a Mercdes BharatBenz 4828R heavy lorry with a 7200cc engine and sixteen wheels and two good guys in the cab, good but pricey. It was the first time in a year that a spring had been in his step because he had been away from his old life for that long. But the itch had been there, had become irritating then insufferable. He had been told he had no need of the shipment, and advised that his investment portfolios were healthy and rewarding. But he had gone for it, retrieved his old life. The lorry was on the move and the dogs recognised his changed mood and had their ears pricked, their tails wagging.

The associates of Lachy Wilson called him *the biggest and the best but a fierce fucker if crossed.* His opponents and competitors, whether in the trade of clubs or girls or firearms or the bread and butter of 'brown' importation, called him *a bad bastard if any idiot challenges him.* His files in secure police premises gathered dust on shelves, and were pushed down computerised lists of priority, and detectives in pubs dropped their voices when talking of him and said, *You'll not know who is on the take from him, right up to high level, which makes him too big to bring down, un-bloody-touchable, what he is.*

He was smiling when he went back into the kitchen, and gave the eggs to Mrs Plumb who did the housekeeping. His paper was waiting for him by his place at the table, and the household bustled around him, and the boys were bawling about school, and the girl's place was empty, and his wife pecked his cheek – and the

Prof would join them, and Softboy . . . and the world seemed in good shape from the viewpoint of Lachy Wilson.

It was the opinion of Jonas Merrick that Human Resources, based on the first floor of Thames House, had made an error – quite a grievous one – when accepting the transfer for temporary duties of Euphemia Bellingham from the Sixers across the river. He had assumed that the intention had been to keep him firmly inside the rail lines of corporate good conduct, not allow him to stray outside and thereby hazard the good name of the Security Service. They should have understood that the Assistant Deputy Director General had his sticky hands in the process: the AssDepDG was long a supporter of Jonas's wilder ventures, was his champion defender, and relished the supreme moments of triumph that were brought home, some by the skin of their teeth, or 'a damn close-run thing'. Perhaps the desk warriors of HR had failed to read her previous history, perhaps they had not been shown it.

His desk, keyboard, screen, and box, were against a wall in the basement Post Room and his small area was screened from the rest of the room by a phalanx of steel filing cabinets, some available to him and some opening on the other side. She had a smaller table, large enough for her laptop and with room to balance a coffee mug, and a stool to sit on. The AssDepDG had described her to Jonas as 'hard as a fucking masonry nail', but then Effie had told Jonas the AssDepDG's description of him to her: 'Doesn't have a friend in the world, has a wife deserving canonisation and a surly cat. Lovable? About in the same league as a slithering black mamba, and with equally unpleasant eyes.'

He thought them well suited. She had come to enjoy working squashed in beside him. He would be dressed in his brogues and flannels, his Tattersall shirt, moderate tie, and jacket of Harris tweed that showed stains of blood, foul river water, untreated sewage that repeated dry cleaning stints had failed to cleanse. She wore trainers, jeans with rips at the knees, neutral T-shirts and fleeces. His hair, grey, was brushed and combed and kept neat on his walk to and from work by a trilby hat, while Effie's hair was dragged into a loose shape on her head by haphazardly placed pins. His voice was quiet, little more than a whisper, and those he spoke to strained to get the drift of his talk; hers was a sharp bark with the snap of a Halifax accent. He shaved tidily each morning but not with extravagant care, and she used minimum make-up and a small stone, which he assumed was from the Syrian desert, dangled on a fine gold chain at her throat, and her fingers had no rings . . . He trusted her; she might have become in the last five months almost fond of what AssDepDG referred to as 'that grumpy old fucker'.

The error on the part of HR was that Effie was now a signed-up co-conspirator in the machinations of Jonas Merrick. As might have been said in that well-lit and comfortable work space on the first floor, she had 'gone native'. Was she a 'gamekeeper-turned-poacher'? They did not know. What else appealed to Jonas about her was that she had no requirement for chatter. Holiday anecdotes were off-limits, TV from the previous evening was not mentioned, diets, wages, overtime rates, and expenses were avoided. They talked work – not more, not less. When not talking between themselves or into their encrypted phones, their silence was broken only by the soft music enjoyed beyond the barricade of filing cabinets by the Post Room staff. When he dozed and his head slumped she did not disturb him, but that would be after lunch and not before. She was in before him and left after him . . . it worked well.

His explanation as to why he was not enjoying the rain and cold on the paths above the Isle of Purbeck cliffs had been brief. She had been minding the shop, putting the last pieces in place for the operation they called *Humble Pie*. It was what they supposed was the appropriate meal in the gaol canteen on the first night of a heavy sentence when the big man was inside and would be for many years, stripped of his aura of invincibility, power, authority.

'Caught out by the cold snap, bit of frost in the pipes of the caravan, frozen, then thawed, and a bit of a burst, and repairs required. Take a few days.'

She had not laboured it, had shrugged, allowed him to retrieve his work space. But mid-morning, a shadow had passed across the entrance to their area.

"Hello, Jonas, fancy you being here! Thought you were supposed to be on holiday, that Corfe Castle had beckoned you. What went wrong?"

"A bit of a leak scuppered us."

"Not done the necessary when we had that mini-freeze? Don't tell me that you omitted to safeguard the water system in the caravan? Surprised at that, Jonas . . . but this is the big week, and good to have you back at the helm."

"Thank you for your concern, but we have work to get on with."

"Glad to hear it." Had Jonas turned in his chair and faced him he would have seen a short smirk, but then the face clouding over. AssDepDG had authorised each step of *Humble Pie*, would take brickbats – heavy ones – if it failed, as would Jonas. "The big week. And we're in good shape?"

"At the moment, as good a shape as we can be."

The shadow passed, and he heard retreating footsteps and then the door to the Post Room closed, and conversation was resumed amongst those who worked there. Once again, Jonas' reputation, and his future, hung by a thread.

Julie woke late, stretched, arched her back. She had been thinking of him.

Thinking throughout the duration of that run in the stinking hot sunshine of the resort city, and through the meetings over the next forty-eight hours when the advance sums of money had been transferred via the covert routes available in that city and in that banking culture, and thinking of him alone in her hotel room, on the flight home, in the car driven by the Prof from the airport. Thinking of their mouths together, thinking of the sheer bloody cheek of him, the disrespect. What no one she had ever known would have done to her.

She was Julie Wilson. The daughter of Lachy and Vic Wilson. The sister of Hamish Wilson, dead three years following the crash when he had – dosed with booze and cannabis – gone off the road with the filth behind him: would now have been thirty. The sister of Gregor Wilson, locked up in maximum security and with nineteen years minimum to go and a conviction for attempted murder: now aged twenty-eight. Also the sister of Connor and David who showed no 'promise' in following in their father's trade or acquiring his skills and seemed to think that he would buy them a semi-pro football team with guaranteed places for them in the starting line-up: they were sixteen and fifteen, and useless.

She was the future. Had had it drilled into her that she would lead the family, would not permit everything he had built to collapse, disintegrate – was the best hope, the only hope. So she had been set apart like a thoroughbred foal, put in a stable and a paddock where the stallions were kept back by a great high wall. Kept there until her father decided who she should be coupled with – something like that . . . Could remember when she was 15 and two smart young lads from the village had pitched up at the gate in an open-top MG and rung the bell and tooted the horn and expected to take the new talent out on a spin . . . and her dad had sent Softboy down the drive and he'd held an angle iron in his clenched hands and both the MG's headlights had been knocked out and one of the boys had pissed himself, and no more had been seen of them. A solicitor's clerk in Dorking who worked for the lawyer they employed, Henry Lyons, had not known the set-up and had come on heavy in the car park a couple of years back and her father had kicked the shit out of him. No more unexpected attention from boys who wanted a sniff of her . . . Time to time, she'd be taken by her dad to a business meeting, and the other party would have brought along his son – usually Albanian or Lebanese, or a Scouser, and she'd say afterwards in the car going home that she found those boys revolting: Lachy would shrug, like it didn't matter to him – not yet. Trouble was that it would, as the years rolled by and his appetite for his work reduced, and he had Vic nagging at him that it was time they put their feet up, and his business slackened, and she – Julie – carried the load, did the heavy lifting.

When she'd showered and dressed, she'd come down the wide staircase of their home that was like a prison to her and waiting for her in the hall would be the Prof. Called the Prof because he acted like he was stupid, halfway to an idiot. But he was not . . . Wally Genge, fifty-three years old and like a fawning kid when Lachy Wilson called him up, was her minder. She went away, he went with her. In Dubai on her most recent trip she had gone running on a pedestrian-only track and had lost him. He would be going with her when they flew to Leipzig, old eastern Germany, in three days' time. His voice wheezed and there was the smell of fags on his breath, and his knees creaked, but he was charged to see that she was kept safe. Because she was the future. Times were when she reckoned herself as much of a maximum security inmate as her brother, daft Gregor who was locked away. Perhaps she needed the protection because men did not rise as high as Lachy Wilson had done, without acquiring 'enemies'. Proper ones, not just the National Crime Agency and the Special Operations people at the Yard, but those who had a brother who'd carry a facial scar to his grave, or those who hobbled on a stick, or those who could no longer shag the missus because of the damage from a kicking, or those who went to a graveyard, and some who didn't know in what part of Epping Forest was the shallow grave. And out of the blue, in Dubai had come this pounding imbecile with his chat-up line about a loose lace on her trainer, and him kneeling, and then telling her about a bet. And the kiss . . . and him telling her she was the 'prettiest' and her letting her tongue go rip. Her eyes closed. She was Lachy Wilson's future, groomed to be head of an Organised Crime Group (not that she had ever been asked if that was what she wanted) and she was treated like some goddamn puppet by her father who sat her on his knee and used her like a ventriloquist's doll. She had not experienced much kissing and thought that was the best she had known.

He had said that he would see her . . . She had told him not to bank on it. He had said that paths often crossed. She had said, *If you say so*. She did not know his name, and there was no way that

he would have known hers, but she could imagine a meeting –
imagine and dream.

Had not forgotten him. The whole thing was so ludicrous and
the kiss so good. She was 22 years old and had only a slight idea
of how formidable were the forces that could be set against her
father – 'too big to bring down'.

One picture on the wall. No wardrobe, just an open rail with suits
hanging from iron hangers and the shirts that Agathe ironed, a
chest where his underwear, socks, T-shirts, and sweaters were, and
his shoes under the rail. A single bed with hospital corners that
would have passed an inspection by a new recruits' sergeant, a
table beside it with a lamp and an alarm clock. A table with space
for two and a shelf with a microwave beside a sink that had a free-
standing draining board and shelves for saucepans and a frying
pan. No family photos displayed.

It was the home of Kenny Harris, Detective Constable, a
member of the Squad. That one picture identified him. He lay
half-dressed on the bed, in no hurry that morning, and the photograph was on the wall across the room from him. A player in
Chelsea's colours, going in for a tackle and the ball flying away to
the side and the opponent was off the ground, near to horizontal,
and that was Ron 'Chopper' Harris in his heyday, and playing on
the edge and the name passed down by a Commanding Officer –
'Well done, Harris, fantastic tackling. Held our midfield from
being overrun. Down to you we've that cup' – and by the company's trainer or coach – 'You sliced them good and proper, Harris,
chopped them up'. After being invalided out of the Regiment, he
had played for a string of police teams, but when his mobility was
slackening and the tackling had become more ferocious he had
gone into outside non-league teams, and was 'Chopper' again . . .
Just the one picture and saw no need for any others. Not interested in one of childhood family holidays on the south Devon
coast, and a kid with a bucket and spade. Or of his mum and dad
holding hands, awkward with having just the one child, or him as
an all-action hero and plunging out of aircraft. His wallet with the

police warrant card was on the table and the one memento that he valued, a sea shell, was wrapped in a handkerchief on the bedside table.

The bathroom he used was down the corridor first right, and he shared that with Agathe and the two of her daughters still at home. They liked having him around. Her man, their father, was back in the Caribbean most of the time. It worked well. Chopper could have afforded better.

What little post he received was left downstairs in the hallway, by the front door of the flat in a block sandwiched between the Grand Union Canal and the Kentish Town Road in north London. Some days he ate food that Agathe bought for him, other days he shopped for himself at the Inverness Street market. Agathe was a cleaner at the New Scotland Yard building and did 'sensitive' offices on a high floor so it suited her to have a detective as her lodger. He was well paid, as a Detective Constable in the Flying Squad, working compulsory long hours: a small and elite unit, much in demand, with an overtime budget that other commanders could only envy. It was possible for him to clear £65,000 in a year, and that was not exceptional. He could have rented a smart two-bed apartment down in the Docks, could probably have bought one by now. Instead he paid Agathe £100 a week, cash, banked the surplus and his idea of what had accumulated was vague. He didn't own a car either, but he did have an old bicycle. His office, that section of the Squad, was based in the east of the city. He cycled to Kings Cross, then left the bike in the yard of the police station with responsibility for the station, and look a train on the Hammersmith and City line to Barking. The pain became severe when he pounded pavements, and it showed.

Chopper was on borrowed time, knew it. Even those in the Squad with weight problems still had sufficient mobility to chuck themselves around when going for what they called 'a pavement job' – a bad boy flattened in the street. Took too many paracetamols, tried not to limp. He had seen the signs: he was kept out of jobs that called for more agility. There was no way that the injury to his ankle was going to improve, no clock would be turned back . . . He would be called in, offered a medical examination, put through tests, and would receive a note that took him out of the Squad and shoved him back into basic detective work or even a return to uniform.

Nothing to cheer about, plenty to mope over – and then a summons and a meeting with a girl in a coffee bar, and a walk with an old guy over one of the bridges across the Thames. Five minutes of the man's time and a parting on the far side . . . and the daftest, dumbest assignment given him, and the flight to Dubai.

Chopper lay on his bed and thought of her, that girl who had the knots on her trainer laces perfectly well tied, and the feeling of her tongue against the smooth skin at the back of his mouth. He'd had no other girl in his life to compete with her, and thought of her every day, morning and afternoon and evening, and dreamed of her when he was lucky.

He eased off the bed, would shave and wash and clean his teeth, would grab a pastry out in the street, then head off on his bike, and after the train ride there would be a locker in a secure police building to be cleared out. Maybe some farewells said because he did not know when, if, he would be back.

Jonas had his briefcase open, had taken out the plastic box and removed the sandwiches. His thermos was unscrewed and his mug was filled. He pondered. Up on his screen were the Persons of Interest of *Humble Pie*, a ragtag crowd and different to anything Jonas had targeted before in London, and with more ability in each little finger than the corporate family in Liverpool who had been 'collateral', brought down in an operation he had overseen on the Galician coast, in north-west Spain.

For heaven's sake, this was in the heart of the stockbroker belt. This organisation, or firm, figuratively rubbed shoulders with bankers and lawyers, accountants and broadcast celebrities, had in common with all of them bulging banks' coffers and investment managers' portfolios. A palace for a home, a park for a garden, wealth unlimited and yet . . . Jonas Merrick and his wife and their cat lived in a three-bed semi-detached house that was now ninety years old, front bay windows and mock-Tudor beams and a concrete stand where a minimal front lawn might have been planted but which was much of the time occupied by a caravan – currently being repaired because he, the man who so seldom allowed error into his life, had forgotten to drain the system during the recent cold snap. These PoIs, his targets, would echo around that massive pile they barely occupied – but Jonas supposed it necessary to display that affluence, and the razor wire on the perimeters of the land, as proof that success had visited. He and Vera felt no need to tell their neighbours that their triumphs were not measured by the cost of their cars, the price of their holidays, and the secrecy with which it was necessary to cloak themselves. He hid from no man, was fearful of no threat, went to work each day on a scheduled train, was not 'too big to be brought down', and he ate the chicken sandwich.

It was the big week. The week it would come together. Little that he could do to affect events. The authority of the AssDepDG and the competence of Effie who sat quiet as a Trappist behind him would have been sufficient, and he thought his recruiting more than adequate. Between sucking his fingers clean and using a tissue to mop his desk surface, he put the pictures of the family and its collaborators up on his screen, used them as he supposed a pornography addict would have, found a little gratification from gazing at the faces. Had the lowest to the highest, and by the time he had eaten the sandwiches and demolished his bar of chocolate, drained the thermos, shaken the box crumbs into his wastepaper bin, and sealed it and returned it to his briefcase he would have devoured the whole gang.

Knew them all, had seen them all, smelt them and noted them – and none would have remembered him.

Their lawyer was Henry Lyons, aged 51, living in the nearby town of Dorking and owning the practice but spending all his working hours beavering on behalf of Lachlan Wilson, and being rewarded. He had a golf course face, chubby with weathered cheeks and a smile of innocence. The minder, who cared for the heir apparent, was Wally Genge, called the Prof, who gave out the image of idiocy, used it to disguise a sharp cunning. He was afflicted with mobility problems and had a lumbering gait and was overweight but the eyes gave him away, sharp and flashing. The housekeeper was Mrs Plumb who ran an untidy kitchen, seemed to live in an apron and had the job of cleaning the home without any help allowed over the backdoor step and would have known some, but not enough, of the family's confidences, therefore was passed over by Jonas. The enforcer, on whose fists and boots so much of the discipline, the certainty of extreme violence depended, was Billy Jones, known to them as Softboy, whose appearance was stunningly normal, with no tattoos and no shaven scalp, but hair that was salt and slate with a dash of pepper and no obvious excess of muscle or steroid abuse. The *consigliere* had pitched up, unwise and should have known better: this was Yitzak Cohn, tanned from a beach on the Mediterranean coast of Israel and with nervous drumming fingers, the man who planned the future of their money and where it should be put, and reaped good rewards for himself. And there was the family, the boys and the older girl and the couple. He had seen them all, had made his judgements . . . it was the barbed hook in Jonas's mouth and the bait was the line of 'too big to bring down'. Without the juiciness of that he would not have been tempted. He had swallowed, was well interested. And how was it possible, this accolade, *too big to bring down*?

By corruption. No other way. By greed. Had to be. By betrayal of badge and office. Must be. By the stench of dishonesty, bent coppers. Made the family a worthwhile target. It was necessary for Jonas to stay in the shadows and to reveal nothing of his identity. Otherwise the outcome would be bad.

2

Effie and Jonas were checking progress.

It was known a shipment was on the way, and could be assumed it was coming from the troubled narco-religious dictatorship of Afghanistan. Monies passed over in Dubai a month before would by now have been cleared through the *hawal* systems favoured in the Middle East, and an upsurge of meetings had been noted involving the principal players among the associates of Lachlan Wilson. Cameras, craftily hidden, monitored the road in either direction from the gates of the mansion in the Surrey village. It was not known when the load was due to be brought to the United Kingdom and not known what route would be used to traffic it. There were still some loose ends. It was an area of analysis, the supposed skill and talent of Jonas Merrick . . . It was what he was, and the pay grade that he held as an analyst, an individual who scoured accessible information, many strands of it, and made some sense of what was in front of him, rearranged the building blocks . . . But he had made commitments, had dug deep into resources, and would need to come up with answers: fatal if the accountants on the first floor – their territory close to Human Resources – were able to find flaws in his work. Except that Jonas Merrick, accused by his wife of being boring and predictable, was also that rare and seldom-tolerated individual: one who could think 'outside the box'. Not tolerated by those on the fifth floor – DG and Brian, the DDG – but winning the patronage of the Assistant Deputy Director who would guard Jonas's back as long as he was able. He would quietly point out to those who lodged alongside the angels of government the successes achieved for the Service by Jonas, but would be unable to cover for him if matters collapsed in chaos, as well they might. At the heart of Jonas's plan if it succeeded would be obfuscation of the detail of the methods, tactics, used to bring down, nail to the floorboards, the man said to be 'untouchable'. If it were to fail then smart lawyers – and he judged his target's man, Henry Lyons, to be among them – would be crawling all over the business conducted from the Thames House basement Post Room. There would be accusations of entrapment and of abuse of power and of ignoring the Police and Criminal Evidence instructions that had near-biblical importance. He should have been on the Isle of Purbeck, should have been walking coastal paths with Vera, exploring campsite hedgerows with Olaf and watching the savage killing of shrews and field mice and perhaps even a young rabbit – and it was more than possible that Effie could have managed this waiting time and didn't need him . . . As day followed night, the intelligence would come through, the point when the family went into the activity they would indicate that the daughter was on the move. Not yet.

The lists were complete.

No way that he could hurry matters to a conclusion that suited better. Vera had told him, during a final countdown when important pieces of the puzzle could not be slotted in, that 'watching the kettle and hissing at it will not make it boil faster'. He thought Effie good under pressure, capable, calm.

She was nominally with the Foreign Office, was actually with the Sixers, had been in Syria, an agent runner. In the war against ISIS it was not a business of meeting suited officials in parks and hotel bars, or in safe houses. It was a question of cajoling, persuading, threatening, or bribing men and women to track prominent Persons of Interest in the ranks of that barbaric organisation and discover their phone identifications – a man makes a call at a specific time and at a specific location and the giant computer systems have a fair chance of identifying from what number the call was made, then of storing it. There was always the possibility that via the cajoling, the persuading, the threat, and the bribe, the wretch on the receiving end of the message that Effie gave would think it worthwhile to sidle close to the wheels of the prominent PoI. They might have a stone in a sandal and need to bend to extract it, and reach under the vehicle and hear the thud as the magnetised tracker thumped into place. The penalty for being caught would be death. Jonas knew that there were porta-cabins at RAF stations in eastern England from which the big drones were flown. The drones carried precision-guided air-to-ground missiles. If that PoI had his phone in his chest pocket, or rode in a car that had a tracker on the metalwork underneath his seat, the drone could be directed to him. It was supposed that every effort was made to guarantee an absence of 'innocents' when a missile was launched . . . a fatality and the other crowd's investigators would hunt for the source of the leak. If they found it then the prognosis for the informant was bad, or worse than bad, and death would come as a blessed relief. It was what she had done: play God with men's and women's lives and the weapons at her disposal, and her nagging persistence with cajoling, persuading, threatening, bribing, made her formidable. Would she have 'lost' people? Of course. Would she have brought into play the wrong car and the wrong phone? Of course. Would she have lost sleep over errors in the 'fog of war'? Of course not. Would she have worried over her part in 'entrapment' or 'abuse of authority'? Absolutely not. They were as far with their lists as they could be.

She had not indicated to him that she resented him being back at work.

"You find this business, Effie, interesting, worthwhile?"

"I do. A good target, quite fun going after him, if rather harsh on the nerves."

The dogs pulling him, Lachy Wilson strode into the teeth of the wind and the hail, going from the car park where the Ford car was left and away towards the myriad of paths that crisscrossed the gorse and brambles and thickets of trees. It was that part of the North Downs that he found most suited to meetings where his money – and his importations – could be discussed. He was shadowed by Softboy.

On schedule, but out of sight of Lachy, a mass-produced

Vauxhall car would have brought Yitzak Cohn to the place known as Newlands Corner, 500 acres of common ground where some of the yew trees were reckoned more than five centuries old. Also out of sight but easing into a parking place would be the vehicle of a solicitor who regarded himself as much too intelligent to make the sort of error that could dump him into the dock in the Dorking courts. By a courier drop they knew which of the five meeting sites would be used and each had brought a dog. Lachy had the German Shepherds. Cohn pulled along an unwilling toy animal that had cost him £1,000 and was only suitable for a woman's lap, and Lyons had a Setter that wanted only to run and run and run some more . . . they converged.

Lachy would have thought it foolproof. He was 'untouchable', 'too big to bring down', because, it was claimed on the upper floors of New Scotland Yard, he owned too many of the senior men there. Claimed to know about any investigations that were launched against him, had the ability to penetrate even those investigations that had taken over supposedly secure premises and used hand-picked detective teams and men and women from different forces. He paid for it, paid heavily, and had now achieved a sort of peace. He reckoned that a decision had been taken, high up, that going after him opened too many potential scandal areas, revealed an excess of corruption, exposed too many raw issues where confidence in the Metropolitan Police Service would be further degraded, that it was better to save the money, save reputations and let the matters carry on beneath the radar. And saw nothing to alter his view since the last search of his home, with a warrant, three months before, found nothing incriminating, their efforts wasted.

But Lachy maintained his standards.

Could have been seen in casinos or fine restaurants, could have flown first class or in executive aircraft, but maintained the low profile that he thought was the best way of maintaining his freedom. Except that he could not withdraw from the addiction of 'one more coup', and another triumph . . . something to talk over with his lawyer and with his main financial guru.

Softboy had the dogs, entwined in their leads, could not curse them because the Setter and the toy were doted on, and the Shepherds seemed uninterested.

The trio talked. Agreed the schedule of the next payment, assessed the lorry's timetable, and talked about the end point on the far North Sea coast and the transfer. Talked about the arrangement in place for unloading and the distribution, and the rinsing of the cash, and the firewalls that were in place. It was a seriously foul morning and the hail which had been merely annoying now came in harder and the stones pecked at their faces, but that was the way that Lachlan demanded his business be done.

Who would argue? Not Yitzak Cohn. Not Henry Lyons. Nor would either argue with the decision taken by Lachy that his daughter was now the front figure in his organisation. They might not like it, the extent of the girl's authority, but Lachy gave not a flying fuck for their feelings. And he rewarded them, what he called top dollar, and neither would have walked away from him because both were beyond the degrees of guilt and could not hope for a minor sentence if they turned King's.

Cohn said, "Seems in good shape, Lachy. Cash is paid out as owed, and the last transfers, both of them, are in place and ready to drop. Nothing bothering you?"

Lyons said, "No shortcuts, Lachy, just keep it clean and safe. That right, Lachy?"

Lachy Wilson answered them, and recognised their nerves and accepted that both men would raise a glass on the day he told them their services were no longer required. Like they were on a roller-coaster, or a helter-skelter, anything that turned their guts over and had no place and no time to step off.

"All in place. All calm and all careful. You boys look like rabbits in the headlights. All going smoothly, and I've no reason to think otherwise."

He was given his dogs' leads.

Lachy walked off and the hail had softened, had turned into rain, and he felt the back of his legs getting wet. Was excited because this was like days long gone when he was young and when he fought for his survival, and always won. No handshakes, nothing, because they were just employees who took his money and were paid for what they did, and no sense in his mind that he had told them other than what was truth . . . All going smoothly and no reason to think otherwise.

"Hello, stranger, how are you doing?"

"Doing all right, thanks," Chopper answered.

He was at the front reception area of the small office block in Barking, off a route away from the capital, the home of one half of the Flying Squad, the other in Putney in the west.

The girl was persistent. "Didn't you get transferred out?' Is your pass still valid?"

"Should be. I was moved to something outside. Seems it may be permanent."

"We'll miss you."

"Doubt it . . ."

Chopper grinned but Daffs behind the desk had a mournful gaze, like she had always fancied him. There was a guy sitting behind her, the security man, who would have been armed because inside the building were files and intelligence and plans that would have made useful reading to the 'bad boys' on that side of the city. Chopper fed his pass into the slot, and the bar came up. He went through an X-ray and satisfied the guy. He turned back to smile at Daffs and headed for the operational area.

It might not yet have fully sunk in that this was likely to be the last visit he made to the Squad, the last time he would present his card and be admitted. He needed families . . . His own had pretty much rejected him but the Parachute Regiment had been superb and he was a sought-after man and one that others wanted to know. Little privileges had come his way, the bonus of being accepted, and the sport had been good and the companionship had been brilliant, and he had been too young to think of any long-term outcome. It had all changed on a dust track in Afghanistan, one shot that was unlucky for him. It hurt to think of it because he remembered Lofty, and going home with him to Brize and waiting on the aircraft till the Honour Guard had taken off his best mate. Had flogged through police recruitment and prised himself into CID training and done enough to get noticed and then win a place in the Squad – an elite place, another family, and top of the tree and good for his ego. Great place to be: the Squad dealt with 'serious acquisitive crime', with kidnappings that usually involved one crime gang nicking the son of another crime gang because of an outstanding drugs debt, and burglary investigations when violence and risk to life were involved, and ATM robberies. The technique they used was to hit those 'bad boys' on the pavement going in or coming out, which required speed of reaction if the great unwashed going about their business were not to get a knife wound or a bullet hole. But it made certain that the charges were for 'armed robbery' and the dread word 'conspiracy' was not needed, which made life seriously hard for defence briefs. It had an excitement, adrenaline surges, but required a degree of fitness . . . It had been noticed that the pains in his ankle were more acute, but that he seemed able to avoid sessions with the police quacks, and put medical examinations on hold. He could do the driving and the shooting (the Squad were permitted to carry handguns as routine), and do the surveillance of which they were proud. But the running was getting difficult, and ten weeks before he had been bumped off a job because he must have been noticed limping and grimacing.

It had not come to a head because the 'other matter' had turned up: a meeting with a girl called Effie, and a walk on the bridge with an old guy that Chopper thought of as Sunray – no name given, whom Chopper always thought of as a military commanding officer – and Effie was Sunray Minor. That too, in a lesser way, was an introduction to a smaller, pint-sized, family.

He went into the Operations Room. Chalky looked up. He was a detective inspector, had stayed on after his retirement age was reached and did stints as the Squad's version of a Gold Commander, and calling the shots on a pavement hit. The cameras in a bank in front of him were accompanied by the eyewitnesses' hissed voices that were supposed to be whispering into micro-phones on their collars but the tension distorted the words. An

ATM with an old biddy drawing a few quid out, counting it, then pocketing the cash and the card, then starting to walk away, then . . . the screens filled with the charge of a bulldozer down the street, its sharp right turn onto the pavement and the impact as masonry and brickwork fractured, collapsed. Glass windows caving in, guys in balaclavas and boiler suits running with crowbars to where the cash dispenser was at an angle, the crazy end of the attack and just starting to manhandle the machine and its embedded concrete towards the low-load lorry that was now on the pavement. Chalky White, cool, calm, and only one word said, softly, but repeated . . . *Go . . . Go . . . Go . . .* Yelling over the sound system. More figures sprinting and reaching the 'bad boys', announcing that they were armed police, to be flat on their faces. One guy ran and tried to make a go of a charge down the pavement, and two went after him, both older than Chopper, heavier than Chopper, faster than Chopper, and caught the guy, had him pinioned and cuffed. Till he had been detached, they had been his family, just about, with him clinging on. They had their own uniform: trainers and jeans and heavy fleeces, cops' caps and armbands. Their Glocks were back in their holsters, hidden from sight, and a little crowd had gathered, gazing in awe at the aftermath, and would have been half-deafened by the alarms and the roar of the digger. A couple of police wagons had shown up, and uniforms were spilling out, and the tape was being unfurled, and the 'bad boys' looked glum and had cause to, and Chopper's family left them without a backward glance and piled inside the wagons and were driven away.

Chalky had his hand over his microphone, shielding it, and muttered, *Fucking good show, great stuff . . . Hello Chopper, how you doing?* He shrugged, nothing to say, smiled which was as good an answer as he knew. Chopper did not need to be told that he would not have been on that pavement with the Glock and the cuffs, would not have been trusted when the stakes were high and fine lines drawn between the safety of the public and catastrophe. Might have been half a yard off the pace or thinking too much about the pain, or . . . would not have been there.

It was another family gone.

Pretty soon, the guys would be back and the air would be full of droll jokes and then they'd be outside the back doors, by the fire escapes and lighting up, then the arrest reports would be written, and later still they'd be in the pub. Chopper felt there would be little interest in his presence and already they would regard him as an outsider. There would be enquiries, of course – *Hi, Chopper, how's it going? . . . Hope it all works out for you, Chopper . . . Look after yourself, Chopper, mind how you go.* He'd no appetite for it, but could console himself, from what Sunray Minor told him, and what Sunray himself had briefly said, that what he was launched into was a stratosphere more important than getting lowlife down on the pavement and safeguarding an ATM.

He went to his locker and cleared out his personal stuff. The kit he left inside with the door flapping and his key in the lock. He nodded briskly to Daffs on the front desk but she would already have had the message that he was history and went on doing her nails, and the security guy took his card and made no comment.

He was out of the building and on the pavement as the vans came past and he kept his head down and doubted he would have been noticed . . . He did not know where the future would lead him, but remembered what the girl's tongue had felt like in his mouth. He massaged the seashell in his trouser pocket.

His life had moved on, and whether he welcomed it or not hardly mattered.

Back from Landi Kotal, the Khyber Pass district of north-west Pakistan, was Rajah. The plane was nine hours late into Heathrow and the meeting had been delayed to accommodate his eventual arrival. He was a Detective Sergeant in the Met's ACU – Anti Corruption Unit, the latest title given to the officers entrusted with rooting out the 'network' of bent cops working in the capital.

Dawson pouted at him. She was 40, and celebrated her fiftieth month as a divorcee. She too was a Detective Sergeant, and said the work was 'better than sex'. Took her son, usually billeted with her parents, on holiday in term time, and didn't give a shit for the school's complaints, and had just come back from a week in Bognor where it had pissed with rain every day. She revelled in the fact they were the 'untouchables' as far as the hierarchy at Scotland Yard was concerned, regarded with fear and distrust. She liked to tell anyone ranked Commander or above that 'fish rot from the head' and then she'd smile sweetly.

"Done wonders for your tan, Raj. Welcome back."

The boss was Plunket, the youngest of them and the tyro who had reached the status of Detective Inspector. His divorce had come through a month earlier, and it was reckoned he'd hardly noticed except that he was now living in a one-bedroom studio and bouncing off packing cases. He had demanded secure premises for a regional part of ACU, hardened security locks, blast-proof windows, regular bug sweeps. He liked notebooks, communication that could not be hacked into, and was regarded as humourless, hobbyless, and a crusader against corruption.

"If we could deal with tomorrow – time and location."

There were half a dozen similar work areas on that floor. Under Plunket's regime they were all called by their last names. Could do the arrest at the target's home in the morning, or at the golf club, in the bar where their man would always be on a Tuesday because of the 'flexible roster' governing that particular Detective Chief Inspector. Birthday parties with the grandchildren present were the favourite setting, but they wanted to push on and were unwilling to hang around for an anniversary. The work sheet was full and needed thinning out like they were sugar beet plants and there were too many of the bloody things as Rajah had remarked before flying out on his break. Plunket could have pushed this to an upper floor at the Yard's main building, had it vetted and approved by an Acting Assistant Commissioner, which would have chucked out a hostage to fortune, so had declined the usual procedure. There would be a moan from on high, and something frantic from the press office as to what they could say but he would not return their calls. The three of them, and a couple of uniforms, would do the lift.

"No chance, boss, of him making a run for it?"

No raucous laughter, but cold smirks in unison because the files were in front of them, photos included, mostly taken by Dawson, who prided herself on the quality of her long-lens snapshots, and most showed a middle-aged man, fifteen stone and counting. Also showed him in the car park of his favourite golf club pocketing an envelope from the elder of the Courtney clan who did protection, girls, and cocaine round the Rotherhithe area. They wanted to know how their personal security played out in that police division.

"Do bears shit in the woods?" Dawson answered. "Walking backwards I'd catch him, and if the unlikely happens we'll have the two lads to hunt him down. I'm for the golf club. Sends a better message."

"And a gin left idling on the bar – what a waste." Rajah might have been a nominal muslim but drank tidily. His father was a senior cop in the Khyber Paktunkhwa force, politically sensitive, headquartered in Peshawar, walking on disaffected eggs, threading through a hair-trigger minefield – a survivor, and proud of his boy in faraway England. Rajah had done conventional time in the ranks, then gone to the Directorate of Professional Standards. Bored with who pinched whose bum or squeezed a breast, he had come to ACU, and his ethnicity ticked a useful box.

"He'll sing."

"They all do."

"Be looking for bail."

"Might top himself."

"We'll want a witness statement out of him. Only charge him when he's done the decent thing."

"Good if he does Crown witness against the Courtneys."

"Would make it hard, his life inside."

It was confirmed for the golf club. Nine holes in the morning, then lunch and probably a shared bottle, then the bar and a gin or three and waiting for his wife to turn up to drive him home ... they might wait till she was there which would add to the occasion. Not their business, but the Courtneys were talked over and their relevance, whether they'd face arrest, charges, convictions, and their status.

Dawson had a perverse habit of breaking up a mood before it had a chance to become complacent. "The joker we're hitting, he's not in any others' pockets, is he?"

Plunket was pushing files into his drawer and turning a key, and would augment that with a padlock. "Meaning?"

"They're only medium range, the Courtneys. Does he service bigger fish?"

"Not that we know, not that we've heard."

"More's the pity."

"You have a way, Dawson, of dumping a bucket of iced shit on us just when we are feeling all smart and chirpy. What's the pity?"

She could do a sweet face, almost angelic. "Going on up, up higher, up above the clouds, right up there. Where you might get to find Lachy Wilson, that poisonous bastard. He must have more of the Met on his payroll than any other villain. Stands to reason."

"That's a graveyard, Dawson. Look at the history. All the bright boys who reckon they have security and intelligence in place go after him, and they end up taking early retirement, on a rubbish heap, broken. That's what he can do, that's what he pays for. I'd give my right bollock to be that close to Lachy Wilson, to have one of his informants, but it's not happening in this case, not that I know of."

"Sorry, didn't mean to take the gilt off the gingerbread." Dawson pushed her chair back and stood. "Out of order, apologies."

Plunket shook his head. "Not out of order, and no reason to apologise, Dawson. One day, some day . . . we're allowed to hope. Meantime we do our job and make it harder for those bent bastards to sleep at night. Have a good evening."

They left him, Rajah lugging his rucksack and Dawson with her shopping list, but Plunket stayed on. Usually did. Had stayed on late ever since the separation, and before that. He dug some photos from the back of a drawer, and looked at the face. Thought he read the faintest grin on it, like he was mocking the camera. Gazed at it a long time before locking it away . . . and started to think of the questioning of the target in an interview room and with a solicitor present but found it hard to concentrate . . . and that other face, Lachy Wilson's, intruded, and Plunket ground his fingernails hard into the palm of a hand and almost drew blood. Wilson was an untouchable, beyond reach.

Two months earlier (December '25)

Because he did not do pubs, Jonas Merrick was confused.

He looked around as the door flapped shut behind him.

Saw rugby shirts displayed in glass-fronted frames, and a couple of mounted stag heads with antlers. Saw the flags of the nations of the United Kingdom. TV screens showed male wrestling. Music was playing, the sort he was thankful was not heard in the Post Room. He did not know what to order. He did not stop at a pub on his way from Thames House to Waterloo, nor at those between Raynes Park station and his home. No one had ever invited him to a pub. A pub was as far off his radar as golf or worrying about the weekend football scores. But here he was in a pub, had travelled from Lambeth Bridge up into Islington, by taxi. Effie had refused to work out the best underground route but instead had come outside with him insisting that he take a taxi and had shoved money into his hand, and Kev and Leroy had been on duty and had waded into the traffic flow and indicated to a black cab where it should pull into the kerb. Jonas rarely used taxis. Felt a fraud. Had been dropped at the pub, a Victorian building.

The barmaid addressed him with respect, but with a hint of amusement.

What did he want? Something non-alcoholic. Did he want a fruit juice, a coffee, a fizzy lemonade . . .?

He would like a non-alcoholic beer. Thought that right for the environment and the cover. It was poured for him, and he paid for it and seemed surprised at the cost. Had sat down. A rather jolly man joined him, introduced himself.

"DCI White, Chalky. You're Mr Merrick. I recognised you from your clothes, what your assistant described. We've spoken enough times over the years, but only on the phone."

His glass was picked up and he was led to another part of the pub, behind two pillars; there were lunch tables and a hotplate and he was shown to a shadowy corner, a fire was burning on the far side and there were Christmas decorations, extravagant in his view.

The Detective Chief Inspector said, "Always been good to speak with you, Mr Merrick, and I'm pleased to put a face to the name, and pleased to be of help. I think I have what you might be looking for, the right sort of lad."

Jonas ducked his head, indicated a measure of gratitude but nothing sincere until he had seen the goods on offer.

Between gulps from a pint glass, Chalky spoke. "We regard ourselves, and deservedly so, as the top detective force in the Metropolitan Police, Mr Merrick. We make it very hard to get into. High standards and when the end-of-shelf time comes we're not sentimental. The toecap of a boot hits the arse and firmly. We have a boy who I think is right for you. Quite pretty, a nice smile, girls adore him but he's not much good to them. But he gets noticed. He has an injury. Not a bad one, but enough to prove increasingly embarrassing to his prospects of staying with us. Caught a bullet in the ankle while he was with a Para unit in Helmand. To us he's Chopper, and that reflects his football achievements, foul play increasing to compensate for sub-standard fitness and deteriorating speed. Bluntly, we're going to dump him, so we've a motive in hoping you are attracted. What else? Fearless, no questions about his personal bravery. Honest, never been doubted. Intelligent to a limited degree. Not top of the range but bright enough. His motivation was spotted by one of my colleagues: wants to be part of a family. What he craves. How am I doing?"

In the world of Jonas Merrick there were a score of men and women such as DCI Chalky White. Jonas disliked face-to-face meetings, he valued impartial advice, best contributed over the phone. The detective had come on to Jonas's radar when working in the Province some fifteen years earlier . . .

"The way things work in the Squad, Mr Merrick, is that two or three times a year we have a binge lunch. Noon in the pub and a restaurant round the corner booked for four o'clock, and we'll be lucky to get home by ten. It's about bonding, about being off-duty, about forgetting, almost, the privileges of rank. Hair, if we have any left, is let down. Just take a good look at him, Mr Merrick, read him a bit and see what you think. Heh, drink up, it's not a funeral."

He was whacked on the shoulder and realised that was a sign of friendship . . . Jonas knew that the Squad was expert in their work, had a reputation for courage, and the fact that he was in this bar, now filling with Chalky's fellow officers – men wearing ties with the motif of a squatting eagle and women who had the same design on pendants on chains round their necks or brooches on jacket lapels, and the drinks beginning to flow. His eyes met Chalky's. He followed the glance. Saw the group and one caught his attention . . . younger than most, full hair and a rumpled suit as if unused to wearing it and a tie that was poorly knotted, and standing at the edge of the group. Maybe he'd never been part of it – or maybe had been once. Chalky was gone from his view . . . Jonas thought it necessary to keep drinking from his glass but when it was nearly finished, the barmaid thrust her way through the crowd, voices rising, and laughter growing, bringing Jonas another beer, and a packet of crisps. He reached in his pocket but she said that it was taken care of.

He watched the young man. Saw him hanging at the edge of the crowd. Saw him sitting with a group but not included beyond what was polite.

Cruel old world, Jonas thought.

He finished his crisps, and the second drink, and found the toilets and reflected that he liked the smile and the openness of the face, and had seen him shift his stance and bite at his upper lip as if that killed the pain.

Had seen enough.

He headed for the door, the bar now raucous.

He was intercepted. "How was he?"

"For what I want, he'll do. Probably do well."

He went outside and might take a taxi and might try the underground. Effie would get the contact details.

Likely to do better than well, with those looks. He gritted his teeth and felt a little shame because he was evaluating the boy as if he were a bullock in the ring at a livestock auction.

Julie's lunch had been a cup of soup and a lettuce and tomato sandwich, brown bread, thinly sliced.

Later she would go for a run on the hill, on public footpaths behind their land.

Her father said she was skinny and needed to put on weight.

Softboy, to her face, said she was a 'runt' and, without muscle, would be a wipe-out.

Her mother would open her hands and look helpless and say that the family depended on her and she'd better 'get used to it'.

Mrs Plumb had looked hurt when she'd ordered her lunch, the half portion of soup and the sandwich, and had said, "I'll not gainsay you, Julie, because that's not my place, but you need some substance where you're going."

What it boiled down to – easy enough to understand – was that in her role of the 'future' she was going to have to protect family interests which might be with a box cutter blade or a lump hammer, or might involve shoving a guy who kicked and screamed into the boot of a car and driving it to a slipway in a marina, parking it momentarily, hopping out, cutting the engine, and letting off the brake – or dropping a lit match into the petrol tank. What her father told her often enough, he had had to fight like a 'fucking wild animal' to get off the ground when he was a kid and had done it because he was clever, also because he was known as a 'hard bastard', and grown men were scared of him, 'scared shit-less'. Lying on her bedroom floor, doing her exercises she could see herself in the full-length mirror and had – she reckoned – a body that was as good to look at as any of those of the actresses, models, and influencers in magazines . . . Now she had proof of it because she had been out running and minding her own business and soaking up the sunshine, and had dumped the Prof far behind her and the guy, the sweet-looking boy, had come after her and said she was *the prettiest girl out running this morning, far and away the prettiest*, and it had been her business to see that his bet was rewarded, made her grin a bit. She was in good enough shape for that, but her dad and Softboy and the Prof, her mother and Mrs Plumb, all wanted her beefed up, like a bloody weightlifter and would have said that being clever, and being the prettiest, would not help her when the time came and she was heading the family firm – unless they found a marriage for her, and her dad and his dad sat down and haggled assets and cash flow and territory, and she was shoved off with some arsehole who'd spend half his nights with a tart – and love was never in the equation . . . all a problem she was hard put to solve. Her dad would get the red mist if she walked out on it all.

She was being groomed. There were girls up north who were made ready for clients: closer to home, a part of their family fortune – what it was, a fortune – that enabled her father to buy the pile where they lived, came off the hard work on their backs of girls from Ukraine and Romania and Bulgaria in the brothels that made serious money and quickly, because the girls looked good and worked hard . . . And she was being groomed, but for different things. The papers, when they had the balls to write it, said her father was 'too big to bring down' and he always flew into a rage if he saw his name in print.

Her form of grooming had started when Hamish had been buried and Gregor had been sentenced to twenty-two years at Snaresbrook Crown Court . . . Julie had been 18 years old. Might have enrolled at an art college, might have taken a law degree, might have chosen accountancy, but all that had gone with her brothers into a grave and a maximum security wing. Taken to London by her dad and Softboy. Going into an old warehouse in Peckham where rainwater puddled the concrete floor and the men's feet echoed and her trainers slithered, and seeing a plastic wall ahead and hearing a low moaning sound coming from it.

Pulling on a boiler suit and shoe covers and a face mask, like the stuff cops used in *Scenes of Crime*. Folding back the plastic wall and, sandwiched between her father and Softboy, going inside and becoming weak-kneed. A man with a bloodied slumped head tied to a chair with masking tape. Two men beside him, in the same gear as she wore, and a chainsaw on the floor, resting on plastic sheeting. Her dad said that the guy had cheated on him, claimed he had lost a consignment but was reckoned to have sold it on and pocketed the return, about half a million's worth. Dad had said, matter of fact, not a big deal, 'We don't tolerate that. Let it go and everyone does it. Both your older brothers did what you're going to do. They were the future, not anymore. You are. You'll take his right arm off, he loses the hand that put stolen money, my money, into his hip pocket, for himself. Not easy the first time, but it gets easier. Promise. Just do it . . . ' She had. The chainsaw had been started up for her. She had small hands and she had to stretch her fingers to get a grip on it, and it was heavier than she expected. The chair was nailed to the floor, otherwise the way the man writhed he would have toppled it backwards. She supposed it was like an initiation, an induction. The family could not sit around until Connor and David were old enough to be put through this challenge. She did not hesitate, surprised herself, went close to him and, at the last moment, as the saw's teeth thrashed, he gave up the struggle and stared at her and she could see that the fear had been replaced by a raw hatred, and that made it easier. He'd no doubt that she was capable of it. She chose a place above the elbow on his right arm. Plenty of blood, plenty of mess. She did not faint, did not feel sick, and cut right through, and he was sagging in the chair. She took her finger off the trigger mechanism and the engine cut the movement of the teeth, and she handed the chainsaw to one of the men and turned her back on the mess.

At the flap in the tent she peeled off the foot covers and shed the boilersuit and they were dumped in an oil drum. A slurp of petrol was poured and a match was thrown. The man, her dad said, would be dumped in a supermarket trolley and taken to an

Accident and Emergency and left there and those who pushed the trolley would be masked. All the plastic sheeting would have gone, along with the unscrewed chair broken into pieces in the drum. The Crime Squad, of course, would want to speak to the man – if he survived – but it was a mark of the power of the family if he refused to say who was responsible. Her father was confident and Softboy said he would bet his last shirt on it. 'Did I do all right?' she had asked her father. 'Yes', she'd been told. And they had driven home.

Different now, because the future was without him in control, day to day. He'd be sitting on a lounger, reading his *Financial Times* and worrying about his chickens, and getting more paranoid as to how the family spreadsheets were looking. She worked hard on her exercise routine. Tomorrow she was in London, talking investments and accompanied by Yitzak Cohn, and she thought it more important that the business suit fitted her well, rather than her being dosed up on muscle-enhancing pills and looking like a freak. If the pills had run riot in her system then a boy would not have come charging after her with the worst chat-up line in history: *Your trainer lace is loose . . . you'll trip . . .* She had stopped, had helped him win his bet, had kissed him.

She had not used a chainsaw again, nor tried her hand with a blade, but Softboy had used both in her name and she had watched. which was thought to be good enough.

"Quite understand," Vic Wilson said into the telephone, and meant it.

She listened to an ever more distressed explanation, and cut it off.

"Yes, it's not easy."

For years Vic's parents had managed to cope with who their daughter had married.

"Good to hear that you're both doing well. Just shout if you need me."

She was the only child of a former detective sergeant who had worked his police lifetime in the West Midlands. When she had married Lachy she had not known the full degree of her husband's criminality. Thought some of his deals might have been 'dodgy', and thought most of his friendships were 'unwise', thought the annual tax bills compared with their standard of living were 'extraordinary', but had married him in a registry office, just him and her and a couple of strangers off the street. She had learned fast, had embraced the new culture, and the price to be paid was the estrangement from her family.

"Any problem, let me know and I'll come running."

She rang once a month. If her father were by the phone and her mobile number came up he would kill it. If her mother answered, she would pretend that one of her friends from the WI had called and the talk was anodyne, non-committal. Vic had not cast eyes on them since the funeral, three years before, and her parents had stayed back and her father had refused eye contact, but her mother had hugged her young grandsons . . . it would have been wasted breath to put out a message that the burial of Hamish should be treated as family only, no flowers. Inevitable that Lachy's associates, and those who wished they were, had turned out, trampling the cemetery grass to thick mud, and behind them had been ranks of detectives from most of the prime agencies at the Yard and at the NCA, and at the edge of the crowd had been a swarm of photographers, but not pushy because there was 'security' to prevent outright intrusion. No wake, but they had heard later that prodigious amounts of cash had crossed the counter of a road-house pub on the Dorking road . . .

Her mother visited Gregor every quarter, but Vic did not know what they talked about. She had once overheard her husband talking to the Prof, and she remembered it keenly. She had been in a corner of the garden, looking at the spread of moss on the lawn and . . . was hidden to them. Lachy had said, 'I want you up there, Prof, and telling him from me, if I were ever to get to hear he had met with, talked to, detectives, then I guarantee he will not see the week out. Wherever he is, I will reach him – ever do it, and inside a week he is dead. Tell him that . . . '

Vic went every month to the prison, no make-up, wearing

charity shop clothes driving Mrs Plumb's car. Gregor always chose a table in a corner, and his grandmother's visits were never mentioned, nor the message that the Prof had relayed.

She rang off. Could imagine her parents in the conservatory of their bungalow. Her father would be gazing ahead, face set in a meld of shame and anger, and her mother would have reddened eyes and her hands would shake on the handles of the tea tray. Meeting Lachy was like freedom descended on her, and he had style and wit, and gave her status. At the functions they used to go to when he was still climbing, brushing rivals aside, she would be the nearest thing to royalty and other gang women would near as dammit curtsey to her. All around her was her affluence, and her eldest was dead and her second was 'away', and her girl was being sucked in deeper and had already lost the art of laughing and joking and having fun, and the next two were poor specimens.

She heard Julie coming down the staircase. They barely spoke now.

She called out to her daughter but was not answered. She went to the kitchen and saw her heading for a back gate off the property, and put the kettle on to boil and would make some tea ... Knew that a shipment was coming in and felt uneasy, did not know why.

"It's the waiting," the AssDepDG said.

"Always the waiting."

"Would have been better off in your caravan, Jonas."

"But I am not in my caravan."

"We have full resources on it, and Aggie's people."

"And nothing as yet showing up."

"Not getting gloomy, Jonas, I hope?"

"Not gloomy, just waiting."

"There's rather an amount riding on this one, Jonas. Please don't forget ..."

"Which you've already told me."

Jonas seldom faced his protector and mentor. He kept his back to him and, hunching forward, obscured his screen from the visitor. He detested that those in positions of authority over him expected to be provided with a running commentary on how it was all going. What fence were they at? How long before the final whistle? What was the score? Would not do it. Actually, Jonas was rather fond of Crime. Liked it better than Terrorism which was thankfully extremely rare but aroused the political elite into a state of near hysteria, enjoyed it better than Counter-espionage and planning the expulsion of members of Russia's military intelligence, GRU, and packing them off on an aircraft back to Czar Vladdy's territory. The times of extreme danger to Jonas' life and limb had, in fact, been in clashes with spy targets. He had been pretty safe, at arm's length, from Organised Crime, had found the challenge stimulating, liked it – other of course than when a Liverpool girl had attempted to sever his head from his body – and been shot dead for her pains, a self-inflicted wound on his part and trying to rubber-neck the end of an operation, and a Liverpool Council Pot Holes Department high-visibility vest was framed and on the wall of Aggie Burns' surveillance section, on the third floor. There was something worthwhile about the opponent in Crime, and the challenge they chucked at him. He regarded most of the terror people he tracked as dim, and their more intelligent directors stayed far from harm's reach. And he regarded the spies as methodical, predictable, and seldom showing any initiative. The criminal element intrigued him; he believed most of them were driven by simple greed, harboured an inability to spend the loot they gathered in, but still found avarice to be an addiction – fought, tooth and nail, to keep their cash safe – and were bright, clever and cunning. Ruthless too, which appealed to him, but greed was dominant.

He had been handed the matter of Lachlan Wilson, 'too big to bring down', and relished it, and had enjoyed being up close with him, having the chance to make assessments. Effie had dug out the police documents, classified, notable by their failure, and he had pored over them, then hatched the plan. The first part, a run in the sunshine along a coastal esplanade in Dubai, which sounded to Jonas like a ghastly place, that was only a prologue.

"You display excellent pedigree, Jonas, for the name I gave you, you grumpy old fucker. Courtesy would be appreciated."

Jonas was rarely polite when stressed. He noted the time, and scraped back his chair. Closed his screen, picked up his briefcase, and reached for his coat and hat.

"And you will appreciate the train timetable out of Waterloo. Be satisfied with my inability to take us forward. When they move? I don't know. Where they move to? I don't know. But where they move to dictates when I can throw our boy, Chopper, into the fray . . . Effie will be here. Will react as necessary the moment those questions are answered, the *when* and *where*. Or try to. We are dawdling now, but when it starts it will be a sprint, and if we are not fast enough then we will lose out, simple as that, and the chance will not return. Please excuse me."

Jonas spoke with a hiss in his voice. As he left his little den, he heard the AssDepDG mutter to Effie, "Poor old beggar, quite flaky isn't he?"

3

Vera followed him out through the front door, and Olaf bolted after them. Jonas had his schedule to keep, the walk to Raynes Park station was exactly timed and did not brook delay if he were to be in his place on the platform when the train pulled in. He looked back and saw the cat close to Vera's heels: it would have been a sudden impulse on her part to go down the pavement with him because she still wore her indoor slippers. He stopped and listened.

"You wouldn't hear me out last night, Jonas. Don't just shake your head and mutter that you were busy . . . after supper you just sat in your chair and closed your eyes and refused to discuss it. Heaven's sake, Jonas, it is not the end of the civilised world we are talking about, it is our caravan . . . More to the point, it is our holiday, already booked and you supposed to be free of work commitments . . . What is there that is difficult to talk about? Jonas, are you listening? Just stop believing you are single-handedly saving the nation from oblivion. Sorry, Jonas, but you are being very trying . . ."

Their road, lined with bare cherry trees, was a rat-run at that time in the morning. Taking the little blighters to school when Jonas reckoned walking, as he did, would have been beneficial to them. Shaving a couple of minutes off the journey to the station . . . allowing time for a ludicrously expensive coffee before getting to the office . . . and noise and fumes, and her rabbiting on in his ear . . . but he realised from the annoyed yowl that Vera had lifted Olaf in her arms and carried the cat as she approached him.

"What I was trying to say and you refused to hear was that the caravan will be ready for collection on Thursday. If I get it, God forbid, it is just the repair to pay for, if they bring it back then that's another twenty-five pounds, and we can pack it on Friday, be off on Saturday for a really early start . . . Jonas, cheer up, please do, it's only twenty-five pounds, and I'll be on the phone this morning and get the camp site booking changed because we've already paid a deposit on the one I cancelled . . . Jonas, will you, please, nod your head at least, show that you have taken it all in, then concentrate again on saving humanity – or whatever it is you do in London . . . Jonas, you are annoying me."

And Olaf was shouting a protest at him, and the Stanhopes were open-mouthed at their front gate, and Jonas Merrick swatted her away in the only style he knew.

"Of course. Pay the twenty-five. Off to the Isle of Purbeck on Saturday at dawn. See you this evening, my dear."

He lengthened his stride and the cries of the cat grew fainter. In his mind, already forming, were a bevy of lies that he would have to employ. He was puffing and his breath came faster, and it was nothing to do with the ghastly prospect of missing his train. In truth, Jonas Merrick was an addict. Like a prolific smoker, he was able to turn his back on work for a limited period, strictly limited. Three days or four, when he steeled himself, were possible but it took mental preparation and solid knowledge that the end game was in capable hands – those of the AssDepDG and of Effie. The trip away had seemed possible the week before and effort had gone into the planning of him being away from the Post Room . . . All for nothing, and the craving was back and it was imminent, the finale, he was sure of it. Like a prize might be snatched from his fingers. He waved his season ticket at the barrier, and cursed because it did not open immediately, but a station worker realised that 'the poor old boy' was having trouble with the system and let him through.

He realised the skill with which Vera had ambushed him, rather admired her for it, and her ground would have been carefully chosen; the pavement was ideal. He chuckled. But she would still have to be lied to, which would exercise him . . . The train arrived. With seats already taken and the corridor filled with standing commuters, Jonas elbowed his way to 'his' window seat and fancied it was known to those boarding at Motspur Park and Worcester Park and even Ewell West that the seat was reserved for him, not available to others. It might have been because word had passed among the daily travellers that the man who dressed as if from a charity shop had – after a few days' absence – returned to his routine, displaying bruises around his eyes, cut lips and abrasions on his chin, his jacket showing signs of more than wear and tear, and his briefcase with the royal insignia looked to have done combat.

Jonas pondered . . . on the judgements he had made on his recruit. The boy obviously revelled in the name of Chopper that had been awarded to him, and could look after himself quite well when he chose to jump out of aircraft and believe in the qualities and professionalism of others – those who packed the 'chute into the bag on his back. Would Jonas have done that? Would Jonas have given Vera a peck on the cheek, then ruffled the hair at Olaf's throat, muttered something about seeing them at teatime, perhaps – then gone off and launched himself and felt the force of the slipstream before it opened, or did not? Would he? He would not. He thought Chopper – young Harris with the war wound in his ankle – complex, quite capable of surprising those who had failed to get close to him, quite interesting, and useful to Jonas Merrick.

The train lurched to a stop, and he was out and propelled over the concourse, and down the steps that would take him along the south side of the river. When he had started out at Thames House as an analyst, a contributor to reports that were never read comprehensively, he had come down these steps and seen the broad smile of a true chancer beaming out from behind a flower stall. Jonas had discovered that his career high spot was as a crucial member of the Great Train Robbery team, as it became known, had done time for it, was well known. He had hanged himself while fortified with an extreme volume of alcohol, and the pitch was never taken up by another florist. Every working day, Jonas went down those steps in the morning and climbed them in the afternoon, and thought of Buster who sold chrysanthemums.

He hurried to work, and his coffee and pastry in the Garden at the back, then his descent into the Post Room.

Effie said to him, in her Yorkshire accent, "I don't have it in concrete, Chopper, but we think it's soon. Vague, I know, best I can do, and we may have little time for a final briefing. You good with this?"

He'd said he was. And she had rung off.

Chopper was shaved, dressed in smart casuals. Had a role to play. The trained man where previously he had been the idiot. His life moved on and he'd precious little idea of where it was headed.

A life that had started conventionally. Older parents, careful, private people. A bungalow in the village of Horrabridge, north of Plymouth and south of Tavistock, up the road from the home of Francis Drake who had shown enterprise and a demand for adventure, neither of which the teenage Kenny Harris was finding at home. He had left school a year early, had taken a bus into Plymouth, found an army recruiting office, and signed up. Neither his mother nor his father had shown surprise or regret at his decision. 'Your life, son, you live it . . . ' He had been a tough but average schoolboy footballer, might have been looked at by Argyle and Exeter City, but not called in for a trial. Had done basic training in the army up in the north, and had been posted to a Rifles regiment, and his reputation on the football pitch would have preceded him, and as soon he was able he had volunteered, and been accepted, by the Paras. He had gone back to Devon, first time in months, and told his father and mother what he was doing and expected them to counsel him to be careful and stay clear of danger, but they had merely listened and then said that they were off to the north Cornish coast in their camper wagon that afternoon, and they hoped, of course, that he would be happy where he had chosen to go, what he had chosen to do. He had walked back into the village and stood at the bus stop. He had only once been back to Horrabridge. His parents were formally listed as his next of kin. He doubted anyone in the village would remember him, the loner kid who had few friends outside the football squad. Pretty soon he had come to regard the Battalion as his family and when they had been urged to draw up wills and last testaments, he had filled in the paperwork and sealed the envelope and had told not a living soul that anything he had was going to the Regiment's fund for Widows and Dependants. There was no girlfriend left behind in the village wondering what had happened to Kenny Harris. He reckoned that a week after he had gone, when they were home from Padstow and Newquay and St Ives, his parents would have cleared his room, binned everything into black plastic bags, taken them to the dump, and likely given it a clean coat of paint and new curtains, knowing he would not be back. He'd sent them a picture of himself in uniform wearing his beret. Had gone back when he was 'walking wounded', on crutches, and off the bus from Plymouth had struggled to get up the hill and to the bungalow, and had not phoned ahead, and the camper wagon was not there but he had rung the bell, and heard nothing, and a neighbour had popped a head over the dividing fence. They were away, out on Dartmoor, had he not told them he was coming? Chopper had never reckoned anything was his fault. Had it been his fault that he had lost that real family, however eccentric they were and he was, then he might have felt a sense of some personal inadequacy. It was easier to be a victim than be open to blame.

Now had a new crowd, a small one, with Effie as the link. Thought he belonged with them, with Sunray and Sunray Minor. The challenge now was to get close and personal with a girl called Julie. Something wicked about her that he might have to match.

Out in the half light, feeding his chickens, Lachy Wilson heard the gravel crunching. Saw Yitzak Cohn at the side of the house, in his best, a £2,000 suit and £1,000 shoes, and a raincoat draped over his shoulders, and lit by the security lights that had been updated to give him even better protection.

"You have a good day?"

"All of it a pleasure, in that company – what else?"

And Cohn gave that helpless Mediterranean shrug that he was so good at. The briefcase, embossed leather and the strap at full length, bounced on his hip. Did Lachy want to glance again at the papers inside? He did not. Was Lachy happy with all aspects of the negotiations to be entered into that day? He was. Yitzak Cohn was by nature a pessimist and would have hoped for further qualification of the family firm's position, so that he was better covered, less exposed. Cohn waved, and Lachy went back to his chickens. The car pulled noisily away from the front door. The *consigliere*'s driver would be at the wheel, and Cohn and Julie would be in the back, and they would be in the City in an hour. He had attempted to brief her the previous evening, but was rebuffed. 'Am I in charge of this meeting or am I not?' Normally, faced with that level of impertinence he would have given her a verbal kick in the arse, but he had grimaced, and turned away, leaving her choosing her suit for the following day. The chickens were feeding well, had laid well, looked well . . .

Lachy disliked Yitzak Cohn but accepted that his expense in employing the man was rewarded. A clever man and inventive, and with a loyalty that was bedded down in the cash paid him. And Julie, the future, was being taken to London for a meeting with bankers anxious to support Lachy Wilson with investment opportunities, and the girl would have to bargain for better terms than those offered, fight hard, and she'd be able to because she was a feisty little bitch, and . . . He loved his chickens, was gentle with them, and talked to them, and his conversation that morning, in a *patois* of grunts, coughs, expletives, and occasional politeness would give him a degree of pleasure.

He held the Courtneys in contempt. The Courtneys might well have short memories. Lachy's was infinite. His ability to recall imagined slights was huge. The senior Courtneys, older than Lachy and seeing him as a rival and an upstart, had once put him down at a charity function, had removed a well-heeled guest from Vic's company, elbowed in, and not apologised. As he explained to his Rhode Island Reds, in particular Doris, 'I'll not tolerate rudeness under any circumstances and especially not if it affects my Vic. The Courtneys are second grade. They have no quality. They showed us up in a public place, which I'll not have. Likely forgotten by them, but not by me, my friends. I get to hear things, hear them and store them away, and I wait. Now's the time. There's a cop, bent as a banana. Old and fat and coming up to retirement. He's been on the Courtney take for more than fifteen years. I don't know him, never met him, and – more important – he does not know me. I can feed things into the system. I hear about this cop and what he means to the Courtneys, like a prop to them he is and they need him. So I tell my people to pass a word into the camp of those real mean bastards, the ACU, and give them a case against this guy. They'll nail him, any day soon, because they'll want him before retirement. Ironic, I suppose, but it's a hard world out there, like it would be for you if the foxes weren't kept away from you at night. A savage world, and the Courtneys won't survive . . . that's life."

He was grinning, as he made sure the door to the pen was bolted . . . then thought of his lorry, a week out, and that gave him more pleasure, and told the birds about it through the fence.

It was what they did to break a chain, to avoid the use of an internet trail.

Extra work for Yitzak Cohn's driver. He left the car in an underground bay, had the envelope in a secure inside pocket, the timetable of the flights in his memory, and set off for the travel agency.

He had not noticed the tail for the whole of the journey from Abinger Hammer, on to the A3, Kingston upon Thames, and Camberwell. Hadn't a sniff of the trackers, nor had he heard of Miss Aggie Burns or of the reputation, jealously guarded, of her people.

"I don't think that would be acceptable," Julie said.

She heard the intake of breath hiss between the perfect orthodontics paid for by Yitzak Cohn. She had no doubt her father would have said to him before they'd left, 'Don't take any shit from her. Lead her.' They were in a boardroom. It was where the firm's directors met before taking lunch, cooked in-house. At a polished table, large enough to have seated a dozen comfortably, was the number cruncher, Cohn and herself. The *consigliere*, what he liked to be called, putting up his hands in simulated protest at the use of a Mafia title, had thought he had done the deal with their host. The company handled investment sums with discretion; they had a wide portfolio of clients and very few of them were open to public scrutiny. His name was George. George and Yitzak, old friends, old business allies, crooks in pricey suits, and with the talent to avoid petty restrictions, legal tripwires, the tedious matters that affected 'little people', had thought the deal done. How much was to be invested, what the rate of return was expected to be, and the size of the firm's remuneration. Julie had no doubt that a generous amount of that fee would end up in an overseas account in the name of a proxy but under the control of Cohn. George gulped momentarily then smiled vigorously. Perhaps he had misheard her.

"What sort of problem is there?"

Cohn interjected. "No problem at all, George . . . not a problem is there, Julie?"

"Of course there's a fucking problem. Your reward is disproportionate to the business we are bringing you. Needs a blade taken to it."

They were in the City, near where St Mary le Bow met Poultry. Smart premises, top-of-the-range rent, and the furnishings to go with it. Nothing as vulgar as a dispute over money should take place here. She was not yet a woman in their eyes, just a girl, a kid sent by her father but safe in the knowledge that Yitzak Cohn, maestro in the handling of financial deals, would be there to hold her hand. More likely, Julie thought, to want to have his hand up her skirt and feeling around. Most of the way into London he had gazed at the length of her thigh between her knees and the hem of her skirt. The suit had cost her what she imagined her father's man and George would have each spent on the silk ties they wore.

"Well," Cohn said, and his face was flushed with

embarrassment, "I am sure a little discretion can ease us over this little difficulty."

And George had the look in his eyes that expressed his admiration that a 'bit of meat' had a voice and a sense of humour, which he would indulge. "I think my team were a touch hasty, and the fee could be eased down a point – and then we'd all be happy."

He paused, caught Cohn's expression and imperceptibly winked . . . Yes, a decent little shag if she were up for it, and was tidying his papers, and was about to drop them in the shredder when Cohn said, "That's a hard bargain you drive, Julie. And a pleasant little victory to report back to your father, and—"

"No way I'm putting up with that shit."

"Steady, Julie."

"I hope we're not at cross purposes, Miss Wilson . . . We have represented your family for many years and always looked after mutual interests. I must warn you that a misunderstanding could lead to serious consequences."

She snapped at him, "Explain yourself."

"What George meant was that—"

"What I meant was exactly what I described. 'Serious consequences.' Baldly stated, for the uninitiated, that implies a leaking of information concerning deals in the past."

"Then you are an idiot, and I do not wish to do business with fools. I advise you that any leakage, as you put it – or snitching, or touting – would see you go down, George, for a minimum of fifteen years, and fines that would bankrupt you. And Yitzak would be in a similar shared cell on the same corridor but probably for an additional three or four years after you have been released . . . As for my father, he is well able to look after himself. Time to go, Yitzak, and I do not enjoy having my time wasted."

The thick pile of the carpet crushed any sound of the chair legs being pushed back. She was standing. A small jotting pad, blank on the page, was slipped into her bag. She nodded her head to each of them, was on her way to the door. There was silence behind her for a moment and she was a pace short of the door.

George called out, "Would ten points off the fee be acceptable?"

"Perfectly. What took you the time?"

There was a lobby outside the boardroom where covered hot plates stored the lunch that she would not share. Instead she would walk around, soak up the sights.

She heard behind her, "Jesus, what a little minx – she'd screw like a rattlesnake."

And heard the Israeli's voice, "Perhaps, if anyone ever gets the chance to find out. Not on the horizon right now."

Three months earlier (November '25)

The convoy blocked the road. The first two vehicles, vans with blue lights rotating, were against the gates. Jonas Merrick, Effie at the wheel, was in the passenger seat of a small vehicle behind them. There was a blast on the horn of the lead van. Perfunctory, and just for the record. Already the bolt cutters were in place, the handles squeezed together, and a heavy padlock bar snapped and fell away. Another beefy guy was shoving the gates aside. Engines racing, the two guys in that little advance party were back into the van and they were heading up the drive, Effie following.

Jonas noted Softboy coming out of the front door of the lodge, recognisable from the surveillance photos. Jonas knew he was the 'enforcer' for the family, and that the man who had given him that name – Softboy – had spent nine weeks in hospital recovering from his injuries. Dogs were barking behind the lodge but wisely they had not been freed – had they been, there was a good chance they'd come forward and be shot. A couple of hundred yards up the drive was an island of rhododendrons and beyond them the tarmac veered to the right and he was able to see the size and scale of the Wilson home.

Effie murmured, "God, what a shit-awful place. Whoever built that saved on architect's fees."

Jonas reflected that crime paid, paid very adequately. The house was built of brick, windows in plenty, enough chimneys for a crematorium, a front entrance with a mock-Roman portico. The grounds had been cleared of dead leaves and the rose bushes had been cut back. There had been frost overnight, and it had been pitch-dark when Effie had picked him up at his front door at five, and it still wasn't seven ... She had made him stand outside his front door, and told him to step into a white garment of reinforced, disposable, paper, and he'd pocketed the plastic shoe coverings. And, rather as if she were a carer and dealing with an incontinent old idiot, had hooked up the hood, then slipped a Covid-remnant face mask onto his mouth and nose, and slung his trilby into the back of the vehicle. If Vera had thought he looked like a pantomime villain she had not said so and he had not seen curtains twitch at their neighbours' windows.

He saw Lachy Wilson on the porch steps, dressed as if he were up and about every morning at this time. Clean shirt, trousers with a crease, polished shoes, hair combed, and nothing on his face to betray any surprise. Likely that he had had twenty-four hours' warning, and Jonas realised the little touch of sophistication: the gate had not been already opened, which would have endangered the contact the 'untouchable' owned, and a man who was 'too big to bring down' did not make that kind of error. Sometime, though, he would, and it would be Jonas' job to recognise it and exploit it. They all made mistakes. Jonas studied him, and tried to read him.

Police, all uniformed, swarmed from the vans and swamped the portico. Jonas saw the paperwork presented to the householder, done correctly, with respect, and it was scanned by the man, and Wilson stepped back and opened his front door wider and invited them in.

A piece of theatre. An audience of Jonas and Effie, and only a Chief Constable in the local force aware of it. Each layer believed this was the real business and revelling in the challenge of having a search warrant and entering the home of the man described in the tabloids as 'UK's biggest villain' and two van loads were inside before Jonas and Effie clumped through the door. Both struggled with the weight of equipment they carried. There might have been surprise that their own photographic people were not there, but it had been put around that other work had taken them already and that the crime-scene couple, old guy and younger woman, had been roped in as replacements.

Effie had the steel boxes. Jonas had a tripod carrying a floodlight, and another on which a camera could be mounted. They were inside the hall, and a line of police boots was in place, and the carpet was white and pristine. Attention would have been drawn to them if they had not shrugged out of their own shoes, so they did so, adding them to the lines and put on the foot coverings they had brought with them. She had a camera out, a pretty basic one because the photographic section in Thames House was reluctant to let one out of their sight, particularly when they were refused knowledge of where it was going. Jonas realised a truth, and quickly. The local uniforms, brought in from Guildford, were up and ready when the conflict was just with a padlock on a front gate, but their enthusiasm was waning fast when they realised the scale of the target and had stared into the face of Lachy Wilson, seen the cold eyes, the mischief of his smile. The search started but without the usual relish.

Plodding around behind Effie, Jonas took in the house, which interested him hardly at all. But he had a chance to study the housekeeper, a Mrs Plumb with no one certain of her given name, except that he knew she was looked after following the death of her husband in Hamburg's prison at Fuhlbuttel. She was in the kitchen frying chipolata sausages and slicing open hot dog-style rolls, and had a kettle steaming on the Aga. Saw Victoria Wilson, police officer's daughter, taking plates and mugs from a cupboard, a well-preserved woman and making a poor fist at disguising the mixture of fury and contempt in her expression as the uniforms in their socks milled around the lounge and the dining-room. It would have taken a week to search a building of that size with conscientious efficiency. Jonas recognised the one they called the Prof, Wally Genge, dog of all trades, handyman, lover of Victorian poetry, totally loyal, the files said, a long-term servant and had done several stretches for them and never hinted at cooperation, and had other responsibilities ... saw the boys in their school uniforms, looking confused, upset, and their mother had hugged them and their father had slapped their shoulders as if to indicate that there was nothing to concern them but they knew that one brother was waking up in a gaol cell, and another was rotting in a grave after a police chase had gone wrong . . . and then Jonas saw the daughter.

A couple of the uniforms stood aside at the top of the stairs.

She would have been in a deep sleep when the uniforms had come into the hall and would have heard feet on the stairs, and voices, and then a knock on her door and guys coming in. Out of bed, wearing only a skimpy nightdress, and grabbing a robe off the hook on the door, and feeling outrage. Out of her room, bed left crumpled behind her, onto the landing and more police there, and an officer trying to get some precision and order into the search and wondering why he didn't have the regular team, who had been spoken for, and her robe was not tied at the front and the belt was hanging loose.

Her mother came out of the kitchen, with a tray holding a heap of rolls steaming in a bowl and plastic plates in a pile and mugs of coffee and a jug of milk and a bowl of sugar with a spoon. 'Nothing to see here, move on please, but a bun and a cuppa to see you on your way.'

"Ma, what the hell's happening?"

Over his face covering, Jonas stared up at her, drank in the entrance the daughter made. The files claimed she was the future. Her mother had nothing to say but went into the living-room where drawers were being opened and they were looking behind pictures, and going through the motions, and . . . Lachy Wilson saw her, and would have seen what the young male uniforms gawped at.

A snapped command: "Get back in your room and make yourself decent."

Jonas watched her. Her head rocked, like a boxer's when the jab went home.

"What's going . . .?"

"Stop flashing and get some clothes on."

A lip curled. Jonas noted. Had seen enough.

The girl turned and went back along the landing, and two uniforms were ejected from her room, and a minute and a half later she was back out dressed, but no brush through her hair and unlaced trainers on her feet. She stomped down the stairs, and she looked through Jonas as she passed him, like he was a piece of dirt and of no consequence, and her eyes blazed . . . Effie raised her eyebrows at Jonas and he nodded, and she would have known what he wanted. Went up the stairs, into Julie's room, did a little snoop.

Jonas hung back. His face mask was doing its job, and when offered a sausage in a roll he declined it politely. There was nothing for them to photograph and the search was perfunctory, and Lachy Wilson was courteous and Victoria Wilson was correct and Mrs Plumb and the Prof and Softboy glowered in different degrees, and the daughter stayed away. Jonas seemed content.

Within an hour the search was concluded. The cameras were stacked away in the steel boxes, unused, and the lighting and the tripods folded up.

A padlock would be provided except that Mr Wilson declined the offer. Effie driving, they followed the convoy, but a mile down the road allowed the others to pull away.

"You happy, boss?"

"Yes, quite happy."

"Something to work with?"

"I would say so, a bit more than 'something'. A morning well spent. Glad to get out of this kit. Yes, well spent. It's the potential for an opening in the family defences. The daughter's a prisoner, isn't she? Not happy to be treated as a child, and not as the future – something to think about and to work with."

He had an anonymous name which suited an anonymous man, and he was as anonymous in his workplace as he was at his home.

Halfway through his life, in his forty-first year, Jacques was a man seen but not noticed, but his comfortable existence was now threatened. He sat in a cubicle in his office and brooded. He was of a lowly rank in the Federal police force in Belgium, and was stressed, which frightened him. His office was in the station of the Scheepvaartpolitie on the north side of Antwerp, the country's second city, and it was from this building that the local authorities attempted to keep some restraint on the burgeoning trade in cocaine coming in daily through the great spread of docks, cranes, container parks. Jacques was familiar with the statistics: a quarter of all cocaine supplies travelling from Latin America came to Antwerp; the port employed 140,000 men and women and boasted 100 miles of quayside, and handled more than eight million containers each year. Policing the harbour area properly was an impossibility. Too many containers to search, too many workers to be PVed – positive vetting took time, effort, resources. Estimates, by self-proclaimed experts, claimed a minimum of thirty tonnes of pure cocaine powder came to Antwerp each year. For a Federal police officer, the dock's police offices provided what an English detective had described to Jacques as 'a cushy old billet', which he hoped to hang on to.

Jacques's role at the Scheepvaartpolitie building should have provided the opposite of stress. It was his job to meet and greet visiting detectives and customs officials from European states and American agencies, and drive them from the airport or the train station, escort them to an upper floor of the building where they would meet senior policemen and the individuals who wrestled daily on behalf of customs with the seeming unstoppable pressure of the imports, now worth billions. Jacques was tasked with taking them on an organised tour of the quays, amusing them with anecdotes, then taking them to their hotel. He would recommend a restaurant, decline politely if they invited him to join them, might pimp a bit if that was required, and would pick them up in the morning and do a brief tour of the city, then on to City Hall and Police Headquarters, in and out of meetings, and back to the airport or the magnificent rail terminus for which Antwerp was justly proud. And somewhere in the day he would have taken them to visit the famed diamond quarter, and also the Rubens house and squeeze his visitors in past the lengthy queues at the cathedral with a flash of his warrant card. He had done the job for

nine years, apparently did it well, and hoped to do it for at least
another nine before retiring on the excellent pension offered to
Federal officers. He found the Germans superior and patronising,
the Dutch arrogant and dismissive of Belgian efforts, the British
pompous, and the Italians chronic shoppers who expected him to
negotiate liberal discounts for then. But for reasons that did not
interest him there were no visitors due that week. Instead he had a
looming date with destiny.

It was two days before his marksmanship evaluation, when
his shooting with a handgun would be judged as adequate or
inadequate. There was a new chief, a bureaucrat, from the
Flemish culture, serious and pernickety, and with a fat volume
of police procedures and standards on his desk. Jacques was
from the Walloon population of the divided state and would
receive no generosity if he fell short – more exactly, if he failed
to shoot straight. His future, it seemed, depended on a higher
standard of shooting in a subterranean range – claustrophobic
and riddled with modern devices that projected targets on to
screens and measured the supposed shots to a millimetre.
Jacques now knew about stress and the way it was debilitating
his life. It was a recent buzzword in the force, and its importance had increased after the suspension of a fellow officer who
had queried it with 'What the fuck did we all complain about
before we'd heard of stress?' A sort of heresy, which in previous
times would have meant being dragged to a stake in front of the
Town Hall or to the castle yard and confronting a pile of
burning faggots.

He would be out on his neck if he failed to get a score above the
pass line. The range was closed for redecoration for the next two days
so he could not draw his FN57Mark2 from the armoury, go down
into the basement, and beg some practice time from the instructor.

Twice that morning he had gone out of a side door into the car
park, and puffed at a cigarette, smoked half of it, chucked it into a
drain . . . He carried the weapon when doing escort duties but had
never drawn it, let alone fired it.

★   ★   ★

Oil drums had been placed across the road.

A main highway between Qazvin and Zanjan. It should have been filled with long-distance lorries, as big and as heavily loaded as their own, using this main arterial route to cross Iran and head for the Turkish border. But there was not a vehicle behind them or ahead. They had skirted Tehran two hours earlier and had thought they were making good time.

Standing beside the oil drums, painted crudely in red and white hoops, were men dressed as militia guards, olive-green tunics and trousers, and carrying Kalashnikov rifles. One of them stood in front of the chicane of drums and waved them down.

Dragan was at the wheel and turned down the music. "Not liking this."

Mehmet was rummaging behind him, twisted in his seat.

"Guard Corps or bandits?"

"Both. Is there a difference?"

"Stopping or going through?"

Mehmet snorted, had his window down, spat through it, had a handgun on his lap, and two canisters. "They would slit our throats."

Not much more to say.

They saw a way through the drums but it would mean slowing almost to a stop and anyway the sunlight caught the nails sticking up out of the planks covering the route through. Would have been a tip from a disgruntled section of the Iran Revolutionary Guard Corps – not on the inside, not on the take – and using a criminal class to do the heavy lifting. And the best part of a ton weight of pure heroin stashed in the back of the lorry by the bulkhead and, hidden by the sacks of nuts, made for a serious weight.

"If they do the tyres we're fucked."

"I think I understand that, my friend."

Dragan slowed the lorry. He was smiling, and Mehmet had a hand out of the window, waving a greeting to the armed men in uniforms. Like they were all fond of each other, and all trusting.

They saw that the hijackers had bought into it, looked relaxed, would have been grinning behind the cotton scarves wrapped round their faces, would have thought that stopping a lorry that had hidden in its trailer a tonne of heroin compound was an easy way to make a fair living. They were coming forward, lining the entrance to the chicane. Dragan pumped on the brake pedal which accentuated the slowing and speared grit out from under the sixteen tyres . . . Mehmet would have thought that if the journey was likely to be easy then the big cats, who stood to make big bucks, would have dispensed with the services of the two of them, would have done it themselves and saved some dollars. But it was not easy, and they carried a valuable cargo – and their weapons, an AK and a pistol, were cocked and the canisters ready. Dragan would put his life in Mehmet's hands: had to, relied on the 'little rat', what he liked to call him, to put down enough gunfire, and enough smoke to screw their volume of firing when he hit the accelerator, and the moment came.

Like the big beast was being held back, straining to be free and then was released. It lurched forward, its full impact cannoning into the pattern in which the drums had been set, hurling them upwards and right and left, and the shape of the route designed to slow a vehicle to a stop was destroyed. Mehmet threw a flash and bang grenade. Dragan had a boot down on the floor, squeezing the last gasp of power out of the Mercedes engine, and managed the wheel with one hand and the pistol with the other. For a moment he saw the faces of half a dozen men, who had been grinning, apelike, ear to ear, freeze in shock and then they had ducked their heads. A hell of an engine was housed below the cab, and they went through.

Shots were fired after them, but they were desultory.

They went on for five or six clicks, and then stopped but only long enough for Mehmet to be out of the cab, and sprinting back to check the rear, and back up inside and the door slammed after him, and he said that there were half a dozen holes in the back hatches of the trailer section, and a few nuts might be spilling out of their sacks.

They drove on, heading for the Iranian city of Tabriz, and then a frontier.

She slapped down her phone, then hesitated. But it was a message too good not to share. Effie slipped off her stool, one stride and was across their tight space. Jonas Merrick, whom she thought of as a kind of genius. His head lolled on his desk and he snored lightly. His lunch was only half eaten, and his coffee was chilling in his mug. His computer screen showed a large scowling cat. She laid a hand on his shoulder and he started up, and his breath came hard, and for a moment he was in a defensive posture while he worked at remembering where he was. Perhaps even who he was.

"Yes? What is it?"

"Next stage. We have it."

"And . . . ?" So damned tired, and age racing after him, and likely to catch him and snaffle his freedom which, Effie's opinion, he'd resent.

"Miss Burns has come through, third floor, the A1 crowd."

"And . . . ?" No enthusiasm shown, no demand for instant access to what she had learned. As if it were all planned, so that nothing would surprise him.

"The family don't use phones or the internet for travel bookings. They have this City firm, off Leadenhall. Done verbally, face to face. So, Julie Wilson and Wally Genge are booked first into a Holiday Inn, Luton airport, for tomorrow night, Wednesday, and have seats on an early flight, half six, Thursday, for Leipzig."

"And . . . ?" She saw a slow smile spread at the sides of his mouth and he rummaged in his desk drawer and took a pipe out, and sucked on its stem.

"An open ticket back to London. From Antwerp."

The boss, assimilating what he had been told, had returned to his lunch. He chewed on the sandwich, and her job now would be to get hold of Chopper, go over the legend with him of who and what he was, and plan the next and most vital link-up where he then barged himself, for a second time, into the life of Julie Wilson. She accepted that a rather naked excitement coursed in her, the elation of plans and programmes working out as predicted by Jonas, and she was grateful to be a part of it.

Had been grateful, also, for the chance to work in Syria, in the Six team, up alongside the Recce troops who escorted her off the Forward Base they occupied to meetings with plants, informers, the idiots either compromised or believing the shite told them about having their backs watched by Her Majesty's people. It had all seemed rather theatrical. But this had a reality to it, and she had a good memory of the house down in the Tillingbourne valley, and of a crime baron, 'too big to bring down' – and now targeted by Mr Merrick, and by her. Real and vivid and with a danger for the boy they exploited. In Syria she had had behind her the weight of Special Forces and their helicopter lifts and the gunships, and a Mess to get paralytic in and a near inexhaustible supply of Jamesons or Bombay Sapphire, and none of that was on offer to Chopper Harris, semi-invalid that he was.

If she did not have this, and succumbed to her boyfriend's gentle nagging and got out and went north with him, Simon, she would become the *chatelaine* of a heap of a building in the far west of Scotland with a jammy roof and historic plumbing and an estate overrun with invasive heather, and swarms of carnivorous midges to feast off her half the year, and eagles slaughtering newborn lambs, and an array of debts stretching round the corner. She would live in jeans and T-shirts, and jeans and waterproofs, and jeans and overcoats and would have kids, heirs, and spares, and excitement would be thinly spread. Might attract her, and might not. But whatever she decided or was pressured into deciding, this was business to be finished first.

Chopper laid out what he would need on the bed. Smart shirts, underwear, socks, and a jacket, and shoes with a heavy tread for outdoors, useful if there was snow on the pavements, and his wash bag with his razor, shaving gel, and toothbrush and some underarm stuff, and his two best pairs of jeans. Under them was a strong anorak that would be proof against the cold. In a separate pile beside his rucksack were his wallet, his phone that was not secure, and a pile of banknotes from a float Effie had given him – and that he had not been asked to sign for – and his passport with the Dubai stamps. Some loose change from his pocket fell and scattered on the bed, and the periwinkle shell dropped out too and plonked on the bed and he hesitated. Part of his past, part of what he was proud of, supposed to be a symbol of the camaraderie of the Squad – elite, whatever that meant – and he had been there but his locker in Barking would already have been reallocated. But the shell was his and as much his right to carry as it was to have a maroon beret and wear it at the eleventh hour of the eleventh day and have a memory of Lofty. Been there, done that. It went on to his pile. Later he would go down the corridor to the kitchen and tell Agathe that he'd be away for a few days.

Jonas stared at his screen, and the picture of his cat.

The former paratrooper, and now former member of the Flying Squad, had asked pertinent questions when they had met on the bridge over the Thames. He remembered them all, and had answered truthfully.

'Is this business legal?' *No idea. Never asked anyone. Shouldn't think so.*

'What degree of back-up do I get?' *None when you're away. Can't have squads from Hereford running around the Middle East or western Europe, wherever the mood takes the tale.*

'How dangerous is this going to be? What level of risk?' *High risk to life and limb. An unpleasant opponent who has killed or maimed opponents to a life-changing degree. Show out and it's bad trouble.*

'What do I get paid for this?' *Not as much as we – that is I – would like to pay you. Not a generous remuneration, but we'll cover the equivalent of your police wage, and overtime without receipts. It may lead to further employment opportunities but may not. The money paid to freelance operatives is not this organisation's strongest point.*

'Why should I do this?' *Because you are up a cul-de-sac and have no future with the Squad. You're about to get the boot. And because this is a job worth doing. Which is why I am pulling it together. It's something important. Certainly better than counting paperclips.*

It was not Jonas's style to issue a cry to arms, to make a motivational speech on the harm to society, its very fabric, of the international narcotics trade. Nothing about the billions of lost tax revenue, or the cost of treating the addicts, or locking them up. What he supposed to be the sort of dressing-room encouragement before people went out to play team games, he thought inappropriate.

He had finished his sandwich, shaken crumbs from the box into the bin, finished the coffee and the bar of chocolate . . . there was not very much more for him to do. Effie would be better at communicating with Chopper – if the man wanted to be known by that daft name. It was not Jonas' job to talk him down from his particular high ledge. Effie was nearer his age. Jonas was old, winding down, but thought his plan was unique and would have blind-sided his opponent, and was worthy of him.

What did irk him was the timing that had now settled on *Humble Pie*. And with it was the clear indication that a lie was to be told. Untruths hurt his wife and fibs were always seen through. It would need work but would have to be done.

Suddenly there was confusion around him. He had been calm, pleasantly so, but anger settled on his face as Effie spelled out the cause of the noise, the unfamiliar voices and the scraping of chairs and tables and the manoeuvring of filing cabinets. The interior designers had gained access to the Post Room, were horrified to see that postcards and photos of loved ones – partners, children, pets – were stuck to walls, destroying the symmetry of the room's design, and had spread beyond the areas designated for leave charts, exhortations from the DepDG on gender and ethnicity tolerance, and the occasional modern landscape that was thought necessary to bring calm to a workplace. He was not moving. Not Jonas Merrick. They could get Human Resources, Public Affairs, Property Management, summon the King and Queen for all he cared. He was not moving and would not permit the cabinets he'd purloined to be shifted back to their designated position . . . It was something of a disappointment when he was not called on to defend his ground and they had thought better of frontal assault.

Effie twitched her eyebrows at him, which seemed to show approval.

He swivelled his chair, turned to face her. "Tell me, Effie, when you lost people, when you were away, how did it feel?"

"Hurt. What else?"

"Matter if you were fond of them? Different if you hardly knew them?"

"Not really – a few drinks in the bar seemed a cure for sentimentality. If the goal was achieved then we accepted the collateral."

"Makes you a hard person, not easy to live with."

"As long as we win, which is what seems to matter. Did I say that? Is that over the top?"

"I don't think you heard me argue. We're into that stage of things where what is critical is *mistakes*, whoever makes them – us or the opponent. Mistakes decide the day."

He turned away and the screen seemed to haze in front of him. He undid the top button of his shirt and loosened his tie, and one notch of his belt, and settled back to doze, and thought of that half-dressed young woman in the huge house, and the former paratrooper who had a bullet wound at his ankle. But he denied personal responsibility for them both – which made life more tolerable.

4

"Do I go with him?"

He sensed she had been building up to the question, wondering whether to ask it with an attempt at justification, or simply blurt it out.

Jonas did not look at her, concentrated on his screen. "To what purpose?"

He had come off the phone to his old friend, a long-retired but arthritis-disabled detective from a crime squad in the disbanded Royal Ulster Constabulary. He spoke softly in that grating accent that floated down the line without interruption, and opinions that Jonas valued were offered.

"Just give me the chance to hold his hand, you know, if things are rough, that sort of thing." Effie shrugged, maybe realised she made a poor fist of it. Normally, Jonas would have declined to expand on a refusal, not this time.

"Absolutely not. To 'hold his hand' you would have to be up close and that is impossible. If he can jump out of aircraft then the chance is that he doesn't need a hand-holder."

He thought she would come back at him. His limited experience was that women often did. Even Vera, who some believed deserved canonisation, usually went for the jugular of a 'last word' or 'and another thing'. He had called his friend in the Province, had listened to him for nearly an hour and could hear rain falling noisily on a conservatory roof and the sound of the wind whistling shrilly down the line, made a sort of symphony to accompany an old, tired, wise voice. The subject matter was clear enough: *How does the undercover survive when isolated and beyond help?* Which was how and where the boy would be.

"I thought it might help, that's all."

"You didn't do it in Syria. Didn't want to hold the hand of a wretch that you had suborned into helping HMG and taken the Queen's shilling. This, believe me, Effie, is hardly different, and with it is a distinct possibility, even probability, that you might show out and put his safety in further jeopardy. No . . . I confess to a bad habit, I am a rubber-necker, like to be around at the final moment, which is stupid because I sometimes end up on the wrong side of a beating, but it is an addiction and I serve no useful purpose. I am not, of course, suggesting anything remotely similar in your motivation . . . No, we keep our distance."

Effie said that when they were in Syria there was always back-up in place. Neither she nor any of the guys would have gone out of the gate of a Forward Operating Base without the knowledge that back-up was rostered, armed heavily, and had a Chinook on 'immediate availability'. She had flushed, and he had hit home which marginally distressed him.

He had written notes on his lined pad, taken the salient points of what he'd been told by the old detective. 'When we had people in place, Jonas, and I am talking about agents, not the compromised idiots who get minimal rewards, but our own people going under-cover, then we had to accept that – for all the brave talk – they were beyond the reach of back-up. These people are outside what we refer to as the 'golden hour' when it might, emphasis on *might*, be possible to intervene. They are alone. Chance is that they are unable, because of location and circumstances, to wear a wire, have a tracker built into the heel of a shoe, and a wristwatch with a pulse alarm that can send a signal that their counter-measures can detect. The clever stuff seldom works, or the batteries go flat when it matters. Psychologically, it may be better to be clear of gadgets and dependent only on the man's nous and sense of survival. Usually, over here, the agent had an ethnic link, so had the accent and the body language, and might hang out for a week or two – not longer. You, Jonas, are I gather on different ground. More potential for a quagmire, a quicksand.' Jonas had grunted his response. 'I put it this way to you, my good friend, if the terror kids laid their hands on you then there is a small chance, not good enough to wager your house on, that they'd hold you as a bargaining chip, see some use for you down the road, keep you alive and think there was benefit from it. Might be an option for them. Crime is in a different league. You are dead. Might not be dead for a few hours, and they might use the time to hurt you a bit because that will amuse them, but the outcome is the same. Dead. A gang is not that interested in the names of your superiors, the structure of the organisation, even the phone numbers and addresses of colleagues. They want the agent out of the way, no longer a problem. That means dead. Is that simple enough, Jonas?'

Effie said, "Understood. I'll have a session with him tomorrow morning. Go through it, fortify his morale."

"Thank you."

The one-time Provo fighter from Northern Ireland had finished making his key point. 'Your boy, or girl, if suspicion is building on him and he gets the vibes, then he doesn't hang around, try to convince that he's what he says he is . . . Might do it with our people, any terror folk, but not with crime. They have different antennae. Suspicion is in their genes, runs in the veins. Won't talk his way out and return to being accepted. Will never be trusted, not anymore. So, the agent should bunk out. Get to the front door, take a deep breath, make a remark about whether it will rain that afternoon – or whether the sun will soon shine if it's already pissing down – and bolt. Run like the devils of hell are snapping at his heels. Run, and keep running. An agent who has been slotted is no use to anyone. An agent who is out of breath and alive has plenty of gaps to fill in during a debrief. He bolts, runs, makes himself scarce, if it's crime . . . Are you keeping well, Jonas, and why the feck are you not yet retired?' He had rung off. Jonas had the headlines on a sheet of paper, and had *Run* underlined twice. He had turned towards Effie, squeezed himself round in his chair, and saw a frown settle on her forehead, as if a different answer had not yet been considered.

"Always another avenue, of course, Mr Merrick, because we might see it sliding into the territory of the Verona syndrome."

"Meaning?"

"A love story. Him and her. There's a balcony in a courtyard in the Italian city of Verona. Into fantasy romance. Shakespeare to blame . . ." She gave it him in a crisp outline, like a school teacher. Two families split by hatred and a couple who wanted none of their parents' enmities, and with their own agenda, and thinking they could break the mould. She was well into the story when her phone went and the thread was lost. His eyes were almost closed and he mulled over what she had told him before the interruption. He was amused that the 'Verona syndrome' might stray into the territory of *Humble Pie* – and it was about danger and that familiar route along which Jonas Merrick led those unwise enough to take employment from him. Quite a decent young man, but without a risk assessment done. Jonas had never done one, feared it would cramp the scope of his ideas.

He turned it over, rolled it in his hand.

The periwinkle shell had survived the years it had spent in a trouser or coat pocket, being buffeted by coins and keys. It had already been pounded by the tides that smacked against a Scottish coastline. Chopper valued it.

His fingertips knew each of the scratch marks on the ringed surface of the shell from the cavity where once its organism had been up to the small pointed tip. In the Middle East, and in Afghanistan, men had worked their fingers against worry beads made from sandalwood and maple, from garnet or gemstone, almost caressing them. He worked over the shell. It had been given him by his first sergeant in the squad when he had joined Team 4, and it was precious to him.

He also had, hidden at the back of a drawer and behind a pile of underwear and handkerchiefs and socks, his parachute beret badge, which was pinned to his cloth paratroopers' wings. They meant plenty to him, but the shell had pride of place. The family of the regiment was important, but the sea shell, so crisp and so clean, had a higher status in his life.

He played with it, toyed with it, and allowed his mind to linger on the meeting that would be concocted with the girl. Could be cool: *Fancy that, fancy seeing you here . . . you do remember me, don't you?* Could gush, *This is just so incredible. Amazing. No lie, I have dreamed of seeing you again.* Could be offhand, casual: *Sorry, wasn't looking where I was going. You okay? My imagination, or haven't we met somewhere?* None seemed right, and he realised that, like the military and a fire fight, it depended how it kicked off and how everyone reacted, and whether to go and bust a situation wide open, or keep smiling.

Was mindful that he was being paid to do a job . . . remembered the kiss, and remembered that the 'bet' had amused her . . . Effie had said there wasn't a boyfriend that had shown up in the files, certainly not a fiancé. Effie said she was a songbird in a cage, and was there for the taking. Effie hardly mentioned the shipment that was on the move, somewhere in Europe, with a cargo that made misery and destroyed people's lives.

He remembered that when he was a kid, in Tavistock or in Yelverton, or up on the moor in Mary Tavy, there were people who looked like, dressed like, spoke like Sunray, and had a quiet and hesitant authority. He knew nothing about him, and felt he should – and could recall every detail of where they had met and what was asked of him, all conveyed at what was virtually fast marching pace, and with sleet in the air. Wanted to see Sunray again, thought he needed to, not the bottlewasher girl.

And he kept on turning over the shell in the palm of his hand.

Conversation buzzed in the bar where members and their guests joshed and squealed, and told and heard familiar stories, and they were well fed, and well oiled – and, for the most part, well heeled. The golf club was on the fringe of the Kent countryside and the boundaries of south-east London, had good greens, unpleasant bunkers, a waiting list, and a hefty joining fee.

The double doors swung open. Detective Chief Inspector Plunket would have anticipated the reaction to their entry. He was followed by Dawson and Rajah. They did not set out to look like stereotype police officers, but managed to. Something about their bearing, plenty about the confidence with which they came into the bar and let the doors sag and swing shut behind them. None of the hesitation that most people would have shown when coming into foreign territory, and behind them was a reception desk where a name had been mentioned and ID was briefly waved and a nervous girl had pointed to the bar doors and confirmed the 'name' was in there . . . Stories died in the telling and laughter was strangled, and demonstrations of killer strikes with various clubs froze. A silence fell. Eyes locked on them. Who were they here for?

It was soon clear. Clear to all except the man, himself a senior detective who managed the membership of the club, owned a small river-going launch moored at Teddington, a couple of cruises a year and . . . He had his back to them but the story he was telling was not being listened to and eyes stared wide and the silence hung heavy, except for the TV screen behind the bar with an item about the state of the economy. He twisted, followed the stares, and focused.

Would have recognised them. Barely a detective in the entire complement of the Met who would not have. Something about their suits, or the fact that it was beneath their dignity to clean their shoes, their hair cut to a basic standard, and the way they barged in, expecting the bloody Red Sea to part in front of them, which it did. A channel was opened and it led to the detective . . . Surprise? Hardly. Pretty much each time that he escorted his wife – due to arrive in a few minutes to drive him home – into the suite on the cruise liner, or when he fuelled up the launch engine, or paid his bar bills at the club, he would have had that chill on the back of his neck and thought of being confronted by these weasels, and knowing that his time was up, curtain coming down on the good life . . .

Would have been those fucking Courtneys not knowing how to keep their fucking mouths shut. His hand shook and the lemon slice floating in his wobbling glass cleared its rim, fell on his jacket and dribbled onto a trouser leg. They speared in on him, and everyone else in the bar backed away. By the time the trio were in front of him he was alone, deserted, had lost the support of all those bastards who had been happy enough to accept his hospitality.

Their boss, hardly out of fucking school, eased to the side. The Asian one slipped behind him. At the front stood the woman. He barely registered what she said. Could have heard the proverbial pin bounce on the parquet floor, but his ears seemed clogged and he had to lip-read what she said. He was familiar with the speech. He was being arrested. The charge that would be levelled against him was corruption, abuse of public office, passing classified information to unauthorised persons. Something about 'anything you say will be taken down . . .' Like it was a TV soap. All the usual stuff, and when others had faced that menu of accusations he had murmured to himself, 'There but for the grace of God . . .' The ceiling lights in the bar, bright on a miserable February afternoon, caught the chrome on the handcuffs she produced. All done quickly. The Asian took the gin out of his fist and put it on the bar. His hands were pulled together in front of him, the cuffs on the wrists, the snap of them closing, too bloody tight and the metal cutting into his skin.

"Nice and easy, sir, let's not make a pig's arse out of it."

The boy who was in charge led them out. The Asian had a hand on one arm and the woman on the other. Two uniforms waited at the main door, at the top of the steps, and in the forecourt was a marked car, its lights flashing. He understood . . . They could have taken him at home and by arrangement, or had him escorted by a solicitor to a police station, but instead they had chosen to inflict maximum humiliation in the bar of the golf club, and give the bastards there something to chirp over for the next five years. He saw his wife, parking the car; she would have thought the police were there because of a break-in, or a spot of pilfering from the Prof's store, and then would have seen him. She clambered out of the car and started yelling.

He snapped at her. "Just get a fucking solicitor, and a fucking good one."

And the Asian behind him said, "Very sensible, sir, a fucking good one – very wise."

He climbed into the marked car. Wanted to pee but would have to bottle it.

Gravel crunched and he was driven away.

The three of them, Plunket and Dawson and Rajah, did their own form of victory dance. No movement of the feet but each exposed the palm of their left hand, and allowed it to be punched by the right fist of one of the others. A mark of celebration because it had gone well, better than well.

Drinks down the pub in the early evening? Not Plunket's style. They had paperwork to get in shape, and an initial interview to conduct. It would be late before the Detective Chief Inspector was back in his bedsit, and Dawson needed to be home to get the washing in and put a pizza in the microwave, and Rajah, jet-lag still afflicting him, would need a pill to get to sleep.

There was said to be just one fear in the life of Lachy Wilson: the informer, the tout, the rat. His mother was quoted as having said, 'I'd rather my boy was shot dead than be a rat.' Lachy had an innate suspicion of strangers, so had no friends. No one with whom he would play golf, invite to dinner cooked by Vic, unless they were in his 'firm' . . . He could not avoid the team that lived around him but they would all have understood the reach of his arm and the fury of his vengeance, and seen both.

Distribution was a big issue, one that needed firm control if the maximum street price was to be maintained. He would see them at a venue at a Catford casino that he owned, and that morning the room on the floor below the gaming tables was his meeting place; they would come one at a time.

Three of them. A man from Manchester, a woman from Birmingham, another man from Liverpool. They were big hitters, each of them, but not as sizeable in influence and in the ability to strike fear as Lachy Wilson. He was a man in control, liked to speak quietly, say the minimum of what needed to be said, cut small talk, gossip, and any unnecessary greeting. He would name a figure and an amount in weight that he would sell when a shipment came in, and expect it to be taken up or rejected. He would not bargain. His visitors were not permitted to arrive in the car park at the back of the casino in smart cars: they were not footballers or rock stars, and they should not boast wealth, draw attention. Fords were suggested, or Vauxhalls. With him was Softboy who would stand behind his chair in the small darkened room and would frisk each of them for a wire.

The woman from Birmingham showed a sliver of impertinence. "What I heard was that you're hiving work off to your family, specifically your daughter. Are you losing your appetite?"

"I am not and don't like to hear that said."

She had grinned, and maybe did not believe what she was told. She was shown out. Ugly as a mule, and needed no calculator for her side of the transaction. The deal had been agreed.

The Liverpool guy liked to be called the Colonel, so Lachy didn't do so.

"This is a big deal, a huge one. The word on the street is that you've got a bit old for it, might be looking for an easy life . . . All right, all right, just what's being said, don't – no offence . . ."

The Scouser was a powerful man in the Birkenhead district of Liverpool, and thought himself 'hard', but had winced as Lachy's fist clamped over his hand and squeezed the bones of his fingers together until there were cracking sounds from the joints and little gasps from the guy's mouth and it seemed an age before Lachy released him.

Could have been that the Manchester boy, a young thruster, with a cold and humourless face, had met the Liverpool man in the car park, had been tipped off about Lachy's five, and wanted only to get his business done, how much he would take, what purity, how much up front and how much on delivery, and the quality of the heroin to be supplied. Rattled through the basics, no handshake, heads nodded that meant a deal was in place, and no hurt done to him . . . A year ago Lachy would have had Julie alongside him, and would have murmured at her, 'Just stare into their fucking eyes, and don't give them anything.' But those times had gone and he did not know how far to trust, and age and weakness were catching up on him.

She would have been there half the night if she had seen them individually. Julie had them gathered, six of them.

She had chosen the garden, set with greying and tilted stones alongside the City of London church of St Botolph Without Aldersgate. It was the first time she had been permitted by her father to meet these people, who worked in the shadowy areas at the back of a distribution operation but as essential to its success as any part of it. The shipment would come ashore in a container, the container would be taken to a secluded car park behind fencing and not overlooked, and the cargo would be unloaded and the shipment retrieved, and the container seals refastened and carried forward, and a tonne-weight of quality heroin would then need – that magic word – distribution. The men she met were part of a clan of self-employed 'logistics experts' and they worked for the highest bidder and were impeccable about their security and owed no debts and had no loyalties other than to the best payers and the most efficient.

She needed to prove herself. She did not have the support of Cohn, the self-styled *consigliere* who had thrown a hissy sulk and would pick her up in an hour for a strained ride back to Surrey. She despised him – had no doubts that he loathed her but coveted her thighs and would hitch the skirt higher all the way from inner London to the village of Abinger Hammer, just to taunt him.

These were men, all men, who would take it badly if they were threatened. If told that a long arm would reach them wherever they hid, they would sneer a reply and walk away, disappear into the log-jammed traffic of the City as the day's trading came to a halt. She was aware, what her father often said, that a reputation was slow to win, quick to lose. All eyes were on her. The drone of traffic filled the garden and an ambulance sounded its siren. They needed confidence that she knew her trade, had the competence. She sat on a metal bench and they stood or squatted around her.

Julie understood.

They absorbed the timings and the locations, and the amounts each would be carrying and gave the estimates of driving schedules to the principal cities of the country, and still stared at her. Her mother had warned her a couple of years back when she had first been out on the road with the learning curve still steep enough to fall off. 'They'll be working out how fuckable you are. Can't dress it up. Not whether you're attractive, have a fine personality, should be taken home for tea with their widowed ma. Taking the clothes off your back, imagining a turn with you in the back of a cab, or a room for an hour at a service station hotel. A bit of a trophy, your knickers, in the cab window – Lachy Wilson's girl, ignorant and innocent. Give them nothing – don't even think about screwing on the side. No ifs, no buts, just don't. These had been the guidelines laid down for her. She gave them the last information they'd need, the weight and what help they'd need. She thought of the boy in Dubai. Wondered that it would be like with him. Surely better than an arsehole at school, a bike shed job, and him spilling down her leg. Her father would have had most of the bones in the kid's body broken if she had breathed a word to him of what had taken place.

Four months earlier (October '25)

"I'm in a hole – I'll pour."

The host was an Assistant Commissioner and headed Special Operations from an upper floor suite at the Yard.

"Then always best to stop digging."

The guest was an Assistant Deputy Director General of the Security Service. A glass was pushed forward, liberally filled.

"Have a problem and don't seem able to solve it."

"Would be glad to help, *if* . . ."

A waiter hovered and wanted to take their order, but was waved away by the policeman.

"There's always a bloody *if*, isn't there?"

"Sadly, yes, there usually is – matters of remit, authority, ability."

"I'll put it on the table."

"Always helpful."

"A rumour seems to be floating around corridors in the top floor of our place that you have a man—"

"Really?"

" . . . a man who gets things done."

"Do we?" A chuckle.

"Don't, old chum, piss on me, please don't." A grimace.

An hour later the first bottle had been emptied, and the second bottle severely damaged, and no order had been given, and both men decided that they were no longer hungry, and a bill was met with an MPS credit card. Outside on the pavement on a dark, dank afternoon in late October, they shook hands, gripped fists, and the AssDepDG said that he would 'see what can be managed', and the AC said for the fourth time, 'Deliver a meaningful hit and we'd be in your debt, big time and for a long time. Substantial debt.'

They parted. One would go back to Victoria Embankment to ponder whether he had appeared too much cap in hand, and the other headed in the teeth of a squall to a side entrance of a building on Horseferry Road. Instead of going up to the fourth floor, he took the lift down to the basement and headed for the Post Room. Saw Effie Bellingham in the corridor, asked how the 'grumpy old fucker' was and was rewarded with the sort of shrug that indicated 'the same'. He laughed, went into the Post Room and clamped his hands on the shoulders of Jonas Merrick.

The AssDepDG scratched his chin, then eyed the smoke detector on the ceiling, recognising the enemy, glanced at Effie as if she were an ally, and she shook her head. No smoking, sadly.

"Something outside my experience, Jonas. There are areas where we lend a hand to the civil power because they do not have the expertise . . . We have resources in surveillance, in matters relating to communications decoding, where we are far superior. And we have you. This is not about terrorism, nor espionage, and were it so we would have kicked their butts, and told them to go away and chase speeding motorists . . . It's about crime. What they are short of is willpower, and what they are overloaded with is corruption. A senior figure has come to me, in clandestine circumstances and without the clearance of a sub-committee, and has talked to me about the activities of one man who the Metropolitan Police Service has decided is too big, too powerful, to bring a case against. You heard me right, Jonas. They have failed in their efforts to bring down a crime baron because his network of bribery, and the greed of enough of their middle-ranking detectives, is such that they prefer to take his money and foil whatever is chucked against him. He hears when select units are set up with the sole job of providing evidence against him. Items that could compromise him go missing, removed from supposed secure storage, and from forensic laboratories. Witnesses who could testify against him are threatened and refuse to go into court. Jurors are intimidated or paid off and decline to convict . . . I am talking, Jonas, about the United Kingdom in the twenty-first century. We are not in Baghdad or Bogota or Buenos Aires. We are in an area of south-east London, close to leafy Surrey, the belt supposedly occupied by stock-brokers, high-flying lawyers, and multi-millionaires in the music business. We are also thought to be in that fertile part of Afghanistan where the Taliban grow high-quality opium in well-cultivated fields. Providing that wretched regime with hard currency because of the demand in our society to smoke, inhale, chew, whatever method is fashionable for the nauseous addiction to heroin. And there are girls from eastern Europe, there are firearms from the Balkans, and there is protection. It's a long list . . . my chum is ashamed at the inability of his force to put this individual behind bars, and has come to me and pretty much – over some fierce alcohol intake – gone down on bended knee and pleaded for help. What's in it for us?"

"I was beginning to nod off."

"There is a no-go area, where secrecy rules. The public must have confidence in the police force that protects them. Any investigations into the criminality of detectives is going to further destroy that necessary confidence. So, we need to keep inquiries into investigations out of the public eye. It is good to trumpet the success of drugs raids by Serious and Organised Crime squads, but actually almost meaningless and not affecting the state of supply. Does the cost go up on the street corner? Hardly. My entertainment at lunchtime today was paid by a credit card. Who picks up the tab? The public, the taxpayer, you and me, Jonas. It's the way things work. Constables at the coalface work their balls off. But high up the chain there is a desire to protect careers and not stray into areas where success is trashed. What we are being asked for is the determination – which does not exist in their corner – to bring down a major criminal and dump him in the dock of the Central Criminal Court. They have not managed it, not in twenty-plus years. Do they have your name? Absolutely not . . . What they have heard is that we have an individual who operates with a high success rate. That's you, Jonas."

Pretty much the way things arrived on Jonas Merrick's tiny desk in the subterranean Post Room – which was both a punishment posting where it was believed he could do little damage to the ethos of the Service, and a bolt hole beyond the view of many of the sticklers for protocol and the guardians of HR and the lawyers in house who preached the need for strict legality: if he was successful then his procedures would be mildly examined and the rap on his knuckles administered with little energy – if he lost and his methods were displayed to public view then he anticipated he would, in the modern-day equivalent, be gently swinging from a rope hanging from a lamp post high over Lambeth Bridge. He was sought out by those who had a problem on the floors above him and it was dropped on his lap, and he would refuse to give a running commentary on his progress . . . some days he had a spring in his step, other days he seemed close to buckling under the weight of responsibility parked with him.

"Why should I be interested?"

"Because it is a challenge. Made for you. They all say it cannot be done. I have made no commitments on our behalf, just that we would have a look. It's good to have the plods grovelling to us. Excellent to have them owing us. We can milk that. Have a look at it, Jonas . . . And come up with something out of the ordinary, and preferably moderately legal. His name is Lachlan Wilson."

"Seems we might need a bucket of luck."

As he left the Post Room, the AssDepDG said over his shoulder, "Isn't that what you always say, Jonas? You earn your luck."

"Would probably need an irregular. I'll give it some thought. A complicated man, serious thought."

*   *   *

Not an easy fortnight for Betty.

Dosed up with antibiotics, she washed her hair early that evening in the one-bed apartment she shared with her partner, older than her and being crucified for maintenance payments. She'd been off for a fortnight and a night stint at Luton airport marked her return to work.

Betty was Border Force. She sat in the Departures section and gazed at passports and swiped them, and thought herself conscientious. She'd never had the red lights flash and the sirens squawk.

A day of home decorating had been her problem. Her partner was National Crime Agency, a civilian recruit, good with computers but pretty useless at anything else. She had trodden on a screw that had come detached from the wall, and it had pierced her tights and the underside of a toe, which had become infected, and had blown up, and she was put on antibiotics. She was on the horrid night shift and would be there when the last aircraft took off and the first arrived and would leave the airport the next morning before first light: an unpleasant place, the drone of cleaning equipment most of the night and then the passengers pitching up, most of them half asleep. The toe had healed, but the enforced absence from work had caused her to reflect on the wisdom of the relationship with Ralph. She had to go to work, had to put on an ugly uniform, had to seem bright and cogent and not yawn at the punters. Her partner seemed able to do at least half of his work shift from the computer in their living room/dining room/kitchenette. Ralph was a civilian. He had been drafted to the National Crime Agency, and was beginning to be quite dull. The fortnight with them both at home had gone slowly, been a pain, and given her a chance to reflect that her life seemed emotionally and professionally to be heading down a cul-de-sac.

She had once dated an 'armed copper', a taciturn bloke who could not escape the reality that he had 'never actually done it'. How many of them had? One a year in the Met, one in ten years in a big provincial force like the Thames Valley, and one in a generation in a small outfit such as Bedfordshire. He had been dumped when he had begun to talk about the need to shoot someone, and soon, to see whether the 'bleeding H&K actually worked'. Natural that on the rebound she had picked up with the present squeeze, but it was wearing thin, and he seemed to offer little. Ralph was out getting the Chinese takeaway, and then she would head off to work, and somehow stay awake in the rest room during the long hours in the middle of the night when the airport was handed over to the cleaners and restocking the outlets. Truth was, her job on Border Control was tedious. Betty would have been uncertain as to how to describe what might be considered interesting. What might have given her work a tad more meaning, and a flurry of excitement? She was uncertain. Would she even recognise anything 'interesting' if it stood up on its back legs and bit her bum? The armed cop she had dated had once been in a state of near collapse because he had decided he could no longer recognise a serious threat – the 'Christ, it's actually happening' moment. She would dry her hair, fasten it in an elastic band, and go out and face the world . . . They would be in an orderly line and would slap their passports down on the panel and would avoid eye contact – except for the few arrogant cretins who seemed to want to smile and duck a head as if they were acknowledging backstairs staff.

She was, mind-wise, a bit of a mess, when she heard Ralph come back with the supper, and she had not even warmed the plates, which always pissed him off. She came out of the bathroom. They did a bit of a clinch, and one of the trays in the plastic bag started to leak, and he reacted like it was the biggest disaster that could smack him in the nose in the next twenty-four hours. He unpacked the containers while she was in the bedroom, tugging on her uniform.

Something might happen on that shift, but – more likely – nothing would happen. Betty smiled sweetly at Ralph and started on a Kung Pao chicken, not her favourite . . . might happen and she could but hope.

Sitting on his bed, feet on the chair, tucked away in the east wing of The Gables, Wally Genge – the Prof – read and savoured.

Remember me when I am gone away,
Gone far away into the silent land.

Except that she would not remember him. Would ditch him as soon as he was beyond the protection of her parents, and she was beyond their authority. He drooled at the work of Christina Georgina Rossetti, knew 'Remember' by heart and many poems of that vintage. At first, when he was accompanying her regularly, Julie had ignored him, but he had noticed that she now avoided him, and the proof in that pudding had been down in Dubai when she had gone for her morning run and chosen a route where he could not follow on his hired bicycle and he had become fearful.

When you can no more hold me by the hand,
Nor I half turn to go yet turning stay.

Used to hold her hand as they crossed the road, take her to school, walk a pace behind her, with a penknife hanging from his belt and a short-handled hammer under his shirt and a knuckle duster in his trouser pocket, and knowing that he would have died in an attempt to protect her from kidnap or reprisals, and loving her. Tomorrow he would resume his duties, and that hideous bloody Cohn would not be staring at her, as he always did, and they would be away together and him with responsibility, and her on a looser rein . . . He was certain she did not mess with him, was merely inconsiderate. He did not blame her, of course not, but assumed she did not understand the weight of responsibility he carried because he was charged with protecting her, given that very precious role by Lachy and Victoria.

He closed his book, would select the clothing he would need to take the next day. The forecast was good after early foul weather, which lifted him.

The Prof idolised her, could not deny it, thought himself privileged to have such trust placed in him by the family.

Coming down Lambeth Palace Road, his phone map telling him he was alongside the Archbishop's Palace, and near to the right bridge, Chopper braked sharply. He was rewarded with the usual volley of motorists' complaints, but was familiar with that. Could have given them a finger, but didn't. It was a small memorial that he had never seen before that had caught his attention. He was on the edge of the Thames walkway, on the south side. It was for Special Operations Executive, showed a woman's head, a firm gaze. He scratched around in his memory; thought it was something about the last war. *Their services were beyond the call of duty. In the pages of history their names are carved with pride.* A life-size statue of a paratrooper was in a garden in the barracks town of Aldershot, and he had passed it, running or marching, but had never paraded in front of it. The words rolled in his mind and a sharp wind came off the river. He felt a sense of confusion because Call of Duty was beyond what motivated him . . . Great to have the big general-purpose machine gun up to his shoulder, muscles straining to hold a steady aim, and Lofty feeding. Great to have the company or even the battalion on the touchline and yelling for him to 'get stuck in', and him doing the 'chopper' bit. Great as well, before he was pulled off, to be on the pavement jobs with the Squad and sprinting to get close to a lowlife bastard. This was a statue of a young woman and she would have been heaved out of the side door of a light aircraft, in darkness, with perhaps one light far below her, and not knowing whether betrayal waited, not knowing but still trusting . . . He felt under the cosh. Had to know more of what he was expected to achieve, and what it would do for the great mass of people hurrying past him in the dusk. So, he had come here, and Effie – Sunray Minor – had told him that her boss always left work at the same hour, to the minute, and walked at the same pace to get the same train. Wondered if this woman had survived, had been eaten by treachery, or had died and been dumped in an unmarked camp grave, wondered what she had achieved and how much it had mattered to her. Tough stuff that bit about the call of duty..

Chopper checked his watch. Was early for what he wanted, and would loiter on the bridge. He had prepared. A baseball cap shadowed the top of his face from the street lights, a scarf was around his lower face, protection against the chill and the wet that blew off the river. A quilted anorak that disguised the shape of his body.

Wanted to be anonymous, use his surveillance skills which all the Squad had, and gaze at the man who had recruited him, try to read him. Didn't want a motivational lecture, what some of the junior officers had tried before leading Brecon route marches, or when heading out of the Helmand compound, what 'Ruperts' did and believed the men responded. No chance . . . Wanted to learn something of this guy, Sunray, and what it was for, the game that he was a part of – and the girl who had kissed him. It was cold, and the wind was unkind and the traffic crawled past. He pushed his bicycle nearer to the bridge . . . and his ankle hurt from the effort of pedalling and he bit at his lower lip, and across the water was the massive, well-lit building that was the workplace of Sunray, where he would be coming from.

At the end of the bridge he leaned the bicycle against the railing and below was the churning motion of a rip tide flushing under the bridge, going up river.

He could see up to the mid-point of the bridge. Streams of pedestrians hurried towards their destinations, heads down. He remembered the hat he should look for, and the type of raincoat, and the briefcase which had, as he recalled it, a fine chain holding his wrist to the handle. Knew what he should look for.

A new family calling for him? He waited.

There were lamps at the centre point of the bridge, and columns of headlights inching across, and he had never felt alone in the Regiment, nor in the Squad, and never alone in the teams he had played with even when his skills were down the pan and his injury dominated. He waited. The place he had chosen was in a cone of darkness, the nearest street light was angled away and his disguise was good, and he had the skills. Could shoot, could drive, could do surveillance to a high standard, and was praised for it, but now had the boot in his backside.

Saw a policeman, an H&K across his chest. He was escorting someone. Someone wearing the sort of scarf his ma gave to his pa at Christmas, someone swinging a briefcase. Saw a second policeman, similar weapon, and both of them paused at the top of the bridge and Sunray went on alone, acknowledged neither. They stood their ground and watched his back and he had his head down and maintained his pace. Chopper shivered in the little corner of darkness that he had chosen – observed the man. The briefcase thumped the man's legs, the length of his stride did not alter. Chopper was not sure what he had gained by pedalling across central London and letting the wind get into him.

They were a few feet apart, close enough for their fingers to have touched if both had reached out their arms. Sunray's eyes were down, concentrating on the pavement in front of his polished brogues, and . . .

A quiet voice, and barely audible above traffic, "Good evening, Detective Constable, a poor night to be out in the cold. Sorry, but I can't hang about, have a train to catch."

. . . And he was gone.

The surprise rippled in him. Chopper had believed there was a possibility that a family, based here, would welcome him in, and realised his error, and cursed.

Olaf asleep on his lap, Jonas interrupted Vera's concentration on her crossword.

"Tell me a little, fact and fiction, please, about Verona."

"Don't astonish me, are we taking the caravan there? Right, north Italian city, known for an opera festival. Bit off the beaten track for us, Jonas."

"And the balcony and the love story?"

"Am I hearing this? Romeo and Juliet, a balcony on a first floor where he climbs to and she waits. All forbidden . . . Is the Security Service now a dating agency? Jonas, what are you asking me?"

"The families were?"

"They were the Montagues and the Capulets – not really. All out of Shakespeare's imagination. Does that matter? They were rivals, both greedy for power, the two top families in the city, loathed each other. Romeo was a Montague and Juliet was a Capulet. Any relationship between the children of the two camps was certain to cause a major ruction. It's all made up. Where is this dose of culture and romance taking you?"

"Protestants and Catholics, a girl from Andersonstown and a boy from the Shankill Road . . . a Muslim girl from Sarajevo and a Serb boy. Orthodox Christian, from Banja Luka . . . kids from either side of the wall in Jerusalem. I have the idea."

"Thought you were doing crime. Are you manipulating, Jonas?"

"Always two sides to a coin . . . The Montague boy and the Capulet girl, did each of them assume the other would ditch their own camp and move over?"

"Did not. A plague on both your houses. Would have ducked out, gone their own way. Rejected both – have to, wouldn't they?"

"As I assumed – thank you."

She seemed to Jonas to be happy to get back to her puzzle. He had his fingers on the ruff of fur at the cat's neck. He thought both of them, the policeman who was Chopper and the gangster girl who was Julie, innocents, unfulfilled. The meeting of those two imagined kids in an Italian city, and written about four centuries before, would have been by chance, and the love would have been immediate, as it would have been for any of those opposites that he had conjured up, Belfast or Bosnia. If it happened as planned, his idea for *Humble Pie* would work well. He was in the process of congratulating himself, and Olaf seemed content. All was well until Vera put down her pencil.

"Jonas, relationships and romance are not your top academic subjects. Are you leading two young people into extreme danger?"

"Don't think so."

"Surely you know?"

His question had been very straightforward, and had been answered. She would not become a snitch for the police. He would hardly dump his background and join the conspiracy of the Wilson family. The answer was as he had expected, but he had opened the can and she was now ready for debate.

"And us, Jonas. Me, the cat and you, are we now at greater risk? Criminals have a more desperate reputation than spies and terror people, and . . ."

He probably was inept at calming and comforting, and she might as well have scraped a serrated edge across his nerves. He heaved Olaf off his thighs and was scowled at and sworn at. He muttered that no additional hazard threatened them – but could recall how it had been for those hours – years before – when armed police had camped in their home, only one night, and had moved out after Olaf had savaged the hands of one of them.

"Absolutely not. We have excellent quality firewalls at work. No problems."

He had exhausted the conversation, wanted it over. Said it was time to take the cat outside.

He stood in the winter late evening air, felt it cool his face. He saw the cat dive into the shrubs, shredded of foliage. Might be sheltering there, might be hunting for a rodent, might be remembering when it had fastened its claws, back legs and front, on the shin and thigh of a wannabe Merseyside-based assassin. The cat had likely saved his life, had wounded the man . . .

The target he aimed at now was every bit as effective as that who had confronted him before, and almost certainly more efficient, more deadly, more committed in hatred. Just for a moment he wondered what he had allowed to fall on his shoulders, and the wisdom of it – and reflected that inside the Post Room at Thames House he had felt secure, safe, and on the pavement were Kev and Leroy, with the H&Ks, except that Vera and the cat were not protected . . . He was almost flustered, but she broke the mood and called to him.

"Jonas, you do know it didn't end well for them. You know that? Not well at all."

He took his eyes off the border where the cat prowled and faced the kitchen, spoke with annoyance. "But it was only a story, wasn't it, a story?"

5

Jonas reflected.

It was going to be an 'in between day' which meant the planning was in place, and the key moments for its execution would come tomorrow. He recognised the voices.

Thoughtful as always, his protector in Thames House, the Assistant Deputy Director General, always seemed able to secure a few moments' warning and would scoot down from his room on the fourth floor get into the basement before Brian. Enough time for Jonas Merrick to have his head tucked down behind the barricade of filing cabinets which screened him from the area where the Security Service mail was sorted before internal delivery.

"I am sure that back in the Stone Age, when card index files were hand-written, when a postage stamp cost threepence, that a Post Room required space. Can't see for the life of me how it can, in this day and age, be justified." Brian, Deputy Director General, was more interested in Administration and Budgets.

There was clucking agreement proving that the DDG had brought a column from Administration with him, and there were suggestions that an overflow gym could be put here, or a music room for those members of the Security Service wanting to 'chill' in meal breaks, or a library, or another conference room, or … Jonas grunted contempt. He was sitting in front of his computer but had not yet unpacked his briefcase, removed his lunch box and his thermos, nor taken out the classified documents which it was forbidden to take from the building, and developments involving *Humble Pie* had not been chewed over. And the wretched man had already intruded.

"A damn good case for this lot will have to be made if they aren't for the chop . . ." the circus had come close to the filing cabinet barricade " . . . and isn't this where Merrick is? Not out to grass yet? Did us well with the Chinese, as I remember, but it was a year ago. What's he at? Trouble? Behaving himself?"

Those in his retinue would not have had the clearance to know of the work of Jonas Merrick, nor would they have recognised his name.

The AssDepDG intervened. "Doing valuable work. I put a girl alongside, FCO, stroke Sixer, and takes no prisoners. Keeping him on the straight and narrow, and you'll remember what we set him to work at, no mischief permitted."

"Which was?"

"Just after you'd taken all that praise from the Agency, for the defection of that little stoat from the Chinese intelligence larceny programme. You felt the need to keep Merrick tethered for fear of something worse. We put him into the 'waste squad', gave him a rather leading role. Anywhere there's poor use of resources, Jonas follows it, like a damned bloodhound, even down to paperclips."

"I've not had sight of that."

"My fault," AssDepDG chimed as if taking immediate blame mitigated the felony. "It was excellent material, and presented with dedication . . ." Jonas reckoned him a devious man, a master of that art. He owed much to him for kindness and courtesy, and were it not for the protection he was given he would by now be in his second or third year of the misery of retirement, with little to concern him beyond the caravan's maintenance and his cat's vet bills, and boredom on an industrial scale. "His report will be on your desk after lunch, and will be excellent reading."

They moved on. The final words from Brian came faintly through the Post Room doorway.

"Is this rest area for the police the best employment of space? Four settees, three hanging-height lockers, satellite TV, micro-wave, sink, foldaway beds. I know we have to keep them happy, but I'm sure we could do a re-think . . . I have to say that I am sometimes frustrated – not saying angry – when my car is held up and I'm cutting it fine getting in for the first meeting of the day, and the police step out into the road and hold everyone up to escort Merrick across the road. We all have to wait because the police regard helping this doddery old thing as the most important item on their agenda. I'm not being entirely facetious, but if I was a planner for Daesh or Al Qaeda, or whatever the Provos call themselves these days, I would aim to hit the main entrance when the guns are escorting Merrick over the road before he goes off for coffee and something in the park. Not a complaint, but—"

"I will look into it, Brian. If knuckles need to be rapped, be assured they will be."

They were gone. Jonas unpacked the briefcase, handed Effie the papers that should not have left the building – assessments marked SECRET from the National Crime Agency on the importation of heroin to the UK, routes, and the prices on the street.

She said, "He spoke well of you."

"And has had his rewards," Jonas said without charity. "Has done well off my back. And will do better if this one comes home."

He felt it himself, the stripping of confidence, and the poor humour that led the AssDepDG to describe him as a 'grumpy old fucker'. Said with a soft humility, "Except we don't know, do we? Can but hope. In other hands."

"I've left it all tidy, Agathe," Chopper said, trying to sound relaxed. "There's a months rent on the chest, and I've cleaned out the drawers and the cupboard and everything else is in a bin bag."

Her face had fallen, and she had no words. It was that morning of the week when she did not go into the Yard to clean the offices of the senior men and women. He would have preferred her not to be there, but hadn't the option of just slipping away, leaving only a handwritten note and £500 in cash in a neat pile on the top of the chest where the drawers had been left open to show they'd been emptied. He thought there would be tears . . .

"Moving on, Agathe, can't say more than that. Being honest, not just hiding a truth. Don't know what I'm heading for . . . Life is taking a bit of a turn for me, and I don't know where."

He had dressed well, his best jeans, shirt and trainers, and an anorak over a sweater. In his rucksack were a change of clothes and a wash bag and a second pair of trainers. No weapon, no special communications gear, nothing personal. His keys and a heap of loose change and his wallet were on a handkerchief on the chest, and the shell. There was nothing personal in the bin bag either. Owned nothing that was precious to him except the periwinkle shell and the cap badge that was fastened to the wings and one well-dented and scarred pair of shin pads, and they were all on the bed. He pulled up the ankle of his jeans on one leg and bent and pushed down his sock, and showed her the scar.

"What I'm saying, Agathe, is that this little problem from faraway places still gives me grief. Put me out of the military, and has just about put me out of the quite happy place I was with in the police. No longer as good as I want to be in the mobility stakes. I'm having a last crack at something and it would be a miracle, a big one, if it were to work out and that might take me off in a direction I'm not really sure about. If that doesn't work, and precious little chance it will, then it will just be time to get on the road, head towards a different sunset, know what I mean, Agathe? That's a bit of a speech from me . . ."

He knew little of her past, her trials and tribulations, but plenty of her kindnesses. It was all she needed to know, and perhaps she had already realised that his circumstances had changed but she was too strong for sentimentality.

She said, "I wish you well, Mr Harris, wish you very well."

"If I'm back at the start of next week it will be to collect the bin bag and the bike. If I'm not back by a week today please feel free to rent out the room, and take the bag along with any of my clothes you've been kind enough to iron and are still with you, to the Salvation Army, something like that, and get rid of it, and the bike is for whoever you think might appreciate it. I've done it before, moved on, and somehow, somewhere, touched base with something. I'm grateful to you."

"May I ask one question?"

"Shoot."

"Perhaps impertinent of me to ask it."

"We call that, Agathe, a double tap. Again, shoot."

"What might be a miracle, what you call a big one – would that involve a girl?"

He laughed and the smile stayed and there was a coquettish grin at her mouth.

"That obvious?"

"When you smile like that, Mr Harris, I remember when I was young and I would have given all I had to walk down the street with my arm in yours, and that smile in my eyes. Given all I had. I hope you find her, and she finds you."

He reached forward, took her ample shoulders in his hands, and kissed her lightly on both cheeks. She turned away to go back to the kitchen and he headed for the bedroom that had been his home.

Into an inner zipped pouch of the rucksack went the cap badge and the cloth wings that he had unpicked from an army tunic, and taken off a beret. He tucked the wallet into a secure pocket of his anorak and his phone, remembering to switch off the power. The shin pads went in another pocket of the rucksack. He slid the coins into a trouser pocket, and his passport into a hip pocket, and picked up the handkerchief, dislodging the shell so that it rolled across the bed. He picked it up and held it for a moment. Gazed at the synchronised lines and the ridges circling it to its top.

He sat on the hard chair by the bed, and closed his eyes . . . Could see the girl's face, and waited for the alarm on his wrist-watch to summon him. Thought calmly of a target that had been given him, and the trust of a sort placed in him.

Vic carried flowers into the graveyard, and a trowel and a stiff hand brush.

The gate wheezed as it closed behind her. These were not the church grounds nearest to Abinger Hammer but they were near enough. She had taken the decision that her son, Hamish, gone three years before, should not be in an obvious resting place which enemies of the family could desecrate, feel they were striking a machete at her and Lachy's hearts. The gravestone had her son's name carved on it, no dates and no message, and it was in a corner and close to a heap of slow-decaying leaves raked up the previous autumn. Her husband never visited. She did not bring her younger children. Hamish was not mentioned when she visited Gregor in the maximum security compound. She was a woman of mind-bending wealth, and that Wednesday morning wore old jeans whose knees and thighs had lost their original colour, and a cheap anorak, and on her feet were trainers that would absorb the rain-water from the sodden grass. It was the price she paid. She had married Lachy – then an advancing career criminal, and her a policeman's daughter – and known where life might take her.

She had made her bed. Only one man had ever asked if she had regretted the decisions she had made, the course she had taken. A quiet and rather feeble seeming man. A vicar who acted as a trav-elling officiator at several churches in that part of Surrey and who stepped in when the regulars were on holiday or ill, or moving on and a replacement not yet available. He had buried Hamish, had done it with dignity and without any 'pious claptrap', as Vic would have described any attempt to pontificate on a misspent youth. Lachy had barely spoken to him. He had done a service similar to many he had performed that year, and more of them to follow in the next months.

She had once listened to a radio programme about World War II which had included a critical statement made by the Holy Father that had challenged the might of 'Uncle Joe' Stalin. The dictator of the Soviet Union, having been told of the remarks, had snapped back, 'How many tanks does the Pope have?' What Lachy might have said himself, with the same contempt. Lachy had tanks, and enforcers, and could call up hitmen, could have jaws broken, cheeks slashed, limbs taken off by chainsaw, cadavers buried in the depths of Epping Forest. She had never asked Lachy if he regretted anything. He would have looked at her first with astonishment, and second with annoyance. Her answer to the vicar had been a helpless shrug.

At the grave, she knelt to use the trowel to clean grass and weeds from the small patch where she had planted a handful of pansies that would soon give some colour to the drabness of the place, and then she would use the brush to clean lichen off the stone. The damp earth soon soaked the knees of her jeans. She did not hear him approach.

"Sorry, Victoria. Didn't mean to startle you. Are you well?"

Peregrine's payment from the Church of England would be a bare pittance. The establishment showed more interest in the state of the roofs of the churches in the diocese, and the standard of the leadwork, and the funds needed to prevent churchyards from becoming rough and unkempt wildernesses. There was money, of course, in the Tillingbourne valley, but often slow to materialise. Victoria Wilson was the prime benefactor, and she was valued.

"Fine, thank you, Peregrine."

Which was true, marginally. She *was* fine. She had buried a son whose grave she tended. The next day she would drive north and visit another son who languished in a hideous gaol. She had two other sons who were tolerated at school and showed little aptitude for anything other than sport. And a daughter who was heading off that afternoon to bring home from central Europe the largest delivery of Class A narcotics the family had ever handled. A husband who veered between tending his chickens and running casinos and cat houses and protection . . . Of course she was fine.

"Good to hear it, Victoria."

His hand was on her shoulder. She permitted it. She was, it was generally agreed in the village, a good-looking woman, well preserved. He was on the edge of emaciation, had a jutting chin and needed large magnification spectacles. If she had spoken honestly to anyone about the predicament of her life, it would have been to him. There was an understanding, what was tolerated, what was not, and there was a 'difficulty' over the restoration of a stained-glass window in a church between Holmbury St Mary and Peaslake, with few parishioners and a deteriorating fabric, and she reached into her handbag, produced an envelope, and passed it to him.

"Thank you, Victoria. We appreciate your generosity."

"For nothing."

"Never too late to change a course of direction."

"As someone said, Peregrine, 'you can run but you cannot hide', and a change of direction would indicate that my husband and I sought to do that."

"Never too late."

"Thank you, Peregrine."

They shared a hot drink from his flask, and sat together on a wooden bench, and the cold wrapped around them and there was a spit on the wind, and it was only instant coffee but it was warm and comforting. She supposed that she bought a sort of peace by passing him these envelopes that represented less than pocket money to her, and would make a difference to the world he inhabited. He was the only man in the community who treated her with a degree of friendship. The Wilsons were not invited to drinks at Christmas, nor did they throw open their own home to entertain. She was treated with politeness in local shops, nothing more, served quickly and expected to leave without gossip or pleasantries. At the school attended by Connor and David, teachers conveyed the bare bones of their academic progress, did not criticise their behaviour. The Wilsons had no friends, were isolated inside the grounds of The Gables. Perhaps tears welled in her eyes.

She would not be embarrassed by him. He hurried to finish his own drink, and she tipped out what was left of hers and handed him back the mug.

It was her bed, and she had made it.

He said, "We are grateful for what you bring to our parish, Victoria, and I don't preach at you. Bless you. Good day."

She had already swept the stonework, but did it again. Had already weeded the surrounding earth but thrust her trowel into the frosted ground. It was rare for her to feel fear, but the future tugged at her, and the past was gone, and she wondered if her husband shared it. She didn't know and he wouldn't tell her because he always needed to win, of necessity, for survival.

✲   ✲   ✲

The caller had a quiet voice, almost a purr, not unlike a contented Olaf. Might have been from one of the northern American states. Jonas asked his name and business.

"The name is Hiram. Hiram Schultz. I am glad to touch base with you. You have time?"

"Perhaps and perhaps not."

"What is my pedigree? Fair question."

"Then answer it, please."

"I am speaking from our embassy in Lima, Peru. The wrong side of Latin America. We exist in a fortress in the Monterrico district. I am not a diplomat. But I am accredited as one. In reality I serve with DEA, and last night I enjoyed dinner with Nikko and he—"

"I have time," Jonas said and the rancour was gone from his tone.

"Always good company is Nikko. He talked of you, Mr Merrick, not breaking confidences but with respect. May I tell you something?"

"I am listening. Don't have all day, but have time. Nikko was helpful."

He could recall conversations with the flamboyant, boastful, delightful individual from the Drug Enforcement Administration operating out of Bogotá, Colombia, and bringing Jonas news of the departure from an Amazon tributary of a semi-submersible that was ferrying four tonnes of pure and processed cocaine across the Atlantic, with landfall on the Galician coast of northern Spain. An incredible voyage for a three-man crew, thousands of nautical miles . . . He had never met Nikko but had been sent a photograph of him, clutching an assault rifle and kitted out in combat gear, grinning with sheer happiness that God had favoured him with such a job . . . That was 'crime', designated as a backwater in Thames House. The value of Jonas' work had seeped into veteran operatives of the Agency, and of the Bureau – and his contacts – always discreet – were at a level that most senior figures on the fifth floor only dreamed of.

It was how Jonas Merrick worked, quietly and out of sight, with confidences shared but in restricted areas, and little put on record and electronic contacts that were bland at best. He took advice, rare for him, but from a trusted few.

"He said you were someone, Mr Merrick, I should know about – a guy who liked to be below the radar."

"Can I help? Tied down at the moment but—"

"No wish to interrupt. Just a touch-base call. Would it be rude to ask what involves you, without compromise?"

"An individual who has risen too high, needs bringing down, and a web of corruption."

"Which I know about. Inherent dishonesty, where I work, the coke production world. It spreads, has tentacles, it's in our society and in yours, burrowed into the culture. Sad and depressing. The attack weapon?"

"An 'irregular' is what I call him."

"Outside the normal limits of a flight path, beyond the usual tram lines . . . I have some experience . . . May I share it?"

"I have limits on time."

Not that Jonas did. Soon, his own man, the Montague in the story, would be collected by Effie Bellingham and driven to a cheap airport hotel at Luton and would await the arrival of the Capulet girl. How the contact would be made was kept from him, and from Effie. Chopper had likely not yet decided and would rely on instinct, sexual and romantic chemistry – an area in which Jonas Merrick was lacking. Soon, Julie Wilson, heir to an empire but identified by Jonas as the weak link in the dynasty's chain, would also head for that hotel, and take the same dawn flight the next day. The plan was outrageous, ludicrous, hatched during Jonas's journey between Raynes Park and Waterloo. And, with advice, he had chosen Chopper, judging him as vulnerable enough, isolated enough, to fulfil the role given him.

"I know what you mean, an 'irregular'. An individual likely to get a job done. Not on a list and not on a pension scheme. Not to be called into court as a prime prosecution witness, if you want a conviction. Hemmed in with anonymity so that deniability is maintained. Dangerous to use, but needs must, as they say. When all else has failed, that sort of thing. They don't take kindly to being given instructions. My experience, you point them in the target's direction and sit back and wait. If it works then you open a bottle, and if it doesn't then you go to ground for a week, forget it ever was an idea, and then find something else to do. A suggestion if you're using what you call an 'irregular' is to make sure, Mr Merrick, that you stay well back and behind a firewall that filters out your connection with the affair. But you know that."

"I think I do."

"Good to have spoken. If you lose one, an 'irregular' then we just shrug and say, 'That's show business', or you shake your head and reckon it's 'win some, lose some'. Tough old world."

"A tough old world and sometimes a hard one."

"Our trade, Mr Merrick, seems to attract them, the irregulars. Have a good day, what's left of it at your end. May I pass your regards to Nikko who I will see again tonight before he heads back north?"

"You may."

"We might get to work together one day as colleagues."

"We might, Hiram. Thank you."

Jonas rang off. That was his work, navigating in a 'tough old world' and putting an irregular into a hard corner of it, but staying, himself, in the warmth and the comfort. It was what he was paid to do.

"I don't need a lecture."

"You'll get a lecture because what Cohn tells me is that you were offensive and rude to an investment manager that he rates."

One more of the increasingly frequent spats between Lachy Wilson and his daughter had started upstairs when he had come to her bedroom and walked in without knocking which she thought unacceptable, then had moved down to the hall and into the kitchen. Where she went, he followed, and it was plain that the odious Yitzak Cohn, who relished the title of *consigliere*, had bleated last evening. Would have driven over and done it face to face, and whined that he had been offended by her attitude to George, that his advice had been ignored.

"That what you want, to second-guess me? Telling you, Dad, you either give me responsibility or you do not. Give, and I do it to the best of my ability. Don't, and I walk away. Your choice, Dad."

"You humiliated Yitzak. I will not tolerate that sort of treatment of the people who have shown loyalty to our family. Got me, girl?"

He could not do it, could not hand her the baton and look in another direction. He was tired, exhausted by the wars he had fought and wanted out. But he had the itch and had put in place what was going to be the last big one, a coup, an importation that showed the trade that Lachy Wilson still had the brains and the influence to pull off, and was not to be trifled with. Her ma had been to the churchyard that morning, had said she had talked to that pathetic priest who seemed to have her wrapped round his finger. She had been subdued and had pushed Mrs Plumb away from the Aga and was making cakes or scones or something, and stayed out, kept her head down. Always did when Lachy showed his temper, and when she cleaned the grave.

What Julie thought, had not said it, was that her brother had been a tosser, ignorant, arrogant, and stupid. Anyone with half a brain would have stopped the car, wound down the window, asked, 'How can I help you, officer? Problem with a rear bulb? Apologies, officer.' Not driven off because he'd had a few drinks and was in panic mode. The police car had followed and the speed had increased, and he'd gone off the road and into a tree, and broken his neck. Stupid and dead. And didn't think any better of Gregor, who Ma would see the next day, bloody awful journey to get there. So, Julie was the future. The way it had to be. Her dad would have belted Gregor or Hamish, not her.

"Ripping you off, didn't you hear me?"

"Decent deals and very decent security."

"That bastard is on the take and what he was offering is sub-standard."

"May not always get the best rates but he's discreet, which matters."

"Doesn't it matter that he's ripping you off? Doing it big time?"

Gregor would have screwed it, the future, given the chance. Had done violence – nothing wrong with that except that a trail had been left that even a copper could follow, and evidence, and there was one god-fearing witness who had allowed himself to be put on a protection programme, and the barrister was having a bad day and had pissed off the judge, and it was possible that her dad had realised the limitations of her brother and perhaps had let him go down. Less of a liability in maximum security than throwing his weight around, and taking on fights, arguments, maimings. They depended on her.

"You walked out on a man who has knowledge of us, and—"

She interrupted her father. "And told him some facts, the Adams and Eves. That he would be found. This George, who cheats us, and promised him he would be found, and would regret it. I promised it, in your name, in mine. I was walking out on him and his deal, had reached the door and told him we were going elsewhere. What happened? He changed his mind. I tell you a truth, Dad, he thought us weak. Enough?"

Definite that George, the investment manager, would not have known it. But, definite that Yitzak Cohn would have known it, and Lyons, the lawyer. Cohn would have wondered what the coming months and years held for him, and she expected now that he would look to build bridges, or would dread the night when his front door bell went, answered by his wife, or the girlfriend, and coming into the hall and seeing a man, or a woman, reaching into a pocket, would have half a second to note the handgun before the finger squeezed. Cohn would know that. She saw her dad's eyes flicker – wouldn't have done that in the past. And thought that the solid mass of his body had shrunk. She reckoned his power was ebbing.

"It'll be fine, Dad. All under control. Spend some time with those bloody chickens. And keep that shitface, Cohn, off my back."

Rather desperate, the question. "You can manage? It's complicated. Can you handle it? Listen to the Prof."

Her mother still worked at the Pyrex bowl, and the mixture for whatever was going into the Aga would have been kneaded half to death, and Mrs Plumb would have heard nothing.

Julie said, "Complicated? Of course it's complicated."

It was a small shipping container but adequate for the contract being fulfilled by the removal company.

The client was His Majesty's Government. More immediately it had collected the personal possessions of a British diplomat from his residence close to the Embassy in the Baltic city of Vilnius. The container on the back of a flatbed was in the queue, where it would receive favourable treatment at the border controls between Lithuania and Poland. It would then travel south and eventually reach the Slovakian capital, Bratislava, and load into the container the furnishings of a military advisor, along with the property of a commercial attaché from Latvia. The load would reach the port city of Antwerp by the weekend and then be shipped across the North Sea to the container dock destination at Felixstowe on the East Anglian coast. The company had a good relationship with Foreign, Commonwealth and Development Office and provided their services at a highly competitive rate and were useful at managing those small areas of collection, storage, and delivery that the principal contractor found onerous.

"If life were easy," Dragan hissed.

"You get boring, and repetitive," Mehmet whispered, an irritated answer. "Give them another one, gas."

Which Dragan did. Lowered the window on his side of the cab and pulled the pin clear with his finger and broke it off the canister and chucked it behind him and heard it bounce on the surface of the layby. Heard the chatter of voices and the pattering of feet and then the detonation. It was powerful, police standard gas, used for riot control. It would not have exploded as far back as the tail of the cargo trailer, but would have been nearer the fucking tyre that had blown.

"If life were easy . . ."

"You've said this . . ."

" . . . every man would be doing it."

" . . . a thousand times before. It is not easy."

They had been on the highway linking the capital, Ankara, with the port city of Istanbul, the gateway to Europe. Had been doing well when the tyre had burst, cracking like a gunshot. Incoming fire, or a tyre. They had by-passed Bolu, were between the Black Sea and the Koroglu mountains, and the way was through pitch-dark countryside broken only by lonely pinpricks of lights. And Mehmet had been telling his friend of the history of the place, of bandits, brigands, robbers, and myths. They had been pressing ahead because this had seemed a bad place to be delayed, with one of their sixteen tyres flat. Could have been a nail or a flint or a screw, could have been a weakness, but unimportant. They had a power jack and, between the two of them, were capable with a flashlight of making the change, and had been watched. A couple of kids at first, then more arriving and finally a ring had been formed around them, and there were signs that this was the equivalent of a foraging expedition from one of the distant villages high above them. Signs of clubs and staves, and perhaps a shotgun. They knew that if they paid a ransom to leave this isolated and threatening place then more would be demanded, capable perhaps of providing the resources to dig a new freshwater well for the community. Hands had tugged at the handles of the trailer doors, and the youngest and fittest had crawled up and on to the top of the trailer roof. Dragan had thrown the first grenade, which had won them two or three minutes to hurry on with the job of attaching the new tyre. Both men knew that if the sides or the tail were breached then the cargo inside would be damaged. The nuts would spill out, and a fair chance – once the first canister was thrown – that their throats would be slit or their skulls pulped. Each time they used a canister, explosion and white light or gas, the kids and young men would float back into the cover of darkness, but would return, and now it seemed a game was being played, and what they needed was a break of only five minutes to fasten the tyre in place, make it secure, then drive off into the dawn light.

"Because it is not easy, there is work for idiots such as you, such as me."

"We are paid for being idiots. The bigger idiots are those who pay our wage, want that fucking stuff up their noses, down their throats."

Grim laughter in the cab. They each had a pistol on their lap but the Kalashnikov remained hidden.

"What do you hear?"

"I don't hear anything."

Mehmet held his pistol and opened his door. The snow of the previous day had not thawed. The tyre, and its spare, had not been touched. Footprints had formed a pattern round the tail, and were on the sides where the climbers had been, and emptied canisters were littered there. Perhaps inside the laws and regulations justifying the courtesies of thieving from travellers it was considered acceptable to use flash and bang and gas, but payment would have been seen as a sign of weakness and would have invited ever-growing generosity. Gunfire on their part would have broken the rules further and demanded retaliation ... Perhaps they had become cold, or hungry. Perhaps they had gone home, back to a village where fires would have been lit, and animals needing fodder. A couple of boys watched them, shivered at the side of the layby. One was still on the roof.

They did what work was needed. Kept the pistol close. Mehmet talked to the watchers in his grated Kurdish accent and with little sign that he was understood, talked in staccato bursts. Talked about slicing off their testicles with a knife, but also with a wide smile.

"Is that the worst that can happen?"

"Worse than inside Iran, which was not easy?"

"It can still get worse. I read it in a book," Dragan said. "Things are going to get a lot worse before they get worse ... Does this have a bad feel?"

"I'll not answer that."

They were on their way. They came out of the layby's feeder road and were back on the highway, leaving behind them a damaged tyre, and the used canisters, and the shambles of foot-prints. The kid on the roof had jumped clear, might have hurt himself but they had not slowed and looked to find out. They had time to make up.

Inland from the port city of Antwerp, crouched on a stool and only half sheltered by a wide fisherman's umbrella, was Jacques.

The policeman had no duties that morning, could not prepare for his shooting examination the following day because the range remained closed, so he had attempted to minimise the burgeoning strain he was feeling by taking his rods to the *kanal* at Turnhout. Beside him were an optimistically large landing net, not yet used, and a bag containing his breakfast and a hot drink. The float on the water did not move. His wife was at work in the warmth of the Town Hall. For Jacques there was only the *kanal*, the chill in the still air, the threat of rain, and the absence of action. He used the traditional method of warming his maggots: clamped his teeth shut, opened his lips, and inserted the wriggling little wretches against his gums and closed his lips. The maggots, trapped between teeth and gums, would wriggle there and get warm, before they were hooked out and dunked in the water. Sometimes he used maggots which had been treated with a crimson dye: it was said by the pessimists among the anglers that this could contribute to mouth cancer. Not that Jacques was by nature an optimist, but he disregarded the warning.

He was hoping to attract some small carp, or roach, or rudd. The chance of carp was not great because of the cold, but the small fish might feed. If he were to catch any, he would change his rod and tackle and use them as live bait in the possibility of attracting a pike ... but there was no tug on his line. There was nothing to take his mind off the problem of the marksmanship test that beckoned in the morning, and the risk it presented, like a kick aimed at his crotch, to his career and his job at the Scheervaartpolitie station.

His phone rang, breaking the quiet and causing a pair of coots to take flight.

It took Jacques an age to get underneath the zips and studs of his gear and retrieve the phone. He answered it grumpily, and was given a clipped message: one lane in the firing range was being opened that afternoon. It would be available in two hours and fourteen minutes. If he passed over this opportunity there was a risk that another slot might not be available for three weeks. And he was told that, under the new regulations, his firearm authorisation would probably be withdrawn if he had to wait that long before his assessment.

Jacques opened his mouth and spat ferociously into the canal. The maggots scattered and left a swarm of ripples. Jacques wound in his line, hastily broke the rod, folded his umbrella and collapsed his stool, closed his tackle box, and tipped the rest of the maggots in the bucket over the canal bank and saw them slowly sinking. He collected his gear, heaved the straps over his shoulders and took a last glance at the water: he saw the dark shadow of a large pike pass under the feeding frenzy of smaller fish.

Jacques began to tramp to his car, panting beneath the weight of his kit.

As preparation for a marksman's examination it was as bad a situation as he could have imagined. But the alternative was worse – the prospect of having the pistol authorisation removed. It would be hard to win back. And without the weapon he would lose the right to escort important visitors, and the title of *Beveiligingsagent*, Security Officer, would be removed and his status would disappear.

The alarm on his wrist warbled.

The alarm would have woken the section in a forward base, inside a compound of mud walls reinforced with a multitude of sandbags, the first light peeping over a mountain ridge away to the east. A stampede to piss and shit if they were lucky, snatch a mug of scalding tea and get to the parapet and the firing positions. Dawn was when the ragheads liked to come and pepper them with RPG rounds. But he was not in Helmand and was no longer a Regiment man charged with handling the heavy machine gun.

He had a look around him, stiff and awkward from sleeping in the chair, and checked he had not left anything in the room. Saw the bin bag and the smoothed bed, and the open drawers, and the wardrobe. There were noises from the kitchen . . . He hooked the rucksack on one shoulder . . . No room key to turn because there had never been one. He went past the kitchen, her back was towards him and she was mixing something in a bowl. She'd have heard him but did not call out, nor did he announce he was going. He walked past his bicycle in the hallway, opened the outer door, closed it quietly, and slipped the key back through the letterbox and heard it fall on the mat.

He stood on the kerb by the underground station, expected her to be punctual, and she was. The car pulled up. He chucked the rucksack on to the back seat, and slid in beside her, and belted up as she swung out into the flow of traffic.

"You good?" Effie asked.

"Not bad," Chopper answered.

She steered with one hand and dug in a big bag with the other, coming up with an envelope which she dropped in his lap. There was a roll of euro notes, a hotel voucher for Luton airport and one for Leipzig, and a one-way ticket from Luton, with an early start the following morning. She drove as if she was at the controls of a main battle tank and she was given space by other motorists, even lorry drivers.

Effie asked him, "Reckoned how you'll do it, the contact?"

"Not yet."

"Play it by ear?"

Chopper said, "See how it works out."

"Fair enough," she said, like it didn't matter to her. Except it did, and he realised it. A sort of blinding truth hit Chopper: he had never felt so alone. In the days of the Regiment he had been hemmed in with guys, Lofty up against him and never leaving his side when they went towards a sharp end. Never with the Squad when they were packed close in the cars, ready to go, and each feeling the body heat of the person next to them. He sensed that she would have pitched at Sunray the idea of going on the flight with him. But then she would have been in the way, a nuisance and a hindrance and trying to call the moves, and he'd not have had that. Was pleased that Sunray had made the right decision: might have dressed like a pantomime idiot but had made the right call. He had been shocked, staggered in fact, when he had been identified in the gloom at the low point of the bridge. All of his supposed expertise in counter-surveillance had counted for nothing. Had he been identified that easily on a training exercise in east London the chances are he would have failed the assessment. His opinion of the man had soared. He didn't ask Effie what the guy was like to work for, who he was and from where, and was he a star in that building, with a host of researchers working for him – nor ask how hard he was, how caring. Nothing really for them to talk about.

What sort of approach would he make?

Had to hope that an idea would show up but could not say that it would.

No more talk. His was a brooding silence.

When it came, it sort of trickled into his mind, and he must have smiled. The car lurched between lanes as they headed for the airport.

"You want to talk it through?"

"I don't."

"You want to go on playing the bitch?"

"Wouldn't know how to."

Dressed as if for a board meeting, Julie sauntered towards the car. The Prof had already loaded her bag in the back, along with his own. Her father watched. The door was held open for her . . . Lachy Wilson thought his daughter needed a fucking great kick in the arse, and her indifference to him was tolerated only because of his dependence. Vic was behind him. The door was closed on Julie . . . At the other end of the line would be a lorry and very soon it would be losing its principal cargo of nuts and whatever and replacing it with a load of furniture. The registration plates would be changed, and the logos on the side, all done in an Istanbul warehouse with the speed of those guys who did pit-stop tyre changes in the motor racing world. What would not be touched was the covert cargo hidden away – the full weight of a tonne, he was assured – that would bring him home some 80 or 90 million, even 100 million, in cash. The biggest, best deal of Lachy Wilson's life, and his hold on the detail was dulled, and his mind less sharp, and he needed her, needed his daughter, the bitch. She did not wave, nor did he.

The car went down the drive, and Softboy would let them out at the main gates. The avenue of old oaks was a feature of his home in the Surrey countryside, each tree subject to a Preservation Order, and inspected every year. He took a pride in that, and in the meadows from which a closely supervised silage cut was taken at the beginning and end of the summer. Behind him were gentle hills and in front of him the ground dropped down to the river. It was a perfect place, and his finances were in perfect order: he had no need of the shipment, had been told that by his wife. Had no need of the fortune that would need to be well laundered before investment. Would spend days of anxiety about the security of the distribution, and nights of tossing worry as to the sums spent on buying silence and whether they were sufficient – and in the right pockets – to safeguard his freedom . . . But the addiction claimed him. He had no requirement for it and could not help himself. And his daughter was a bitch and he needed her. He heard, carried on the wind in the falling afternoon light, the big gates scrape open, and the car would pull out carefully on to the road, and be gone.

He thought his wife's face sombre.

Lachy went to Mrs Plumb for a cup of tea, and then would go and feed his chickens. Vic would leave to collect the boys from school – some pricey shit place where they had blazers and ties, and looked crap . . . He had no need of the money, everyone told him, all ignored . . . and there was talk of a problem with the man who would distribute in Liverpool and doubling back on agreed prices, which would need sorting. Sorting within a 24-hour span, not within a month . . . He thought the deals kept him alive, and without them he was a spent cartridge. And problems needed fixing, not left to hang about. A grey and damp evening and he sensed danger – prided himself that he had a nose for it – but could not locate its source.

The 'in between day' so dreaded by Jonas moved at irritating slow speed.

The workers in the Post Room gathered in a far corner or at their tables and did not speak to him, as if an order had been given that 'Mr Merrick should not be disturbed, left to himself and his heavy thinking'.

Soft music from a radio on the manager's desk, which was allowed after the lunch break and when work slackened off.

Even a visit from the AssDepDG badgering him for updates, times, locations, and him able to snarl back that he did not do 'a running commentary', might have been welcome. The time when he might have slipped out the back and into Thorney Street and paced up and down and puffed a cigarette – except that he did not smoke. Or gone to the mini-market and bought a box of chocolates and taken them to St John's Gardens, and gorged – except that he was disciplined and did not do binge eating. He sat at his desk. Or he could have gone home. Flashed his ID at Reception, seen their shock at his departure an hour and a half early, walked across the bridge and along the embankment and taken the first train to Raynes Park – except that his season ticket was only valid for the 5.27 departure.

He made a poor fist of doing nothing.

The General Secretary of the Republic of China's Communist Party was known in mass circulation papers as the Helmsman. From that lofty office he would not know of Jonas Merrick, but would be keenly aware that a principal agent of his nation's espionage programme in the UK had been 'persuaded' to defect to British and American agencies . . . the Helmsman was a good title. The head man of a remote Albanian village steeped in serious organised crime, with huge success, brought down by Jonas Merrick and now languishing in a ten-by-seven-foot prison cell was the 'Shefe' . . . the Chief was another excellent title. In his own little bailiwick, the Post Room, he was the Guv'nor to the staff . . . and he thought of the boy now being driven to Luton airport on a mission of outrageous presumption and optimism, and danger . . . and the girl doing the driving, Effie, had called him the Architect: he was for *Humble Pie*, the man who had conjured up the planning, and thought up the idea and put flesh on it . . . Jonas sat alone, his screen blank in front of him, and it was always like this on an 'in between day', with nothing more to be done, and success dependent on others and his influence diminishing by the hour. He felt uncertainty and wondered if it were shared in their own terms by the Helmsman, or the Shefe – or by the Czar, perhaps eating on his own at that gigantic table where he had once been served, from a silver platter, a severed head that his own people assured him was that of Merrick . . . Did they, like any self-serving architect, feel the strain when control moved far from them?

He laughed. Thought of himself ambling among the great and the good and the seriously bad.

Laughed out loud.

Heard chairs shifting behind him, and the radio was switched off.

Heard the volley of queries. "You all right, boss? Guv'nor, you okay? Please, sir, is something wrong?"

He sat up straight in his chair, and poked his head above his wall of filing cabinets, and smiled.

"Fine, thank you for asking. Don't know why you thought I wasn't. Sorry to have disturbed you."

Jonas might have thought a black dog mood had nuzzled against him, but now reckoned it was back in its kennel.

6

Almost the end of the 'in between day'.

Jonas ignored the nod of greeting from the official at the exit barriers of Raynes Park station. The man often gave him that acknowledgement and was never rewarded with a reaction. The gesture might have been because the official had worked at that station, on that shift, for more than thirty years and so the chances were good that five days a week, when the 5.27 came in from Waterloo, he would have seen Jonas Merrick step off the train and hurry through the station to make his way outside. The official was now a few months short of retirement and looked forward to when his time would be up and he would be able to commit himself to his allotment, and his delight in growing over-sized and inedible parsnips. He kept well under wraps the secret that he harboured about this particular passenger. He knew Mr Merrick, and he had once had reason to scrutinise the season ticket card, to be a man of importance, part of the apparatus of security that kept the country safer. He had noted when Jonas travelled home after the initial short breaks when he had been forced, damn near tied down, to take time off from travelling to London, after being 'roughed' by an Isis bomber on arrest and after being 'dunked' in the Thames by a home-grown spy operating inside the brother agency across the Thames, and there was the time when he had been saved by armed police from having his throat cut in a Liverpool street, and when he had been 'pulped' by a hired hitman. The official had noted those transparent strips of Elastoplast on his face and the stiffness of his movements – and, most important, had long ago spotted the chain that linked the briefcase to a fastening on the right wrist. A man of stature, a man deserving of respect.

Jonas passed him. Perhaps he realised that a degree of his cover had been broken by this fellow, perhaps not. The act of rudeness, not acknowledging the momentarily ducked head of the official, was typical and reflected a sourness in Jonas that seemed to wash ever thicker over him . . . not that he cared. However, that evening he felt at peace and the calm was created by the movement of the hands of his wristwatch, the end of the day coming on him with the thickening dark of the evening, and with that peace came a sense of hunger. His plan, his game, and the countdown about to start. Almost a jauntiness in his step. And then, in mid-stride, he hesitated, almost tripped, tangled up in his own feet, and looked back and the official had his back turned and would not have seen him. Jonas realised that he missed the wretched man on the days when he was sick or on leave, when a substitute took his place. Same as he felt when the scarred veteran who kept the gardens behind Thames House unnecessarily tidy and swept up the leaves was not in place.

The cold settled on him, and his Christmas scarf was insufficient to protect his neck and the forecast was for rain overnight. But in the morning – Jonas had that iron resolve – there would be the signs of the sunlit uplands. Pedestrians hurried past him, scampering for their homes, and might have wondered if the sound from him was bilious.

He was a winner. Cared about little else . . . had the official turned and faced him, had their eyes made contact, Jonas might well have asked him whether the signs were good for giant parsnips (he knew about the man's obsession because once a rosette had been pinned on his chest proclaiming First Prize for Largest in Class). He, too, would have been a winner, as was Jonas. He left the shops behind him as the shutters were coming down. He had no interest in working unless the opportunity was presented for him to succeed, to have destroyed an opponent of proven worth. These last several years had been a rollercoaster of triumph, and he had shared it at that intimate place, the front line where the end game was played out. His step was brisker and the possibility existed of unlocking his front door a full two minutes before he was expected.

Might be 'a grumpy old fucker' as his protector in the building, the Assistant Deputy Director General, described him.

Might be an 'old shrew, a gossip who knows everything about everybody gives fuck-all but does the business', as he had heard Effie describe him on the phone to her man and him pretending to sleep and thinking it both apt and deserved.

Might be 'a miserable bugger but one I'd want on my side', as Vernon the Post Room manager had described him at a staff birthday bash, Jonas behind his barricade of filing cabinets.

It was not a popularity gala, what he did. All that mattered was ending up the victor, with his brogue shoe across an opponent's throat, pressing down with whatever force was necessary . . . Of course he would win.

Jonas Merrick indulged himself. Who would he have accompany him to witness the success? The probable location would be that ludicrous house down in the Surrey hills, close to the River Tillingbourne. Who would he favour with such an invitation? The laughter welled in him – and Derbyshire, his neighbour, who was now in management in the company that sold conservatories, was getting out of his car and paused and seemed transfixed by the sight and sound of Jonas laughing. He arrived home and Vera would greet him coolly but Olaf would be warm and loving – two predators, two in love with the chase, two winners.

She manoeuvred the car into a bay on a far corner of the airport hotel car park, switched off the engine, folded her arms, and turned to face him.

"So, Chopper boy, how you going to play it?"

He smiled, his star turn.

"How? Last time of asking. How do you go at it?"

Chopper read her. She would have been to enough briefings where a boss shone the light from a laser marker onto a board or screen where headlines were written or a military map was on display and each of the mission leaders would have had to confidently explain how they planned to achieve whatever was set them. He imagined that old Sunray would be expecting a full statement on how he would attack this critical moment in the targeting. He had been plucked out of the Squad, recruited without much chance to decline, had been flown halfway round the world, had a bank account opened for him in which dosh was deposited, had been given a bet and had smiled enough to persuade a high-grade gangster girl to kiss him, pull a face at him and then resume a run along a seafront esplanade before the temperature climbed above thirty degrees. Flown home, then dumped at a loose end for a month and have the 'mushroom effect' heaved over him – *kept in the dark and fed a diet of bullshit* – and Sunray would have wanted a chew on his idea of the next stage, mull it over, pick a few holes, and make a few suggestions. *I was just wondering, what if . . . ?* Not Chopper's way.

Perfectly polite, "What did I say last time you asked me?"

"Didn't say."

"Why would that have been?"

"You said you didn't know, like you'd decide on the hoof."

"And what is different now?"

"What is different, Chopper, is that we are running out of time . . . Do not forget, please, that I'm the piper and call the jingle."

He could have replied that she was sounding similar to all the Sunray Minors he had come up against, the Ruperts and the Admin Chief Inspectors at police training camps, but he did not. Might have said that he would not have shared his plan because if she rubbished his idea and its timing then he was left with precious more than little. Did what he did well, his smile.

"Truth is the same as last time you asked. Don't know . . . will suck it and see. I don't know until it's in front of me."

"The best I'm going to get?"

"I'll know when it's right – if it is right. Last word."

He sensed her annoyance and recognised that failure came rarely to her. What Chopper was certain of was that any idea he had would not benefit from being run past a committee. He said he would see her again and suggested it might be appropriate if she wished him luck, but he was scowling and the clobbering of her self-esteem had hit home. He did things his way, leaned across and gave her a peck on the cheek, and smiled helplessly, and she said, 'Go fuck yourself,' but gave him a wan smile.

He reached behind her and lifted his rucksack and pulled himself up and out of the car. Chopper did a gesture with his fingers as he walked away, a sort of 'goodbye' flick, but did not look back. He hooked the bag over one shoulder and headed for the growing light at the entrance to the hotel . . . His idea of what to do, and when, remained vague. One solution to the problem appeared to have superiority, merit because it was so bloody ludicrous . . . and another difficulty loomed. He went through revolving doors and into the brightness of the empty lobby area.

He checked in. All charges taken care of, including the mini-bar in his room and anything from the breakfast buffet. He scribbled an indecipherable signature, then wandered into a more remote area of the lobby where he could see the entrance and the park forecourt, and the reception dark. He settled into an uncomfortable low chair and started to wait – and remembered her, and what she had done with him, as if it were an hour before, and thought some more about who she was, why she was of interest, and what the file said in the dry language of reports that were *Confidential* and made hard reading.

The Prof, Genge, trailed behind her, darting forward at the outer doors to flex them open for her, acted like he was a hired servant . . . which he was. She crossed the lobby, headed to reception.

The hotel, to Julie Wilson – daughter of Lachy Wilson, target for at least half a dozen crime squads – was hideous. She blamed her father who, with the support of her mother, loathed anything smacking of ostentation. No private jets, no taking over of boutique hotels, no booking of restaurants where no other clients were accepted. He liked to say that drawing attention to themselves was 'a feckin' lunatic way to behave', and her mother bought into it. It was an airport hotel, minimum charge and minimum service, and had that mid-evening scent of what was third rate. A vacuum cleaner was already being wheeled round the lobby and towards the bar area. A cheapskate place, which was what her father would have wanted. She was almost at the desk, then stopped and backed a couple of paces away and let the Prof pass her. He gripped a printout of the reservations. Blue-arsed flies they were, on the run and buzzing and clattering against doors' windows, and going at speed to make more money, 'have one last big one', and for what? The Prof used his card at the desk and she stood aloofly at one side and wore a loose scarf over her hair and Ray-Bans that covered half her face. More money coming in, wheelbarrows of it, and plenty for George in the City to get his hands on and slice off his cut, and some more for Cohn to spirit away . . . Julie had a story she liked when she had been trawling on her laptop. 'God's banker', a Mr Calvi, had managed to lose money that rightfully belonged to the Vatican's treasury, and wrongfully was the property of Sicily's *Cosa Nostra*. He had been found one dawn in the early 1980s dangling by the neck from scaffolding under Black-friars Bridge over the Thames – which kind of sent a message to those losing the Pope's cash or the Mafia's. A poor career move. She wondered if George knew the story, and would have bet that Cohn did. She was handed her key, a plastic card.

There was a desert of empty tables in a coffee shop that doubled as a restaurant.

Did she want to eat with him?

Not sure.

She looked around her. The bar was quiet, just a few customers. They'd mostly be business class, on an early flight out and a destination in time for a breakfast meeting. Two couples, each with a buggy, and two single men were now queuing for attention as the Prof sorted out the back-up early calls, and a guy was sitting in a shadow, mostly hidden behind a colour magazine from the last weekend.

Was there Room Service?

A consultation. There was.

She would eat in her room.

The Prof led her to the elevator . . . He had been her escort since she was a child. She had tried to shed him and had failed, and no longer attempted it. Loyal, devoted, and boring. Probably muttering under his breath verses from Rossetti or Morris or

Swinburne which he now accepted she would not recognise. They went up in the lift – she accepted that he would die if she were threatened in any way, would protect her with his life. She took her bag and went off down the corridor to her room.

In the corridor of locked doors, no slivers of light from inside the rooms – except for one door where a computer was still alive with a bright screen. The teams from the Anti Corruption Unit had all left, but only after some grudging praise had been given to the group led by DCI John Plunket. Both Dawson and Rajah had also left to head for their homes in the thickening darkness. Perhaps it should have been a moment for celebration and a meal together and some drinks in a discreet bar but not his way and not theirs.

Might have been satisfaction enough that a middle-ranking detective was languishing in the cells of a suburban police station, alongside the usual list of clients – druggies, drunks, muggers, abusers – waiting for a solicitor to pitch up. If that solicitor had common sense, had read his runes correctly, then he would advise total contrition, humility, and a guilty plea. Unlikely, and for a small fee would attempt to concoct a blustering defence . . . Not Plunket's concern. The cop, 'bent as a Brazilian banana', was going down and a judge would pucker his face in distaste. The fact the accused, now convicted, was wearing a quality suit and a laundered shirt and a gold club tie and would have made a Masonic sign towards the Bench would not matter. He might be standing in the dock alongside one or several of the Courtney crowd. It was a grim future the disgraced policeman faced in gaol, but that gave Plunket, in this case, minimal satisfaction.

Others in their corridor, also leading a secretive professional life, had muttered congratulations to him – put their heads round the door – and they had been curtly received. It was the nature of ACU: the work stretched towards an infinity point, and none of them on his team, or hidden away behind any of the other rooms off that most secure of corridors, would have believed different . . . It was a mantra in all police work that they were supposed to 'make a difference', it was what the posh graduate kids coming in as recruits had told the first interviewers and had gushed on their application forms. There was, of course, a way to make that difference, have it shouted off the rooftops and splashed across news screens and front pages, a mug shot accompanying the headlines, but he was not close to that moment.

He had half a packet of chocolate biscuits and that would be his supper, and a soft drink in a can which he would open later in the evening. Eventually he would lay his head beside the keyboard and maybe sleep for an hour or two and then would splash his face with cold water in the wash room and would head to his studio apartment and an unmade bed – and imagined that Dawson and Rajah faced the same emptiness.

They were a driven team.

Could not have slid a razor blade between this attitudes to work. He supposed he was – as Sally, his former wife, had claimed – 'rather sad'. He knew, of course, of those cops, decent men and mostly in uniform, who sang in choirs, helped in youth clubs, and were good people. People who did not flagellate themselves as he did, did not set themselves up to fight, bare-knuckled, against the most significant target on the territory.

Might have been an addiction.

He knew of no way to let go of it, go cold turkey, lose it. And so he spent the evening working on other files that should have given him some solace but failed on that evening, and most evenings.

Jacques cleared the pistol, squeezed the trigger with the barrel pointing into the sandpit.

He removed his ear defenders and the protective goggles.

The instructor's face was inscrutable. Jacques was still breathing heavily, and his blood pressure must have soared, and he had not eaten, nor drunk any coffee. A disaster.

Arriving at the range for his rescheduled shooting stint, he had found himself in a queue. He had complained, had hissed criticism of the way the place was run, had been invited to put his problems on paper and skip that day, and wait until there was next a vacancy. But that would have meant losing the authority to carry a firearm, as well as his self-respect, and a job that gave him satisfaction and which was convenient, comfortable and cosy. He had already been in a puddle of self-pity when called forward. Hearting beating like a sledge hammer, blood pounding, and there was something unfamiliar about the grip of the weapon, and even as he had stepped forward his mind had been clouded by the sleek outline of the fish that had roamed under the sinking scattering of the maggots he had chucked away. There was a clear indication that the instructor wanted to get away, that time was not on his side.

He had fired, had emptied two magazines, handed back the weapon.

It must have been clear from his expression that he needed some sort of an answer.

The expression was inscrutable, but accompanied by an eloquent shrug of indifference.

Jacques said, defensively, "The Five Seven, it did not feel right."

"You are used to the old model. This is the new specification. Time marches."

"How did I do?"

The shrug was repeated. "*La ligne de demarcation*, it will be evaluated. You'll hear tomorrow . . . Now I have to clear up, shut down the facility – you will be told."

So he was on the borderline and a stranger would see his results with the FN Five Seven and would decide. Perhaps positively, perhaps negatively – and he would sweat. Borderline. On the edge. Out of his hands . . . He went out into the evening and because of the unfairness of it and the odds stacked against him, a sense of misery welled in him: in Jacques' thinking a glass was always half empty and he struggled to imagine how he could redress his situation.

Betty said over her shoulder from the front door, "And try, just try, for once, not to have left the place looking like a tip when I get back."

Her 'partner', Ralph, failed to look up from the table where he struggled with a crossword in the newspaper. "Have a nice evening, sweetheart, and a nice night, and a nice early morning, and come back all cheerful."

"Because the last time—"

"And don't be late for work," he interrupted. "Terrible to be tardy for the important job of safeguarding the nation's borders. Maximum alert – the order of the day, the night. Sweet dreams."

She was gone . . . it had been growing on her, the feeling that his time in her one-bedroom apartment had reached the end of its shelf-life. Had seemed an excellent idea for the first month, with vigorous bed-time and happy laughter, but had palled in the second and third and now, in the fifth, he had begun to bring cardboard removal boxes from his mother's home, as if a permanence loomed. It would take some strong words to move him out. She recognised that he seemed to harbour a poor opinion of her intellect, and a feeling that she was useful, filled a niche in the job market but had no particular talent. Sod him. The time she had come back from a night shift just before her injury and the infection, he had left the table in their living-space cluttered with papers and with the packaging of his supper . . . Sod him and big time.

She chucked her bag on to the back seat – spare clothing, overnight toiletries so she would swell sweet in the morning as dawn came up over Luton airport, and a home-made sandwich, coffee and an apple. She drove off.

Always had that feeling that 'something might turn up', nurtured it on the journey north. By the time she reached the destination, parking area reserved for Border Force, she was usually convinced that nothing would, that surprises would boycott her.

Her foot still hurt, and her mood was poor, and Betty went to work and would be doing the late flights into Arrivals and the early flights out of Departures.

So far he had not expressed it to Olaf, the Norwegian Forest cat with a pedigree as long as Jonas' arm, but had he done so he would have chosen a chilly night, and late, when the Derbyshires next door would have been in their beds and their light out, and Vera was upstairs, snoring lightly, and the cat was foraging in the herbaceous bed. Would have said, but had not shared yet with Olaf:

Don't know them, dear friend. They'll turn up, certain of it. I may, perhaps, hear of them after they have appeared, or may not. Probably they will flicker into the beams of the headlights and then back off but that intervention may upset whatever applecart I have fashioned, or may not. You cannot budget for them, Olaf, but have to accept the fact that they lurk, loiter, close to events. Means we have to fly by the seat of our pants. Means also that those to whom we have entrusted responsibility from our bunker in the Post Room must be able to carry on with a mission – what I have called Humble Pie *– without my having an ability to intervene, for better or worse. I don't know who they are, these lurkers. Will likely never get to hear of them but might just have to retrieve the debris from where they have loitered. They are always there. Have never heard of me, have no interest in my plans, are illuminated briefly and may leave me in a better place, or may disrupt my intentions, and may fade fast to insignificance. I have no idea of who they are . . . which, Olaf, makes for a degree of fun.*

But had not said it, not even in a whisper, while the beast hunted for prey among the bare winter beds.

Close to the end of the 'in between day'.

Jonas was sitting in his caravan. He had done his inspection of the work carried out, but with only lukewarm interest. Rare for him to have admitted to himself that the fault lay with him and could not be slid off his area of responsibility and into another's lap. As an operator in Thames House, Jonas Merrick relied on mistakes, but not those made by himself, from opponents, and thought he was adept and able at exploiting them. He would say to the 'disciples' who worked for him when he had been on the third floor and in a cubicle in a corner of Aggie Burns's territory of A Branch, Surveillance, 'Hang around long enough and keep a good eye on them and the mistake will be made, always is, and the trick is to see it, note it, exploit it. Them making a mistake is inevitable and provides us with the opportunity to get the hobnailed sole of a boot on to their windpipe and pressure should then be applied, and done with rigour – and that's when we win. If there is a difficulty it is in being insufficiently vigilant in seeing the mistake' . . . All rather complacent, and verging on the pompous, but still part of Jonas's creed and integral in his Bible . . . He could not fault the caravan park's work, except for the size of the bill that Vera had settled on its return, and it had received a serious valet standard clean, which he had generously paid for.

He quite liked Effie Bellingham, but found her marginal impertinence almost mocking, unpleasant. On receiving the creed, she'd pouted a question at him, 'And what if it is us who makes the mistake, what then?' He had answered sourly that 'Mistakes are not accidents. They are the result of carelessness, and should not happen.'

He had the cat on his lap. The beast was relaxed, purred softly, kneaded its fierce claws in and out of Jonas' trousers, and had seemed in poor humour after doing the rounds of the caravan and inspecting the interior of each cupboard and failing to find signs of mouse habitation. It was time for Jonas to allow competition to jostle for space in his mind, and for the matter of the all-important 'mistake' to be challenged by the harder issue of the blatant lie that he would tell his wife when the caravan was loaded and they seemed ready to head for a south coast idyll, a site in Dorset. Two bits of business and competing hard, and both relevant to bringing down an opponent of quality.

Off the main Dorking road, set back from the one linking Westcott to Coldharbour, was a newly built roadhouse, that doubled as a gastro-pub, also as a bed and breakfast, where a couple of rooms were always vacant should Lachy Wilson need them.

His muscle, Softboy, had already headed there; Lachy followed. Softboy would reach the premises and park close to the back door. Lachy would leave his car in the rear car park, where it would be recorded by the CCTV. Lachy would go into the pub, would drink a couple of cokes in the bar and show a picture of health and warmth and politeness to those who met him, and then would make his excuses and would seem to head off to one of those rooms that were always available. That was the routine. Tacked on to it was the fast hustle when one of the bar staff would slip out of the back door and into the passenger seat of Softboy's vehicle, with a scarf round his face and a flat cap low on his forehead and an anonymous blue anorak that had come off a line of hooks behind the bar. Except . . .

when they were needed, the barman could shed the soft tartan scarf, the sort half the male population over forty years old received as a Christmas present, and the cap, and the anorak, and Lachy would put them on. Softboy warming the car, Lachy in the passenger seat, and the vehicle gone . . . Not foolproof, not capable of throwing a half-decent detective off the scent, but good enough to fool the average juror if the prosecution were calling it 'crucial evidence'.

Softboy would drive. It would have taken fifteen minutes longer to get from the Wilson residence to the pub and the delay was because there was a lock-up garage on the way, a small diversion, where the Astra vehicle he drove, ordinary bodywork but with enhanced engine power, was checked for a bug. A necessary routine and the procedure for all the vehicles from the big house, all the way down to the little compact used by Mrs Plumb and into which the boys had to squeeze to travel to and from school.

They drove north, would reach the motorway ringing the capital, and would come off it at the exit that would take them north-west to Liverpool. A bit over a couple of hundred miles, and the Astra would eat it, and a pair of allies would be waiting for them, and a man who had caused Lachy 'a little bit of difficulty' would be in ignorance of the vehicle coming up the M40 and then the M6, with false plates for the 'recognition' cameras, which was as well for him because otherwise his sphincter would have been under extreme strain.

He was told by Softboy when they were likely to arrive, and Lachy closed his eyes. Slept like a baby, a happy baby, well fed and watered. His age seemed to him to have dropped off his shoulders and it was a joy to have a lorry on the way, and the sniff of action in the air, and both of them with their phones left in the rooms in the Surrey pub and no distractions . . . Only the one where he could imagine how it would be for the Scouser who had shot his mouth. It was how Lachy had operated in the early days of his meteoric climb when he had overtaken rivals, left them dead or maimed or terrified or going to ground. Happy days they had been, and he craved to recreate them.

Slept well, felt good. What might have been a worry was dismissed – the chickens would be fed by Mrs Plumb. *Depend on me, Mr Wilson. It is as good as done.* And her promise that they'd be shut up for the night, secure as Fort Knox.

Not the exact detail of what would be done, but he had talked it through with Vic. Her questions: had the target reason to believe that Lachy Wilson was coming after him? Or had the target merely fired off with his big mouth and not realised, or been too dumb, to comprehend the stupidity of his actions? Had the target decent security at his home? Would Lachy's intelligence be good enough? He'd answered, and she'd shrugged, was the policeman's daughter.

In bed and on her back, Julie listened.

Had no option. Thin walls. Not going at it like rabbits, but slow and careful, like it mattered. Julie was a master in the arts of money laundering, and the extraction of quality deals from the 'brokers' who did the transactions with the Afghan people, and could face down the pimps who brought the girls in from eastern Europe, and knew how to negotiate with real estate and could pick any worthwhile investment site . . . All taught her by her father. Had kept her away from pretty much all of the boys who had come sniffing round her. Imagined it as all frantic and hurried except what she heard through the wall was measured and slow and like it was gentle.

She rolled over on her stomach – felt fucking jealous – and grabbed the top pillow and dragged it over her head. Tried to shut it out, and clamped her eyes shut. Wondered how long it might last. Pressed the pillow hard against her ears.

Chopper lay on his side.

There would be one chance, one chance only. One chance to be up close, make his statement, half a dozen words, and it might work and might not. Had only been one chance when getting off the first blast from the general-purpose machine gun, and Lofty feeding the belt and putting down the heads of the Tommy boys wanting to get close and personal. One chance only when they jumped out of the cars and the unmarked vans and sprinted towards the bad guys and needed to achieve mind-deadening surprise and put them down on the pavements before – God forbid – they'd a moment to get their handguns clear of their belts. Liked the concept of 'one chance'. That same one chance when the other crowd's striker was coming towards him and his momentum would carry him past for the one on one with the keeper unless the tackle came in. Tackle was the pleasant way of putting it, as Sunray would have called it out, or 'chop him down' or 'kick the legs from under him' which was the barely coded message. One chance was enough.

She had walked past him in the lobby . . . Had she been on her own he might not have recognised her. A smartly turned out businesswoman. Sunglasses and scarf, and the demeanour that went with entitlement. It was the man who trailed behind, carrying the bags, who told the story. Flagged up in the file: Walter Genge, or Wally, or the Prof. Age 53, dog of all trades who could fix a leaking tap, mow the grass, paint the walls, mind Julie, do time for the family, and do violence for them and would go to his grave rather than betray them. One bag that was a shambles, unzipped and a sweater sleeve trailed and a folded length of coiled newspaper was visible; the other bag was discreet and seemed half filled. Effie and her guy had said that Genge had been there in the Gulf but had not been able to follow her along the esplanade, had hung back, leaning on a push bike's handlebars, and sweating like a horse.

She had 'style'. 'Class'. Had walked ahead and lined up the girl on Reception then let her man do the business, fill out the forms, and sign. Had a taste of her still? Not really but could imagine it . . . What hurt him was that she was a different individual. Not jogging in the sunshine, waves slipping against rocks beneath her, sweat running off her neck and shoulders and staining her T shirt, and relaxed. This was a young person at the top of a tree and knowing it, but checking into a cheap airport hotel and there would have been a reason for it which was beyond Chopper.

He would say what he planned to say, do his best, and she might walk past him as if he were a troublesome nuisance, best ignored . . . might flick her fingers for Genge to come close and shove an elbow in his face that would pitch him backwards . . . might have a choice volley of abuse in his ear or might have a polite request to stop bothering the lady . . . Might try his smile and might be rewarded.

Chopper grinned.

Might get the reward Sunray craved, and might not. If it went against him he doubted there would be an inquest, and he'd save them the airfare because there would be no reason to be on the flight to Leipzig, doing a shadow job on her which might just as well be given to the local police. He would be signed off and whatever paper trail he left would go into the shredder and the electronics would be deleted, and Human Resources at the Yard would find him a berth in some corner far away from Agathe's apartment and it would be time to start out again. Chopper sincerely doubted he would see Sunray again, but might have a ten-minute slot with the girl and Effie would read the riot act against him blabbing about where he had been and what had been his target, and he would be 'history'.

The end of the 'in between day'.

Jonas climbed the stairs to the bedroom and the cat padded after him.

He was a man governed by instinct. He did not deliberate nor look for alternative planning, but kept a void in his mind and only filled it when a solution nagged hard enough for him to find its enthusiasm no longer resistible. He would not discuss an idea even with the AssDepDG until he had rubber stamped it. And true to form was *Humble Pie*, and the job dumped on him. His intuition allowed to run riot, then identifying the weak link followed by the recruitment of Chopper, and the launch of his plan, rubbished by all. He had shrugged, suggesting that if the plan were not liked then they were welcome to walk away and approach another source with another idea, and then would have ducked his head below the filing cabinets. The AssDepDG had run with it. Of course he had. Instinct was followed by the slow march of the preparations, and led up to the final 'in between' hours, which were over as the hand on his alarm clock crawled towards dawn – then the stampede. Always worked that way . . . a careering charge towards the tape, and he would want to be there, a sort of vanity, but one that required a shameful lie to be told. He eased open the door of their bedroom, and the cat leaped onto the bed, securing a position halfway across, curled and, settled.

Jonas sat on his chair. Took off his shoes, began to undress. On the back of the chair were clean socks and an ironed shirt in his Tattersall check and a fresh handkerchief.

Vera was still awake, waiting to interrogate him.

"Jonas, what I need to know is—"

"I doubt you do, at this time of night."

"You have been peculiar all evening. I could say you've been peculiar ever since our holiday was postponed."

"Peculiar? I am not aware of it."

"And I can time pretty much to the minute when your mood started to become evasive."

"Vera, you know very well that I don't bring my work home and lay it out on the kitchen table and expect my decisions to be dissected, and—"

"Claptrap, Jonas, piffle."

Beside the bed was a dark wood chest. He was allowed the bottom drawer. The one above was filled with Vera's jumpers, the next her blouses, at the top were two more, the right one containing what Vera described as her 'this and that', and the left drawer was stuffed with underwear, her knicker drawer. At the back, far from sight and disturbance, was a medal box in which was the QGM, a gallantry medal, and with it a bar. Jonas had been sent to a country residence of a Royal some years before and had received a personalised investiture, and then a year later the QGM had again been matched and a bar awarded. It was to be assumed that the AssDepDG had put the word in the correct ear. Jonas Merrick's name had appeared on no public list and the citation was known to a minimum of people in the Security Service, certainly not by the majority of high-flying graduates that were the recruitment target for the Fivers. Without a degree, the anonymous analyst had managed to disarm the vest worn by a would-be suicide close to the Palace of Westminster, had done it himself rather than calling in the back-up. He had been sharing the bench while sitting out the last hours of his employment in Thames House before the dread guillotine of retirement had fallen on him. Retirement had been cancelled. His talent had been belatedly recognised. The bar was awarded after he had identified where an Isis activist would be in the cathedral city of Canterbury and where he intended to detonate himself along with teams of pilots in portacabins in Lincolnshire who remotely flew the Royal Air Force armed drones over the Middle East. Had he, again, called for an armed police intervention, the man might well have slipped away. Jonas had shown no fear, acted without hesitation twice, and not entirely sensibly. He had not been afraid.

In truth, the only area in his life where he might feel fear, demonstrate it, was when challenged by Vera, his wife of more than thirty years. He cringed.

"You're having doubts, aren't you?"

"Not that I am aware of."

"You are involved in a matter that is troubling you?"

"Am not aware of it."

"You asked me about Verona."

"I did."

"Verona is about Romeo and Juliet. About a boy and a girl from opposite sides of a river or a peace barrier or a political culture, who come together and put themselves in danger. Do I have to spell it out?"

"You do not, and I have a busy day tomorrow and I need sleep, not an inquest."

"Is that what you have done, Jonas? Pushed the opposites together? Is that *convenient* for you, Jonas? Are you, now, uncomfortable with what you've done? Is that why tomorrow is busy, Jonas? Are you easy with what it is that you have done?"

"Have to be, Vera. It is the way things get done. The people I work with are adults and, after a fashion, are volunteers. Nothing for you to worry about . . . I do very much need it, my dear, a good night's sleep."

Light out, his back to her, and saw the young man and his smile, and the hours until dawn slipping by.

7

The alarm clock showed it was not yet four o'clock.

Jonas heard rain pattering on the window.

The cat snarled.

It was the most important morning of *Humble Pie*. He had been awake for two hours, tossing and fretting. The one relief was that he had put to the back of his mind the challenge given him by his wife and her concerns about the couple of youngsters for whom he played an amoral role as a matchmaker. Not that Jonas was skilled in the customs of dating websites beyond what he had eavesdropped in the Post Room and the chatter he had heard through the flimsy cubicle door of his room on the third floor. He had not seriously believed in the possibility of failure, but he was tense. Probably anyone who conducted similar business as that practised by Jonas, in Five or Six or Special Forces, understood what it felt like waking up on the critical morning, lying in bed before the traffic started up, before the street cleaners were at work, before the police and health staff changed shifts. Would have comprehended the loneliness of rising, showering, dressing, clearing the mind . . . chin forward, and best foot, and facing the day. In the next few hours he would have it rammed down his throat: had his instinct served him well, had his intuition pitched him into failure? He cleared his throat, coughed, spat into the handkerchief in his pyjama jacket pocket.

He pictured Chopper sloshing his face with warm water and splattering the floor outside the shower door, cleaning his teeth and scraping his cheeks with the razor and dragging on last night's clothing, then running his fingers through his hair and looking in the mirror, and grinning. Star choice, and Jonas believed in self-congratulation . . . And Julie, whom he had seen half-dressed, coming out of her bedroom onto the landing above the main staircase of her home, spitting in anger, and being put down by her father. He had seen her nascent hostility at being publicly chastised and Jonas had thought her alpha quality more than useful . . . And Effie who would be longing for a shower having sat in her car through the night with a clear view of the entrance to the hotel and waiting for the shuttle bus to turn up. Had checked them both into the hotel, and felt that Genge, the bag carrier, was loyal, and was not stupid. She had messaged Jonas that Julie Wilson and her escort, had arrived an hour after Chopper.

Jonas sat on the side of the bed, waited, and was rewarded by his phone coming to life.

The transport was there and he was on board, well muffled against the morning cold, and raining in Luton, as it was in Raynes Park, and his face was covered. She was last on the bus, with her minder. Seemed more critical than what had gone before in his life, as if the stakes were higher . . . It was worth picturing the face of the target, Lachlan Wilson, the untouchable, remember the self-control he had shown when he had welcomed the search party into his home, and followed what was clearly a routine where his wife made tea and coffee and warmed up sausage rolls and produced plates and paper napkins, and suggested that the police remove their shoes so that the white carpet was not dirtied. His self-control had been total, and Jonas wondered for how much longer that lifestyle was possible – and wondered where the lorry was, and its destination, and . . . He coughed.

In a small voice Vera asked, "Was I a bit of a bitch last night? Sorry. Prying too much . . . A troubled night?"

Jonas – who very seldom apologised, and then only to regain high ground – said, "Not bad and not good – best you try to get back to sleep."

Passengers had begun to go through the metal detector arch and their bags and outdoor clothing were on the security X-ray belt, and a queue had started to form at Betty's pint-sized box, and the guy from Border Control next to her wasn't hurrying, and no reason why he should. She pinched her cheek, a good way to get her concentration up and running. She noted a good-looking boy, but he didn't look her way.

Chopper was in the right-hand queue.

She was to his left, and two places ahead of where he waited for the passport control people to get their act together. He could remember when he had been a young cop, a probationer, and there were always arseholes in an older group, PCs and WPCs, who liked to show off their authority by holding up motorists, or pedestrians, just for the hell of demonstrating authority. He was heading for the Border guy in the right-hand booth, and she was in line for the miserable-looking woman on the left. Her minder was a pace in front of her and carried the two bags and held their passports. If instinct was to be let rip this was as good a time as any. He could be ignored, could be kicked, could be slapped, could be . . . Chopper took a deep breath. Exhaled, and murmured the words. Had a momentary thought of why: nothing to do with the old guy who was spare with his time and incapable of an officer's motivational spiel, or Effie, who was so full of herself and her status and him being the hired hand. Nothing connected with the benefit of the state and allegiance to the Para wings and the warrant card and the little shell in his pocket.

Chopper had his rucksack half on a shoulder, his scarf wrapped over his lower face. He left the queue, heard a grunt of annoyance, took a few steps to the left and she was unaware of him. He went down on one knee, kept his head low.

"Excuse me, miss, but your shoelace is loose and you might trip over it."

She had heard him and seemed to stiffen.

"Very dangerous, walking around with a loose shoelace. I'll fix it."

She could have taken a pace forward and caught up with the Prof as he offered his passport to the woman behind the screen.

Or she might have kicked him out of her way, or might have kneed him in the face, or bent and slapped him. When Chopper looked up, he saw she was blushing like a schoolgirl. If it had been an extra-time goal he had scored, or a freefall jump like the Hereford folk did, or a judder on his shoulder from the machine-gun, then Chopper would have raised a clenched fist and punched the air. He looked into her face, wiped a hand gently over the buckle on her shoe, and stood.

She held the eye contact. He ducked his head.

What any of Chopper's sergeants, Para or Squad, would have called the 'bloody bleedin' obvious', she asked, "Are you following me?"

"Trying to."

She was staring straight ahead and for a moment seemed pole-axed. He resumed his place in the right-hand queue, saw the minder turning to her and handing over her passport like she was an unaccompanied minor. She handed her passport to the woman in the Border Control booth. She did not look behind her. He took his own passport out of his trouser pocket, felt coins and the seashell, and went forward.

It was enough to wake Betty. The travel arrangements of *Walter Genge*, an address listed in Surrey, were 'of interest' and would be logged ... And there was more to amuse her because right behind him was a classy little madam, playing 'businesswoman of the year' and travelling with Genge. And the good-looking boy had come to Madam and knelt at her feet and said something about shoelaces, which was ridiculous because she wore shoes with buckles and not a bloody lace in sight. The passport was given her and she fed it into the scan, and choked a moment. Name of *Julie Wilson*, and the passport number matched and the date and place of birth: 'to be logged as priority, but not delayed'. That was all a bit choice, out of the ordinary, and no way what she had seen and heard about the shoelaces cam from a stranger. Did her corporate smile and indicated that Julie Wilson, logged *priority*, could move on, and the next punter could stew for a moment because she was watching the guy with the smile at her colleague's booth.

The Prof had fixed her with his eye, unpleasant and lazy, a reminder of a beating years back that had carried 'consequences' for the lowlife who had done it. "What kept you?"

"Nothing kept me."

"I was waiting for you."

"Tough shit, it's a hard life."

"Did you have a problem with your passport?"

"No."

"Just wondered."

"Don't then, don't wonder."

"Your father pays me to wonder, right?"

"Whether he gets value for money, that's his problem."

And the Prof seemed to back down. "Sorry was just asking. Didn't get much sleep."

The Prof was poison, and she trusted him not an inch, but he would not have seen it, nor heard it, and she looked again at her shoe, and remembered every word he had said.

"Nor did I. Go get us a coffee each."

He went away in search of coffee. She did her own searching, but without success, could not see him. What was more than obvious was that he would be on the Leipzig plane, had locked on to her travel details, probably knew where she was booked in for the night, which meant he knew pretty much everything about her, which meant . . . It was too much for Julie Wilson, the future of a crime family, to cope with and the sun not yet in the sky and the rain pounding the plate glass wall . . . which meant that she was the target they had chosen. Part of it was a kiss, and a bullshit story about a bet, and she had bought into it. And as the blood seeped from her face, her neck went cold, like it did when the world seemed to build walls round her, and she was alone.

From her Border Control viewpoint, Betty had watched him. Had seen him scrabble on the ground in his own queue, and present his passport after getting the stuff back in his pocket. Betty dealt with the last passengers for the Leipzig flight, and mixed in with their dregs were the first of those off to Sarajevo, and God alone knew why any human wanted that destination, and her shift was nearly done.

Good looker, great smile, doing business with some kind of shoes worn by Julie Wilson, who rated as *priority*. His passport in his hand, and his boarding pass, and coins spilled on the ground and he was scrabbling on the floor, searching for something. Finding it and the panic diminishing. A fucking seashell? A periwinkle . . . one of the millions that washed up on the UK shore, on any beach, any shingle, any stretch where the incoming tide rippled. But it was something that mattered. She had witnessed the relief when it was found – almost under a fellow passenger's shoe, half an inch from crushed extinction. Pocketed, and up to the booth where her colleague sat, and an apology for holding him up, and a smile to go with the apology. Not long now until the end of Betty's shift.

Effie had told him that he would be at the back of the aircraft, with a view down the length of the aisle. He could not see her, not even the crown of her head above the top of a seat rest halfway down, but he recognised Genge's scalp.

There had been a delay. Might have been twenty minutes. He wondered how she was, whether her degree of turmoil was as great as his. Seat belt signs were already on and a couple of stewardesses walked the length of the plane to check that the belts were fastened, then the engines started up. He had been on enough flights to have a decent recollection of every moment of the race towards the speed needed to get the crate into the air, and hoped that the guy at the sharp end had enjoyed a decent sleep and wasn't in the aftermath of a domestic, and they were up.

Chopper lowered himself in his seat, and turned his head to the cabin window, closed his eyes, and had good leg room with the seat adjacent unoccupied. Not much talk around him, and no laughter, but soon there was gentle snoring. He reflected on how little he knew of her, had only instinct to guide him.

Everyone had said that Sunray's plan was idiotic, a lunacy, but it had not yet fallen arse over tit, was still above water.

A tap on the back wall of Betty's cubicle. Her replacement had arrived. In a lull between the boarding for the Sarajevo flight and the one for Sofia, she had sent the details of Walter Genge, *of interest*, and Julie Wilson, *priority*, into the system. Not her business where it went after she had fulfilled her task. But the excitement had managed to clear the ache in her foot, and the pain in having Ralph in her home and the usual dreariness of her work. Barely a word passed between Betty and her replacement. She was off through the darkness to the staff car park – and home, and sleep.

Julie knew about the nuances of police surveillance, how many of them it took to follow a pedestrian suspect, and how many vehicles and motorcycles were needed for a road journey, so what had happened made no sense to her.

She thought about the voice of the guy, soft but clear and with a trace of humour like the stunt with her shoelace was the best joke in town. She hadn't had a satisfactory look at his face: he had looked as different as was possible from the business on the sea front when she had done her run before going into a private meeting room and signing off for the transfer of big bucks for the initial part of the deal that was bringing the 'brown' out of Afghanistan and across Iran and then Turkey, and all done with speed, and the currency gone from a proxy account run by Cohn and into the fund held by the proxies of the people who preached the purity of their religion in Kabul but needed to get the best deal on the annual crop. The next stage of monitoring the progress of the shipment was when it came through the eastern German city of Leipzig. All that had happened, in the Gulf and in the passport queue, was contrary to everything she knew about the police and surveillance, about 'showing out'. Nothing fitted. She went through the permutations. Could not work out how a guy who had messed with her on the shore front, and been left far behind when she had run off, had managed to nail her identity, where she would be, penetrate the security procedures that the family used, and was now on the same flight.

When she could not solve a problem, she became annoyed, and when she was annoyed she was angry. Also, when Julie Wilson did not get what she wanted she was worse than angry. She was bloody infuriated. What had been a laugh between strangers was acceptable. But what was happening now was intolerable . . . but he wasn't police. They didn't have the intelligence to have tracked her and then put an oaf, a hell of a good-looking oaf and with the sweetest smile, on her tail.

Julie elbowed the Prof.

He grunted, shifted, swung his legs into the aisle, made room for her to pass.

She manoeuvred herself out, into the aisle, hesitated for a moment, and adjusted her hair. As if it mattered. Her minder gazed up at her. She said she was going to pee, queried whether he needed to know, snapped at him. She could have gone ahead, to the bank of toilets nearest the cockpit. There was turbulence because of the thickness of the cloud and the seatbelt sign had been switched on and she chose the other direction. She knew he had been behind her when they had boarded, and knew that he had not passed her. Clinging to the backs of seats, raising annoyed glances, she made her way down the length of the cabin. It was not an airline where the crew were up and down with trolleys of food and drink, so the way was clear.

She saw him, stood stock still.

He seemed to be asleep.

Easy to recognise him now with the scarf removed from his face. His mouth was a little open, the shaving had been clumsy, seemed to be wearing yesterday's shirt. He had slumped sideways into the vacant seat near to his own.

What did she want from him, she asked herself. She was a girl whose position made men afraid. An eye opened . . . and the plane lurched, and she rocked. An arm came out for her to steady herself against. He held her so that she did not fall on him. She thanked him, but curtly. He shrugged.

She said, "Are you a cop?"

He shook his head, seemed to indicate the question was extraordinary.

"Do you know who I am?"

He shrugged again.

"Why are you following me?"

And he made a little frown and followed it with a smile, as if to say that conversation was unnecessary.

"Do you know where I'm staying tonight?"

No answer required. Beside the rocks on which the esplanade in the Gulf had been built, he had said to her, *I'll see you around* and she'd replied, *Don't bank on it*. Of course he knew. If any of the crime squads that went after her father had known where she would be the night before, that day and where she would sleeping that night, they would have been crawling all over the hotel, and round the airport, and would have been shoulder to shoulder on the plane. There was a woman standing behind her, pale-faced and perhaps about to be sick, growing anxiety on her face, and there were two toilet lights and one was already red, so Julie eased aside and the woman passed her and might make it to the door and might not.

Julie turned and went back to her seat, climbed over the Prof and sat for the remainder of the flight with her legs crossed. She lived a controlled life, was a 'subject of interest', and sensed a chance – not knowing how it had arisen – to be her own person. The aircraft's nose was down, the bumping fiercer and nothing to see through the cloud wafting round them, and she was reassured to see the Prof gripping his arm rests.

'Her own person' . . . Was unsure what that meant, had read it somewhere, but it seemed a freedom which she had not known.

Jonas re-read the message from Effie Bellingham.

The hotel he stayed in was ghastly, but he must have survived and I saw him leave, ahead of her and her minder.

He was on his way to the station, the briefcase flapping against his thigh, and he managed a rueful smirk . . . had still been in bed when it had come through. There had been a succession of young people who had worked for Jonas since the days when the AssDepDG had permitted him to go 'free range' and find challenges that stretched him and which had the barest relation to legal requirements. He had never considered their comforts. They stayed at the cheap end of town, expenses were at a civil service minimum, did their work on shabby street corners among the pimps, dealers, and addicts, in ill-lit car parks and seedy bars. They were exposed, left to come through as best they could. Their feelings were not considered by Jonas. And when they were signed off, they disappeared back into the fog he had dragged them from.

The airline we've sent him on is equally grim with everything an 'extra'. Lifted off twenty minutes late: the end of my night out in Lutonshire.

Jonas was perfectly happy with his lot, towing the caravan behind the elderly car and not feeling envious of those who demanded that holidays were necessary and should be spent in skin-broiling heat or in ankle-deep snow. Jonas had little time for the benefits of education. There had been no talk of him going on from a grammar school education to a university. He had needed to get a job . . . a father who was erased from his memory, a mother who offered him little, and family meaning next to nothing. He was, after a fashion, self-educated and had a distaste for those from Oxford colleges who could reel off a list of all those who had done well enough to collect knighthoods and the civil service gongs . . . There was a generation of bosses and managers in intelligence-gathering agencies who met in those absurd quiet rooms in Pall Mall clubs, sat in leather-upholstered armchairs, and knew the waiters' names and patronised with little jerks of the fingers for attention. Men who believed that targets could be identified more by brain work than by the slogging grind of the surveillance teams of Aggie Burns and by the efforts of detective sergeants and the old squashed-nose professionals going west across the ocean, not the trim young men and women who came for sherry in the suites of offices of the DG and DDG up on the fifth. Truth was, Jonas Merrick liked humble men, and soft voices without a bray in them. Another message from Effie Bellingham.

The Met report on their route shows a bumpy trip, being chucked about a bit. Good for romance? I wouldn't know!! Am off to sleep – in later.

He had gone through the barriers and was on the platform, at his usual place in front of the giant-sized poster offering the best seaside holidays on the Welsh coast. Last month it had been the Cumbrian coast, and last summer it had been Devon and Cornwall's shorelines and the especial advantages of train travel. It would have been a nightmare for Jonas Merrick to be strapped in on that flight although he remembered the previous year when he had been given an American-built executive jet in which to fly round Europe which had been passably tolerable. When he boarded the train there seemed an unwritten law that he was not impeded: somehow he managed to get through the door easily and by another miracle the seat he favoured was always available. As he settled, his mind roamed. He did not think about an aircraft careering through storm clouds for a landing in eastern Germany, nor of the fortunes of a young man who might be on the edge of mortal danger unless he was sharp enough to watch his back, nor of a girl to whom Jonas did not acknowledge that he owed anything, who was merely a conduit for getting a target brought down. He had exchanged brief words with Vera about the coming weekend, and when the caravan should be loaded, fridge filled, grey water tank topped up, the stowaway bed made up, Olaf's rations measured out. Should it be Saturday or, at the worst, Sunday when the van was hitched up and he drove out into their avenue and cursed the restrictions of the parked cars, neighbours watching to see if he scraped the trees or his own boundary posts. The lie was hatching because he had that feeling, as his friend in the Province would say, 'Deep down in your water, Jonas, my old friend, you know you cannot hurry matters like what you've on your plate.' Would likely be Monday so a lie of some considerable weight would be required. He felt the burden of the lie, but thought he could manage it. His phone pinged.

Sunray, she's the cat that's just had a saucer of cream put in front of her. I think she'll scoff it. Chopper.

He reflected, even at this early stage of developments, that it would be a worthwhile lie, and felt no shame.

They came into the familiar Surrey car park at the back of the pub that was off the Westcott-to-Coldharbour road. A mixture of sounds, each one of them crystal-sharp, played in Lachy Wilson's mind, as he recalled a conversation that he remembered, word-perfect, unique between him and Softboy who had driven him back from Liverpool.

Any other time they had been out on a night of that length, and with a similar job done in the night hours, before Lachy had left the passenger seat, he and Softboy would have hugged, bonded as two men who had been together in tough times and the best of times for many years. Softboy had stared ahead like he was just a fucking taxi driver and not happy with the gratuity. Lachy had gone inside, changed his clothes, and in a few minutes would be on his way home.

What he had heard rang loudly in his mind, didn't usually. Different this time, but that was because of the talk in the car, what Softboy had raised. The sound of a lighter snapping open and a fag lit by Softboy, gloves pulled on by both of them and balaclavas dragged down to their upper lips, and then the noise at the front door of the small terraced house in Toxteth. The home of the mistress of the Scouser with the big mouth who thought it clever to shout his contempt of Lachy Wilson. A compact Mercedes parked half on the pavement. The Scouser's main home, where his wife was and his teenage kids, had a wall round it, and cameras and coiled wire, and dogs loose in the darkness and a couple of men who shared a caravan and monitored screens. But his 'bit on the side' had just had a new Yale lock on the front door and a bolt if she remembered to push it across. The Scouser came out and the girl had little on and clung to her man and must have been half frozen. The door closed, and the guy was at his vehicle door and was about to slide into the driver's seat when Lachy on one side and Softboy on the other had him pinioned. The gurgle of a gag being slipped home, and of the Merc's boot opening – all clear in Lachy's memory. The Scouser being thrown into the boot and a belt across the back of the head to briefly stun him, and one set of fingers trying to drag himself clear and being chopped off when the boot lid came down, not remarkable to Lachy or Softboy. Lachy drove the guy's car, and Softboy led with their own wheels, a straight route to the heritage docks. A hell of a noise coming from behind Lachy – banging, thumping, an attempt at yelling – he had cause, didn't he. There was a place where the vehicle barrier was always left up so that the corporation's refuse carts could get in to empty the bins and have the place neat and tidy for the coming day. Both cars went through. Engines off, and a moment of quiet and then the noise from the back came on heavier. Lachy didn't have a message for him, didn't bend down and put his mouth close to the boot lid and say farewell. Pressed the windows down, climbed out. He and Softboy took the strain, not that heavy because it was a compact, had it moving, and a final surge and a push and let it roll, and the yelling reached a pitch and the car went over the edge and had enough momentum to get clear of the quay and the tide was up and the splash as it hit was gentle. There was a last thunderous beating from the inside of the boot. The water was deep and the car went down fast and there were not enough lights behind them for them to see it being swallowed. The last sound was the murk of the dock water closing over the Mercedes.

They were into their own car and gone. Down the road out of the city, off onto side roads. Over towards Cuddington, but not as far west as Chester, was a Forest Park where they had done their only stop on the way up, and where the registration plates had been changed, and they would have been well short of Stoke on Trent before they hit the motorway. Nothing to talk about and Lachy had been happy to leave Softboy to concentrate on the winding lanes, and what seemed to be abandoned villages where nothing moved except for a scurrying cat . . .

Lachy felt good. Had no tension.

Softboy seemed bothered.

Lachy remembered everything Softboy had said, and his answers . . . They had been together since the start of the climb of

Lachy's fortunes, not much out of their teenage years and muscling on protection in south-east London street markets, then in fast-food places. Had been together when people needed persuading that this was the right time to sell a property, and at a generous discount, and so had gained useful premises to lodge the first batches of girls coming in from behind the old Iron Curtain, and on into vehicle robbery: there had been setbacks when people on the fringes of the firm had been lifted, but a near solid wall of silence had protected Lachy, and Softboy had stayed safe with him. Onwards and upwards, and some big import deals, always the heroin market because that was what Lachy understood, and then the move towards better laundering procedures and better protected investments, overseas, and the 'old-fashioned' life had been nudged aside, and it had seemed that gentler times were ahead of them . . . but the itch had needed scratching. One big shipment out of Afghanistan, same route as before, same team as before, same market as before. If Softboy hadn't liked it, he had not said so until they were on the motorway coming back from Toxteth, spoken with an intensity and language that didn't fit a hard man.

"I'm not apologising for saying it, Lachy, but that wasn't necessary."

"Sorry, come again."

"Not necessary, what we did."

"What part of it wasn't necessary?"

"Doing that, sending that message, doing it that way."

"I'm not hearing you right."

"Think you're hearing me fucking well, Lachy, loud and clear. Didn't need to do it."

"Need to do what?"

"To behave like a cheapskate scumbag, a kid trying to get noticed. He opened his fucking mouth, which was stupid, but not on the level of what was done to him."

"Don't tell me my Softboy's gone soft?"

"I said stupid because that was not the behaviour of a man of your status. You draw attention to yourself and you kick more crime squads into a reaction. Stupid, which means not sensible. It is headlines stuff, attention-seeking – like a vanity exercise. It's the way you'll get done, and the rest of us."

"Seem to forget something, Softboy."

"What am I forgetting?"

"Who I am . . . Lachy Wilson. Remember. Lachy Wilson. Not a small-town hustler, but Lachy Wilson. Nobody takes a liberty, not a fucking Scouser . . . and no crime squad. I am, Softboy, untouchable. Remember? Too big to bring down. Owns too many cops, has the best connections. They can't lay a finger on me . . . They can't touch me and I'm yards ahead of them, so cut that crap. I know the names of all those big cops, and where they live and what they work on, and they can't get near me. I know all of them who are lined up against me, and know they are shit. Got me, Softboy? So, cut it."

Nothing said after that. Lachy thought of Softboy as a friend, a confidant, trusted, and his voice might have risen which was unusual. Most people said that when Lachy's voice went quiet, and people strained to hear what he said, then the anger was deep. He had spoken loudly, like he was flustered. Softboy did not come back at him but drove carefully and the termination of the argument further angered Lachy.

"You don't like working for me, Softboy, then don't. Pack your bag and get on your bike. Got me? Fuck off out . . . and don't even think of having any clever ideas."

Softboy did not say, *I am hearing you, Lachy. Out of turn. Should not have said that. I apologise. Of course it's what you are, Lachy, untouchable. Forget I said it, Lachy.* But he *had* said it, loud and clear. Back at his local pub Lachy went inside, changed his clothes, collected his phone, went home. Vic was out. Boys on their way to school with Mrs Plumb, Julie in bloody Germany. No one to talk to.

Lachy went to feed his chickens, but the sounds of the car meeting the water stayed in his ears, and the words in his mind.

Away and over the massive bridge that spanned the gulf between the continents, and the city of Istanbul was behind them.

The lorry hammered north-west. New cargo was listed on the

documentation, and new paintwork on the vehicle and a fresh logo. The nuts had been unloaded and the interior stripped to the bulkhead where the principal cargo was hidden. The substitute load to fill the lorry's transportation space was furniture, manufactured in Turkey, top quality and high price, much of it made from walnut. Loaded, packed close and a small army of men had done the work, crawling with chimpanzees' dexterity to fill the lorry and create the maximum complication for premature unloading at any international customs bay. Mehmet and Dragan were also new people, with fresh papers that showed no evidence of having been east of Istanbul. They were cleanshaven and wore fresh shirts and company ties and looked like a couple of salaried workers representing a dull, old-fashioned haulage company from western Europe. The engine had been checked over again . . . What was secreted behind the panelling of the bulkhead more than justified the expense and time spent in the warehouse.

All drivers of contraband had a habit that distinguished them. They kept to the speed limits, did not cross lane, kept the plates clean, all binding on the cargo impeccable. Dragan's phone advised the time to Leipzig as twenty-one hours and on the bridge there would be traffic cops. The two cursed the type of person who volunteered to become a police officer on the highways of Italy and Germany. Men and women on their bikes, and in their performance vehicles, who seemed to get excited if they spotted a faulty brake light, or a broken indicator bulb. Would be the officials least responsive to finding a hundred-euro note tucked into a passport when they demanded documents . . . it was said that every man had a price but he was hard to find if he was a traffic cop. And they'd want a look, and if suspicion were kindled then the lorry would be directed to their search depot and the full works ordered and no interest in schedules. So, best avoided – if that were possible. Millions at stake, and years of imprisonment.

Mahmet and Dragan talked.

They had families who managed without their man, weeks at a time – years if they were caught plying their trade. They had kids who they hardly saw but whose futures were financially assured because the money was stashed away. They bantered and joshed. Sometimes they noticed a cop car in a layby . . . Moving cargo was what they were paid for.

The gaol had its own smell.

If it was summer when she visited, then Vic Wilson always stripped off in the utility area at home and piled everything into the washing machine. If it were winter, then her outer clothes went into a sack and Mrs Plumb would take them to the dry cleaner in Dorking. Difficult to identify the smell. Part perpetual damp, part the stuff they used to clean the floors, and part the sewage from the old and overloaded pipes, and always the stink of running urine though it was never visible. And there was a smell of unwashed bodies, of stale sweat, always boiled cabbage. All of it might have been in her imagination, but each time Vic Wilson came to visit her useless son, bloody pathetic, she had those smells in her nostrils.

But she had appearances to keep up. Would have been known from the top-ranked high security prisoner, down through the ranks of those who worked in the kitchens or the library. And on the other side of the place, every man and woman who wore a uniform, going up to the governor and his entourage, knew who she was. No liberties taken with her because of the reputation of her husband.

In spite of her status, or because of it, she moved at the same pace through the searches and paperwork into the visitor hall. She stood in the queues of girlfriends and wives and other mothers, and spoke to none of them. Seemed to hear nothing and see nothing of what was around her. Lachy had never been there. Nor had he attended the trial. He wasn't interested in talking about the kid, whether he'd benefit from a new legal team and another pitch for an appeal. She visited, thought it necessary, thought also that, without her presence and the commitment it demonstrated, Gregor would have been in danger.

He showed little sign of wanting to see her. Each of them seemed to count the minutes until it was decent for them to split.

He would scrape his chair back and peck her cheek when he stood, squeeze her hand, and mutter something about telling the family that he missed them, and would spin on his heel and be gone. But nothing was ever said about her own parents, the retired cop and the woman who represented all that was 'respectable'. And never a question about his father, like he was airbrushed out of Gregor's life.

When the time came for her to leave, she waited her turn. She was certain that her man, her Lachy, was right not to come to this soul-destroying place where hope was long dead, and she'd not forgive Lachy if an error of his took him somewhere similiar, and would fucking strangle him, and use a stocking to finish the job, if there was a chance of her ending up in the women's equivalent. They would do her on a conspiracy rap: if they were ever close to banging him up then they'd have made the case against her.

How was business, Gregor had asked. She'd shrugged. Business hardly mattered to them because now they were pretty much at retirement age ... She knew about the lorry, of course she did, and knew where her daughter was and what Julie had to achieve, and it would have mattered not a flying fuck if she had urged Lachy not to stage an importation of this size. She, too, also had the whirring buzz of excitement, like blood coursing in the veins, and felt the thrill of it. Knew nothing better.

It was a hell of a long way to drive and then go through the search procedures, for a visit that lasted no more than eleven minutes. She headed for the car park.

She did not know how to get off the treadmill, did not know how to jump clear. Had no idea, and when her breathing came hard, and spray was thrown up on her windscreen from the tyres in front, and the smell clung to her ... she found comfort from it. Lachy said that if a crime squad or an agency was getting close to them, he would see the warning signs, a swarming of surveillance. She had seen nothing, and drove hard for home.

*   *   *

Jonas sat on his usual bench, with the chaffinches around him anticipating he'd shake his coat and scatter the crumbs from his pastry. He was waiting for the gardener to reach him with his wheelbarrow and broom and the shovel.

There were only a very few in his world of counter-this and counter-that – terrorism, espionage, and crime – whom Jonas trusted for one-on-one, face-to-face advice. The gardener, a damaged veteran of infantry fighting in Iraq and a covert assassination mounted in a supposed Costa paradise, was one of the few. He was happily short on words and high on discretion . . . There were many men and women working in the building behind him who might have made a satisfactory job as a gardener in this one-time cemetery. But they would have been adequately replaced by this gaunt and unhappy man when it came to common sense, experience of total buckling pressure, and survival. It was Jonas's habit to lift his legs at the knees, make a space for the broom or the rake to clear the ground, then drop them, and sometimes he spoke to the gardener and sometimes he did not. The man seemed not to care whether a conversation ensued or both stayed quiet. That day it seemed necessary to engage. Jonas did not even know his name.

"Something I am doing, friend, is at the tipping moment."

A shrug for a response, and the broom removing imaginary dirt from under the soles of Jonas' shoes.

"And might as well, bar one brief message, be happening on the far side of the moon."

Another shrug, and little sign of any interest beyond what the broom was gathering.

"In my own work, friend, I don't expect to give running commentaries, not the three-thirty over sticks at Wincanton. Don't really know how we are doing."

"So you have to rely on the people you chose, put your trust in them to get on with it."

"Accepted."

"Or tell yourself your people have nothing of real note to tell you."

"Also accepted."

"The problem you have, sir, is you hope for reassurance. Don't look to me for it. Beyond my capability . . . Have a good day, sir."

The wheelbarrow squealed mournfully as it was pushed away. Jonas said nothing but thought, 'Thanks for not very much. I get that sort of advice from my cat. Can you imagine what it's like to have an operation running? Actually it has a name, *Humble Pie*. Which seemed clever at the time. Any idea?' Age was seeping into Jonas's joints and bones. He relished the challenge of bringing down an 'untouchable' but found the detail exhausting, and felt no joy in being reduced to the sidelines.

Perhaps he did not require the 'running commentary', perhaps he could imagine, and perhaps he knew enough of both of them – should have done because they were his choices, identified by him for their suitability. Back at his desk, he typed the name of the hotel into which they were booked, stared at the lobby area . . . and imagined how it would be, or how he *wanted* it to be, expected it to be, the key contact and all he had worked towards. Not the messing about and the play acting, but the moment when the serious business began, and high stakes were scattered on the gaming table.

8

Not the greatest test for the attributes of Jonas Merrick's imagination.

His man was sitting in a low chair, a coffee table in front of him and a house magazine to act as a mask if needed, and doubts whether Chopper spoke a word of German.

His target would have gone to her room, dumped her bag, and had now come down to the lobby and looked around her. Would have seen him. A couple of paces behind her was the minder, Walter Genge, the Prof, and unwise to judge him – so the files said. She wore a thick anorak, and he a heavyweight fleece and a baseball cap. She looked around her, would have taken in the main glass doorway and seen the snow flurries blustering haphazardly across the wide road. Some of the vehicles already had snow on their roofs and over the engine bonnets, and salt had been laid on the pavements.

Not hard for Jonas to imagine. He was hunched over his desk, still had that view of the hotel lobby, and his eyes were close to the screen, like a spider protecting its web . . . She had seen him. If she was going to slurp for the cream then she would need to get herself clear of Genge. Predictable what she would do.

Cold outside and a temperature hovering either side of freezing. What would she do? Decide what she had left behind in her room. Gloves, another scarf? Most likely it was gloves. Get rid of Genge. Perhaps there were no extra gloves in her bag and she had only brought with her the lightweight pair that might have been good for driving but not out on the Leipzig streets by the rail station or the Town Hall or the main church, or the market area. She did that, and made it clear with her gesture that she was boss, he was employee, and a relationship was different here to that he enjoyed when they were in the village, Abinger Hammer, on the pretty little River Tillingbourne. This was Leipzig, in former east Germany, and this was work and a destination for a lorry to come through, and she was the future and was in charge. Different ground. He came to her. Yes, gloves . . . pointed to a hand as if to indicate she rated the man as such an imbecile that he would need such an explanation spelled out.

Chopper watched her from behind his magazine as she passed the minder her room key. If he felt resentment at being treated like a maid he didn't show it. The lift doors closed on Genge and lights flickered as it climbed.

Julie made her way across the lobby. Chopper put the magazine on the low table in front of him. Two kids, each their own master, and both realising that the chance to speak would be brief. She stood over him and Chopper smiled up at her. She had an advantage at that first moment and was standing and was dominating, and he allowed, was not casual, not take it or leave it . . . and that grand smile was spreading and Jonas would have realised that this was a different guy from the isolated loner who had become separated from his supposed colleagues,.

As Jonas saw it, heard it, she would speak first. Hands on her hips, the tea-pot stance, and trying to take charge but not comfortable with it. A rasp in her voice.

Would be direct and sharp, and would seek truths, and look for reactions. And wary . . . a snap in her tone. And Jonas realised he had hit the wall, that imagination had limits. His last thought, they were two young people, and were attracted, and were drawn to each other and that put them on a pedestal and concerned about each other and overwhelmed the anxieties of the cultures, and their 'families'. Montagues and Capulets but trying to break free – as he had intended, and now imagined.

'A cop, is that what you are?'

Chopper fixed on her eyes, and spoke quietly. "Not exactly."

He could see that the elevator had reached its destination. He could see the line of slots, one lit, that marked the floor reached by the elevator Genge had taken.

"What is 'exactly'?"

"I don't have a warrant card. I'm on the outside, signed off because of an old wound."

"What do you want from me?"

"Honest?"

"Be a start."

"I am looking towards my future."

"Which means?"

"My future. Maybe yours. Maybe ours . . ."

"Do you know who I am?"

"Julie."

"Julie Wilson. Do you know who my father is?"

"I do."

"Gangster's kid. Top man's kid . . . Best you were never in my life."

"Not after what you did when your lace was loose. My name is Kenny . . . but called Chopper. About chemistry. You and me. I've never said that to anyone before. Certain of it – us."

And that was the truth. Chopper had never spoken like that to a girl, let alone one such as Julie Wilson. He thought, if he had been able to hear it, Sunray would have been cheering him on, quite excited and maybe congratulating him on his inventive use of B movie dialogue . . . But Sunray would have been wrong. He meant every word. Never said anything like it before. The experience on the paving by the Gulf seaboard was a first in Chopper's life.

Women had looked him over, liked what they'd seen, and must have thought him worth an effort, and some had managed to reach out to him, get a bit closer. If they'd all met up there would have been a brief exchange of their disappointments . . . Tracy was the most recent, in Admin, and an NCO's daughter at the Colchester depot, and one from a flat on the same landing in Camden Town, and two girls from school in Tavistock: all said the same, a mix of sadness and complaint. *Looks bloody terrific, but doesn't know what to do . . . Nice enough, and attentive, but no chat up and half scared to death . . . Great, so I hear, with a machine gun, but bloody useless once your knickers are down . . . Liked him but hardly a bucket of fun.*

"Certain of it." He said it quietly, but it was to her back and she might have heard and might not. She had walked away from him with that impatient pout on her face that meant she was not used to being kept waiting. The elevator had stopped, and the door opened and a woman with suitcases was pushed aside by Genge, and he was scurrying to get alongside her. A shrug from him, and something said that told a story. Would have been that he had found no pair of thick gloves where she had said they would be, and no thanks given him, and her heading for the doors and the flurries of snow and whitening pavements.

"Maybe I left the gloves at home." Julie said, She did not apologise, and they headed outside into the snow.

She knew nothing of him except that he had the power to stop her dead in her tracks down in the Gulf with an excuse that was ludicrous, but laughable, and now had broken the security codes of the family and had trailed her through an airport, onto a flight, and was here in Leipzig and knew who she was but did not have the apparatus of state security in back-up. She had not seen it, nor had the Prof who was reckoned to have a nose better than a spaniel's. And the guy – Kenny, Chopper – talking about a future together, their future, him and her, repeated that he was certain of it. Julie was in turmoil. Options: could tell the Prof to take him down, which might be messy. Could say it herself: 'Been sweet, a little joke, and that's not how life works out, so piss off and stay away.' Could manufacture another moment, or rely on him to do it, draw big red lines, what was possible, what was not, and let it rip and say to him that she cared not a fuck for the consequences . . . and might just get round to telling him that she was handy with a chainsaw . . . Her phone rang. She recognised the number.

She had met the two men in London, one Turkish and one Serbian. Found both of them unattractive and no doubt they were disappointed, despite their ogling, to be seeing her and not her father. She heard the noise of the engine pounding, and could imagine the big bulk of the lorry dragging its trailer load along a highway. Just a few words, and all of them agreed, and locked in her memory. There was a schedule, of course. They had expected to be flogging through Leipzig in the late afternoon or middle evening . . . were not going to make that timing, and had been held up in Romania by a highway collision, which was bad luck. She thought it was worse for the drivers who were being cut out of their vehicles and carted off by helicopter or ambulance to intensive care. But the schedule was important because of the nature of the rendezvous and the need to offload and to fill up for the next stage of the transportation. Likely now, at best, to arrive in the small hours of the following morning. Now on Highway 442, clear of Slovakia, just into the Czech Republic and hoping for a good run across the German border, then Dresden, then Leipzig. A new schedule was set, and a new rendezvous with the lorry coming from the east, dragging a shipping container behind it.

She swore.

"Do we have a problem?" asked the Prof beside her.

She snapped back. "Do you have a problem? I doubt it. Do I? Just a bit of logistics. Do we need a conversation? Don't think so . . . so let us enjoy our walk."

Which was rude, unnecessary. They walked. He had talked of *together – us* and had said in his quiet voice, *Certain of it* . . . and the lorry was running late.

'Don't take any crap from her,' Lachy Wilson had told Wally Genge.

'I won't,' he'd answered.

'Getting to be a shirty bitch, and full of herself. Cohn came back from London moaning about her. She needs to calm down, ease herself into where she's going.'

'Thanks, I'll remember that. Seems to be getting difficult, and it started, or I first noticed it, when we were down in the Gulf. Not that I'd know, but a girl growing up wants to flap her wings, and . . .'

'Fuck that. She has work to do, and I'll not have her give you shit.'

Lachy Wilson, head of an empire but, the Prof reckoned, uncertain about the dynasty's chances, had slapped his man's back, the sort of gesture used for a jack of all trades who could change a light bulb, get the mower started when the drive belt came unfastened, and keep an eye on a girl barely out of her teenage years who was becoming a bitchy little creature. It was good for the Prof to have the support of his boss, and all of it had been heard by Vic and she'd nodded, like they were together on this.

But they weren't here, and he was. Could not have said, if it came to the shove time, whether he would be backed. He was wary.

They went off up the street outside the hotel and came near to the railway station. To what purpose? Not told. God forbid a trip to a museum or a castle. They were walking as if she had a purpose but he did not know it. He was worried about the state of the pavement as the snow flaked down, wet and skiddy once it had settled. Did not know what the Wilson family really thought of him, and what loyalty they harboured for him. Had had chest pains before Christmas, probably indigestion, and he'd gulped pills, but there had been one dark night when a sort of mental constipation had gripped him and he had imagined himself being carted up the hill and into a cemetery, not near where Hamish was but up at the end where the paupers were buried, and he had quoted Miss Rossetti to himself to break the mood. *When I am dead, my dearest, Sing no sad songs for me; Plant thou no roses at my head, Nor shady cypress tree;* and repeated it now but only to himself. The Prof had relations in the west of England but they'd disowned him when the gaol time stacked up and he was the committed 'gang gofer', their name for him. He was dependent on the Wilson family, and the cake on his birthday came from their kitchen, and the only presents at Christmas were from them. Had no one else and without them would spend his last days in a bedsit on the Kent coast in one of those falling-apart resorts. *Be the green grass above me With showers and dewdrops wet; And if thou wilt, remember, And if thou wilt, forget.* She'd forget him, the bitch, and probably the rest of them.

"Betty, not messing? You sure on that?"

"Like I told you, everything. It was Julie Wilson, for God's sake. I followed all procedures. Bit out of the ordinary . . ."

"You could say that. And the guy down at her feet and having some little private joke with her, he then went and dropped a shell from his pocket? A periwinkle shell. And you had his name from your pal in the next booth? Is that what you're saying?"

"Is . . . didn't you know, Ralph, we do actually have some hot water in this place, and taps, and washing up liquid, and a rubbish bin, and . . ."

"You are, my opinion, a very clever lady, Betty. Super clever."

Like he was a penitent, Ralph swept up the mess from the table and binned it, then was at the sink, squirting bubbles and running the water, sluicing and wiping and stacking. Then, he dried his hands and went to her and gave her the longest, sweetest kiss she had had off him for bloody days, and told her he loved her, and she was wonderful, and 'super clever' was an understatement, and took her into the bedroom and helped her undress, and get under the duvet and drew the curtains, and went out and closed the door after him.

Did it by secure phone, what his mobile could not manage and not on his laptop, and called through to his supervisor at a building on the south side of the river, an agency that commanded an annual budget of close to a billion pounds a year.

Ralph said, "Thought you might like the sound of this. From my girl who does border checks at Luton. Let me run it past you . . ."

*   *   *

A caustic message was received by Jonas.

Not had my shin kicked – so far so good

He imagined that the girl would be mightily confused and had cause to be, and would be uncertain how to react – except that she liked him and he brought a freshness into her life . . . which was what Jonas had predicted, had planned for. Would have liked Effie to be in by now but thought she was probably in bed after a night at Luton airport.

Jonas, however, maintained his rigid schedule and would not deviate from it unless threatened with dire consequences by a medical team, and had always found it unreasonable for others to play the exhaustion card or out-of-hours worked. He might be on the 5.27 home but would have a briefcase full of classified papers – expressly forbidden to take such material from Thames House – and often when returned they carried the stains of the cat's paw prints – and half the damn night he would lie on his back and have a focus point on the ceiling and worry through the points that were unresolved. None of that now.

He had a good picture in his mind of Lachlan Wilson, crime baron and regarded as beyond the reach of the law and a target. From the photos he could see each wrinkle on his face, each small mole that made a blemish, and the depth of the lips and the sharpness of the eyes, and he had his own memory of the man in the hallway of his house in the Surrey countryside. Had seen the moles and wrinkles himself and had an image of them. And the eyes. Jonas believed that for a man such as the gangster who was 'untouchable' his eyes were as much a weapon as his fists or his feet. A smile on the face and an apparent gesture of hospitality as refreshments were offered to the search team, but meaningless because the man was incapable of altering the set of his eyes, and the penetration of the gaze, and the way it would have had the power to chill the resolve of an opponent.

He was charged with bringing Lachlan Wilson down, and would not let the eyes bead on him, would guard his anonymity. He heard the footsteps approach his corner of the Post Room, and the chatter was silenced and the radio was switched off, which told

Jonas all he needed for confirmation of his visitor. He turned off his screen, killed the images of a webcam that he had found and its views of churches and public buildings in the city of Leipzig, 640 miles away.

"So, you grumpy old fucker, how are we progressing?" The Assistant Deputy Director General, down from the fourth floor, never destined to reach the fifth and with a reputation for adventurism which was almost fatal inside the walls of Thames House. That he had survived for so many years rested on his ability to bring in the gratitude, and the resources, of the American 'cousins' and because he had the ability to find work for the elderly analyst now hidden away in the basement area. "Going well, I trust?"

Jonas did not look up. "It is going."

"And a favour, don't chuck at me your usual riposte, 'Don't do commentaries'. Where are we?"

"In the city of Leipzig. She and her shadow are out walking, it is snowing lightly. He, sensibly, is hunkered inside the hotel."

"Too cold for your boy? Not picked a fragile petal?" the AssDepDG teased Jonas, a regular and appreciated sport.

"To show out to the minder would be an error of judgement and—"

"Enough bullshit, Jonas. I have an anxiety."

Jonas was dismissive. "I don't. It is not shared. If you have cold feet then wear thicker socks."

"Should we have taken this on? Easy at the time, nearly six months ago. A buffoon from the Yard who was bloody near on his hands and knees and begging, and flattering, and it seemed a chance for us to get a hold over the plods. And them in debt if we pulled it off, thanks to your endeavours. Brought the man down when they had failed. Seemed attractive."

"Late in the day – too late."

"Some truths that I should have examined months ago. You run loose over the Putin people, and over the cocaine importers from the Amazon delta, and over the Chinese so that we have a valued defector, and when there is an Isis boy then we have enough forensics to be able to keep your name back from the witness box . . . Here, we are riding roughshod over entrapment and God knows what else and those bloody lawyers and double bloody judges would like to get their teeth into an unscripted operation against a man with no criminal convictions, and his daughter, and . . ."

"Stiffen up your spine a bit, and enjoy the ride."

"What I'm saying—"

"What you are saying is that you are hoping I'll give you a spurious guarantee that all will be well."

"As best you can, Jonas."

It had been a long time since he had seen his protector so hesitant. "Don't lose your nerve. Things look well as of this hour, but a bit to go."

"That as good as I am going to get?"

"Yes. We are well down the road."

"I am at a hockey tournament tomorrow, my daughter. Sort of bullied into it."

"The big day, I imagine, is Sunday. That's when I think the pieces will be in place. Tomorrow and Saturday seem premature . . . are you going soft on me?"

"Don't snarl at me, you miserable creature. Get it done and keep your nose clean. Snaresbrook Crown Court on a wet Thursday might just be, from the viewpoint of the witness box, and the undivided attention of a sleaze-bag defence lawyer, a quite unpleasant experience, Jonas. I am not, repeat, *not* going soft on *Humble Pie*. Just offering wise counsel and you would recognise that if you were not – but you are – a grumpy old fucker. Good day, and a safe journey home."

"Enjoy your hockey, and don't shout too much."

Not where he had expected to find weakness. Jonas waited for the next bulletin. Would allow, of course, for his man to set his own pace, and could not second-guess the decisions he made . . . and had little hostility for the target.

Lachy Wilson never asked her about her journey and how she had found him.

And she never told him whether the drive up the motorway was good or bad, fast or slow, nor how Gregor was and his news. Understood between them that the prison visits were off limits to Lachy. Kept to herself, and Lachy not enquiring.

Still a good-looking woman, with only minimal flab, and there was a mirror in the utility room and she could confirm it, and had loaded the washing machine, made a point of doing it herself, then had walked out, passing Mrs Plumb. The housekeeper would have liked her to have taken cakes to her son but, at the level of security he enjoyed, that would have been a pain, with each bloody piece having to go through the X-ray. She crossed the hall, went up the stairs. Lachy sat on the bed, naked.

Outside, up by the chicken shed, was the incinerator. An oil drum with holes hacked in it so that the air blew through, made a draught which kept a fire burning well when there was rain in the air. Smoke billowed from it, which meant the job was well along the line. She did not think that he was in as good condition as herself. There were signs of a paunch developing at his waist. He had been the love of her life when they had started up and the efforts of her parents to block it had been doomed. Now there was a degree of a working relationship, and she rated them as stuck with each other. He was waiting for her.

They did not often talk business. When they did it was because a matter was on the agenda that he needed help with.

If Lachy Wilson needed help then he had a problem.

"Not in a good place, love," he remarked but with caution.

"Did it not work out?"

"That part did. Perhaps they've lifted him out by now. He was in the boot. Made a hell of a noise but not for long."

"But, Lachy? But what?"

"It was Softboy – that's the what. Turned on me. Tight as a bloody drum, then turned on me. Actually said, to me, *That wasn't necessary*, and then, *Didn't need to do it*. To me ... Softboy. Reputation second to none. My guy and looked after by me, and treated like fucking family. Criticising. Couldn't believe it."

"How did you deal with it?"

"Straight. How else? Like I always do. Don't stand around and argue. He said that it was beneath my status, whatever that means. It was stupid he said. A vanity exercise. Gobsmacked me."

"What did you say?"

"Told him I was Lachy Wilson, told him to shut the fuck up. He was driving, kept driving. Said if he didn't like it to pack his bag and get on his bike. Nothing more said. No apology, no settlement."

"That's how it was left?"

"It is. Don't like it, Vic. Softboy has been more than a friend. He's been part of our household, and the kids' family. He must have weighed it up and decided to give me shit and not give a fuck. What is he saying?"

Vic said, her arm round her man's shoulder, her bare skin on his. "About ourselves. We live here, huge house, could sleep twenty. An ordinary house would do for you, me, and the boys, and without Mrs P, and without the Prof, and ship Julie off to London and a flat down in the Docks. Turn our backs on it all. You have an allotment, and a garden big enough for your birds, and we live out our lives. But it's not an option. Need the space, need to say who we are, need the wire round the boundary and the cameras. Need Cohn and that weasel Lyons, because if we are weak then we are gone. Don't get to where we are by being everyone's nice folks. Wouldn't last a week. Trouble is, Lachy, his appetite is sliding. Wants a bungalow in Bournemouth, with a glimpse of the sea. Make a bit of peace with him – and if he is dumb he'll believe you. Seem to settle it. Like a bloody hand grenade, isn't he, and the pin's loose. Not out and it's activated, but loose – not to be trusted. Make some peace. He likes a bit of Italian. I'll do a risotto with some prawns, his favourite, and show we love him. You go along with that?"

"Will go with it."

She said she would do the Italian for the next evening and sent him off to have his shower, and she dressed and went to pull her clothes from the washing machine. Felt it might all be crumbling, the walls they had built around this fortress and did not like the feeling of decay but was confident her man would fight to hold back the clock, fight like a cornered rat.

The heating was on, but she felt cold like a chill wind came into the rooms.

An investigator at the National Crime Agency said, "That Ralph, my opinion, is a bit of a tedious beggar, but I rather fancy he may have come up with something juicy."

"Off his girlfriend, right?" A wide grin from his line manager.

"Good lady, done well . . . We have Julie Wilson, said to be the heir apparent travelling at sparrow fart from Luton. And with her is that scrote, Wally Genge, who is real lowlife and long term on Dad's payroll. And she just happens to have a silly little chat with a guy in the passport queue, and he goes into panic mode because he's dropped a seashell. Who carries, rite of passage, a periwinkle shell?"

"Only the Flying Squad. Part of their 'legendary uniqueness', how they describe it." The line manager was almost chortling. "You've run it through the machine?"

"Have done."

"I'm liking this – and came up with?"

"What I said . . . on the Met's main database. Kenneth George Harris, calls himself Chopper and that's about football. Rank of Detective Constable. About to be invalided off the Barking team, old Afghan bullet hole when he was a paratrooper, causing more and more aggravation and affecting his fitness. Didn't go any deeper because of making waves . . . Travelling on a red-eye flight with Lachy Wilson's girl and one of the stooges. I think I know the pigeon hole for this one."

"Don't mind saying it – someone has fucked up." A hand was closed to make a tight fist, and it smacked the investigator's shoulder, like a badge of congratulation handed out.

"What you call a 'mistake'. I'll send it to those miserable sods wherever they're hiding out right now. A good definition of a mistake."

★　★　★

Jacques was told, "It is a short-term authorisation to carry a firearm. It will be evaluated. I'd call it temporary and you will need reassessment. For the moment, that is where we are. Good day to you."

A message from the administration that governed the use of weapons issued to serving police officers of the Federal service working in Antwerp. *Stuck-up, arrogant bastards.* It could have been worse. He was almost at home but would be back at work tomorrow which was a small mercy.

It was quiet in the room used by the ACU team. The end of an afternoon, and another team was still taking the statement from the detective lifted the previous day. So there was not much for this trio to be busy with, and getting near that time when the others could slide off – but not the boss who near as hell slept there.

At his desk, Detective Inspector John Plunket had been fielding grief and his temper was raw. The light on his phone screen flashed.

Detective Sergeant Hasan Rajah was hunched over his expense sheets. Always filled them in by hand, thought they'd seem more truthful that way.

Had his phone cradled against his ear.

Detective Sergeant Peggy Dawson was doing a shopping list, and hoped to be away from the building an hour or so early.

The boss had the phone against his ear and scribbled on a pad.

Calls had come from senior officers. 'Why the fuck did you have to do that? Real hurtful stuff, and over the top. Don't you people have any sense of occasion, no value for dignity?' An objection that a 'senior and valued colleague' had been humiliated by being arrested in his golf club surrounded by his chums. Anger that his wife had been there to see it and her suffering from bowel cancer. 'Don't you smug buggers do your homework?' They had not known of the medical link, no mention on the intelligence given them, and what should have been a matter of congratulation had turned sour. Not that exposing the Met's shortcomings was ever likely to be a celebration at the Yard.

Plunket thanked his caller, rang off. In front of him was a foolscap lined pad covered in his spidery writing, and two more beneath it. His face was impassive.

"Hope neither of you were looking for a feet-up evening in front of the box, 'cause you'll not be getting it. Rajah, a starter for ten, does Flying Squad do deep penetration investigations?"

"No, off their limits."

"What *do* they do?"

"Call them pavement jobs. Arrests of robbers, sometimes armed with shooters, and looking to get their hands on the cash going into holes in the wall when delivered. They also do serious and violent larceny cases where burglars on premises are using heavy force. A few kidnaps, but that's mostly inside the crime world and involves gang-on-gang, cash disputes . . . Do I get an A star pass for that exam answer, boss?"

"So, if a detective constable from Flying Squad is leaving the country with a blood member of an Organised Crime Group, that is the Squad and an OCG player up close and personal, what do we say? Dawson, that's your starter."

"Haven't reached Weetabix yet, let alone Shiraz. We say, *Lord, thank you,* say it quite loud."

Rajah's expenses forms went back in a drawer along with a stack of receipts. Her shopping list was dropped into her handbag. Plunket started to reel off what he had, and his demands of the two of them.

He murmured, "Fucking hell. Wilson . . . Happy times."

She said, with a little puff of pleasure, "I don't see that 'sharing' is appropriate."

From Plunket, "Sharing is not appropriate. Against their culture. We're not sending a signal to the Squad, or to the Wilson crowd, of where we are and what we are looking at. Keep it close, within this room. Julie Wilson has a checklist when she goes abroad, and one of the big crime squads will have a notification on that. I'm not looking to go into it and blaring out that we are taking a show involving that family. They don't know who I am, nor who you are, and long may that last. We need to find out where in Leipzig Julie Wilson and the Squad guy are. What's their business there, where are they booked out of? Should all be easy computer stuff . . . What I think is that someone on their team has made a mistake. These are people, both parties, who take an excessive pride in avoiding a mistake . . . I'm looking for a start point. Want to know that all this is real, and hear it from a source. We begin with Betty. Border Control, and home from a night shift at Luton. This, guys, might get rough round the edges, but already has a feel to it. Would you get us up and running, Dawson?"

She put the phone down. Had worked through the night. Had no worthwhile sleep. Was not going to get it now.

Betty yelled, "For God's sake, Ralph, what have you gotten me into?"

She told him about the call. Not given a name, nor a department, but asked in detail about what she had experienced that morning, what she had seen – and a feeling gathered that she was now in a world where those experiences and sights had a weight of importance she had not known before.

"It's the price you pay for being clever, Betty. You've said enough times you wanted your life to perk up, seems it just did . . . Perhaps you're going to help save the world."

"Perhaps I should have kept my bloody mouth shut."

"Except you didn't."

Chopper watched them come back to the hotel. The Prof had more snow on his head and shoulders than she did, but inside, within seconds, it had melted and dripped depressingly around him. Chopper heard him say that he was going up to his room to make a proper cup, courtesy of the tea bags he'd thoughtfully brought with him. Did she want a cup? She did not . . . Heard her say that she might take in a museum if they were still open, or walk some more, and that she did not need nannying. Her minder went off to the lifts and she hesitated, looked around and would have seen Chopper, and turned back to the double doors and pushed her way through. He followed. She was walking away from him, back towards the rail station, and darkness closing on the city. Chopper thought that what he could see of it was well tarted up from the days when it had been part of the east of divided Germany, but off to the side streets there were drab alleyways. Brightly lit shops on the main drags but small and poorly lit stores in the back roads.

He had the feeling that she had little idea where she was going, was just walking, and he would follow until she stopped. He would allow her to set the pace. She did not look back, but there might have been counter-surveillance techniques that she knew like using shop windows to reveal what, who, was behind her, and she seemed confident enough that she had him in tow and could reel him in when it suited. He sensed her conviction that she was in charge . . .

The lorry came off the autobahn, on to a clear straight road where the cameras were not covering each kilometre. They were making good speed. Suddenly a deer appeared. Without the wit to wait for this monster lorry doing well in excess of 100 klicks, it charged towards them. Going as fast in the outer lane was a solitary motor-cycle, its rider wrapped against the cold and the road surface under his tyres going greasy.

The deer cleared the barrier separating tarmacadam from white-coated, Christmas-card woodland, and then froze in the huge headlights of the Mercedes long-distance truck. Mehmet swerved, Dragan cursed. Mehmet kept swerving to avoid the deer and the central reservation, but in his way was the motorcycle. The lorry clipped the bike and sent the rider careering up and ahead, bashing into the lorry's windscreen, then falling back, and a lurch from the front wheels. It happened in not much more than a blink of an eye, or a single gasp of breath. They drove on, and neither suggested otherwise.

He was maybe thirty paces behind her. A small garden loomed out of the gloom, undisturbed snow on the ground and empty benches. A summer water fountain in the centre of an extravagant stone decoration that would have been drained against freezing. The road was filling with traffic, headlights spearing the snow-flakes, and there were people walking cautiously, and in the distance he saw a gritting wagon. She made for a bench, cleared the snow with her hand and sat. Made a gesture to indicate that he should join her. Chopper accepted that she expected to dictate the action, was familiar with decision taking. He'd have bet his shirt that she was in unfamiliar territory, but felt happy to let her struggle. He slipped off his gloves, rubbed his bare hands together. Put the gloves in his anorak pocket and laid his hands on his thighs. Her call. He waited.

"Should we have stopped?" Little conviction in Dragan's question.

"No," Mehmet answered.

"Couldn't have missed him."

"You could not."

"It was the fucking deer."

"You think he was still alive after we zapped him?"

"No idea. How would I know? Possible, not likely."

"We're paid to get the load through, not to play blue lights and paramedics."

"Wrong place at the wrong time. That's life."

"And death . . ." They both laughed and when they had gone through the next town they'd find a layby and pull over and Mehmet would scramble up on to the bonnet and use the leather to clean the windscreen, remove the impact marks.

She had picked up his right hand, held it in her own. Did not look at his face, still unsure of the ground, didn't know if she played an idiot's game or was entitled to follow her instinct.

Julie said, breathlessly, almost a gabble, "You think you know who I am, but that will only be a little part of it. I am protected whether I want to be or not. Being Julie Wilson is like living in a straitjacket. You don't know anything about me, except perhaps what was in a file that you were fed. Half a page, or do I get more?

If this meeting were known about, you – whatever you are – and me and who I am, known to my father, then I would be dead. Non-negotiable. Dead. *I would have strangled you, or might have done you with a knife, or shot you in the back of the head, execution-style, but since you are my daughter, you get to walk away with a rap on the knuckles and a very firm reminder not to behave like that again. Be a good girl and all forgotten.* Do not bank on my dad talking like that. And with me being dead, expect the same chat-up for yourself. You do not know who I am. We meet on a seaside jogging track, and you told me a story, and we had a bit of a laugh, and I wanted you to win your bet. It was worth a kiss. Actually a hell of a kiss, and it was also a hell of a chat-up line . . . And to tell you the truth, I have not forgotten you, what you did, the way you did it. But you are a cop, some sort of cop, and that would be enough for my father to condemn you. No hesitation. You hearing me?"

"Hearing you."

"So we understand those rules, and still have a way to go if we are to be honest with each other. Move on. You do not know anything about me, what I do, who I am, my loyalties. I am believed by my father to be the heir to his empire. Why me? Because one brother, an idiot, is dead. In a car crash when the law were following him and he was over drugs and drink limits, and another older brother is banged up, still has half a lifetime to serve and is going nowhere and is an even bigger idiot. That leaves me, and my father and mother are slipping off the pace. Another fact. As a little teenage girl I was taken up to London and handed a chainsaw, a Stihl of course, top of the range, what else, and a guy was tied to a chair – can't even remember how he had offended. I cut his arm off. They took him off and dumped him at A&E, and he never squealed on us . . . I don't lose sleep over it. Didn't then and don't now. That is a bit more about who I am."

"I can match that. A bit older than you but to put it in context."

"Have you killed anyone?"

"Three times at least. I took them down with a general purpose machine gun, and my mate – Lofty – he fed the belt. I never blinked. Never had a nightmare. Never regretted it."

Needed reassurance, one last time.

"Say it again, please – which is not a word I often use."

"This is about your father. Dropping him. Bringing him down."

Julie Wilson did not reckon she needed to speak. She thought about what he had just said. Was she surprised? No. Saw her father when he was smiling and out with his chickens. Saw her mother, and the boundaries of their home, the wire and the cameras, and the whole empire that was Cohn and Lyons, and George in the City, and what it was to be the future.

"Is there another place to be?"

"There's always a place, somewhere beyond reach."

"And you?"

She thought he must have thought it through, rehearsed it. His mouth was close to her ear. "Your father is convicted, that's my deal, what I have signed up for. Only that. I don't then slot back into law enforcement. We're on the move, gone you and me. Us."

She might have turned him in. Gone back to the hotel, hauled the Prof off his bed, announced she was being followed, tracked by one of the Agencies. Had him knifed, beaten, and then disappeared into the night to the rendezvous with the lorry, and him left as a crumpled shape in a ditch or a culvert . . . Might have done that.

She held his hand and the snow fell on them, and felt a freedom unknown before and had made up her mind that it was worth hanging on to. They might already have looked like two statues, still, without expression. It was cold enough for the snow to stick, and their features were lost to sight, only outlines, and snow was settling on the bench, and a few car and van lights caught them and might have presumed them to be pieces of modern art. Each shivered but controlled it. Two kids came by, throwing snowballs at each other, but they ignored them, might not have even noticed them. They were wrapped in themselves

He came through the barrier at Raynes Park and his phone warbled. A little frown appeared on Jonas Merrick's forehead. Who rang him on the way home, out of hours, away from his desk in the Post Room? Up on his screen came a smiling, almost impertinent image of Effie Bellingham. He answered curtly, without familiarity. He was in a queue of fellow commuters who carried rucksacks and shopping bags, none with a briefcase with a chain from the handle to his wrist.

"Me, boss . . . You free to talk?"

"On my way home."

He detected an excitement in her voice, like she had important news to pass on. Something that had brought a bubble and a little stammer to her words and a breathiness meant she had heard from Chopper, meant that *Humble Pie* was over the tipping point and on the way towards that line which Vera sometimes quoted: 'There is a tide in the affairs of men that taken at the flood leads on to fortune', and 'flood' and 'fortune' seemed apposite, but . . . He should have been the recipient, not her.

"A bit of news for you, boss, and wanted you to hear it . . . Going to marry my chap. Simon. Got the ring off him tonight. Says he bought it in Dubai, and got a good price there. Thought I never would but we parked in his flat this afternoon and shifted a bit of fizz and he had the ring. Be a ghastly experience, up there in Scottishland, midges, frozen pipes, leaky roofs, stags hanging in the cellar and dripping, kids running round out of control, scaffolding all over the place, money worries morning, noon, and night. But it might be fun . . . Anyway, there's going to be a family gathering up there this weekend so the kith and kin can run a rule over me. Flying up tomorrow so I won't be around at the weekend. You'll be okay, won't you? Of course you will – you can manage. Be back with you on Tuesday – grateful if you can copy me in while I am—"

He snapped her off, and strode on. Would have had that petulant grimace on his features. He had planned to invite her to help him with the 'lie', keep him company and protect him from Vera's brickbats, and now she had reneged on him. He went past the parked caravan, also an integral part of the lie, and opened his front door. The cat eased against his legs and Vera emerged from the kitchen. Any vestige of a welcoming smile went from her face: she read his annoyance.

"Beyond the strictures of the Official Secrets Act, am I allowed to ask what irks?"

Rueful, "Best not to."

"Is it about your boy and your girl? Your match-making."

"Not that I know of."

"Your social engineering, Jonas. Playing God with the Montague family and the Capulet family, is it troubling you?"

"I'll be told when I need to be told."

"Pasta tonight."

"Excellent."

"And let us hope that the boy doesn't slip off when he's climbing up to that balcony . . . Sorry, Jonas, it is only a story."

"That would be nice if it were, only a story."

9

Past midnight, and the church clock in Merton was chiming.

Jonas lay on his back, his hands behind his head. Enough light came through the curtains for him to see that his phone did not flash, and the cat slept securely, and Vera had her mouth open and was gently snoring. As he had prepared for bed – calling Olaf in from the garden, switching off lights, climbing the stairs, he had kept an eye on his phone

Hooked onto the webcam that covered the hotel's front entrance, he had seen them return. Two snow creatures on the move – snowman and snowwoman – and important that gender be separated in the workings of Thames House. The man taller than the woman, but the woman carrying more snow on her head and shoulders and less of her face visible. He had taken it to be a sign of the promised bonding . . . no other explanation why the pair of them would have sat outside for so long, while the snow wafted steadily down on them. He wondered if they had spoken, or had sat in silence . . . he was confident of his man's ability to manufacture deceit.

Jonas was certain that his Chopper had achieved what his own mentor, and protector, had claimed to be impossible – and *ridiculous*. Would not be for Jonas to tell him 'I told you so'. Triumphalism was always, in Jonas's opinion, vain and pitiful. He might indulge in little bursts of self-adulation, but it would have been an attractive thought to parade a few of the cronies, or the acolytes, down to Surrey and stand a couple of paces behind them as they formed an orderly line, and watched the glint of a winter sun reflecting off the frosted ground and catching the metal of the handcuffs, to see the savage frustration of a man who had believed himself 'untouchable', beyond reach. Jonas imagined himself standing on tiptoe, peering over their shoulders, watching as the blue lights circled and engines revved, and dogs strained on leashes, while other members of the same criminal conspiracy gazed on in numbed shock. Another murmur: 'Was that Jonas Merrick's work? Did Jonas manage to put all that in place? Wasn't the man supposed to have erected a firewall to prevent this happening? No messing, have to hand it to old Jonas, curmudgeonly old boy, but delivers doesn't he?' He might have touched the brim of his trilby, acknowledged them, and dropped his head as if that were a sufficient gesture of impatience at the tributes paid.

He lay on his back and accepted the plaudits, and noticed a spider weaving a web on the underside of the centrally hanging lightshade, its lair too high for Vera to swipe it off. And Jonas would not have agreed to remove it because there were many nights when the spider kept him company and he admired the endeavour of manufacturing the web, and the patience of the spider as it waited for an entangled meal to show up, and be paralysed and then scoffed. He could have said that this *Parasteatoda tepidariorum* specimen was as effective in its use of tradecraft as was Jonas himself, and as bloodthirsty as was Olaf who slept soundly.

His attention was jolted off the spider, safe from the attention of a feather duster. The phone vibrated.

Coming together. About to go on a lorry hunt.

Appreciated that he was kept inside the loop, probably would not have reciprocated had he been at the front end of *Humble Pie*. But he had chosen this boy, had brought him onto the team after no more than a couple of hours' observation in a public house, surrounded by detectives said to be at the top of their trade, and had noticed this boy's isolation.

Now he would doze.

Jonas Merrick was a predator, would not have argued with the description. Was also, he was told, a grumpy old fucker but regarded that as an accolade. He was also a killer of those who stood across his path – and that also pleased him . . . He wondered if his boy had managed to thaw out, and perhaps had found a cup of vegetable soup to restore him – And the girl, must not forget the girl.

When he had the movement of the lorry, in which the cargo would be secreted, then the business would be wrapped, and the prey would be as helpless as any house fly caught in the web over his head, and the occasion down in Surrey – for which a lie must be told – would be worth inviting guests to watch.

He turned on his side and was soon asleep, thoughts of Montagues and Capulets, and balconies on which grape vines grew, and the division of cultures, and the use of young people for whom he had a purpose, disappeared.

"We need a hose," said Mehmet.

Dragan agreed. "The wipers cannot cope with the man."

The huge, high-powered lorry, product of a factory at Worth am Rhein, the world's largest truck assembly plant, built for performance and reliability, hammered north towards the outskirts of Leipzig. The driver was anxious to make up this lost time, and maintained the maximum allowed speed. But the cab windscreen was becoming harder to see through, colours distorted and distances reduced, and Mehmet complained to Dragan that soon they would have to stop, find a gas station and sluice water over it. They were running late, and the schedule was unlikely to be made up ... the beast charged and moved into the centre lane of the highway. Other motorists, seeing it coming up in their mirrors, to backed off, gave it free passage.

The value of the cargo, not the furniture which, in comparison might only have had use as firewood, had justified the 'incident' which had caused the problem with the driver's ability to see clearly through the windscreen. The quality of the Turk's driving, the swerve and then the impact which had led to the problem of the windscreen, was not a matter of discussion ... the two were only a pair of men who understood what was at stake, what they carried. Many anxiously awaited news of the lorry's arrival further down the route laid out for them.

There were the syndicates who fretted and wondered why they had not yet been notified that the money, American dollars, had been transferred although the cut-off time was not yet reached.

There were dealers at the top end of the trade, who handled bulk of 100 kg at a time, and who were prepared to play a delicate game, highly choreographed, where they took and they gave, and the taking was in plastic-wrapped parcels, and the giving was in the region of $13 million per transaction. And that night, throughout the length and breadth of the United Kingdom, such dealers wrestled to cobble together such sums, and men down the line would be looking to buy 10 kg, and further along the trail would be those for whom it would be a considerable investment to purchase one or even two kilograms of the stuff, uncut, and fresh because it had been on the road barely a week since leaving the poppy farms . . . and in every city there would be addicts hanging about on street corners, languishing in crack houses, waiting for the arrival of what they were assured would be good 'brown', best quality.

And the big man, the main man, would be waiting for confirmation that his consignment had cleared Iran and Turkey, was deep inside Europe, was about to power on to the last leg of the journey. That individual, vastly wealthy and with the trappings to show that he was on a par with a small coterie of the most successful entrepreneurs, took – predictably – no blame for filling up the clinics that were trying to wean addicts off the habit that could ultimately kill them inside the walls of a filthy squat. *Not my fault. I just answer a demand. People want to shoot themselves, that's their problem. Don't come moaning to me because people don't have self-control, discipline.* Surprisingly, that individual, and his family, and the people he needed around him, for the smooth running of his affairs, and for security, only ate one cooked meal a day, and otherwise relied on snatched sandwiches or cereals, did not feel it necessary to park their bums on gold-plated lavatories – and collected cash until the bell in the old register had lost its capacity to ring . . . Not that the individual intended to find himself having to defend his trade, not in an interview suite at a cop shop, not in a court of law, not anywhere.

So, there were many who waited for the lorry to reach that city in eastern Germany in the region of Sachsen-Anhalt – where the book publishing trade once flourished, where the 'heresies' of Martin Luther had first been taught, where there was a trade fair known throughout Europe and where Napoleon's military ambitions were crushed before the final throw at Waterloo.

The Turk said, "It'll take some shifting."

And the Serb said, "We'll need a powerful hose with a proper jet on it. Not that I'm saying you should have done anything different. The fucker got in the way, his fault, not ours. Getting the stuff through is all that matters."

A well-thumbed map, pages frayed at the edges, showed the plan of Leipzig, and where they were expected to rendezvous, and where they might find a hose pipe, and see the big man's daughter – the thought of which made them snort: did not rate her, did not trust her. They turned off the main drag to the city centre, away from the hospital and the Wildpark and towards the JET Tankstelle, the meeting place. The fuel station was closed but there would be a hose there, whether the pumps were useable or not.

The wheel was heaved across. They turned off the road and into the darkened car park at the back of the fuel bays.

They were in a mosaic of those little personal patches of possession, so loved by German city dwellers. Handkerchiefs of land, individually cultivated, weeded, with hand-built huts proof against the year's weather where a family could sit in summer and down beers and devour sausages – and enjoy the quiet.

Chopper had followed her and the minder from the hotel. His coat was still damp, and his hair was plastered down. Shoes and socks wet. She had flicked her fingers for his attention, as a Chief Executive Officer would have done. He had been in the lobby and she had swept past him, allowing her minder to go ahead. She passed him a slip of paper with the name of a fuel station and the road it was on, and made for a line of taxis that were paid off after the journey to the city fringe.

Its lights had caught him full in the face, had caused him to blink. The lorry had loomed high over him as it had swept past, and there had been a light on in the cab. Enough for him to see the mark staining the windscreen and the rusty red stuff that had gathered at the edges. Obviously an impact, and blood spilled, and the wipers were going hard against the weather but were not shifting the stain. No chance it was paint, had to be blood, and the remains were being sloshed and smeared backwards and forwards by the wipers.

She went forward, and the minder tailed her.

Chopper could drive fast, shoot straight with a Glock 9mm, and also keep out of sight but near enough to have a grandstand view. The snow had eased, was now a mixture of sleet, short flurries of hail, and rain. It was easy to walk in the shadows.

He was not sure of where she led him, or her motives. He was certain that her mind would be febrile as it contemplated betrayal at this level, and that it was a fair enough possibility that she would change her mind, her right, and give the nod, the wink, the tip, to the minder – and he would be killed.

Chopper noted the registration plate of the lorry, and the logo on the trailer sides, and saw the men who had climbed out of the cab, and stood respectfully in front of her, and she had to play the role of a kingpin . . . It was blood on the windscreen, and he made a record of that, sent that message. He noted that the Prof seemed ill at ease and had started to pace around the lorry and around Julie Wilson, and around the pair from the cab, like they had been there too long and were exposed.

She did it in her way and in her time. He saw her point up at the rear fastening on the trailer and there was a scramble between the two men to get up and unfasten the entrance, and a torch was shone inside and seemed to reveal a dark tunnel between a forest of furniture legs. She was lifted up and wriggled off out of his sight. He understood. There would have been a pen knife, and a small slash made in a wrapped pack that she had chosen at random. A bare finger smeared over the stuff, and the finger going between the lips, no makeup on them, and the chance to get a taste of it. Not like a woman in a smart restaurant, sipping wine from a freshly opened bottle and mulling over the quality, but with the same purpose. Had to be checked and passed for inspection, and if she had not been satisfied then it would have been a killing job and pain first.

She came back from the tunnel, feet first and arms went up to ease her drop down but she waved them away, hesitated, and then dropped. He saw her tongue wipe fast across her lips and she nodded. Quality control and the test passed – and he loved her, good to say or sad to say . . . he thought it a good chance that her father would have beaten what they called 'seven shades of shit' out of her if he had thought she was a user. She wiped hard at her mouth with a tissue. She shrugged. Work done. The trailer was sealed.

A hose was in a roll, against a wall, and the taller of the drivers had unwound it, used it to squirt water over the windscreen, and the redness of what Chopper knew was blood was running down the bonnet and puddling on the ground.

The hose was dumped in a tangle, still running water. The men climbed back into the cab. The Prof was waving to them from below. The engine coughed like a lifetime smoker before engaging. It edged away, going past the narrow ranks of the weekend huts and handkerchiefs of garden, turned out onto the road, flashed the lights like a farewell gesture, and pulled into a stream of traffic.

She walked past him.

Chopper had no idea how she knew where he sheltered in shadow.

She didn't turn her head.

No hesitation, no stammer, an instruction given.

"Back at the hotel, check out. Lose yourself outside. Wait."

Julie kept walking, and the Prof had to scurry to catch her up. They went to a corner where the road had a slipway to the garage, and the Prof was on the phone calling for a taxi. Hours of darkness still to come, and the sleet and hail had eased but not the rain . . . How would he get back to the hotel? Not Julie's problem . . . A decision taken.

How he returned to the hotel near to the rail station from the suburb area of the city was the least of the problems confronting her.

The decision she had taken overwhelmed all others.

Outside her experience, beyond anything she had known, and would need him – the one-time paratrooper and the one-time cop, what he told her – to fortify her. All her life she had been subject to the disciplines of the family, like a wall enclosed her and it would need taking down with a sledgehammer. Either she was as vacuous as any girl who read the magazines that talked of sudden love, or she needed to believe.

Enough … the taxi came. They were driven into town, still desolate, hardly a car moving.

She went upstairs, and on the landing told the Prof where she would be the next day, and where she would see him.

In her room was a pencil and a pad of hotel notepaper beside the telephone. She had no need to stiffen her morale when she began to write and the mini-bar was not raided. What Julie wrote was an act of treachery. Used four sheets of paper, and covered them on both sides in an ornate, copperplate script. Folded the pages carefully and slipped them into her underwear, and decided she had time for two or three hours of sleep. She set her watch. Then rang the SIXT company and arranged the rental terms for a car. The rain had come on hard and she was at her window, staring out into the night, and saw the ambulance approaching and the lights going, and then heard the siren. Saw an emergency unfolding in front of her. It pulled into the forecourt of the hotel and two uniformed paramedics came from the front and walked to the back doors. She had that cramped feeling that anyone would feel – even her bloody father – when they anticipate the misery caused in someone's life by the need to call out the wagon and get the pick-up ride to hospital. A stroke, a heart attack, a fall and a fractured hip, some guest in the hotel and far from home and in a state of crisis. They opened the doors and reached in and she expected to see the wheeled stretcher being eased clear, and then them sprinting with it for the hotel entrance – and saw him, head first and bent and then stretching and straightening and shaking the guy's hand and giving the girl a hug. The lights caught his face and he was smiling, and thought . . . 'For better or fucking worse this is what I have chosen.' He would have seen an ambulance going by, would have waved it down, encouraged it to stop which probably broke every regulation, had shrugged a bit and told them something about a girlfriend and where she was, and they'd let him ride in the back and maybe he'd made them laugh, and him with pigeon German and them with *patois* English. And he was gone from them and inside the hotel, and they drove off, shift over.

Doubts gone. Perhaps they never existed. Would get two hours of sleep, then would go and find him.

The two men loathed each other.

"He's losing it, losing his bloody marbles," said Henry Lyons, solicitor.

"To put it gently, and no reason to, these are difficult times," said Yitzak Cohn, *consigliere*.

Two men who appreciated that they needed each other, but distrusted the other to the point of paranoia.

Lyons said, "Old truism – probably not from your neck of the woods – 'better to hang together than to hang separately', know what I mean?"

Both were well aware that the conversation was unique. Never before had the two principal aides of Lachy Wilson, who competed for his ear, met together in strict privacy and dropped their guard sufficiently to unburden the other of anxieties, of failing confidence in the 'project'. Each had been phoned late at night, roused from sleep in their respective mansions, by the man they knew only as Softboy, and protocols had been broken because the supposed muscle of the 'firm' had choked out a description of the taking of a Liverpool loudmouth when leaving his girlfriend's home, locking him in the boot of his own car, driven hollering and bashing at its lid with fists and feet, and put over a quayside and into deep enough water for death to follow speedily: not more than a couple of minutes, they had been told. Told also that the supposed 'insult' to which Lachy Wilson had reacted had been so insignificant that – Softboy's opinion – the mere sight of a blade would have proved sufficient to ensure it did not become a habit.

Both warmed to the task in hand, vilifying the employer who had plucked them from the obscurity of conveyancing and doing useful mortgage deals, had made them envied by those who knew of them . . . their loyalty had seemed assured. Would have been if life had continued on 'an even keel', as Lyons put it. More than three years since they had last spoken together, and then only with others at hand and close enough to be proven witnesses that no betrayal was planned. Why would there be? Lachy was their milch-cow, their sustenance, their ladder to extreme wealth. Loyalty, for both the legal and the financial minds, depended on a smooth ride.

Lyons said, "The daughter, is a nightmare."

Cohn slapped the table with his hand. "Not to be trusted, not a centimetre."

"He wants out, but no sign of how he will achieve it."

"Nor of where we are, our futures."

"Like the end of a summer cycle, which was never going to last."

Cohn said, "Stormy times ahead."

In the Surrey town of Dorking, the two men – wrapped in over-coats, one of tweed and one of cashmere – sat in a windswept garden outside a coffee shop and a shivering waitress had brought them their drinks and a muffin each. Their voices were muted, and their speech brief and gabbled, as if both men entertained a profound fear of the reach of the man who had brought them such affluence.

"What is his appetite for the future?"

"Don't know."

"Will it crash and take him down?"

"The empire? And take us down?"

Lyons, a careful man, picked at the last crumbs of his muffin and the wind ruffled the paper it had been served in. "I tried, not with any enthusiasm, to discuss security with him. A year or so back. Never left first base, refused to think of it. I would have suggested that it stands to reason that one bright spark in the Met or the Agency, wherever, will take him on, and won't have been bought and won't have been intimidated. Will move with the cunning of a bloody stoat, and he won't know of it. Will be like dry rot in a roof, and slowly weakening him, and all unseen. It's what I lose sleep over. He won't consider it, and now we have the big run coming in with the poppy stuff, and . . ."

Cohn, ill at ease and with a slurp from his mug spilled on his scarf and his hand shaking, interrupted. "I think it is time to dust off the shredder, and to change the hard drives, and to get that boy in – the keyboard wizard."

"And maybe take a holiday, a bit open-ended."

"Are we over-egging it?"

"Maybe we are and maybe not . . . if we are, and he hears of it, then we go into a concrete pillar or a ditch. If we aren't then we go in the cage with him. *If.* Couple of great options . . . If – big word – if there is someone on the block, I have no idea who, who will stand up to him, fight him, challenge. Will not be me, and I doubt you're in line. If . . . Good luck."

They went their own ways, were troubled.

His dogs at his side – and Lachy Wilson was confident they would tear the throat out of anyone who tried to harm him – and with his chickens fed, and the kids gone to school, and a message in from the Prof confirming a meeting in the small hours, he set off down the drive. The rain had eased, the cold was sharper, his advice from Vic clearer.

'You got to do it, Lachy, get it smoothed over.'

Went as far as the iron gates, electronic and secure, told his dogs to sit, and went up the short path to the front door of the lodge, paused, rang the bell. He did not do apologies, not with any sincerity. And doubted Softboy knew much about the business of 'regrets' . . . He heard a bolt drawn back and the grate of a key turning in an old lock. The door opened. His man looked like bloody death, like he hadn't slept and maybe alcohol had been taken, and he was not shaven which at that hour, every day, he usually was. Looked a bit pathetic, which many did in the eyes of Lachy Wilson. Softboy was slight, with a neat head of white hair, no tattoos and no misshaped ears and no out-of-kilter fists. Said to be, seen a leaked police file, 'without a conscience'. This was his home and the Wilsons were his family. He paid, by a bank order supervised by Victoria Wilson via Cohn, the money man, who also organised his ISA accounts and investment portfolio.

Lachy took him in his arms. Spoke in his ear.

"This isn't us, Softboy. Isn't how it's supposed to be. Not after what we have been through, where we started, where we travelled, where we are today. Joined at the fucking hip, eh, Softboy? Both tired, you and me, and shooting our mouths, and none of that called for. Don't need it . . . we are together and I need you and you need me, and that way – together – we take on the world and we walk all over them. They don't stand a fucking chance, not against Softboy and Lachy. We are the top team. You might have been out of order and I might have been out of order, but that does not divide us – and a friendship like ours does not get fractured by some Liverpool lowlife. It does not . . . I told Vic that both of us might have said things that were not thought through, both of us, ill considered, and best not said. I said that to Vic. Tell you what, Softboy . . . she gave me a regular bollocking. You know what she is. You know what a Vic bollocking adds up to. What she told me, to tell to you, is she is not having any division between us and you, Softboy. Won't have that. You are coming to dinner with us, tomorrow night. That is Vic's instruction. You are coming to dinner with us, and this afternoon she is going all the way to Leatherhead, where the best fishmonger is – only the best, Vic says, for Softboy – and there she'll get some prawns, and a risotto with prawns is what she'll cook and that is for you, because you are that important to us. Been with us for years and we don't even imagine a life when you are unhappy with the way things are. It is like we are the same family, same blood, and take care of each other . . ."

Lachy slapped the man's shoulder, and Softboy seemed to be trembling.

Had done the job, as he'd needed to, and they'd work out over the next few hours how to play it further down the line. Stepped away, smiling, oozing his friendship before turning away. The dogs came to heel and he started to walk up the drive. He heard the door close behind him.

Pathetic creature, he thought and walked faster.

"That you, Jonas?"

"It is."

"Chalky, my old cocker, Chalky White."

"Indeed." He knew the voice of the Detective Chief Inspector, a man who still enjoyed an envied reputation – even as retirement, which would be purgatory for him – had tried to snatch him from the Squad.

"Something to fly past you."

Jonas would not have expected that Chalky White would have rung him for gossip. He thought he detected anxiety. If Jonas were ever asked if he wanted first the *good news or the bad news* it was inevitable that he would require the serious and difficult stuff first. Good news was rarely sufficient to lift his mood. "Fly it."

"We've just been trawled."

"A fishing expedition?"

"It went to Admin. None of the top boyos could field it. It was ACU . . . the Anti Corruption Unit . . . They called in. The sort of spiel you would expect from them, said it was just a routine check on one of ours. The one of ours was Chopper Harris. Got me?"

He did not answer. No need to, allowed his silence to prompt.

" . . . I don't do a regular shift pattern any more, bloody lucky to be in work at all, and Admin found me on the twelfth hole and patched it through. Had to think on my feet, never a strong point."

"Where are we leading?"

"One of those tarted-up casual inquiries: did we have this guy working for us? And then, in a roundabout way but seeming to matter: what sort of job is he involved in right now? Investigating what? Not in any trouble or anything, just tying up some loose ends . . . I let the silences hang again. What I am assuming, Jonas, is that they would have gone into the Met's data banks and learned he was with us, but not up-to-date enough, because they are idle bastards. Supposed to keep files to the hour, and so they would not yet have logged that Chopper boy had lost his ID and been moved on. No reference to your outfit anyway. Natural they called us and Admin found me. My mind, Jonas, is now going like a bit of a flywheel. These are humourless grey bastards and no man or woman with a decent mentality would even consider joining their ranks. They are not into small talk, nothing that might be a waste of their time. That is a bit of cliché, but carries some truth. Serious people and you'd not want them close in . . . And I am getting the alarm bells clanging. Thought it was my turn to play interrogator."

"Did you now, Chalky. The question?"

"My question was natural enough – 'What is all this about?' Fair enough? Reasonable? Came back all glib. Just an inquiry, a matter that remained unclear, need to clean and dust a bit, better housekeeping, winding a matter up and repeating the bit about tidying the loose ends. Then the question was repeated."

"You said?"

"Caused my friends on the twelfth a bit of a laugh, and buggered up one of their drives. I told him, Jonas, to fuck off. Clear and to the point, don't you think? I thought he might not have fully understood. So I said, 'Just put anything in writing and in an envelope with a second-class stamp and post it on Monday, and we'll have a look at it when it arrives, and in the mean time do us all a favour and just *fuck off*. Then I went on with the game. Happy?"

"Thank you, Chalky."

He ended the call. Jonas could not imagine how, why, where, the Anti-Corruption Unit had latched on to Chopper, unless it was proximity to the Wilson daughter . . . A cause for anxiety? He doubted it. ACU operated wheels that ground slowly and whatever lead they had come across, fastened onto, they would be well distant by the time *Humble Pie* came to a conclusion and then far beyond the bailiwick of Jonas Merrick and his relationship with the lad . . . intriguing but not interesting.

A new message had arrived. *Keeping calm. Driving north on a magical mystery tour. Destination not revealed.*

He thought a free spirit such as Chopper Harris always attracted the adverse attention of the bureaucrats, rather as he himself did with the Human Resources on the second floor with their kangaroo courts. And that could have led to a fondness for the boy, one enjoyed at a distance . . . But it was a rule of his not to become emotionally attached to any of his employees, those who took his shilling.

Chopper drove.

Recognised it was the same situation for both of them. The leaving of a family. Like when he had gone from Devon into the city down the road and enlisted, or when he had cleared his cubbyhole at Colchester and emptied the locker and accepted that his army time was up, and when he had walked out of the front hall of the Barking building. Said goodbye, perhaps with regrets and perhaps not, to a family that had once mattered but was now beyond its shelf-life. The same for her.

She had set the car's SatNav. Four and a half hours, 250 miles give or take a few. Two big autobahns, either side of Berlin. A clear route and little traffic to slow him. He cruised. She allowed her head to sag against his shoulder. Would have been easy to have wrapped an arm around her and felt the warmth of her body, but he kept both hands on the wheel, and concentrated. Might as well have been driving a surveillance vehicle for the Squad or powering an armour-plated brute along a dirt track in Helmand, needed to be alert: would have been pitiful to have screwed up on a violation of road laws and been waved down. Chopper felt that her withdrawal from the blood ties would be more acute than his. He had moved on before, turned his back on an institution, on guys whose backs he had watched, and walked away – that was 'weakness'.

She hadn't. Might have thought about it, had never done it. Might have dreamed it, but not done the walk, reached the bus stop and looked at the timetable. She rested until they were, his map said, halfway to Berlin and just getting onto the big ring road. No build-up of traffic yet and the night was black, and the rain sheeting. She had straightened up, had said nothing – might have forgotten that he wasn't a hired hand, her chauffeur, and had shoved her hand down her front and produced some folded sheets of paper, and then had started writing. Had used her passport as a surface to press on, and had needed to write into the edges of each page to make space.

Only when they had circled the capital and were heading north, not much more than a hundred miles left on the route she had selected, did she cap her pen and refold the sheets of paper. Did it carefully and with purpose. Looked at him but he kept his eyes on the glistening road ahead, driving through more waves of water that the occasional heavy-duty lorries threw up. She leaned across him and her hand went under his anorak, and fiddled to get below his sweater, and then was exploring his shirt until she found the breast pocket. He felt the paper slipped inside.

He said, "That was?"

"Like a guarantee, a certificate. A confirmation – something like that – where I'm coming from."

Julie watched him. Had to be sure that he realised the enormity of what she had done. Plenty of times in her life betrayal had been discussed over the kitchen table.

Other families, she assumed, those who had the kids who shared her class at school, would have talked about holidays, and their mum's and dad's work situations, and about the football team or permission to go to a gig . . . Her family talked across their table, over toast and cereal, or a takeaway curry or a pizza or Mrs Plumb's Sunday roast, about the penalties exacted on those who betrayed them, played them short by cheating, bragged about success in a deal. Discussed like it was nothing special, and the big boys, Hamish and Gregor, used to squirm with pleasure at the description of the pain done by knives, saws, drills, plastic bags and suffocation, and other more inventive methods, even talked through when the younger boys were there.

It would happen to her, no doubt of it.

And happen to him, another certainty.

Good that he realised what she was doing.

"It's what you need, what can get you killed – and me. What do I get in return?"

"Not much of a trade-off . . . you get me. You are backing off your family, doing the big turnaround, heading away into the mist, and I am beside you. That's the trade. Your father goes down, and you and I are far away lost from sight. My family gets the heave, doesn't mean anything special. It is us, it is together, because that's the chemistry we make, you and me. Enough of a speech?"

"Good to hear it. What is in your pocket is the battle order, best as I have it, of the shipment that comes into Antwerp and then gets moved to the UK. I have to be there when the switch is made. If I am not, then the abort button goes off. Then it is back to my father and a new plan gets put in place, and I don't know it. Have to be there . . . Are you up for a bit of madness?"

"Madness? I feast off it."

"Insanity?"

"Can do that, insanity."

"Regardless?"

"Regardless of how it ends. Reckon that madness and insanity are worth it. Yes I'm confident."

She sagged back in her seat. She had read once, in a magazine, that love could come easily enough from a chance encounter and be realised pretty much immediately. Did not take a six-month romance, did not need a year's bedding down. The article had said that the ingredients were a trio of Ls – Lust, Laughter, and Loyalty. She elbowed him in the ribcage.

"When they hired you. Took you on their payroll, briefed you, told you about me and about my family, flew you down to the Gulf, they were looking long term. Were they just betting on the bump when I was running that we'd do something that was not forgotten?"

"Yes, right."

"Then breaking into the family security?"

"They have good kit."

"Sent you off after me, and were confident that a second contact would go further?"

"An original mind planned it, and he stays off-limits."

"Clever guy?"

"Pompous old arse, but a bit of a genius."

"And assumed you would score and that pillow talk would do the business?"

"Yes."

"Screw me, and I'd spill it?"

"Probably . . ."

He was staring ahead. The light was growing. Signs said how many kilometres until they reached Rostock, and the screen showed him there would be a swing to the west, and . . .

"I might need a hand to steady me – in fact, that's definite, I will."

"I'll be there. Rely on it."

*   *   *

The coast between the centuries-old Hanseatic trading ports of Lubeck and Rostock, facing out to the Baltic Sea, was notable for wildlife reserves, nudist beaches, dunes and spiky grass, and the abandoned decaying buildings formerly occupied by the Soviet military, except for one little corner that had done well from the ignominious retreat of the Red Army, the Red Navy, and the Red Air Force. The town of Rerik, with a famous thirteenth-century church, had pristine sandy beaches and flabby-skinned naturists, and also boasted some of the best conversions of armed forces accommodation to suit the vacation needs of German civilians, mostly from the old west. A few sharp-eyed and financially aware foreigners had seen the opportunity of acquiring property at a keen price and had invested in the refurbished blocks where once tank teams and fast patrol boat crews and aviation maintenance technicians had been housed.

A British family had been amongst them: a girl from that family took her boy by the hand and led him from the car to the front entrance and punched in the code that released a lock, and led him across a ground-floor lobby to an apartment and repeated the code, and kicked the door shut behind her. In summer, Rerik was overwhelmed with visitors: now it was deserted but for its few full-time residents, and its ghosts, and the winds coming in with the waves – and a young couple needing to learn about each other, and what was their future, and consider the magnitude of their deceit.

Few knew who he was or what he did. Amongst the mums and dads at the touchline, cheering on the girls' 2nd XI hockey team representing a school that ranked few stars other than its convenient location for the principal breadwinner of the family, he was a solitary figure. His daughter had come on with the side losing 6-0, and the wag in him had muttered: 'Lucky to get the nil'. He stood apart because he smoked incessantly and it was the sort of school, with the ethos of condemnation of most of life's luxuries, that taught the anti-social evil of cigarette smoking. He stood under a tree on the far side of the pitch, where most spectators huddled in the poor weather, and nursed in his hand one of those little boiled sweet tins, and the ash went into it, and then the cigarette stubs. The Assistant Deputy Director General had used his official driver to get here. Harry was in the school's car park and would have been reading a red top. He thought the majority of the parents opposite, silenced by the girls' limp athleticism, would have been uninterested by the presence among them of a man so versed in the detail of threats against the realm, and combating them – and just as indifferent to *Humble Pie* and the net closing on a particular heroin importer. Had it been cocaine, taking that off the streets where they lived, then such a dislocation of many of their weekends would have been cat-called with abuse. His daughter had asked him to come, and he had agreed. Thought it necessary to show willing. The dear little soul scored. Her father hopped one-footed on the squelching turf alongside the all-weather surface, pirouetted, did a little jig, shouted his congratulations, not once but three times, and might have seemed 'over the top' when those on the pitch for longer had so manifestly failed. A couple more shouts of 'Bravo', and another jump of exaltation . . . and down he went. Down like a sack of bloody potatoes, down as if he were shot (and he had avoided that in incessant tours of the Province), and landing on the tip of his left shoulder. A foot had caught a root of the tree where he sheltered, and had brought him low. Full-time called, the final whistle. He lay, unable to get up, unnoticed. The pitch was deserted, the parents and players gone for tea in the pavilion . . . Harry found him. Harry helped him back to the car where his daughter sat, and she complained that he had made something of an exhibition of himself when she'd scored. The AssDepDG vowed the afternoon would never be repeated, asked Harry to take the miserable teenager home, then take him to the nearest Accident and Emergency. He was starting, rare for him, to feel almost sorry for himself.

Harry said, with sympathy, "Rotten thing to have happened and this being a big weekend for your show, sir."

"Right now I could not give a damn for my show."

In the crowded waiting area, while forms were filled out, details taken, he fainted.

That Friday, approaching the lunch hour, a party kicked into action in the Post Room. It was to celebrate a woman's birthday. Bobby was not her name but it had stuck. The subterranean area had long managed to behave in an atmosphere of autonomy. Such an occasion could not have happened on the ground floor or above, but no one without specific business came down to the basement. Beers, shorts and mixers were brought in, and nibbles, and a radio was playing music. From their rest room next door, the armed police, off-duty, came in, ponderous in their belts and vests. The chauffeurs from the drivers' pool, white shirts and ties, like the cops, could make a noise but stuck with orange juice. Bobby was popular on her own territory, would have been unknown to Human Resources other than as a statistic, and led a conga. Drinks had been dispensed into cardboard beakers and were carried high, and the room rocked and no letters were deemed important enough to send to the heights of the building, and what came down in the antiquated lift system was left unsorted, but might catch a late afternoon collection. The conga meandered around the tables and chairs and the filing cabinets, and phones went unanswered, and cakes and rolls were snatched off plastic plates as the procession navigated the floor space. It arrived at that distant corner which staff in the Post Room usually avoided, but the mood was lighter than on any other morning, and Bobby brought the dance to a halt, leaned across the top of the filing cabinet.

"Sorry to have missed you out, Mr Merrick. Apologies. I see you have a coffee mug and a thermos . . . can we fortify it?"

He was irritated, about to start his packed lunch, regarded the din as an intrusion, had poured his half measure of coffee, saw the interruption as impertinent, and abruptly changed his screen from the biographies of the Wilson family to the saver of a scowling image of Olaf. He shook his head.

"Come on," she cajoled. "I only have one a year. We're actually harmless, you know. Come on, pass up your mug."

And, rather surprising himself, he did. He held up the mug, on which was an image of a mountain view in the west of Scotland, and she produced a quarter bottle of the cheapest blend of Scotch available in Asda, poured liberally, pocketed the bottle, and giggled.

"Well done, Mr Merrick. A bit of brown milk in coffee never hurt anyone."

He said rather weakly, "And a happy birthday to you."

She was gone, and the conga resumed, and a chirpy smile from Kev who was draped in his gas and cuffs and truncheon and taser kit, and raised eyebrows from Leroy. Jonas assumed that he had been on leave, and getting himself near beaten to death on the Devon coast, when Bobby had celebrated a previous anniversary. He drank, felt the warmth in his throat. Had shocked himself . . . Normally, alcohol for Jonas and Vera was limited to rare glasses of dry sherry. Felt comfortable, almost chortled. Then remembered.

Remembered who he was.

Remembered his poor opinion of the men and women on the third floor and above who needed 'sustenance' to get them through the afternoon.

Remembered that Lachy Wilson did not drink.

Remembered that the hours ticked away. That he did not have Effie there to hustle through their emails. That Chopper was on assignment and walking a bouncy tightrope, and what he had done to a girl to achieve an aim . . . And remembered that his life enjoyed few of the moments of sheer pleasure as expressed by Bobby who he thought was responsible for deciding what incoming mail went to which pigeonhole and would have been paid a civil service pittance – and wore no ring, and was in no way conventionally attractive, and seemed so happy.

Was he? Was it possible to be happy, to be simple, and uncomplicated, and to do his job?

He could not be a part-timer, could not be slumped in his chair at home, nodding off with the help of alcohol . . . Could not do his job with other than total and unashamed concentration. On Effie Bellingham's desk was a small pot plant, a species of orchid, with a mauve pattern on a white background and two flowers that day. He leaned across and tipped his coffee, and the 'brown milk', into it and watched it soak away into the soil and felt better for it. The noise went on round him, but he was not interrupted again. Would not have been able to do his work, and that justified the wearing of any necessary hairshirt: had precious little to sustain him other than his work. He started on his sandwiches.

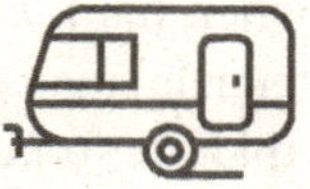

10

A pub, within walking distance, would have welcomed the birthday celebrants from the Post Room.

Only Vernon, the manager, remained on duty.

Jonas had quite enjoyed the disturbance, might have given the sour appearance of resenting the interruption but the bustle of the dance and what had been poured into his coffee had cheered him. There had been a fast clean-up before the exodus and little remained to show that a celebration had taken place. The chauffeurs would have been back in their drivers' pool, and the armed police were in their own rest room. He had the quiet, but not much to do with it.

Funny old world, the one he inhabited. Moments of sudden intuition that startled him: the time when he had walked over the bridge, high above the river, and realised that an outsider should be introduced to the family, put alongside the vulnerable element. Minutes of extraordinary clarity such as when he had been inside the home of Lachy Wilson, been treated with politeness and overt courtesy, and had noted the flash in the daughter's eyes when reprimanded by her father – and had known where he would target. An hour when doubt was replaced with certainty when he had sat on a bench in a public house and detectives had joshed and laughed and told their anecdotes, except one who had been hunched, no longer of the tribe, and had felt certainty, made his decision.

Moments, minutes, an occasional hour, and then having to compete with entire days, sometimes whole weeks, when nothing happened that in any way lifted him. He was left then with tedious business to hack through. He supposed it was how counter-intelligence, counter-espionage, had always been, and likely would

always be – until the day when his ID was rescinded. He would
have liked to have Effie Bellingham there, to witness the complexity
of his plotting and the way that the strands knitted. But he did not,
and there was not even an answer message on her phone . . . had
given up on her. Jonas knew very little about sport, had regarded
athleticism in the distant days of his education as a tyranny, and
had only a vague idea of how long a schoolgirls' hockey match
lasted, and had rung the AssDepDG and would have quite happily
endured some of the man's barking rudeness, except that his
phone was switched off. Had tried it several times. The driver,
Harry, ought to have been able to patch him through. No sight
nor sound of him either.

Jonas, as the afternoon passed, felt almost lonely.

Nothing from Germany. He waited, and the afternoon wore on.
Spurts of activity, sloughs of inactivity, he knew them well. His
sandwich box and flask were back in his briefcase, and his screen
showed Olaf eyeing him without affection.

Chopper stared around him from the front step of the entrance to
the block. Development had obviously been started, then discon-
tinued. Some buildings were finished and habitable: others were
decaying with holes in the roofs and beams exposed, and signs of
recent history enacted. On some walls, where the windows were
fractured or the glass broken, were the faded outlines of the shapes
of active service military aircraft. He recognised the different
stages of the Soviet Union's bomber, fighter, and interceptor
generations: the Yak-25, the SU-24 and 27, the Il-28, the Tu-22,
the MiG-25 and 31. There was a lawn of rough grass in front of
the block, but further away, where the buildings showed evidence
of the old military occupancy, and where undergrowth had flourished, he saw the sneaking movements of emaciated feral cats. He
heard the sea's beat on a beach. There was brittle sunshine and a
wind carried the sharp cold. It would have been a community like
that of Colchester, or similar to the permanent sovereign base
camps on the island of Cyprus: would have represented power,
and had been stripped away. Rather liked the image forming in his

mind of a once-great authority brought down, now strangled by brambles and overrun by the half-starved animals, or had a change of use and was being used as a playground for the affluent. It suited him to think the thoughts of the new world where odds-on favourites had collapsed . . . as they would in his relationship with the Squad and the Battalion, and the empire of the family firm. Liked the image.

She'd shown him a store of chilled food in the kitchen. Staff came each month to replace it. She'd said that she was 'bloody useless' at cooking – all done for her at home – but would try, and there was the sound and smell of sausages and bacon cooking. He assumed everything was now planned. For the rest of the time they were given, he should get used to doing the cooking. Had not argued. Could teach her to cook after a barracks style, and could teach her how to fire a handgun better. Both of them were leaving their dependence on an existing family – two kids from opposite sides of the street and moving away from everything they had known. No turning back, no looking behind. He sucked in the chill air and tasted the tang of the sea, and she called for him.

He went inside.

Still in his pocket were the folded sheets of paper she had given him. They would be sent to London, when he was ready – not a moment before he was ready, and happy to do it.

She put her hand on his.

"My mind's made up."

He had a slice of sausage on his fork, put it down.

"And mine, Julie."

"I'm not agonising."

"Which is right. Not going to spend the next days, weeks, however long we're given, chewing on what we've done and whether it was sensible."

"It is a breakout. We become our own people."

He said, "You were in the Gulf because you were put there. I was there because I was sent. Our meeting was engineered. End of their story. Finish with them. End of gibberish, bring a curtain down on it?"

"I think so. We will have gone free . . . It's what you see on wildlife programmes on the box. They bring a caged animal to a jungle or a mountain or a moor, one bred in captivity – like us – and unfasten the door of the cage. What happens? Could be a cat, could be a young eagle. What happens is that it stares around, very tense, sniffs, evaluates where the risk is. Decides to accept that risk, takes a step forward, comes out of the cage, then . . . That's where we are now," she said and her hand tightened on his.

"Then, if it is an animal it steels itself, then hustles for cover, the shortest number of paces and the greatest density of foliage. Puts distance between itself and anything from a former life. A bird? A few flaps, then up, away, and climbing, getting into the hang of soaring and looking for peaks and crags and perches where it is beyond reach. Then . . ."

Julie grinned. "Gets peckish, needs to eat. Won't have what is cooked and put on a plate. Has to go and look for it, do its own killing, find its own meal. Never return to the cage. It is breakout."

He kissed her hand. She shrugged. Would do for now. A winter evening gathering on that cold shoreline: no risk of snow or hail, but a chance of a frost if the wind allowed it. A boy had come after her: none ever had before. Too fucking frightened of who she was, where she came from, her family. Had knelt at her feet and fiddled with a trainer lace and had made her laugh. Had won a kiss from her, and had captivated her. She knew what would happen, later, and what he would do with her: do what none had been permitted or dared to do before.

"Eat your sausage, and your bacon, and don't bloody complain about your egg."

He did. She thought he might have to get used to doing what, when, she told him, and not *why*. And might learn to do as she was asked, told. Might learn a whole lot . . .

"When will you send them what I've written?"

"When I'm ready."

"When you're ready?"

"It means that I let them sweat. In my own good time, and then they scramble."

"Which does not make it easy for them but increases the chance of success. It is not that I hate them, my family, but unless I do this I have no chance ever of being free. Let's go and walk on the beach."

"A trail has been left behind her that a bloody donkey could follow." Dawson grinned as she flapped the sheet of paper in front of her boss. Detective Inspector John Plunket.

He snatched at it, read what she had scrawled.

"So, she and Genge flew from Luton to Leipzig which we knew, and the Germans have done their homework, very cooperative, and the hotel – except they have all moved out of there, cheap and not particularly cheerful – sort of sales rep place, but they've told us the next step."

And back to Dawson. "Which is Monday out of Antwerp, back to the UK."

"Conclusions?" The boss was also finding it hard to mask his own pleasure at where they were.

"The shipment comes into Antwerp, will be pushed on from there to the UK," said Rajah. "They will see it between the two stages. She has that authority, pretty little Miss Julie, but Dad has to be involved because he needs to sign off the big payment. The stuff is delivered, he needs to cough . . . putting it mildly, for him to have stepped out of bed it needs to be a hefty load, big money – so more than just a snort, a hell of a cough."

From Dawson, "That's good, but getting better. The Squad boy on the flight to Leipzig, and in the same hotel there, and routed back out of Antwerp. Is that better or best?"

"Choice – like a Lottery win."

The next business of the day was hurried forward. Contacts in Antwerp were explored, exploited. Travel fixed, not using the Met's system because it was outside the practice of ACU to rely on arrangements that could be overseen by the great mass of employees in the Met family. Unlikely that their names were known but possible . . .

They would leave that evening.

Nothing out of the ordinary. No extra kit, just their phones and their base would be double-locked and the alarms on.

By the time their return was noted, there was a chance that word would have seeped out that the *untouchable* himself, the one his thought himself *too big to bring down*, would have been photographed in handcuffs, being led towards a marked squad car by a pair of nondescript uniformed constables, dropped onto the back seat . . . There would be promotion, and cynics' praise from those who had criticised a lift in a crowded golf club bar, and fear among those who decided they had reason to expect a knock on the door in the middle of a grandchildren's party. Would be accolades . . . and would be smouldering resentment from an elite unit – and all of them so loved the word *elite* like it made their work worthwhile – when one of theirs was awaiting a place in the dock at Snaresbrook Crown Court. Happy days.

Peggy booked the flights.

Rajah organised the cash float using the credit card locked away in the team safe, and early cabs arranged for the morning.

And John Plunket would do more badgering of the Belgians for escort facilities and transport. He believed the status of his unit was not yet properly recognised. It was accepted by the three of them that the reaction of the squad to their general enquiry concerning the work of Detective Constable Kenny Harris was predictable and defensive. And accepted that the Flying Squad had no role to play in investigations against a crime baron as prominent as Lachy Wilson, were better suited employing their talents against thieves, cash delivery hijacks, gang-on-gang kidnaps.

A cheerful atmosphere settled on the room.

They survived on success. Needed it to justify the secrecy surrounding their work and the necessity of the budget, not inconsiderable, to be beyond the prying eyes of the number checkers.

Survived also on their deep unpopularity – which was a blessing, appreciated – and all of them liked to think that hostility meant a job well done.

With what sounded like grudging reluctance, the Antwerp Federal Police Service came back to them. The liaison was booked. Their flight would be met. Cooperation would be of the highest standard.

"Which says . . ." Dawson intoned, "we'll have a right bottle-washer in tow."

"I have passed my test? I am 'firearms enabled'?" Jacques asked more in hope than expectation.

"It means that we are short-staffed."

"I will be permitted to draw my Five-seven?"

"You will be, Jacques, but that authorisation does not affect your subsequent need to undergo a firearms examination because of the poor score you registered when you last—"

"Circumstances were against me."

His supervisor was not to be shifted. "I have a busy day. This matter has landed on my desk. I want to go home. I have messages to clear before I leave. This is a small matter . . . on a pygmy scale. Three British are coming. What for? I am not told. Their tone implies they are not prepared to share with us the reason for their visit. They need to be ferried, they need facilities, but I do not know what it is they require. They are British: they will regard us as *paysans*. Do federal police going to London have a red carpet rolled out for them? Do they hell. They expect it from us. They will have a most pleasant surprise, Jacques, because it will be you who will meet them. Every courtesy, Jacques, and the tourists' view of the city which you excel at. Please, I want to go home and my tray is still full. Any more questions?"

"Do I only get to have my Five-seven reinstated because you are short-staffed?"

"For fuck's sake, Jacques, you are given this role because you are the most innovative, talented, hard-working officer working out of the Scheepvaartpolitie station." The sarcasm gushed but he seemed not to be aware of it.

"This is a weekend assignment, and the hours are not stipulated, so do I presume I will be able to bill administration for weekend work and over-time hours?"

"And charge for your croissants when you are waiting for them at the airport in the morning."

"Thank you."

"I sometimes, Jacques, wonder if you keep those fucking maggots in your mouth too long and whether every month or so a few manage to get inside your system . . . Go away, leave me in peace – and do not fucking embarrass me because I am scraping the bottom of the barrel to fulfil our personnel requirements – that conference in Brussels, the flu epidemic, the football in Liège, the funerals, all the usual fucking excuses. Still here, Jacques?"

A slip of paper was passed him. A signature was scribbled on it, and was stamped over, and the armourer, on the receipt of it, would issue the FN Herstal designed semi-automatic pistol that fired 5.7x28mm bullets.

A step forward for Jacques, not as far as he would have preferred, but sufficient. He went back to his work space and started to badger for a fully fuelled people carrier to be available from the pool. The British had a reputation for awkward superiority, but he would manage. And having the holster weighted on his chest and the harness tight on his shoulder would enable him to absorb rudeness, superiority, lack of respect . . . might actually be enjoyable, even amusing.

Jonas was annoyed. Beyond irritated.

He was peeved because he needed reassurance. Jonas had not lost faith in his boy's delivery. No question of that. Would not have entertained any suggestion that he was about to be 'stood up', that his grand scheme was built on shifting sands. But he had assumed that he would by now have received the detail of the plan put in place by the Wilson clan. Had expected that by now it would have been nailed down, that he would be savouring the moment when he would get to speak with the Assistant Deputy Director General and pass the jewelled timetable into his hands, and be told with a smile that would have been more than patronising, 'Never in doubt, eh? Isn't that what we say, Jonas? Took your time, took a few buckets of resources, but we are there. Yes, I will check over what you have presented me with, Jonas, and run my intellectual eye over it so that the Service is not led into a quagmire of legal difficulty. Which I believe has always been a difficulty of yours, Jonas. The inability to register that some matters are destined for a court of law, a distasteful outcome, and one where your shortcomings are pretty damned obvious. Will check it out and will then pass what is appropriate to the relevant people . . . Almost forgot. Well done, Jonas. Yes, as they say every Saturday afternoon, never in doubt.' That was how it would finish. But he was impatient.

He had sat out the afternoon. Other than Vernon, the Post Room had been deserted. The afternoon had passed slowly. His impatience had manifested itself in him switching his screen on and off, gazing at his cat scowling back at him, then blanking the beast, and making a list of those he expected would face arrest when the family was brought down, and then realising the futility of such preparations before his briefing material was in front of him . . . Perhaps he was beginning to tire of the process. Might have been that the target rather wearied him. He missed those long calls from the retirement homes around Langley, Virginia, and sweet things said to him by veterans, and could have done with one of those rather jolly monologues from Bogotá or Lima when DEA men talked about 'wasting' and 'bringing down' the big-time bandits. Probably it had, at a maximum, forty-eight hours to run. Then he would meet Chopper on the bridge, would say something that was both gruff and saccharine. Would inevitably get a stumbling request for future freelance employment, and would deflect it with practised vagueness: expected the young people he fed off to disappear into the sunset, not to bother him again. But that was all for later . . . Right now, Jonas Merrick waited for the information to be sent him that would further enhance his reputation.

The big clock behind Vernon's table showed that the window had closed. Coat on, trilby rammed down on his head, scarf knotted at his throat. He had his briefcase, containing the sandwich box and the thermos, locked to his wrist. He went out into the dusk, and the chill caught him. Up Horseferry Road, and his café was already shuttered for the weekend, and he paused at the roundabout and gazed into the walls of traffic inching forward, lights bright and tempers short. He was sufficiently annoyed that he was prepared to step into the road, head for the haven of grass and concrete in the centre. His name was called.

Leroy, arm raised to hold up the bumpers and fenders and silence the horns. "That's it, Mr Merrick, in your own time."

Kev following him, and gaining equal respect because of the Heckler & Koch machine pistol dangling on its strap across his chest. "Very wise, Mr Merrick, to have skipped the pub session. Have a good weekend, sir."

He ducked his head, a gesture of grudging gratitude, and they'd have expected no more.

Kev said. "We've a lieu day on Monday, both of us, and the girls have one off work. We're in the Welsh hills, a hotel, some archery and some drinking, and a quiz or two. Bit of a switch-off."

Leroy said, "Safe home, Mr Merrick and you have a good one too, and see you on Tuesday morning. Look after yourself, sir."

He was on the pavement, the bridge stretching ahead of him. He clung to the trilby's brim, and the lie churned in his mind, and he wondered if the stakes were worth it.

A clear sky, the blanket of clouds gone, and stars for Chopper to look at. And planets up there, not that he knew their names. And something bright that was likely a space station on the move and doing its revolutions.

When he was not kissing her, his teeth chattered from the cold.

Sand had worked inside the sleeping bag.

Her idea and Chopper had not fought it. The walk on the beach had taken them past the former defences of barbed wire that marched into the sea on collapsed posts and broke the incoming waves, and past signs that warned of the dangers of abandoned munitions. As they were leaving the block she had passed him a bulky plastic bin bag. They had walked, fingers linked, stepping over seaweed dumped from a previous storm, and there was moonlight to guide them. They were hemmed in on one side by the darkness of the abandoned camp and on the other by the dark expanse of the Baltic, and only a single tramper's navigation lights. The glow from the town of Rerik was almost hidden by a dense plantation of pines. She had led him into the lower stretch of the dunes where the spiked grass grew in clumps, had taken the bag from him and shaken out its contents. One sleeping bag, single occupancy, and an already-opened half-bottle of Scotch. She kicked her shoes off, and he followed her, then took off his socks.

Then they took off their anoraks, and he folded his and she dumped hers in a heap – old habits died hard: one had been trained for a private soldier's barracks inspection by an uncharitable NCO, and one had a housekeeper to pick up after her.

Then her trousers, and his.

She wriggled into the sleeping bag leaving precious little space for another body, and stared up at him.

He took his fleece off and his shirt. She had opened the zip of the sleeping bag, to make it easier for him, and he knelt and his ankle – the old bullet wound – hit her knee and it was like he was stabbed. He shifted and his weight was across her.

He felt the warmth of her. No laughter, no giggling, steady breathing and he wondered whether this was perfect, or beyond perfect. Had her head in the crook of his arm and did not want to move for fear of breaking the dream. Didn't need help from the bottle.

In each other's arms, and their heat melted the cold off them. He said nothing but started to count the stars, and thought it was beyond what he could have hoped, was fearful of losing it.

He had broken clear, Chopper realised. Was no longer the man who took the step forward because he was ordered to, let his weight go off the balloon platform or out into the violence of the slipstream gale, and drop. *Theirs not to reason why, Theirs but to do and die,* as the resident humorist on the Forward Operating Base in Helmand liked to intone. Nor the strictures of working for the Squad and what was expected of a detective with the right to carry a periwinkle shell, and a Glock . . . all gone. Proof of the ruptured links was the feeling of sand in his groin.

He would have struggled to express himself, say what he thought, so said nothing, and held her as loosely as the bag allowed.

She put his hand where she wanted it.

Chopper thought her as inexperienced as he was.

Thought them a match.

The lights from the tramper had disappeared, and darkness descended. The wind became fiercer, and he thought that within a few minutes the rain would start.

Hoped it would never end.

Had broken free and all else in his life was behind him.

Thought himself blessed.

Julie's promise to herself: nothing faked.

Nothing between them was pretend, and him in no hurry, nor her. No acting required.

Julie Wilson had no confidantes. No one who she trusted with the innermost workings of her mind; no one from whom she could have mined experience.

They were like two kids, glorying in their ignorance.

Better here than a hotel room, in a bed where a couple had screwed the night before, and another might have the space for two or three hours the following afternoon. She thought this was perfect. *Perfect*, and had never known it.

He asked whether her face was okay. She told him, a whisper against the rush of the wind in the grass, that her face was good, that the weather did not matter.

"Tell me that this isn't ordinary."

"It is not."

"And special?"

"Better than special."

"Because . . . ?"

"Because we do not look back. It is not about how I have been treated, how you have. Not about misery, what is past. All gone, like a curtain's over it. Finished. We are changed. How changed?

Broken free, that amount of change. Ditch your family, and big time. Ditch mine and go off their radar. They come looking for us. They will. Search and hunt for us, like a pack. Won't forgive us because we ignored the rules [that] they set. Enough of a speech . . . ?"

"Maybe, maybe not."

Her hands moving, and his, and a happiness that was mutual and the sleeping bag stretching and arcing and rolling a little on the slope of the dunes and shipping more sand inside.

"Don't think about the past, only the future."

Julie said into his ear, "The future is anywhere I want it to be – say that again. The future is anywhere *we* want it to be. Anywhere. I have passports anywhere I want them, and people who deal in passports, and documents. We have, of course, the guys who deal in passports and identities, and they give a start and we move on, and then find someone else with the same skill and use them. That is what is washing and rinsing, but you know that . . . and break the chain again, and we are anywhere. When it is broken, that chain, Chopper, what will you miss?"

"Don't know of anything."

"Nobody will own us."

"I will miss nothing."

"Is that enough talk?"

"More than enough."

Pitch-darkness around them. Thunder rumbled far out over the sea. No lights from a ship, and none above as the moon was obliterated, and the hail hammered them.

Had an image of them in her mind, and they were the past and Julie savoured it. Saw Lachy and Vic and her four brothers. Saw the gang that tiptoed around after the family. Would be shot of them all in a couple of days. Let her mind go blank before replacing the image with her and this guy who had come into her life, and who she did not doubt.

She reached outside the sleeping bag. Groped for the zip and pulled it down so that her back and her thighs and all of him were exposed.

"I think we need some fucking room. Right?"

"You heard from our beloved daughter?" Lachy Wilson came into the kitchen.

The kids were already eating. His own plate was held by Mrs Plumb, and Vic was serving a cottage pie. She shook her head.

Which puzzled him. Puzzled him as much as the message received from the Prof. *Confused. A note from JW this morning under my door. Said she was going off for shopping and sightseeing. Would meet me in Antwerp, Sat morning. Nothing more. Don't understand.* He had rung Julie's mobile. Twice, breaking the protocol of keeping communications to a minimum. Not answered, switched off.

Perhaps there was truth in what she had written. The need for time on her own, maybe some fucking church to go and look at, or a museum, maybe a shopping binge, though God knew she had enough in her wardrobe and most of it never worn, and . . . most likely she could not stand the thought of another twenty-four hours in the company of the Prof. Wally Genge was among the most boring people that Lachy had ever come across. 'Boring', but loyal and therefore valued, and perhaps the daft bitch had not yet taken on board the value of loyalty. And then his plate was on the table and Vic was complaining about the weather.

"No way I'm going into Leatherhead, best part of twenty miles round trip just for prawns. Cost a fortune anyway. The ones in the freezer will do. Won't know the difference, anyway. Defrosted prawns in a risotto is hardly going to be noticed. You all right with that?"

He had started eating. The cottage pie was a recycling of the last of a beef joint, one of his favourites. Always liked the last meal of a joint, knowing that nothing was going to waste. Lachy could not abide throwing away decent food, taught that by his mother when times were hard, before he had started – aged eleven – to run his first little bit of protection in Peckham. Mouth full, he nodded.

Vic said, "Just asserting herself, isn't she? What girls of her age do. I'm hardly an expert. Must have been doing that, asserting myself, when I went out with you for the first time. Suppose that's it."

She gave him her smile. The sardonic one. The one he loved because it proved they were a partnership . . . He had not yet worked out how the matter with Softboy would end. A hole in the ground? A renewal of trust? A boot in the arse and him turfed out of the lodge? A pretence that nothing had happened? Softboy had not walked up the drive and found him with the chickens and made a stammered attempt at making peace. Hadn't gone the extra yards to settle it. Others had. He'd had a message that cousins had effortlessly slipped into the space in Toxteth where a vacancy had come up. Respect had been shown and a deal would go through. The cousins would be salivating that an opportunity had arisen for them to take charge of that end of a shipment and decent money would come their way. He would think some more about the future of Softboy and would run it past Vic.

He cleared his plate, and the boys had toyed with theirs but they knew not to leave anything, not if their father was at the table.

Vic said, "You worry too much, Lachy. If she wants to go shopping, decent clothes in Germany, top of the range, and smarten herself up for what's in front of her, we shouldn't complain. Bad enough to have you following me around, but if it were the Prof, mouthing his bloody poetry, then I'd consider jumping off a high balcony."

They laughed. She kissed him. The kids cleared their plates.

He'd talk it over with her, the options to take with Softboy. The matter of his daughter was eased sideways, and the matter of the shipment. The payment for it – a crucifying amount, but for top quality – nagged at him, like it always did when the cargo was on that scale . . . But it was where he was, that position of importance that the 'untouchable' dealt with, and where he intended to stay.

"Can't sleep, Jonas. Am in my conservatory, in my chair, and I have the heating on which is costing me half my pension, and the wife's share. Feckin' hips and feckin' knees, and they are killing me. Not a joke. Just pulled the cap on a new Bush bottle. Don't know who else to talk to, Jonas. Where are you?"

"On my back lawn, with the cat. Not for long. We have a cold snap if you didn't know."

Not many would have received that degree of politeness from him, not when they phoned him at the time of the evening when he let Olaf out to prowl among the shrubs bordering the lawn, and delay him when he would have called the cat in and climbed the stairs . . . He did not object.

"Bad night for me, and no escape from it. Working out for you, Jonas?"

The caller was that long-lasting friend from the disbanded, vilified, Special Branch of the Royal Ulster Constabulary. They had never met but had had telephone conversations, mostly dominated by the old policeman, now a virtual cripple from the ravages of rheumatism, over a long span of years. Much of what Jonas knew of the world of counter-terror came from this man's wisdom. He had not risen to high rank but elucidated truths, and Jonas valued him. Jonas was grateful that he could still work, could still walk briskly to the railway station and over Lambeth Bridge. The policeman was a mentor. The 'truths' were not from analysis of where terror was spawned, but was from experience, the face-to-face, eye-to-eye, nail-and-tooth level of the men and women who had given themselves the right to kill and maim in the name of a cause, and how they went about their trade. Good understandings for Jonas to absorb. In that great grey Portland stone building, once home to Imperial Chemical Industries, also to the Prudential, few would have understood his longing to be down at the gutter level of the thinking of his opponents. It was the same with espionage when probing for weak points, and the same for crime. He humoured the man across the Irish Sea, and thought it in his interests to do so.

He answered the question. "Think so. Uncertain of how far down the line. Not been told yet."

"It is audacious, Jonas. Big word, but a big plan."

"Quite pleased with it."

There was a scrabble of movement in the shrubs, a suppressed squeal, and Olaf appeared, a late snack dangling from his jaws. Jonas shrugged, concentrated on his call.

"But not buttoned?"

"Sadly, not. But I am confident."

"You have to be, Jonas. Confident. It's the only game in town. No plan B to fall back on. Hope your back is covered. He is what we've called an 'irregular', right?"

"Right. An 'irregular', which seemed a good fit for what we are attempting to achieve."

Extraordinary how much noise Olaf made when he crunched the head of a creature in the moments after it had failed to provide any more fun.

The voice of the one-time detective murmured in Jonas's ear. "Probably the best sort of man. Unlikely to get emotional about loyalties. A free thinker. You don't own him, you are not his lord and master. We had them, adventurers, and used them against the bad boys and they were good as far as it went. Not for spick and span parade-ground discipline, but getting where you wanted them, provided that you did not demand too great an allegiance. They walk away when it suits them . . . Nor, Jonas, will they take a bullet for you, not that amount of commitment. But you knew that, didn't you, Jonas?"

"Think I did. Think I knew it."

The security light showed only a back leg and a whippy little tail. Nothing else on the grass. Olaf stalked away, heading for the kitchen door.

"The target, worth this amount of hassle?"

"It will be a victory on a grand scale for my masters, if the irregular achieves it. Cork-popping time. Me? Didn't someone write, *They also serve who only stand and wait*? My wife likes that line, keeps one in one's place, she says. Yes, I manage. Good night, friend – and I'll remember your wise words about my irregular, but I'm very confident in his loyalty, such as I need it."

He rang off. The cat waited for the kitchen door to be opened. And Jonas waited for a text, a detailed one, to be sent him. His lips pursed in frustration.

11

A Saturday morning in Raynes Park, the dormitory suburb in south London where many houses' design mirrored the 1930s' obsession for mock Tudor semi-detached buildings with bay windows for the front room, and a bit of pebbledash, and shared driveways to twin garages, and concreted-over front gardens. Only the bold or the stupid were outside as the rain came hard, and the weather forecast indicated little change.

Jonas Merrick, neither bold nor stupid, was among them and paced irritably. Usually, the cat would be under his feet if he was outside but had taken one look through the open door and turned its back. He had already inspected the caravan since its return from the repairs required after he had failed to drain the interior water pipes before the 'cold snap'. It required no work inside or outside. It was dried out from the leakage, and the carpet had been cleaned, and the units were wiped down and the gas bomb canister safely stowed ... He should, that morning, have been loading it, and then hooking it up to their car, edging out into the road, holding up traffic if necessary, then heading for the route that would take them down to the Dorset coast, a good stint of it using the A31. But the departure was on hold and he had delayed a final decision until the following day. Vera, eyes and mouth reflecting a comprehensive image of thunder, accentuating her mood by refraining from comment but making her point more eloquently by dumping his bag, her bag, the cat's cage and bed and food in the hall by the front door.

He paced around the caravan. He did not know what else to do.

The Derbyshires, money made from conservatories and double-glazed windows, would have seen him and wondered if the 'silly old beggar' had finally lost what plot he might once have had. The new people on the other side, quiet as church mice, would have wondered why he was going to work on a Saturday.

Jonas supposed that the majority of those who followed him each morning into Thames House were able to switch off their commitment to the cause at 17.30 on a Friday evening, leave it dormant until 08.30 hours on a Monday morning, and go off and pursue hobbies or keep company with friends. He had no hobbies and probably would have admitted to having no friends . . . He had Vera, of course – now with the hump because the long weekend break was on hold – and he had Olaf, the Norwegian Forest cat . . . nothing and no one else mattered to him. Again and again, spattered with the incessant rain, he circumnavigated the caravan. In his pocket was his phone and his hand clasped it. He had barely slept.

He could not abide any display of weakness. To have phoned the boy, his irregular, and disguise his annoyance at the delay in being kept up to date, would have been unprofessional and shown weakness. He was supposed to instil only confidence. To nag for a progress report would have shown signs of a concern that would easily build to panic. He remembered a custody officer at a West Midlands police station who was a pigeon racer – high-quality birds, some worth more than a month's wages. They would be crated up, loaded onto a lorry, and taken off to Portsmouth, put on a ferry, and driven down to the Spanish or Italian or German border. Fed and watered a last time and, as the clock started ticking, they were let free and went off in a swarm, did a couple of circles and headed for home. The custody officer said that all he could do was sit by the loft, fill a pipe, scratch a match and wait. 'Can't go off down to the south coast cliffs and holler abuse if the peregrine falcons are flying, waiting for them. Have to show patience and hope they make it back, and in good time, just stay safe.' Good advice . . . Did Jonas Merrick care too much? Should he have been in the greenhouse, or on a golf course, or helping to renew a steam engine's life, or pushing the trolley for Vera – God forbid – round the supermarket aisles?

Would have preferred to have been in the Post Room, no natural light, no sign of the rain other than the trail of wet footprints from the door. He had no other life.

The boy did not call him.

Neither did the AssDepDG. Nor did Effie Bellingham. Vera had the wit to recognise his torment, and left a mug of coffee on the front step and the porch roof would keep the rain off it.

Eyes closed, but not asleep, Chopper heard bacon spit and smelled it frying.

Felt the wrap of love.

From the bedroom, he had a view of her in the kitchen. She wore only a T-shirt from the pile of his clothes on a chair by the window.

Was devoted. Had given himself. Thought it mutual. Knew it would take a powerful amount of planning to work through the potential difficulties of their lives ahead. A mass of fences to be cleared and ditches jumped – possibly a pack of baying dogs closing on them.

Had no doubt about her. Did not cross his mind that she might be the sort of girl who would gush interest in him, then change her mind. That he would soon enough fail to excite. That she would want to move on . . . That he might wake up one morning and see the other side of the bed empty, find a note propped against a bottle on the table . . . Would not happen.

He thought she was giving up more than he was.

Lay on his back, stretched.

Had been in the shower for a full fifteen minutes when they had come back from the beach. Had left the sleeping bag out on the grass, had brought the bottle in and binned it. Each had carried an armful of sodden clothes. Him in the shower, and her, and the steaming water sluicing down on them. Had thought the shower, even more than being outside in the sleeping bag, had marked the commitment each of them had made . . . the paratrooper and detective constable with the multimillionaire daughter of a premier-tier gang boss. Both moving on.

She brought his breakfast. The T-shirt hem was far above her knees. Had mugs of coffee in her other hand.

He knew the answer but asked it. "What do we owe them? Our families?"

She might have said that they were owed plenty. His had sent him down to the Gulf and had positioned him with his 'carers' on the breakwater. Hers had sent her down to the Gulf to oversee the *hawal* stage of the transaction, hidden money movement and based on trust, that paid a first-stage transaction of a 1,000 kg weight of uncut, pure heroin paste.

"Nothing. We owe them nothing."

"My people, your people?"

"There is that cord, whatever the name of it, and we've snapped it."

"For all time?"

"All time."

"Which takes us?"

"Wherever we want to go."

"I would be frightened, Julie, for you to walk off, find you gone."

"Never."

"We do not belong to them anymore. And will not be separated."

"A good place to be. Together . . ." Julie said. "You have walked away from the people who hired you. Afterwards they would have cut you adrift. I mean it. Let you float away, let you drown. I will destroy my father and then I am free. No regrets."

"I don't know where the bitch is," Lachy said.

Lyons, the solicitor, and keeper of the secrets, shrugged.

Cohn, keeper of the money, spat on the tangle of brambles and dead heather beside the path.

"Difficult age," said Lyons.

"Finds it hard to show gratitude," said Cohn.

"Gone from the face of the earth," said Lachy. "Phone switched off. No idea where she is. Dumped the Prof, hired a car we assume, disappeared."

He led them on. He know there would be more criticisms of his daughter, of Julie who was nominated as the future. They were wary, had the right to be. They would have understood they were being tested. The trap for both of them was to weigh in with a condemnation of the girl and then he would know they were not there for the long term, had no loyalty to her. Lachy Wilson's life – his climb to the top of the ladder – was about loyalty and trust.

He trusted these two – with limitations. Believed in their loyalty to him and to Vic, and ultimately to Julie, their daughter. They had been with him from the start. Had been picked up when he needed a decent brief and who now had no free slots in his diary for another employer. Lachy had been 19 years old when Yitzak Cohn had sent a junior from his office with a sealed note to tell Lachy that he and Vic were now valued at a million. Had been 21 years old when Henry Lyons sidled like an interloper into a gaming house and looked more out of place than a giraffe, and delivered the foolscap envelope that held the deeds to the property that was Lachy's first brothel, good-quality Estonian and Latvian girls, and cocked an eyebrow when asked if he wanted to stay. Two good men, he had always thought them, except that now the doubts seemed to pile higher ... too fucking comfortable. No longer fighting, no longer pulling the legs out from under a police investigation ... A detective who'd thought himself the bee's bollocks and who might have been closing on Lachy but found himself subject to a disciplinary inquiry and wiped off the board. A block of apartments in Bournemouth with a sea view for sale, and potential buyers flaking off when an asbestos problem had been discovered that other surveyors had missed, all except one – and him a friend of Yitzak. They had eased aside problems, they had constructed advantages, and when their talents were not appropriate then there was always Softboy's persuasion which had a record of success.

Lachy was fond of his chickens, all hand-reared, and he expected them to last a good ten years, but if they went off laying in summer, and ate too much, and messed with the ones that had the top egg record, then he would go in, pick up the offender, take it round the back, and wring its neck, fast, and take the corpse to the far edge of the property and chuck the carcase into the undergrowth. It was too old to get Mrs Plumb to roast the next Sunday, and stripping the feathers was a shit job anyway. Too fucking comfortable, both of them – and too clever that morning, the rain in their faces, and out on Newlands Corner, the high vantage point, to fall into his trap and criticise his daughter.

He tried one more time. "Just gone off. Phone's not on. This is a fair-sized deal, and we have a fat amount of capital about to be paid over, and she's disappeared. No word – which is not respectful. I give her everything, all the slack she needs, but she always wants more, and moody around the house to me and her mother. She's too fucking comfortable which is not something I like."

And neither of them rose to it. Might be loyalty, and might be that he was too obvious in the ploy, not as good at being devious as he had once been. He needed to trust his lawyer and his *consigliere* because he would never be able to find another pair of men, two who were clever enough and dishonest enough and reliable.

They talked some more about the payments that would be coming in once the shipment was inside the UK, and how the final payment would be made to those fucking people in the Gulf, and he felt a tiredness that rocked inside him, like age had caught him . . . No one ever retired in the ranks of the big men. He had never looked forward to spending his last years on a lounger beside the pool inside a complex of discreet villas at Estepona on the Costa. No one ever did. The big men kept running or were shot dead by some bastard they'd not even remember slighting, or shuffling along the landings of a maximum security place and needing the screws to give them a hand down the steep flights of stairs. Better to keep running, the only option.

Nothing he suggested was challenged. They went back to their cars.

Lachy Wilson prided himself on his ability to sense danger, see it building like clouds before a storm, and prided himself that he shelled out enough money to enough guys in the crime squads and among the senior detectives to give himself a trip-wire alarm system if that danger became serious. Rated himself, and rated the people he had bought.

"You'd have thought they'd have given us breakfast," was Rajah's first complaint of the day.

His anger might have been directed at the late take-off of the aircraft from London City, or that the car that had picked him up was filthy, or that the landing was against crosswinds and had done some bumps after hitting the tarmac.

"First stop will be for a plate of chips. Aren't they big on fries in Belgium?" said Dawson.

Not often that an ACU team had permission to travel abroad. Difficult because there was little chance of a senior authorising officer being given a thorough briefing on what they hoped to find, at what level of criminality, and how long they would need. Simple fact given was that it was 'an important investigation, one with a reasonable chance of progressing, and needed at all stages to be protected with abnormal security'. Peggy had done the negotiation and had seen the boss wince at the use of *important* and *security*. Their cash float and bookings – and the liaison with the Belgian Federals – had all been completed before the journey was rubber stamped. They were something of a law to themselves.

"Right, guys, heads down and at them," and a merciless grin from Plunket. They went through the passport checks. Was it so obvious they were cops? Must have been because the scanning of their faces and their travel documents was as fast as the machinery permitted. Each of them carried a holdall, and Peggy Dawson had a couple of laptops in a sagging rucksack hooked on one shoulder. She had been up before her kid, had left a bowl of out-of-date cereal on the kitchen table, and a glass of milk, and had requested that her neighbour came in to make sure the little beast hadn't nicked her fags while she was away. Plunket had expressed no regrets over the lack of food served on the plane, nor mentioned his car ride, nor spoken of the erratic landing. He was a man on a mission and had a somewhat manic look to him – about as near as he came to happiness.

They had been assured they would be met. Who by, what rank, what unit? Jacques, bottle-washer, Federal attached to the liaison team working out of the Port Liaison unit.

She said he would be a 'total plonker', Rajah said he would be an 'utter wanker'. They had known who was meeting them, and his pedigree, the night before, but going through it again was a sort of necessary ritual condemnation. A good stride, in step, from the three of them.

They had agreed that Dawson would lead the negotiation with the liaison, and Rajah would back her and, if necessary, Plunket would demand more senior help, better facilities. The trio had never been abroad before as a unit, and none spoke much French, and not a syllable of Walloon, but all would have been confident that a firm voice, spoken slowly and with volume, would get them through.

The stakes were about as high as they get, Dawson would have said. What every ACU officer would have dreamed of in Rajah's estimation. The jewel in the crown, Plunket's definition . . . He was the only one of them who had actually laid eyes on Lachlan Wilson: seven years before, in Serious and Organised Crime, six months before transferring, watching comings and goings at a casino and the Person of Interest was not the short stubby guy that was Wilson. But the woman in the car with him had hissed excitedly on recognising him. Seen him just the once but for long enough to see the authority and the confidence. Since then he had heard plenty. Had read all the files, prised out those ones that were supposed to have restricted access. Knew enough to comprehend the value of such a catch, and what it would do for his career . . . The daughter was a highlighted individual and Intelligence said she was being groomed for the future. There was a conduit that would lead them to the target – a member of the Flying Squad, a detective constable, who had flown with the daughter to Leipzig. No explanation given by his outfit who seemed to Plunket to have more interest in obstruction than following up a query. It was the route in, and they were like three out-of-shape bloodhounds who had been given a well-worn sock to sniff and now had a trail to follow. The doors yawned open in front of them.

"There he is – stands out like a bloody lighthouse, total plonker."

"Utter wanker."

In front of them stood a middle-aged man in an ill-fitting grey suit, a bulge below the jacket breast pocket. His hair needed the attention of a comb and he had shaved poorly so that he had a nick on the upper lip. He glanced at his watch and fidgeted, and . . .

Plunket said, "Gratifying that they've sent the top team to meet us."

'Let you out, have they? Thought you were on 'further consideration'. Weren't you supposed to hit the target nearer the centre?'

The armourer at the station had turned away to examine a shelf behind him for an appropriate Five-seven to hand Jacques. The man was known for his gallows humour, bordered on rudeness, and always got a laugh from other officers in the queue. Just a titter earlier that morning, crack of dawn and him first in the queue and waiting for the grille to be lifted, not a minute before opening time.

The weapon was passed him, and two magazines, and forty rounds clattered out on the counter.

'Should be enough for you, Jacques, even on semi-automatic. Just make sure you bloody well behave yourself.'

He had managed a weak smile and could hear the shuffling behind him from the 'expert' firearms people, those who protected the VIPs running the port and the Customs section. He signed with a shaky finger on a screen. At the back of the armoury he had slipped off his raincoat and jacket and had eased on the holster straps, and then had taken the time to load the two magazines, and his fingers had been clumsy and one bullet had fallen on the floor and had rolled, and the queue had allowed him to scrabble at their feet to retrieve it. He had slotted one filled magazine into the pistol butt, and one of the Close Protection team had sniggered, 'Don't use them all today, mate.' Had one consoling thought. They were as much innocents as himself. Had never done it. Excellent chance that they would spend twenty years on the detail and never fire an 'operational' shot, had no cause to sneer but they did, and wore dungarees and ankle coverings and bulletproof vests and had kit loaded on their chests. They were arrogant but without cause, which made him feel better, considerably better.

The three came towards him. Perfunctory handshakes. He introduced himself, just his first name. They were DI Plunket, DS Rajah and DS Dawson. Had they had a good flight, apart from being late? Not particularly because the weather was lousy, winds in Antwerp were gusting to strong, the pilot had brought them down but without obvious talent, and that was it.

He had been allocated a people carrier, a Renault. Not from the pool, because there was a shortage, and he had been late getting through the paperwork from the garage and then had flipped a speed camera on his way to the airport. Not the best start . . . but one aspect of his life pleased him. He had the weighted shoulder holster. They walked with him to the police compound where he had parked.

Reasonable enough question for Jacques to ask as they settled in. What did they want? What programme did they have for the day?

The woman said, "Good question, Jacques. But we don't have a good answer. What we know is that two men and a woman are coming through here in the next twenty-four hours. Names are Kenny Harris and Julie Wilson and Walter Genge. All UK citizens. Don't know how they are arriving, or when they leave. They have open tickets and we are assuming departure is tomorrow, Sunday, or Monday at latest. We are looking for help . . . big help. Harris is a collaborator. Wilson is a part of an Organised Crime Group, and a relevant family, Genge is her minder. It is sensitive, and—"

"And you are hesitant, Miss Dawson, in trusting us – in particular *me*?"

She blustered, "I didn't say that."

He spoke confidently, and had that necessary weight against his chest, and the tightness of his buttoned jacket to prove it. "Seemed implied. I will help if I know how I can help."

"They matter to us, but we don't know where they are. We believe a shipment is transiting through Antwerp."

Jacques said, "We have become a narcotics lavatory because of the size of our docks. My superiors say that this city is on the front line in the war against Class A drugs coming on to the continent of Europe. Neighbouring Holland is almost a narco state, their own admission. We have the highest percentage of cocaine users of any community in Europe, higher than your capital city. Even our racing pigeons are doped up for better performance. The sewers of south Antwerp are laced with benzoylecgonine – cocaine after it passes through the human body. We discover some ten per cent of cocaine coming through the port, but the trade is worth perhaps sixty billion Euros. We have in our country the rotting pillars of society. We have desperate levels of corporate corruption, and even the customs men working at the port, more than three thousand of them, have to protect their identities if they are to avoid bribery or intimidation. The Mafia is more important as an enemy than terrorism. Are you absorbing this?"

"We are," she said. "Except that we are not interested in cocaine. Not our problem. We are not concerned with Class A stuff coming *in*, only what we believe will go *out*. We do not need a lecture on your unfortunate statistics."

Jacques felt powerful. He felt also they were unwilling to share their degree of helplessness, but were forced to put a begging bowl on his lap.

The rain dribbled on the windscreen. They would have had an early start. Probably hungry and tired, apparently at the edge of their experience, and he sensed the fear they demonstrated that precious intelligence could be dissipated in loose talk, or by simple corruption . . .

"Those names. Where do we find them?" asked Dawson.

"And then?"

"Surveillance, which we will do."

"Without the paperwork and bureaucracy?"

"Without."

Jacques was smiling broadly. Everything now seemed attractive, desirable, as worth following as that huge shadowy shape that had swum in front of him when he had tipped his supply of maggots into the canal.

"Which name is the priority?"

They said, in unison, that it was the name of the one they called the 'minder'. Chimed the name.

He fed the information into the system. Walter Genge, his age, and his passport number. Did not say for what reason, or for whose benefit. He asked them if they had any accommodation, and felt happy and wanted, which was rare. He drove them towards the city, and began to tell them about the history of the country's most famous artist, Peter Paul Rubens, born in 1577 and died in 1640, and where he had employed his 'factory' of apprentices. They had to listen, because they were dependent on him, and it was the same talk that he had given to a German team from Stuttgart and a French squad from Marseilles.

As if his resolve had fractured, and approaching the time that Jonas would have a mug of soup in the kitchen, he phoned the Assistant Deputy Director General. The number rang out. Normally it was answered, within seconds, with a brusque one-word acknowledgement. Each time the connection was made, the AssDepDG would have known it was Jonas, and would give the same blunt response as to a stranger . . . the same degree of enthusiasm as Jonas himself used. But it kept on ringing. It was a mark of his desperation to speak to a colleague, someone with a keen knowledge of *Humble Pie*, that he kept the phone at his ear. Vera had gone to the Co-op, then would go on to the gallery where she worked and would be helping with a new catalogue. He was alone, could manage a mug of soup, powder in a sachet and hot water from the kettle, would not be stretched by the necessary procedure. He was severely taxed by his inability to talk with either of the colleagues inside the loop. He tried again.

Heard the breathing, then a smoker's cough. Announced himself.

"Of course I know who it is, Jonas. You're all over my screen and that bloody cat of yours."

Said that he supposed the AssDepDG would want a catch-up résumé . . .

"Don't waste your breath, my friend. Just keep on being our much loved grumpy old fucker. Want to know where I am? Probably not, but I'll tell you. Am waiting to be collected from hospital which means that my darling wife has had to cancel a game of tennis in order to fetch me. Fell on my bloody shoulder. Clumsy, stupid, painful, I don't advise it. Needed an operation. Had a window last night, end of their busy day and they squeezed me in . . . I've become rather self-interested, Jonas. That means my shoulder, the backside of a nurse from Turks and Caicos, the guy opposite having a hard time, the lunch menu and I've ordered 'meatless meat balls', how to pee into a cardboard thing, when I'm having my next dose of codeine and paracetamol, when the constipation will kick in to a serious level, all of that is at the top of my agenda. Got me, Jonas? The dear old Defence of the Realm – whatever it is that we are supposed to do – has slipped down the pecking order. A physio has just given me a grim list of exercises that I am going to have to work on to get mobility back. That is the key word in my life now, Jonas, *mobility*, and it comes way in front of worrying about what is going to be shipped into the UK, who is doing it, and why I should give a flying fuck. Extraordinary how being here has put things into an altered perspective, and all for a hockey game where my girl was bloody useless, on a well-beaten side, and she managed a goal that changed nothing . . . Could be the same as *Humble Pie*, Jonas. Changed nothing. Anyway, you stay all excited and please don't bother me again, unless you can give me the recipe for meatless meatballs. A new perspective, friend, and quite energising . . ."

The call ended. Almost in a state of shock, Jonas laid the phone on the table.

He went to the unit beside the sink and took the dried soup packet from a cupboard, cut the top off, put the contents in a mug – one that had a transferred colour photograph of Olaf on it – put water in the kettle, switched it on.

And he was shaking. Only the squeal of the kettle broke the quiet, and he felt betrayed . . . Took the mug outside, and collected a hoe from the shed at the end of the garden.

He put the phone back in his pocket.

An officer in Charlie Company had once talked of a 'Rubicon moment', something about 'no turning back' and the casting of an arrow along with the crossing of a river, and something to do with their dawn mission of going into a villagers' compound and searching for weapons, and putting all the hearts and minds crap on to a bonfire.

Pretty simple. Photos of each page that Julie had written, done in her posh girls' school hand and easy to read. Attached a note that was cheeky, verged on impertinence – neither of which concerned him. *What you were looking for?*

She had loaded the car. Their clothes were still damp, and a wind cut through, and the coast looked grey and the clouds scurried but the hail might come later. The next stage, the Rubicon moment, would come that evening. The drive to Hamburg and then another ring road, and then across to Bremen and the *auto-bahn* down to Osnabruck and Cologne, seven hours – not more – after the turn into Belgium and another fast and busy route on to the port city. The BMW saloon would eat it. They fastened their seatbelts and kissed, but with the naturalness of age-old lovers, neither frightened of losing the moment, like all of that was settled, had a permanence.

"Your people, if they had their hands on us, what would they do for what we have done?"

"Do to us?"

"To us."

"Depends on how much time they had. Top of the list would be us. More than sorting out the mayhem would be us. They would like to think about it, if they could, and then they'd come up with something clever. Kill us, of course. Inflict pain, of course. Do it slow, if possible. If they had a chance to do what I'd call clever then they would enjoy that challenge. It is the way it is. Always has been . . . part of the fabric of life, and important because it ensures the faint-hearted stay disciplined. Not just a kick on the shin against their authority – my dad's and my mum's and their names and reputation. What I have done is why they will be sitting in separate cells on a landing that is only for serious people. And they will be there for months and years. Their muscles will atrophy and start to collapse through lack of exercise, and their minds will go stale, and they will have time for hatred. All they can cling to is how bad it was for us who put them there . . . it is what you signed up to, Chopper. Hot coals and a fire, pincers that can peel the skin off your back, fingernails and toenails off. Which is why we will not be around when they have the chance to think of what we deserve. Did you want to hear that?"

"What I expected to hear."

Chopper gunned the engine. He supposed that anyone with a faint heart would have anticipated the answer, and would have stayed well clear of the bridge, and meeting the guy on it. Remembered seeing him come over the crest, and hiding in deep shadow and being seen, and Sunray scurrying off towards his station.

"No turning back," she said.

"Onwards and upwards."

"Necessary?"

"It is. Doing it put us together. It is like a contract. Pledged to do it, you and me. Like we signed on the line."

"A bit bloody awesome, Julie."

"A bit."

A hug and a squeeze and the power taking them forward and gravel crunching under the wheels, and work to be done.

Julie Wilson had gained the notoriety that entitled her to a label which designated her as the lowest of the low.

She was the snitch. For as long as she could remember, it was the word for those who scraped the bottom of any barrel. There were also 'tout' and 'rat', and in police terms there was 'confidential informant'. But for condemnation, an offence for which no form of mercy was ever shelled out, 'snitch' was unique. She understood that.

Believed it about the only thing that scared her father.

A man vulnerable to a snitch was regarded among contemporaries, and equals and those down the ladder, as a man who could not control those he allowed close to him.

She knew that successful prosecutions using the information provided by a snitch depended on the evidence of a protected witness. Such a person was usually hooded and masked and hustled into a court building – Snaresbrook in east London was the usual one – hemmed in with armed police, and would give evidence from behind a screen that prevented all but the judge, the barristers, the jury, and the accused from seeing their face. They would be savaged by defence counsel, treated as lesser vermin and with a perpetual sneer below the perched wigs. Admired by nobody, outside of society . . . Then taken out, again inside a security bubble, and into a vehicle with privacy windows, and lost in society. New name, new identity, funds that might last a few months, cut loose . . . If found, they were dead. If not found, they were forever looking over a shoulder, fearful of dark nights, terrified of shadows.

She had the title, but not that future.

She would not be behind the screen, would not be seen by her father. Not seen by any of them. Would be gone . . . lost . . . disappeared . . . What she had provided on the four sheets of paper – and had watched Chopper use his phone to photograph them – was enough to give *them*, those who fed off the snitch, the evidence to follow and which would convict, and her name not necessarily appearing, and her part in bringing him down irrelevant to his guilt. All done, all wrapped up. She owed her father nothing. Julie believed that if she said it often enough in the privacy of her mind then it would be true.

"Could always put him in a bath, an acid one," Lachy mused.

"Do we know anyone who has one?" Vic murmured. "Not a cup of sugar, not what you borrow from a neighbour."

"Or put him in a wood chipper."

"Often wondered – he'd be alive, of course – better to go in feet first or head first?" Vic pouted at him.

"He'll go in something, I'm thinking – hope he enjoys the risotto."

"He will, and the prawns will have defrosted," and both laughing and forgetting that they did not know where was their daughter, their Julie, who was the future.

Hard times were facing the shipping and removal company which repatriated diplomats' possessions and brought them home. The British purse had shrunk, and the number of men and women employed by the Foreign, Commonwealth and Development office. Enough remained to keep the company in business, and of course there were fringe benefits negotiated by the company's chief executive which eased the pain of diminishing orders.

Outside the Embassy of the United Kingdom on Kawalerii Street in the Polish capital city of Warsaw, the last furniture was loaded into a shipping container. The men who did the heavy lifting were from Hertfordshire, north of London, and were considered by their employer to be diligent and helpful. Not much to be loaded but just enough to trigger the right of this diplomat, on the consular staff, to require the shipping facility. The crew had also made sure there was access behind a particular chest of drawers and access wide enough for a tonne of wrapped cargo to be manoeuvred to a false panel against the far end of the container. A girl, bright as a button, had come up with the solution that minimised the risk of a search. The diligence and help came at a price.

The doors were shut on the container that was astride a trailer and towed by a Ford truck. They hoped to be in Antwerp on Sunday afternoon so that their iron crate would be into the port area and shifted by Monday midday, and they would return home on a ferry from Calais. Quite a cushy life, as the security man remarked to the carriers, and wished them well.

Only a severe bout of impatience had driven Jonas into his garden, which he hardly visited even in a balmy summer.

He worked with the hoe as if a fury gripped him.

Could not fathom what his protector had said, the AssDepDG who fed the tasks in his direction, shielded him sufficiently from the kicks of the bureaucrats, the kangaroos on the second floor, made the resources available, and without scrutiny, kept him safe and deflected talk of retirement – and now showed a professed lack of interest.

Vera usually did the garden, was dedicated and conscientious, and little remained for him to cut, loosen, kill.

There was mud on his hands, his ankles were drenched, dead leaves were stuck on his brogues, and his trilby was at an angle.

His mug of soup was untouched on the patio table and was now overflowing with rainwater.

To have said, and it had been, that *Humble Pie* 'changed nothing' was as grievous a personal wound as he had ever received. He hacked between the shrubs' roots, disturbed sleeping crocus bulbs, and vented his anger at the ground, and had no message, and . . . her voice was clear, almost sad.

"For heaven's sake, Jonas, what are you doing? Show a bit of phlegm. Your phone is flashing. Why didn't you take it outside with you? . . . In case you are interested, I've done our gallery catalogue, my part of it. Olaf hasn't been fed. Hope you're not expecting to tramp that muck into the kitchen . . ."

She was holding up his phone. Vera could manage a world-weary look, as if she carried crosses, and could milk a moment.

He dropped the hoe. His trilby fell off.

She was his wife of thirty-five years, and some said she deserved canonisation, and her look now was droll as she handed him the phone.

He read, *What you were looking for?* Read it four or five times, as if fearful the message deceived him. Jonas barely realised that the kitchen door was closed, that he was not permitted entry. He typed the code that revealed the confidential message. He scanned through it fast . . . when a lorry would arrive at a rendezvous on the outskirts of Antwerp, when another lorry would haul a container to the same place, when a transfer would take place and the container would move into the port area for shipment to Felixstowe on the English east coast. Where it would be met by Lachy Wilson in person. Before that, Lachy Wilson would authorise a transfer of monies . . . and Lachy Wilson would be using a phone with the number of . . . and the contacts for Lachy Wilson were the accountant Yitzak Cohn and the solicitor Henry Lyons . . . and Lachy Wilson . . . and Julie Wilson must, *must*, personally supervise the transfer . . .

Jones wiped the rain from his face and his spectacles and could barely see, and his cheeks ran with water and his trousers were tight on his shins and his small amount of hair was plastered down, and his shoes were caked at the uppers.

Jonas raised his fist towards a leaden sky. He let loose a guttural cry that represented, in his world, triumph. Perhaps the Derbyshires, from an upstairs window, spotted him: perhaps those on the other side would have seen over the top of the laurel bush, and wondered what pills he was swallowing. A clenched fist lifted. A shout to wake the dead and alert the living, and maybe frighten Olaf, and perhaps amuse his wife. And did it again. He had never made such a gesture before, or such a sound. His work, his instinct, his idea and his recruitment, and his ability to weather the sneers and the tutting of disbelief from the few who had been briefed on what he would do. His sense of fatigue had fled. Jonas Merrick had accomplished what was considered impossible.

He was allowed inside, made to stand on the mat, and told to shed his wet clothing.

12

Did Jonas want to go to the garden centre?

"No."

Didn't they need more pansies and primulas, Vera suggested, since the previous planting last autumn had been so damaged by rain?

"No."

Did he not need *something*?

"Yes."

Not *something* but *somebody*. Somebody with whom he could share that treasure trove of the enterprise detail soon to be played out close to the port at Antwerp. Had had his little moment in the garden, behaving similarly to a football hooligan. In previous years, before he had debunked from Room 12 on the third floor, he had occupied a cubicle, partitioned off from the territory of Aggie Burns who ran a section of the surveillance crowd. They had moments of disaster, usually when one of the team on foot 'showed out' and a target went missing, an operation in a state of collapse. The rest of the group could only shrug, agree that such was life, and an investigation would start, and two years' work might be binned, and a bad boy given the wink that he was being watched. Then, the team would leave the room, drift away in broken groups, no doubt slagging off the unhappy beggar who had blown it . . . and there were also moments of triumph. A guy, a mobile phone off the radar, picked up and showing on the screen. Because of them an arrest was being made, they were on the ground and calling in the armed muscle and a bad boy was face-down on the pavement, wrists handcuffed in the small of his back, and the bomb due to go off wherever and they'd return to the building on a high. Later they would head off down to the pub on Horseferry Road and would camp there for the evening, and stagger in the next morning, wan and pale. Either way, win or lose, they could share. Not Jonas.

Had he explained his feelings, which he had not, Vera would have understood. But it was a law inside the Service that wives, partners, girlfriends, boyfriends, should not be used as cheapskate confidants, not in good times or bad. It was a big moment, the receipt of the battle plan for the importation to the UK of a tonne of heroin, fresh off the Afghan poppy fields, and indicated that a task had been set for the rounded shoulders of Jonas Merrick and he had triumphed.

The AssDepDG had retreated into the self-satisfied world of a patient. His assistant, on whom he had lavished attention, in his view, was off in Scotland and apparently planning a wedding there and had ditched him. Even the two weekday 'friends', Kev and Leroy, who carried the big machine pistols and saw him across the road – and had saved his life – were off for the weekend. If he were not able to enjoy a brief spurt of pleasure, excitement, and elusive triumph, then what was the point of slaving at this treadmill? One man . . . he knew of one. The chance of him being within reach was doubtful. He thought he had no other option.

"I'm sorry, Vera. I know it is Saturday. I am also aware that tomorrow we are supposed to be hauling the caravan to the Isle of Purbeck. I am aware that my explanations are sparse, and that my intentions and actions are occasionally less than obvious, and . . ."

"Oh, for God's sake, Jonas, get to the damn point. Stop waffling."

"I'm going out," he said. Seemed a big moment. Saturday afternoon, leaving Raynes Park and heading somewhere, going to meet somebody, for the purpose of sharing and getting a degree of peace of mind.

"Where to?"

"To London, to the office."

"Is that all? The way you said it I presumed you were at least crossing through Checkpoint Charlie, or wading over the wire on the 38th Parallel, strolling up the High Street in Crossmaglen."

She turned away, went into the kitchen, and the cat followed her. He was alone, his coat within reach, and his hat, both sodden, and would need to exchange his slippers for his shoes. He had expected to be asked what should be done about his supper, always a chop on a Saturday. And what time would he back? Not asked. Nor any suggestion that this was about the Verona couple, his matchmaking, his manipulation of the Montague boy who was Chopper and the Capulet girl who was Julie Wilson. Coat on, hat on, both cold from the wet, his briefcase locked to his wrist, nothing in it except a woollen scarf. Had his wallet and would need to buy his train ticket.

He called out that he was leaving. She did not answer.

He went out into the afternoon. He needed first to share, then to get business done. Because that is what it was about: the business, not the individuals for whom he was not obliged to take responsibility.

The destination?

Chopper said, "Where no one knows us."

Julie said, "New lives, the past washed away."

"Anywhere . . ."

"Anywhere is good enough."

Soft voices, mixing easily with the radio's music and the station was in Belgium VivaCité, Liège Radio.

She was nestled against his shoulder, still Julie Wilson. Would be the girl of that name, that passport number, for another few hours, perhaps forty-eight, then would have disappeared. Might go to Cologne to buy the new documents with electronic back-up into the systems of governments and Europol, or might go further, to Prague: it was said there were good technicians who could handle 'identity renewal' in Sofia or Bucharest, and some said that the very best were now in Kyiv because that was a fractured society that required the ability to lose old records . . .

Behind them, on another *autobahn*, was the lorry loaded with the stuff for sale produced in Turkey, and also the more precious merchandise hidden away on the trailer bulkhead. Also coming west, and observing all the laws of the road, was the cab that pulled a shipping container with a load of diplomats' furniture and personal possessions and with space for a further tonne of cargo. This part of her life had an ever-diminishing time to run. She had no doubts, felt secure; his breathing was steady, he would protect her.

"God, how can this guy be so fucking boring?"

Jacques, the Federal policeman, was spinning out minutes, then hours . . . driving the three British police visitors around his home city, taking the opportunity to acquaint them with aspects of its history. He ignored the remark made by the Asian. Jacques drove, the woman beside him, and the two men shared the bench seat and he registered the impatience that shimmied at his ears, and thought little effort was made to hide their frustration.

"This is the Grote Market, the centre point of the city. Very historic, and you will see the statue where the nude figure holds up a severed hand. Silvius Brabo had heard of a giant who controlled access to the city down the Scheldt river, and charged big tolls to merchants attempting to trade. If they refused to pay him, he cut off their hands. The Roman legionary fought the giant, who was named Druon Antigoon, and managed to slice off his hand at the wrist and he hurled the hand over his shoulder, and that is where the name of our city comes from. And now, on your right, is the house of the Crossbowmen and there many British-based merchants were active. I think we should drive further . . ."

"Fucking hell," the Asian muttered.

Not much else that Jacques could have done. The names had been fed by him into 'the system', and a promise given him that they would be processed, checked against hotels, guest houses, short-hire apartments, anywhere that required production of a passport, and his phone had only rung once when his wife had asked if he would be back for dinner. Doubtful. He had checked them into their accommodation: near the station and the zoo, a clinical and modern place, that suited business people who were subject to budget restrictions. He felt good, confident, had already formed the opinion that the trio were outside the parameters of their experience, were thrashing in the water, were dependent on him. He drove to the river and its esplanade and pointed out the intricacies in the architecture of the castle – which had never been fought over, never attacked, was mostly a royal residence, and now a museum ... He added that the city was short of military experience and remarked on its 'quiet' war during the German occupation when collaboration had been marginally acceptable, and the Resistance had been slow to form.

"Mostly the castle was a prison. Much feared by the men who were brought here. Very few who went in came out alive. It was a place of executions. We cannot see it now, which is unfortunate, but there is a carving by the gate of a religious symbol and it was there that condemned people were permitted to pause and say a prayer, for the salvation of their souls but not in the hope of mercy. Even today, the dungeons are frightening ... I am starting to receive information. I can tell you that at this time we have no knowledge of the woman, Julie Wilson, being in Antwerp, not at any accommodation where she might have checked in. No record."

He heard a concerted hiss of disappointment from beside and behind.

Jacques drove on, at a snail's pace and with time to kill. He told them that to the right was the 'red light quarter' of the city. "It is based on the streets of the *schipperskwartier* and an effort has been made to keep out organised crime groups, and the mayor signs off each 'window' where the girls can be viewed by the customers before they enter. There is, the city authorities say, a very high standard of cleanliness in all the premises ..."

From behind him, "Has he shares in the place? Do we get a fucking discount?"

They were away from the river, and all had lapsed into silence. Jacques said that it was ten euros to see inside the cathedral but for official visitors it was free, and they would qualify, and he pointed out the statue of a boy and a dog, cuddled together and covered by a blanket that was in fact cobblestones. "The boy and his dog were from a story written by a British woman and they were refused entry to the cathedral in the dead of winter, and they slept together outside in the bitter cold, and in the morning both had died from hypothermia . . . not a happy story."

The woman beside him turned, grimaced, as if her patience was required, buckets of it.

Jacques said, "Nor do we have any record of a man named on his passport as Kenny Harris booking accommodation in the city."

Enough said, and he lapsed to silence.

Lachy Wilson sat in the deep chair in the snug off the hall which he used for his more serious thinking.

"I suppose I could always strangle him – take a bit of an effort, but possible."

Opposite him sat his wife. The snug was where their deep and far-reaching decisions were made, and the room was swept at least once a month, and always the radio was on loud when they talked.

Vic Wilson shrugged. "How long would that take?"

"I read that one of those Sicilians, fucking great hands they have, said it might need as much as four minutes, but I suppose if he were bashed on the head first and not struggling then it might be quicker."

"Too long, Lachy. I'd say you'd aggravate your hernia – and you wouldn't want that."

"No, Vic, I wouldn't . . . Hurts, that hernia. Should get something done about it. Best would be to bash him twice."

"Maybe the risotto'll do the job. Between us, Ma Plumb and me, we didn't fully defrost the prawns. They'll warm up a bit, but not fully . . . I'll serve him the most."

She laughed, but coldly.

He laughed, but warmer – like food poisoning was an added option that he had not considered. The dogs hadn't barked and would have been licking Softboy's hands because they had known him all their lives, but Lachy was alerted when he heard the voices in the kitchen.

They went out of the snug, and he locked the door. Both showed pleasure at the sight of Softboy, and hugged him because it was a friendship that went far back. Had been beside each other since the glory days.

He ended the call, shut down the strident complaint. Did the guy want the information that Jonas carried on his phone, or did he not? Did he want a sharing of Jonas's information, or did he not? Sitting on his familiar bench, Jonas reflected on its source.

Any weekday morning he would have been there, whatever the weather, among the gravestones of St John's Gardens with his beaker of coffee and a pastry. The birds would have been clustering at his feet awaiting crumbs. Quite different on a wet Saturday afternoon as it merged into early evening. On those mornings a solitary gardener pushed a barrow around the paths and between the lichen-coated stones and used a shovel to lift up debris that had been meticulously swept into small heaps. There was no sign of a barrow loaded with gardening tools, but the gardener sat on a bench on another path, his head sunk on his chest, and from to time he convulsed as if stifling a coughing fit. To Jonas Merrick, the gardener was a kindred spirit.

He knew something of the man, but much too little for the detail of expression and character . . . Jonas was happy with just the generalities of personality when he pushed people forward – all, of course, volunteers. The gardener was a former soldier, a veteran of that awful campaign out of Basra in southern Iraq, and invalided home with the symptoms of post-traumatic stress disorder. A charity for disabled servicemen had found him maintenance work in this garden, and spotted there. A woman from the Fivers who ran an operation – without strict legal sanction – to bring a form of justice down onto the head of a Russian born crime baron, and the gardener recruited as 'deniable', and the mission clouded in an absence of detail had ended, it was said, successfully. But the man believed to have reinvented an old life and pulled a trigger, was left with further and more acute symptoms of that debilitating condition. He answered Jonas's questions with short staccato responses. The interrogations always dealt with the morality of command and its responsibilities. He was a sounding board for Jonas, and greatly valued, though voiced thanks were sparse . . . Had been used, had been cut free, and kept the garden in a good state. That evening the only occupants were Jonas and the gardener – and Jonas clapped his hands sharply, made a gesture with his hand, like a summons, and the man reluctantly, with effort, stood and began to walk towards him.

Jonas was not proud of his call across the park, thought it both pompous and rude, but had done it from need.

"I want some answers, friend, must have them better to know myself."

A scratchy voice, sandpaper on seasoned wood, "Ask, but I make no promise."

"Nor should you. My question, to whom did you owe loyalty in the deployment to Iraq? To the Crown, the State, to your Regiment, your officer, the rest of your platoon? Who mattered to you?"

"To myself."

"You did not feel a loyalty to the symbols of power, or even to the men you lived with?"

"I did the best for myself . . . When I was lost, cut off from a patrol, alone, they did not come looking for me. Or if they did, they did not find me. I did it for myself, was my own rescuer."

"That was your first contact with extreme danger, then I believe you were sent to kill a man, which you did. Were you then welcomed home?"

"I was not. Went back to my digs, down the road from here, found a letter on the floor. A note from the bank about money paid in, and something was deducted for food and accommodation. And the council confirmed I had been on unpaid leave and was expected back at work on the following Monday."

"Not acknowledged where you had been, and what you had achieved?"

"Not then, not now."

"Which means?"

"I go my own way."

"What does that add up to?"

He saw, from street lights beyond the garden's railings, a smile slowly appear at the gardener's face, wry and without humour. "I look after myself. Expect no one else to, sir. Would you excuse me?"

The man turned away and began a shuffling walk through the shadows back towards the bench where he had been sitting. Jonas assumed these gardens were his real home, not the bedsit address to which his brown envelopes and junk mail were delivered. He thought a truth had been given him: Chopper would follow that same route, go his own way, look after himself . . . Which suited Jonas well because then he would be free of all responsibility.

The ACU team had been offered food and had declined it with various levels of politeness.

"No, I don't want any food."

"Thank you, not hungry," from Plunket.

"Not even mussels and chips, though I might just get round to murder if that was the way I could get my hands on a pint of gin with a dash of tonic," Peggy Dawson said. They were in a corner of a car park and the overhead light was in need of maintenance. Jacques droned on. Her stomach growled and her bottle of water, nicked from the aircraft trolley, was long finished. Actually, she had come to rather admire the man who hosted them. Could have said that it was the end of his shift and time to be getting home, dumped them at their hotel and told them what time in the morning he would pick them up, and who he would take them to see. She sensed that he realised they wanted as little contact with the police spider web as was possible, were fearful of becoming enmeshed in its bureaucracy.

But he had not abandoned them. What she also liked was that he smoked incessantly and that the fumes were blown hard at the dashboard where an *Interdiction de fumer* sign was stuck, and she had felt emboldened and had rolled a fag, slim as a knitting needle, and he had lit it for her.

He said, "We had colourful rulers here because of the wealth of the city in mediaeval times. It was long recognised for its safe anchorage. Julius Caesar understood that. Yes, he was here. They enjoyed grand names, the rulers . . . we had Baldwin the Iron Arm, and we had Charles the Wild. There was John the Fearless and Joanna the Mad – and Philip the Handsome, and the city's importance was recognised in the time of Charlemagne. Do you think you have had sufficient history fed to you, or would you like more . . . ?"

A groan from behind her.

" . . . Or would you like me to take you, dear lady, to a bar where they will serve you a very pleasant gin, our national drink, the *Genever* variety? For your colleagues there would be the chance to take a local beer, very popular and light on the stomach, the Pintje brew, which is like a *pils* drink. Or, you might wish me to drive you to the hotel where the British citizen, Walter Genge, is already booked in. Which would you prefer? Food, drink, or the address where Genge stays? Which?"

From Peggy Dawson there was a spontaneous kiss for Jacques.

A grunt from Rajah behind her, and a blow from a clenched fist against the Federal's shoulder. "You are a fucking genius, my friend. Up there with the bloody angels that my team worship."

From Plunket: "And don't spare the horses, as they say."

She sensed it was a long time since a virtual stranger had kissed him on both cheeks with such sincerity. And had a momentary thought of the KISS principle of which she was an avid believer. Keep It Simple, Stupid. Liked it, and thought it the basis of decent, proper, old-fashioned policing . . . and liked very much the way he had dropped that jewel into their laps and wondered whether he had nurtured it for one minute or ten before letting them know what he had . . .

Jacques drove fast up a main drag, the pavements nearly empty, and veered past oncoming trolley buses. Ahead of them was the huge and ponderous front of the train station, a statement of the place's importance, hotels on either side, and he parked in a side street.

She took a camera out of her bag, a big lens attached, and snapped the illuminated front entrance Jacques indicated. Just an ordinary street in an ordinary European city, and the start of the waiting time.

The room was at the front of the hotel.

Wally Genge had expected that Julie would have arrived by now . . . Had a sense of failure and the nagging of it increased by the hour. He had moved the one comfortable chair in the room close to the window and sat there with a volume of his beloved poetry. Wally Genge had been sliding towards a state of despair – Robert Browning, Charles Kingsley, Coventry Patmore – and was about to go into the deep and sentimental misery of Emily Brontë . . . He used his phone as sparingly as he thought possible, had told his employer of her disappearance, would send a coded message when she arrived, had tried her phone but it had rung out. It was the first time, since he had been given responsibility for the security of Lachy's daughter, that he felt himself nudging failure. Felt sorry enough for himself to indulge his unhappiness with her lines from 'Remembrance': *Cold in the earth – and the deep snow piled above thee,* and read in a soft whisper with his whiny voice which gave the words, his belief, more meaning.

He saw a BMW saloon with German plates; it was slowing and the vehicle behind it acknowledged the manoeuvre and was pulling out to pass. *Far, far removed, cold in the dreary grave!* It stopped at the hotel entrance. Engine still running, a front passenger door opening. Legs appearing and a holdall chucked from the vehicle and landing on the pavement, and here she was. The line stared up at him from the page. *Have I forgot, my only Love, to love thee.* God, they must have been a miserable lot, back at the end of the nineteenth century, forever harping on about graveyards, failed love. The book slid off his lap. Julie looked clapped out from the light thrown down on her, like she'd hardly slept, her clothes crumpled and her hair a mess. She leaned into the car and the driver would have been stretching across. Saw a boy's face. A young man. Lips together, a kiss. She was reaching inside and tousling his hair and he was running a finger across her chin. Lovers . . .

Not supposed to happen without the blessing of Lachy Wilson. No romance permitted unless sanctioned by Lachy Wilson, like she was the fatted calf and reserved for when the time was right. The Prof's job was to keep a gimlet eye on her so that it did not happen. Failing that – at the start of a possible romance – he was to pass on the detail to her father. What they employed him for – to mind her. The car eased away from the kerb. She stood on the pavement and watched it till the lights held it at the end of the street, and it waited before turning onto the Keyserlei. Only when it had turned did Julie hoist up her bag and head inside. He picked up the book, and contemplated. The line leaped at him. *Severed at last by Time's all-severing wave?* Would have been good to have been able to ask Miss Emily Jane Brontë if what he had seen represented lust or passion or love, put the question to her because she would have been the expert . . . The Prof required guidance on what to report back to Lachy Wilson. Everything, or nothing? Play the faithful servant or the dumb fool?

The boy? Nice-looking, and he had smiled as their mouths slipped apart. The image of the face stayed with him. He scratched at it. Was supposed to have a good memory for faces, one of the talents that had been recognised by Lachy Wilson at his recruitment so many years before – and was supposed to have a good nose, and . . . He stood, pulled the chair back into place beside the mini-bar, put the plastic room key into his hip pocket, and left the room.

Crossed the foyer and made a line for Reception.

"Hi, Julie . . ."

She turned. She flushed. "Hi, Prof – how you doing?"

"Good, and you?"

"Yes, doing good."

"How was your jaunt?"

"That, too, good. Had a look round Cologne and Dusseldorf, just a look."

"Nice . . ."

Did not need to know much more. Could have remarked that

there was sand caught in the uppers of her trainers, and he did not know of beaches or dunes in either of the cities she had mentioned, and the bag she had by her feet was as full or as empty as when she had carried it off the plane at Leipzig – so a shopping binge was unlikely. Perhaps she thought him an idiot, perhaps she bought into the cover he cloaked himself with, but should have known better. She scrawled a signature on the indicated space on the hotel register and pushed it back to the girl. Did not have to, but said to the Prof that she had taken a train from Cologne, and a Brussels change, and a leg to Antwerp, and a walk.

The Prof said, "Nice to get a walk when you've been cooped up on a train."

"Yes, nice."

The problems, more acute with each of the lies, kicked and scrapped in his mind.

Without prompting, Jacques followed the car. Plunket had his weight pressed forward, against the back of Dawson's seat, and Rajah competed for the space.

They were very decent photographs. Dawson was congratulated. The light from the open door had been key, the overhead brightness had doubled quality. They had a passport image to match against the pictures Dawson had taken, and the file photo. No argument ... a serving officer of the Flying Squad, a Metropolitan Police star detective unit, caught in a gentle and romantic clinch with the daughter and heir of the top-rated figure in London's deep and dark underworld. And her already with a hands-on role in brothels and firearms importation, and Class A shipments, and all the rest that went with the trade, and leading onwards and upwards and into the sunny horizons where the trail would lead them to slipping handcuffs on the wrists of the great man himself. Would be quite a crowded dock area for the accused, and extra armed police deployed to Snaresbrook, and search teams to go through any member of the public wanting a seat in court. Would be Wilson himself, and his missus, Miss Julie and her Squad boyfriend, and also the Prof and Softboy, and a lawyer and an accountant, might even have to ask for two rows and an atmosphere of mutual simmering hatred as the gang were marched in each day. Considerable fun for the little unit of Plunket and Dawson and Rajah, and them revelling in it. And fall-out on a grand scale as the names were tossed around of all of those who had taken the money over the years. And jury protection on a grand scale.

Plunket turned away from the pictures and said to Jacques, "This has distinctive implications for organised crime in the UK."

"Understood."

"Big men who are supposed to be on the right side of the law will be crapping themselves when we go to the arrest stage, and wondering if they will be going into the net as well."

"That also is understood."

The car they followed stopped in the centre of the wide Keyserlei. The driver killed the engine, climbed out, and pocketed the keys. He carried a bag and it matched what he had been shown as carrying on the CCTV at Luton, courtesy of a woman from Border Control who had called it up – Betty who had told her boyfriend who did junior analysis for the National Crime Agency. The guy was Kenny Harris, called himself Chopper, had once been a very minor football star, at unit level and then at the clubs messing in leagues in the Thames Valley, and had run out of steam after catching a bullet in Afghanistan which seemed a century ago and the wound never properly healing and the standard of his football in free fall, and the fouling worse and red cards catching up with yellow cards, and all getting sadder and more vicious and Chopper being squeezed into history, unwanted. He seemed to be heading back the way he had come.

Plunket said, "We are an anti-corruption team. We are that side of the fence, Jacques. Bad news for us, Jacques, if you are on the other side from us."

"Very bad news."

"And you would be in possession of information that would be embarrassing to us if passed to them."

"Very embarrassing."

"Corruption enables those people to stay above levels of investigation, their safety is bought."

"You believe it is different here?"

"I read that corruption at state level is acute in Belgium."

"On the streets, yes. In the justice system, yes. In the police, yes. Of course. In government, yes. Everywhere? Of course, not. Most have a price, but not all. I assure you that I do not have a price and that is because I am so far down the chain that I have never been offered a bribe that would make a difference to me. Nor have I ever faced intimidation that has left me frightened and cowering. I am just a pathetic little foot soldier . . . do you comprehend that?"

Dawson had the camera started up again, the lens aimed through the front windscreen where the wipers worked hard.

The target went up the steps of a hotel and through a revolving glass door.

"We are all fairly lowly in the food chain," said Plunket. "We do not do luxury cruise holidays, have second homes facing the sea, pay for memberships at smart golf clubs, buy new tailored suits, or—"

He was interrupted. "My luxury is a fishing rod, or a landing net, and a quarter litre of dyed maggots."

"We are the little people. We attempt to nail corruption. Are we good with you?"

"We take each other on trust."

Neither Rajah nor Dawson would speak over their boss. Both realised that loyalties now dominated. Their loyalty to their work, and the Belgian's loyalty to his badge, his profession. Plunket would not have accepted that he 'had a price', that there was a rate at which his morality would crumble. Could not envisage that Lachy Wilson would come calling at his bedsit late at night, and make a proposition and pass him a brown envelope, brimming with £50 notes. And him taking it and leaving it on his bedside table in the morning and going early to his workplace and unlocking the security, going inside, and blanking the files. Switching on the computer and wiping away the information gathered painstakingly by himself and by Dawson and by Rajah. Could not imagine it.

Plunket said, "Some people say that we all have a price. I do not accept that . . . I'll give you an example. We have a national crime agency, our version of the American FBI, but not as self-congratulatory. This line of inquiry came from them. Close to their headquarters in London, beside the River Thames, is a small memorial to what was called in the last war the Special Operations Executive. It would have handled agents in your country, Jacques, and through occupied Europe. Many of the men and women, the agents parachuted in, were captured, subjected to the most revolting torture, and stayed silent, and died protecting their secrets. They did not have a price . . . You said it, we have to take each other on trust – and that is a dangerous place to be."

The Belgian pulled a clown's face. "Very little that is dangerous or eventful crosses my life. You offer me hope that being *boring* is not the ultimate for me . . . And tomorrow?"

They were driven to their hotel. They would get burgers and chips, perhaps a beer, they would sleep. Would start the stake-out before dawn. Plunket thought it was tangible and beyond any level at which he had previously worked, was almost nervous.

Lachy had been looking across the kitchen table, examining Softboy's neck: saw the old shaving scars and the brown mole on the left side, and the small lump, mostly sunken, of the Adam's apple, and the shoulders, and their obvious strength. It would require, Lachy accepted, a formidable effort to strangle Softboy. At the head of the table, where she could dish out the risotto sat Vic: he thought she was looking at the water bottle they had used . . . Lachy did not drink alcohol, only served water at meals: it was a deceit practised by the Wilsons that the glass bottle with the label claiming the water was from a Highland spring had been filled with water from the kitchen tap. Vic would have been wondering how alert Softboy would be if she manoeuvred herself discreetly behind him, braced herself, and then raised the bottle and brought it down on his scalp. Would he have twisted in time to catch her wrist, turn it, drop her down to the floor? What then? Bad times, like a stick had gone into a wasp's nest and did them no damage but tested their tempers. They had talked nostalgically during the meal (the worst prawn risotto that Lachy had known, and the bloody things were tasteless and hard and barely warm . . . which did not seem to matter to Softboy who had scoffed what was in front of him and taken a second helping). Principal in the good old days chat had been the big confrontation with the Green Lane gang of Turks trying to move further south in influence when he had been looking to stake territory north of his own empire.

The Turks had thought he would be easy meat and had come lightly armed – a crossbow, a couple of machetes, and a single-barrelled shotgun, sawn off. Supposed to be not more than four a side for a 'clear the air' meeting in an Enfield car park, far from his own safe ground. He had taken Softboy and they had a pair of Smith & Wesson pistols, the .32 long version, each with a silencer and hooked into the back of their belts. Epic stuff . . . Overhead lighting had caught the blades and the crossbow had been raised for the aim, and the shotgun was produced from under a windcheater, and Softboy had fired first, saving the day. All four of the Turks in trouble because the firing with that dull and distorted thump was too fast. Softboy had heaved Lachy down to the grease and oil and filth of the car park surface, and had lain over his body while he had tracked to get an aim on the guy with the crossbow. They had been clear winners, the two of them. The Turks had run, not that far because three had needed A&E, and one was in for days, and a message had come south to Lachy two days later offering a new ceasefire line and new terri-tory boundaries. A good evening's work, and the moment they both remembered was of Softboy spreadeagled over him, giving protec-tion. Two man-hugs after it was over . . . lifelong friends and that secret preserved. Friends for ever, never called into question.

Except that people changed, and so did circumstances, and guarantees lost their lustre, Lachy would have said.

That evening Softboy was free with the talk. Did not seem suspicious of the warmth dumped on him.

Softboy said, "I'm reading a hell of a good book at the moment – about the Mafia in New York."

"What, you actually reading, Softboy?"

"Yes, I am actually – don't ask me who wrote it, nor what it's called – great stuff, realistic."

"How realistic, Softboy?"

"Fallout in the gangs, and this jerk is looking for protection in case the bosses turn against him."

"What kind of protection, Softboy?"

"Sits down one evening. Gets out a ballpoint and some paper. Gets into remembering. Writes it all down – where he's been, what he's done, who gave him the order, when down to the hour, why the jerk who was zapped was a target. All on paper, and all in form for evidence at a prosecution. Puts it in an envelope, a stamp on it, the address of a big law firm in Manhattan. To be opened in the event of my death, which of course would be reported in the *Post* or the *Times*. Sent it, let those bosses know . . . and lived out a good long life."

"Great story, Softboy."

"I thought so. Thanks, Vic, for supper, really excellent. Thanks, Lachy, and we're joined at the hip. See you Tuesday for the Felixstowe trip . . . Great feeling, isn't it, when you're into a book and enjoying it?"

He scraped back his chair smiled at Vic, ducked his head slightly to Lachy, and was gone through the kitchen door, closing it firmly after him and the keys dangled and rattled.

Lachy said, "He knows. Clear as anything."

Vic said, "Reckon you're right."

He said, a little smile, "Not much seems to be going well for me . . . but that'll change, love, when the product comes through."

"Yes, right – not much going well. What happened? Why has it all changed?"

They were on the last ferry of the evening. It had taken them from the quayside by the castle and the museum, and off downstream, where the gulls chorused them and the waves thrown by other craft slapped the sides. This was the Scheldt, a wide and deep and murky stretch of water running from the southern tip of the North

Sea coast into the heart of the country. Floodlit on either side of them were the shapes of a massive petrochemical industry, cavernous storage tanks, linked to each other by miles of metal piping, and away to their starboard side were the false vertical mountains of the shipping containers, piled on top of each other, and moved by overhead cranes. Nothing stopping for the night because the port of Antwerp did not have time to rest, so the ferry ran downstream and a couple sat in a bitter wind on an outer deck, and were snuggled close for warmth.

His arm around her shoulder and her arm inside his coat and they clung to each other. Her head against his chest, his chin on the top of her head, her hair blowing upwards and fastening to his cheeks. A few gulls, bored or hungry, flew alongside them, and some squawked at their presence on the otherwise empty deck, and clouds ran fast over the moon and darkened the river, then passed and it was lit again in a silver wash. The ferry reached its destination. A few scrambled from the heated passenger cabin, bent their heads, and made their way along the tossing gangplank, and about an equal number, held at the quayside, were permitted forward, and came aboard at what was almost a run, and ropes loosened and the surge of the engine, and a ticket inspector coming from inside and looking around the deck and shrugging at the stupidity of the couple sitting there and gone back inside. The ferry turned back towards the lights of the city and the illuminated castle walls and the few tower blocks.

Julie said, "There's a place I read about, in South America, where three countries share a border. Argentina, Paraguay, and Brazil. An opportunity like nowhere else?'"

Chopper said, "Be on the road, crossing from one to the other. Maybe banks and maybe the trucks that carry the cash for the ATMs. In fast and out fast. Exhaust it and move on."

"Up north in the Baltics, good pickings."

"And Romania and Bulgaria, and Serbia."

"Hit, and scoot. But have a base and a farm or a little industry as a cover, and respectability. Our place, our home, and we answer to no one."

"And if people are in our way?"

Julie said, "I'm skilled with a chainsaw and you with a machine gun. They would not be sensible people."

And they laughed and both cold, and both obsessed with love for the other.

He had heard the rattle of the chain loosely holding the gates together, and had seen the glow of a cigar end. Jonas eased up the scarf at his throat so that it masked the lower part of his face, and his trilby was rammed down on his head: his face was effectively hidden, and he blinked without his spectacles.

The voice had the irritable pitch of a man who needed to be there, but resented it and with some bitterness . . . getting late in the evening of a Saturday night, but responding to Jonas's call.

A Geordie accent, likely cultivated, "For fuck's sake, where the hell are you?"

One of the lights on Horseferry Road caught him as he walked further into the gardens. A black tie job. Dinner jacket. Shiny shoes and a mauve cummerbund encircling an ample waist. Now Jonas saw the black saloon, with a driver that had stopped on a no-parking line outside on the street. Would have been a fancy dinner, only to be interrupted by a matter with a measure of importance . . . which was a phone summons from Jonas Merrick.

He whistled a brief greeting, just a couple of bars.

The guest spun on a heel and nearly tripped on the kerb, and cursed some more and had likely scuffed his patent shoes. Jonas did not possess a dinner jacket for the simple reason that he was not included on any invitation list that required him to wear one. He did have medals, and a bar, but had no occasion to take them from Vera's underwear drawer and pin them on. The guest was an Assistant Commissioner with the Metropolitan Police Service. He had come to the AssDepDG with a begging bowl and a decent lunch and pleaded that he was 'in a hole', had been advised – and the Five man would have smirked in saying it – to 'stop digging'. Jonas had heard chapter and verse on it, of an individual ranked as 'too big to bring down', 'untouchable', and protected by layers of corruption. Jonas was interested because he had been instructed to be, had been told that Thames House would appreciate having Scotland Yard in debt to them – a big debt and one needing a considerable reward in its paying off. In any normal time, Jonas would not have been in London at a weekend, sitting on a park bench in near darkness, no food in his stomach, no tea, no coffee. But nothing that weekend was normal. Not for him, and not for the AssDepDG who should have been fielding this and not sitting somewhere complaining of a damaged shoulder.

The figure came close.

"Is this the best we can do?"

"'Fraid it is." Jonas Merrick was never at his best in the company of senior men, had inherent hostility to their rank, the baubles on their shoulders that showed off their authority, and was rarely polite.

"And who am I meeting?"

"I doubt my name is relevant or necessary to you."

"You said that it was in connection with *Humble Pie*, which I have never heard of, and I would not be here unless I had been told by your senior that I would be advised to swim the width of the Thames to get to you . . . Fatuous idea. If you are not prepared to name yourself that implies a lack of trust."

"A fair analysis."

"For fuck's sake, I am an Assistant Commissioner, and—"

"You can be a plenipotentiary extraordinary to the Imperial Court in Peking, and it would still be a fair analysis . . . Do you want the answers or not?"

"I want them."

"If there is a security leak then I promise you will be destroyed. We have that ability. What would happen to you is the modern equivalent of a hanging and a drawing and a quartering. The instructions on what you should do, who you should use, and when to activate them, are enclosed."

"Are you, little man, threatening me?"

"I hope so. The instructions are non-negotiable, are to be adhered to."

"You've a bloody nerve."

"As have the people who work for me, are responsible for achieving what your force has failed to. Goodnight, sir, and a safe journey home."

Jonas took an envelope from an inside pocket of his Harris tweed jacket, a small envelope, somewhat insignificant for the value of what it contained. He gave it to the policeman. No handshake, nothing as respectful. He stood, felt his limbs creak, and walked to the gate and was gone into the night. From that same inside pocket he took his folded spectacles and put them on. At least, now, he could see where he was going, and he loosened the scarf that had given him an acceptable disguise. His mood was sour which was usual at this stage of an investigation. It was commonplace among investigators to resent that moment when they passed on diligent work to a customer and lost contact with it.

13

He heard the voices, but Jonas Merrick showed no sign of being woken by them.

Aggie Burns, who ran the A section surveillance team, said, "Looks almost human, doesn't he? Almost kindly."

He had, in a sense, come home.

A young woman spoke. "Is he the one that all the legends are about?"

They worked in a room designated as 12/3/S, which was behind the twelfth door on the third floor of the south-facing corridor whose offices overlooked the river. In the centre of the area was a large circular table capable of seating a dozen individuals, each with a computer terminal and keyboard. Facing the window was Aggie Burns's personal desk and the display board to on which she could pump up maps of target areas and the photos and covert film of suspects that the unit would track. Above her desk, stained with blood and street filth, was a local government bib on which was printed *Liverpool City Council, Pothole Department* and she had had it framed, had hung it in a place of honour. The street dirt was from urban Liverpool, the blood was that of a young woman who had been shot dead by armed police as she was about to do fatal damage to Jonas Merrick.

Aggie Burns said, "If you could see his eyes you would be reminded of carpet tacks, that sharp, that merciless."

A second picture frame held a photograph, blown up and in soft focus, of an armoured car, a group of cutthroat soldiers draped over it, and an old man in a filthy Harris tweed jacket sat with them, a three-legged dog on his lap. Equally precious to her.

A young man said, "What I heard, and reckoned it couldn't be possible that he even existed, was that he had no training in what was legally acceptable, just ploughed on like times were mediaeval – and we're constricted left and centre and right."

After his rude bludgeoning of the senior police officer, and reluctant handing over of the detail that would lead to the arrests and convictions for the man described as 'too big to bring down' and his clan, Jonas had phoned Vera. Had said that he would stay in London that night, sleep at Thames House, and be back with her on Sunday evening, and they would be on the road, with Olaf and the caravan, on Monday morning. To his surprise she had passed no comment. Nothing impatient, not even resigned. Something like 'all right' and 'whenever it suits', and had queried whether he had clean socks for the morning, and a razor . . . He had both. Had gone to his basement den in the Post Room, retrieved them, had been eyed without comment by the duty girl, and had gone upstairs in the great echoing building, and patrolling security people had nodded a greeting to him as he passed. He had once had a cubicle in the room. Frosted plastic panel walls, a lightweight door, a single desk and a chair, and a filing cabinet. He had come back from the Post Room once and found it had become the property of the dawn cleaning team and was filled with buckets, mops, dusters, all the junk of that trade, and in temper he had hurled it all into Aggie Burns's territory. Then, he had gone back to the Post Room and his privacy behind a wall of filing cabinets . . . as if he had never been away.

An older woman said, "I feel bloody ancient, but look at him. Why isn't he retired? Anyway, doesn't look special, not like he'd bite."

Aggie Burns said, "He's as hard as bloody granite and without morality. Too precious to our revered masters to retire him, and anyway it would kill him. We are all he has . . . Can we, *please*, stop gawping and get on with some work?"

Almost a chorus, and some giggles, "Are you fond of him, Aggie? Is he special to you?"

Aggie Burns said, voice dropped so that Jonas barely heard her, "Would walk on hot coals for him if it were needed. Yes, get on with some bloody work."

They were gone. He had come into the room, past midnight, bringing with him the spare socks and an ironed and folded shirt and underwear, and a shaving kit and toothbrush that had all been stored in the Post Room den. The cubicle was pristine, no sign of cleaners' kit. He imagined that Aggie Burns had let it be known that she was not again prepared to divert her people to cleaning up after the mess that had been left when Jonas had cleared his one-time space. Forbidden territory, off-limits, but no bed. He had put down his briefcase and that would serve as a pillow, and would use his coat as a blanket, had loosened his laces and eased off his brogues. His feet would be under his old desk and his head would be by the door, and it had taken him no time to drift off. Not a sleep where he dreamed, but rather a blank episode where other people and their problems were excluded. Did not think of Lachy Wilson whose time of freedom, he assumed, was short, and the rest of the people the man employed . . . nor did he think of the girl with the bobbed hair and the proud chin and the strong deep eyes . . . and not a thought of Chopper who had been his choice as the man best-equipped to do the job: a good lad, and pliable, and might even get taken, if Jonas broke all old habits, to the pub across the river where the NCA investigators gathered, and might even get a drink bought him by Jonas before they parted, might even get a handshake. He was awake, stretched, grunted, an excellent sleep better for not having Olaf sprawled over him . . . Had not thought of the targets and those he'd involved in the work of toppling them, nor dreamed.

"Do that," Chopper said.

She would get a map from Reception.

"And do that too," Chopper said,

She would mark on the map where they were headed.

Maybe Chopper should have slept more, and maybe he should have eaten breakfast. Always good to have food in your gut at the start of a long day in the field, what the sergeant used to tell them in the Afghan compound, and if they were likely to spend half a day at the sharp end and him feeling the whack of the GPMG's butt against his shoulder. It was going to be another of the 'big' days. As big as the one when he had first chased after her and panted to a halt beside her and told her of a trainer lace being loose, and been kissed for a reward . . . and for confronting her in Leipzig . . . and for doing the business they wanted, both of them, in amongst the sand in some bollocks-freezing place on the Baltic dunes. The sergeant might have burst a blood vessel.

He had come to her room. Door unlocked, catch off. Had come barefoot down the corridor. Had dumped his clothes between the door and the bed. Neither of them – not Chopper, not Julie – had the slightest anxiety that the other was a temporary item in their lives. Was for all time . . . Net result, had screwed too long and had slept too little.

She would be with the toad who was supposed to watch over her, and was going to do the final location check. She would be looking over the ground where the exchange would take place, a load from a long-distance lorry that had travelled close to 3,000 miles and would still be needing a hell of a good scrub round the windscreen to get rid of the last of the blood, and would also be needing another change of livery and registration plates because there would come a time when even the German cops would have put together the need to get into the bank of cameras that operated on the main highway stretches. The lorry would be coming, and another cab would be hauling a shipping container, and they'd need space to park up and do the swap. Julie had to be there and to witness it because it was her family money that was going into the pot. She would sign it off and leave the guys to have a night out wherever they could find some satisfaction in Antwerp, and she would see the container fed into the port system for its onward journey across the Channel and into the port of Felixstowe. Without her witnessing it the deal did not happen, all bets off.

Chopper was going with her.

Could not imagine sitting in a bar, watching football replays, eating pizza, while she was doing dangerous business.

There had been times when he had been fit enough to do 'pavement jobs' with the Squad. Over the earpiece they'd hear the call for the 'Go'. Swarming out of vans, from doorways across a street, from a building site or where an engineer seemed to be fiddling with phone cables, and in front of them the bad boys in their balaclavas and boilersuits and some with shotguns and piling out of their transport and about to hit a bank or a casino or wherever there was a hoard of cash or a place where diamonds were flogged. The bad boys should have been concerned about a leak in their system, worried that their security might fail . . . But the absolute shock on their faces when they were aware of the speed, agility, commitment, of what was coming for them, and the sight of the Glocks and then the yelling of instructions. White-faced, frozen, well-fucked . . . and cuffed, hands behind their backs, dumped on the pavement. Nothing much to think about except that the sentence would be heavy. Had seen it, had been a witness, and his team were in trainers and faded jeans and fleeces, with police baseball caps worn jauntily, and maybe their hands in their pockets and maybe rolling a fag, standing around and waiting for the wheels to take them back to their workplace . . . The bad boys might have wet themselves sitting there waiting and soon enough the vans would arrive, and the uniforms would haul them off to face a slow future. And the team would have expected to be in the pub when the doors were unlocked, and the first pints pulled.

Would not tolerate Julie facing danger, would be close, would be watching over her. Did not know how he might need to protect her, but would be there.

And a brilliant night . . . but not enough sleep . . . and no breakfast. Not at his best, but all behind him within twenty-four hours – and gone from the Wilson family and gone from the guys in the Barking office and running. And free. Something like that.

"God . . . unbelievable. You kids are so careless." The Prof had watched them.

A mezzanine floor was poorly lit early in the morning. Julie had said at what time they should leave the hotel for the reconnoitre drive. He had given that a half-hour clearance, had settled himself in a low chair in the gloom, and more cover was given by a screen hiding a stand where a small band, or a single musician, might have performed. A carefully chosen position, but that was the Prof's way.

"Slack and unprofessional – like there's a death wish."

He had seen her come out of the elevator, and the guy had emerged from the doors that led to the stairs. Both of them still blinking sleep out of their eyes, and her without make-up, and him with his clothes crumpled as if they'd been dumped on the floor all night. Nothing that she was wearing had looked straight off a boutique's shelves which gave the lie to her claim she had been on a shopping binge before joining him in Antwerp. She had gone to the Reception and asked for a map. He had joined her, but after looking around, as if suspicious, wary – and had good reason to be suspicious and wary, and cautious of consequences. The map had been marked. The Prof had noted the touch of their fingers, and a smile from the guy, and had seen her look up into his face adoringly, like she was a captive, but willing.

"Going to give me a heap of a problem, pet, aren't you?" the Prof murmured.

He thought of what he was paid to do, why he was on the Lachy Wilson gravy train. The guy had looked around him again, scanning all the corners of the lobby, and been satisfied. He held the map and folded a sheet of paper and headed for the doors, and out into the street. All adding up to something that was as near to a crisis in Wally Genge's life. Had known bad times before but sitting in the semi-darkness of the mezzanine, he could not recall worse times. He thought she looked younger, more like the innocent teenager he drove into Guildford each morning for her accountancy course. He would wait for her across the street at the end of her day and would watch her coming out, sometimes with a gang but never seeming a part of it, and cross the road, maybe cursing what she was born into. The Prof had done that double journey every weekday in her first term at college: bright kid, had passed her GCSEs . . . She had been watched over by Wally Genge, known as the Prof. Some thought he was stupid and that the nickname was to mock him, and a few knew better.

"You tell me, pet, what have I done to deserve this?"

She settled into a chair, and yawned and then rubbed her face. He thought she'd that look that he felt was reserved for a woman who had spent the night on her back, or on her stomach and who had shagged for hours. Mostly beyond Wally Genge's levels of experience, but that was his instinct. And if his imagination was up to its usual standards it represented a massive failure for him. If she was getting the arse screwed off her, under his supposedly watchful gaze, then the failure was as bad as it could get. He let her sit there, bided his time, did not want to appear too fast off the mark and have her wonder what he might, or might not, have seen.

"You going to give me a hard time, pet, aren't you?"

He could not be accused of lacking caution. He made his way to the elevator without being seen and pressed the call button. He took it all the way to his floor, and stood there for a full minute with his shoulder preventing the door closing and the lift descending, then let it have its way and pressed for the ground floor. Anyone, which meant Julie, who had looked at the lift's lights would have seen what floor it came from.

He walked out into the lobby and set his face so that it looked concerned at being late.

"Pretty."

"Full-frontal."

"You got it sharp?"

"Course I have."

"You'd think he would have had some tradecraft."

"Not good, sloppy."

"Have to say it, nice-looking boy."

"Dawson, fucking concentrate. He is not a nice-looking boy, he's a Person of Interest. He's going to get you, and me and the boss, promotion, and lead us to that short squat fucker who is Lachy Wilson."

They had been parked for three hours. The cardboard coffee beakers lay in a plastic bag with the pastry wrappers. All provided by the driver . . . not such a 'plonker' or a 'wanker' as had been suggested. Jacques had killed the windscreen wipers and allowed the rain to dribble down the glass. Dawson was beside him in the front. Rajah was behind her, leaning forward and emitting little grunts of excitement with each picture she took. Plunket did not speak. The wipers were still because the guy, their POI, was near level with them but his attention had been drawn to a jeweller's window and something must have caught his eye. Dawson would have suggested that any guy getting that load each night would, should, be looking for a ring to put on her finger, and Rajah would have suggested that those huge sparklers were the least a guy could give a girl who left him so very obviously shattered the following morning. Plunket showed no reaction, and perhaps was dreaming of a maximum security courtroom . . . The guy passed the van, never gave it a glance, and then he was in Dawson's mirror. A moment of quiet, then the Belgian cop got the wipers going and the windscreen was clearing.

They saw her coming towards them, the minder struggling to keep up with her. Dawson had the pictures. Jacques killed the wipers again and they all ducked low. But fortune favoured them because a lorry had to slow down and blocked them off from the far pavement, and when its driver moved it forward she was gone, and the guy with her.

"Like Christmas come early," Dawson said, hunched over her screen.

Plunket laughed, dry and cold.

Rajah said, "I thought they'd be better at it."

"A pretty girl."

"Thought she was heir to an empire. The minder is not earning his corn. What you said, Pegs, sloppy. Would have expected better."

Not much of the file collected by the Metropolitan Police Service on the life and times of Walter Genge told a story that painted a relevant portrait of the man. He was described as a 'bottlewasher', a 'gofer', and a 'handyman'. Little was known of his true value to Lachy Wilson and the crime family, or their reliance on him.

All shaped a long time before ... when Lachy, aged 20, was beginning to make a mark for himself in south-east London where his home was – running girls, cannabis, protection, anything forbidden and that made fast money. Walter Genge was a year older and the height of his ambition was nicking cars, driving them to a garage where the plates could be changed and then north up the motorway where he flogged them. Decent cash but a crowded work area, fearsome competition and a buyer's market ... one that did not need too much of his particular talent: his nose.

He had been hanging around outside a pub in Peckham, watching for punters who might leave a set of keys in their motor out the back. Everyone in that network of streets knew of Lachy Wilson, of his temper, and of his ambition. Wally Genge had seen Lachy arrive, had seen the clapped-out motor following him, and had registered its driver. Scruffy bloke, acne on his cheeks, several days' stubble, and an oil-stained shirt ... Noticed that the rust-coated bodywork did not fit with its sweet engine. The driver had left his car and gone into a CTN, bought some fags, and dropped back into the car. For a guy wanting it thought that he was enduring hard times, he didn't look the part. His arms were well muscled, his walk was wrong, not shuffling or scraping. Wally Genge's nose told him what he needed to know. Not a special-looking nose, moderate in size, bent where it had been broken in a playground fight, bit too much hair growing out of the nostrils, its talent not visible. A cop, obviously a cop, an undercover cop. Genge had gone into the pub, had gazed through the wall of tobacco fumes, had spotted Lachy Wilson at a table with cronies who listened to him and looked at him as if he was the Second Coming. And up to this God figure had stepped Wally Genge, and had told him that an 'undercover filth' in a bottle-green Cortina was a tail. Lachy Wilson had gone from the table, had walked out to the car, had rapped on the windscreen, and the cop had paled. 'Officer, I fancy you've a problem. You're driving around with a faulty indicator light, which ought to get you a ticket. I reckon you ought to fuck off back to your station and get it fixed, and now, officer, *now*.' The cop had gone puce and edged back in his seat, and then Lachy Wilson had gone round to the front of the Cortina and kicked in the Perspex that protected the indicator light, and the bulb and the shards tinkled onto the pavement. Lachy had walked back into the pub . . . but inside the door had paused long enough to ask, 'How did you know?'

And Genge had answered that his nose had told him the man was a cop and had listed the triggers – and he was on the team, and allowed to know that his instincts were appreciated. Had sort of slotted into place . . . Had never cared much for the boys – one dead and one banged up, both arrogant and looking down on him – but had worshipped the girl from the time he was allowed to push her pram. He had no family: only Lachy and Victoria and the girl, and the two younger boys were conceited little shites. His loyalty to the family was unquestioned and he had risen with them, and it was a place of honour that he now owned. He was her minder . . . also was the informant who reported back to her parents, where she was and who she met. He was trusted, and knew it, and the burden near crushed him.

Julie would have expected the Prof to lead the way and make sure the opened doors did not swing back on her. But he had gone through first and let them half close, and hadn't looked back to apologise . . . They walked along the pavement and then on to the main street, the Keyserlei, and she had not bothered to look at the jewellers' shop windows.

He had parked on the wide centre strip. They had a parking ticket. Not her problem. She would be far away by the time that the ticket was chased, and Genge would have gone into the cage back in England. He had screwed it up between his fingers and dropped it into a gutter of stagnant water where it sank among old leaves. He smiled at her, limply and without humour.

Whatever Wally Genge's problem was it did not concern her. She responded with a tepid smile. And reflected . . . no need to think of him again. Would dismiss him from her memory. He had been around her pretty much as long as she could remember and she had rated him as lonely and sad, one of those people that was short of a family and clung to the one he had found. Harmless.

They were, that morning, to follow a procedure laid down by her father. Necessary to check whether a road was open or closed for resurfacing repairs, whether a parking area was shut to the general public because a circus was in town, whether gates into a woodland and a massive city cemetery were now closed. Her father had always prided himself that he had the right mind to administer what he owned and to keep it from merely marking time, then shrinking. She accepted that her father was clever, intelligent. focused – and might have wondered whether he realised the extent to which she loathed him . . . He would find out in a few hours and, by the end of the coming week, he would be looking at the walls and the bars and the locked door. The thought put a little more spring into her step.

She was told that she had her father's reservoir of certainty. Never a doubt from her, not a hesitation. And not true.

It was part of an act, and inside the shivers would consume her. Had talked tough to the guys she had met in the churchyard in London when they had been visually stripping her down: *Come on forward, you fuckers, and see what you're made of.* Same treatment handed out to the investment manager, George, when his figures were corkscrew crooked. She had 'kitchen-sinked' him, and had flattened him: *Heh, shit face, you going to stand up to me, got that number of bollocks?* And, years before, had looked into the face of a guy, strapped down with adhesive tape to a chair, and she had been handed she chainsaw, and it was coughing into life, the teeth racing. She held his eyes until he had closed his and started to cry. *You thought I was going to cop out? Well, that was another mistake you made.* All an act . . . but now had Chopper – who she did not understand and likely never would – beside her when it mattered and always would. Best moments of her life were being with Chopper on a bed, in a sleeping bag. Felt secure with him and thought nothing of ditching her father, and her mother, the whole fucking lot of them.

She slipped into the front passenger seat.

The chickens were fed, and Lachy Wilson felt such pleasure that when he came to open up their quarters they squawked so energetically and clustered round his feet, and dived into the meal he'd prepared for them. Such loyal and loving creatures. They were so cheerful, and the reward he had for keeping them safe from the marauding foxes was to have fresh eggs for frying and scrambling and poaching. Had done the chickens, and now did the dogs.

Walked them around the perimeter of the property.

And they were as loyal as his chickens.

He checked the wire and the fencing, and looked for footprints in the wet grass and allowed the dogs to roam and was confident they'd have found anyone hiding . . . And it came to him like a blade was skewered up under his ribcage, pressed in deep, then twisted . . . He had done that in his time and seen the horror and shock on the face close to his own, and taken pleasure from turning the blade full circle. Came hard at him. What if there was no one there to let out his birds and bring them their food? What if there was no one there to take the dogs out and tramp around the boundary of the house he owned? What if there was no Softboy in the lodge, watching the screens and minding the gate onto the road. What if everything he valued was taken from him, and from Vic? Who would guard them? A fucking stupid thought. The lorries were on the move, his daughter – moody bitch, but his future and she'd grow out of it – was in place. A tonne weight of the stuff, and the distribution locked on, and he was still the big man in the market. And a guy had gone into the Mersey in the boot of a car, and his cousins had let it be known there was no vendetta, and he had the right money guaranteed and in place to pay off the final tranche of what he owed. He was a man of stature, untouchable. It had been a bad moment just then, but he reckoned he had crushed it. Had heard of big cats, not just a major gang leader, but Prime Ministers and Presidents, who had been chopped by their own bodyguards. Would have looked into the faces of men who had been around them for ever, longer than forever, and knew the names of their kids, and where their parents were from – what part of the Punjab, what suburb of Cairo – and seen hatred when he believed they felt love and respect, and seen the pistol lifted, heard it cocked.

Lachy Wilson shouted, into the mist and the damp, "No, that is not the fucking way. *I* am safe, *we* are safe. *I* am too big to bring down."

The dogs were still, ears back, staring at him.

And he bit on his lip, drew blood, and the spasm of pain killed the thought.

"Here you are, you sad old beggar, a mug of tea."

Aggie Burns was framed in the doorway. Behind her the room was empty. He had heard her despatch her team: usual stuff, the hope that an 'activist' would use that Sunday morning to go back to old haunts. The biggest part of the team, and the one with the least chance of success, was deployed, watching for him to try sneaking home to his wife and the two kids, but a better shot were his brothers and cousins. That was her life, getting her people in place, picking up trails that had gone cold, long hours wasted on street corners and in vans, and upstairs rooms with big lenses. When things worked out and arrests were made, it was never a time for celebrations and congratulations for her team. Aggie Burns had never been called up to the fifth floor and given a glass of sherry, not even a Mention in Despatches. Jonas would have said that she administered the most important team in the whole great machinery of Thames House. Provided more joined-up lines between the dots than any other section in the building.

"Thank you."

She said, "You smell a bit, Jonas."

"More's the pity."

He had already been down the three flights to the atrium, and down another to the basement, and into the Post Room. Had collected his clothing from a filing cabinet, and had also inveigled the solitary staff member on duty in the Post Room into 'volun-teering' to unplug his computer. Together they had taken it back up to the third floor. Had powered it up, and thanked his helper, rather as an afterthought. Jonas turned away from his screen.

She said, "I can manage a piece of cake."

"What sort?"

"Dundee."

"Is it that you are so pleased to see me?"

"Not really. Apart from the smell you've brought, there is also an atmosphere of crisis. I have enough of that here without it being added to. But sleeping on the floor made you a rather diverting sight for my team. Quite cheered them up. Sent them off on a difficult task and one that will probably end in failure, but in good humour. Actually it's nice to have you back ... So many people wonder why I have that Liverpool bib on the wall. Makes for a diverting conversation when I say that it was worn by the sad old beggar from next door – our neighbour. I'd get kudos from that."

"I'd like a slice of cake."

She had her hands on her hips. Quite intimidating. Feet a little apart and rocking. It was the posture she held when pushing her teams to go the extra mile or – more likely – the extra hour with the overtime budget exhausted. "Is it the stress?"

"That obvious?"

"Horrible and lonely ... all set up, ready to go. Everything perfect and in place ... What could possibly go wrong? No one around to rest your funny little head against ... Don't think, abso-lutely do not, that my shoulder can take the load ... It's the stress that hurts us, the ones left behind by the phone and the screen – maybe with a live feed and maybe not ... Anyway, why aren't your gang helping out?"

Jonas told her of a broken shoulder, and of a marriage proposal, and of his favourite cops doing a weekend away with their ladies, and of the lie in his head that festered, but gathered credence.

"Well, my advice to a sad old beggar would always be simple. Snap out of it. And change those bloody socks. And ... you can have tea and cake here but I'll not tolerate you feeling sorry for yourself . . . Not that I care."

He remembered what he had heard her say. *Would walk on hot coals for him, if it were needed.* And did as he was told, changed the socks, went to the gents and finally came round to running the razor over his face, and changed into the clean shirt.

Wished he could call the boy off, get him out and home. But he could not if he were to win . . . seemed to hear it all fitting into place, nuts and bolts, rivets and cogs all knitting together. Aggie brought him his cake.

Rows of heavyweight long-distance lorries were parked trailer to trailer in neat ranks in the designated layby on the approach to Antwerp. Like a jar that had once been full of rich and sugary jam and was now almost empty but was attracting a host of poison-stinging *vespidae* family, wasps and hornets and yellow jackets, the haulage industry relied on the park to filter off the cargo from arriving too early at the port. Old friends met here. Fast food was available. Toilets and showers could be used. Drivers set their alarms and took the opportunity to rest up.

A Serb and a Turk slept side by side in their cab. They had come further than any other of the drivers and the distance had taken a toll of their endurance, and they had seen off more than their fair share of emergencies, and left behind them a trail of destruction, chaos, blood . . . But it was worth the disruption to others' lives because of the value of the 'goods' packed away and hidden against the bulkhead of the trailer. Had any thief been idiotic enough to attempt larceny in the cab then they would have been confronted by two men seemingly dead to the world, snoring contentedly, but the hazard would have been great because they guarded a cargo worth some $100 million when refined and prepared for the streetmarket dealers. Close to the Turk was a loaded AK47 assault rifle, and within a stretch of the Serb's fingers was a handgun. They would be there for the rest of the day and into the evening, but by the dark, cold hours of the Monday morning, Mehmet and Dragan would have used the facilities and dumped the clothes in which they had travelled, and spruced themselves up, and would set off for the final leg of their journey – and by midday on Monday, healthy sums of money would have been deposited in their bank accounts.

Out beyond Maastricht, inside Holland, a cab pulled a trailer on which was perched a twenty-by-eight-foot shipping container, the perfect size for the transportation of family possessions owned by a coterie of diplomats returning to the UK from service on the European continent. The crew had not slept that night. They were tired and pushed the limits of the hours they were permitted to be at the wheel. A puncture had delayed them. A front wheel had begun to wobble because a sharpened length of twisted metal had fallen from a refuse lorry across another frontier, north of Aachen, and the call-out services had been slow in the early hours of Sunday. A carefully planned schedule had been disrupted at a last stage. The drivers would have been aware that timing was all important, they performed a role in a more complex and financially more rewarding area than the mere shipping of knick-knacks of sentimental value. They drove fast but kept within the law. There was an incentive. An additional payment awaited them for a smooth transfer of cargo, considerably more than anything paid for by the Foreign, Commonwealth and Development Office . . . Lucky to have the trade, and worth popping pills to stay awake, and recover lost time.

Three vehicles parked up. Furthest back, behind the shelter of a tram stop, in a side road, were Jacques and his passengers. Up the street and leading to a wide bridge that spanned a motorway was a BMW with German plates, and a single occupant, and ahead of it was the hire car that was driven by Wally Genge and with him was Julie Wilson. All in place and ticking over nicely.

Jacques prided himself on his ability to mix the culture and history of his city with the information his visitors required.

" . . . it is Silvertop bridge. And the tram stop is for Halte Kolonel Silvertop. Then there is a street, Kolonel Silvertopstraat, and there are tower blocks of apartments, twenty-two storeys high and they are De Torens Silvertop . . . Ahead they will be checking out the route leading to the docks, and this is the way their cargo will come, and we will follow them because we do not know how it is being transported. They stop here, which means by road, and very close in time . . . He was Colonel David Silvertop, from the north-east of England, and a tank commander. In 1944 he was responsible for the liberation of our city from German rule, and had many decorations, and was outstanding. In this country he is revered . . . I believe they do reconnaissance. What I do not understand is why the male suspect, the young man, is separate from the girl and her guard. It confuses me . . . The Colonel had about one month to live when he was here, and he went into Holland and was killed there in combat, and that is where he is at rest. Many, many people in Antwerp know his name. In England, in the north-east, I suggest that many, many people do *not* know his name . . . This place is significant but not of the greatest importance, and my expectation is that they will take us there now. I warn you, gentlemen, and you too, lady, to be very careful from this point on. If they are significant players then the stakes for them are high and the rewards great, and they will demonstrate extreme violence to protect their cargo and their freedom . . . Colonel Silvertop is—"

Peggy Dawson said, "I think we know that, Jacques."

Hasan Rajah said, "Have been around the block, all of us, once or twice."

John Plunket said, "Grateful for your insight, Jacques."

But Jacques was not a man easily deterred and irony and sarcasm bounced right off him. He patted his shoulder, where the holster was, its leather polished that morning at the same time as he had cleaned his shoes, and it shone as new, and he had told his drowsy wife, still in her dressing-gown, that he was hosting a 'most senior team from the famous Scotland Yard' who were as blind babes without him. His tribulations with firearms assessors were eased aside.

"You, of course, are not armed, but I have this to keep us safe, and will do that, depend on me."

The cars ahead were moving. He followed.

*   *   *

A Sunday morning. A trace of wintry sunshine with just enough strength to throw flimsy shadows.

Julie looked around her. She had been here two years before, to supervise a small shipment – amphetamines – like it was a training day from an office.

There was a wide plaza, and a covered waiting area for the tram passengers, and a car park that was overlooked by a block of apartments. At the far end was a school building, locked and silent, and a side street that led to cafés and bars and a mini-market, and on the last side was a main thoroughfare, and the signs said it was a direct route to the docks, and there were lights to help pedestrians cross, and beyond was a forest of high, wind-stripped trees.

She could see Chopper's back as he turned into the entrance to the forest.

Julie asked Wally Genge if he were satisfied.

"Yes, the place is good. Could do with some breakfast."

She said she needed to walk, stretch her legs, get some exercise.

"Me, I'm going to eat."

The Prof shuffled away from the car, past the tram shelter and into the side street where he could fill his face with pastry and eggs, whatever Belgians tucked into on a Sunday morning. She watched him go, then turned and loped away, crossed the main road where the lorries were backed up at the lights, and went into the forest. She looked around and at first could not see him. Paths led in three directions. She did not know which to take. The start of a small panic.

And then she saw him, and started to run.

Plunket said, "It's where it's going to be."

Rajah said, "Pretty humdrum, pretty ordinary."

Dawson said, "Not the sort of place you'd bring busloads of tourists to and shout through a megaphone that a big cargo consignment came through here, nine-figure value. A hundred million smackers' worth. Wouldn't be any less if the great man was involved."

"Has to be big enough money to justify the take for a Squad guy. Little Kenny – stupid bastard." Rajah snorted.

"Humdrum and ordinary, which is where they would want to be. It'll be the small hours . . . Thanks, Jacques, all feeling good."

In the people carrier, the driver eased off his jacket, and they could see that he had worked on the holster, but the weapon was old, and would not have been issued to a top marksman. But the holster looked good, Rajah thought.

There was a big poster advertising toothpaste.

Wally Genge had gone into a café, bought a bottle of water, had come out and taken up position behind the vivid white gnashers. Had seen where the guy had sloped into the trees. Had played it easy for her, so that she imagined he was going to be happily tucked up in a café, and noted her stare after him, then start to run. He went after them, as best he could.

Holding hands and walking. A forest path, opening out into gardens, and a château. They heard the drone of lawnmowers and saw rows of white stones.

She had been almost hysterical when she had found him, alerted by his whistle. Crying out and desperate.

Not such a big deal for Kenny Harris. He was used to tearing up his past and moving on . . . had done it as a kid when leaving school and home. Done it again with the walk away from the barracks, a few guys chirping that they hoped he'd do well, and a hint of a limp when he went past the guardhouse at the main gate, and again when he had left the building where the Barking team were based. Used to moving on. Not her. The emotion was shaking her and he thought she realised that her life would be totally altered this time the next day. She would know what betrayal meant better than he did. Would have seen the results in the news photographs as bodies were dug up, and would have heard it chatted about over the kitchen table. Getting close now to the ultimate moment, *no turning back*, beyond recall. 'Sorry, Dad, that you're banged up in Belmarsh, in the High Security Unit. Next time I'm in Western Way, SE28, I'll find the time to pop in and see you, and apologise to your face, for the evidence I provided to the Crown, and for fucking up a deal that was worth 100 million. Seemed right at the time, but getting fraught now.'

Didn't see her doing that, because it would have taken half of Charlie Company, Parachute Regiment, to give her decent protection. They were clear of the woods, and walking on a manicured path towards the mowing team, and ducks were splashing in the drains between the hedges, and away to the right was a cemetery with ornate headstones. They went in the direction of the mowers, and he led and she allowed it and did not question him. He understood the crisis.

"We are all right, Julie, because we are together. You and me, and cannot be wrenched apart. You and me, Julie. Beyond their reach, and safe."

Her hand gripping his tighter. Fingers locked. Dependent on him.

They reached the mowers, four of them, carving neatness on dew-soaked grass. Lines of Portland-quarried headstones.

An air gunner, not yet 21 years old: *Too dearly loved to be forgotten by his loving wife and daughter.* A Royal Air Force, sergeant, aged 19: *You are always in our hearts, even though you lie far from home.* And another stone: *Our beloved only son. He died that we might live.* He read them aloud, in a whisper, felt he had to. No Brize Norton and a colour party for those boys

He took his hand from his pocket where it had fondled the periwinkle shell, all that remained to him of the past. Felt the need to stand to attention.

They walked some more, then turned back. Would separate under the cover of the trees.

Almost there. Wrap up tomorrow morning.

Jonas put his head out of the cubicle door. It was his intention to hand back his plate and perhaps be offered another slice. Knew what he would have said to Aggie Burns . . . something about it all going very smoothly and the end near for an intensive operation of which he was rather proud, and all down to him. Would have liked to have told her that, except that the Deputy Director General was sitting beside her and was poring over a screen while she talked. The DDG had his back to the cubicle door, but Aggie Burns caught his eye. No break in her briefing, but she managed to use her eyes to tell Jonas, in her inimitable style, to 'Get lost and don't show yourself'. No more cake, and no chorus from her of what a clever old man he was. He eased the door shut.

Pretty much all of *Humble Pie* was illegal and covered areas of coercion and entrapment, whole rafts of it – as known at this stage – were inadmissible down at Snaresbrook. Any mention of the use of who he called 'my irregular' would ditch an entire prosecution . . . all immaterial. The conviction would come from the next twenty-four hours, what the principals did, what they said, where they appeared. He had provided the Yard with what they needed, the problems lay with them . . . There was no requirement for the DDG to see Jonas Merrick on the cusp of a wave.

He went back to his desk, disappointed he could not share, nor be congratulated.

He sent back a message. *Looking forward to seeing you in the next few hours.*

Treading water, nothing else to do.

14

Jonas sat in the dark and pondered, his eyes resting on the blank screen in front of him.

Before going home, Aggie Burns had tapped on his door and, not waiting for his answer, opened it, pushed a hand through, waggled her fingers at him in farewell, and closed the door. None of her team was there, and she had switched off the ceiling strip-lights and gone on her way.

He was hungry. Could have done with a sandwich. Would have welcomed a cup of coffee . . . There was a canteen in the building but Jonas had no idea whether it was open on a Sunday night. He was tired, which was self-inflicted, had aches in his shoulders and in his knees, again his own fault. He was also lonely, another problem laid at his own door because he had never encouraged friendships. A noticeboard along the south corridor, and another one in the Post Room, advertised the extra-curricular activities available to officers and lower ranked staff at Thames House. Unlikely that Jonas Merrick would have signed up to a ballroom dancing class, or a mixed badminton weekly opportunity, or pride marches, or bridge and whist tables, even a feline appreciation group where he might have shown photographs of Olaf. He despised them, had no comprehension how people were able to belong to such groupings and also do their work. Was lonely because he had had no call from the Assistant Deputy Director General, who might or might not still be in hospital, nor from the Absent Without Leave Effie Bellingham who had turned her back on him. Nor the armed police to whom he owed his life.

He sat in the darkness. Within a few hours, *Humble Pie* would be out of whatever oven it was being cooked in, and would have been consumed, and a victory would have been chalked up. He supposed that several of Aggie's surveillance youngsters would have marked a major success by taking a penknife blade to a wooden bedstead and scratching a notch there . . . he was far away, and he could not identify a new sound that tickled the quiet, a very soft rumble . . .

A steadily decreasing time until the operation was wound up, and the attrition of it seen to have won through. He supposed he would feel a sense of private elation, and be back in a week or so, after his caravan holiday to the Isle of Purbeck, and would be sitting either here or in the Post Room waiting to be talentspotted, or have an idea and then pretty much bite his backside for further attention: might be terrorism, might be counter-espionage, might be crime. His mind rambled and he had no clear preference as to which would fall in his lap, and the noise came closer.

He allowed himself that little luxury, not to be shared, of contemplating how it had been when he had won through, and always against the toughest of opponents – the man who was like a crocodile, submerged except for half an eye or a part of a nostril and who watched and waited for the chance to kill; the identifying of a Sixer who betrayed the organisation across the river; the progress of a semi-submersible loaded with four tonnes of cocaine sailing from an Amazon tributary to the Spanish coastline; the turning of a long-term agent of the Chinese Ministry of State Security and now in protective anonymity; the tweaking of the Czar's nose; and a journey to a fortress village in the mountains of northern Albania . . . and also permitted himself a momentary smile, acceptable in private, perhaps to be shared with his cat. Good times. He allowed his smile to widen, supposed that *Humble Pie* would have a place among them, except that in this case lives were not on the line, all relatively safe, and his own security not threatened.

Early in the morning, he assumed the news would come as a trickle down, in dribs and drabs, and he would tell the lie with as great a conviction as he was capable of, and they would be off in the caravan. And that brought an audible chuckle – and the rumbling noise swallowed the thought.

Lights lit Aggie Burns's territory. His door was opened. Noise belched around him. An electric-powered floor cleaner swept inside. He cowered away from it, shrinking from the brightness and the noise. He supposed Sunday evenings were the time for a 'deep clean' in the corridors and rooms. The woman who piloted it let out a short squeal, then spoke in the rolling tones of the Caribbean islands.

"You gave me such a shock, sir. Half frightened me to death."

"I apologise."

"My first time here, sir. It's the gastro bug. They sent me over from Scotland Yard. Short here. Hope I haven't done anything wrong, sir."

"Absolutely not."

"I have top cleaner security clearance sir, at the Yard."

"No problem, none at all."

"I am Agathe, sir. But you'll not tell me your name," and she giggled.

"A late shift, Agathe."

"I'll get the last bus back to Camden Town, sir."

"Carry on, please, I'd not want you missing it – nor me missing my last train."

He smiled as well as he was able. He knew. Strange old thing was coincidence. Always played a big part in Jonas Merrick's world. Some called it luck, some called it misfortune. Came out of a clear blue sky. He lifted his feet and she pushed the machine under them. He had read all the preparatory briefings that Effie had dug out. Chopper's childhood and his service in Afghanistan, the football and the wound, the transfer to the Squad, and where he lived, and her name . . . He would rather have enjoyed sitting her down and encouraging her, and learning so much more of Kenny Harris' life, what his character had only superficially shown in the pub, the detail of the man. The machine roared as it skirted his briefcase, then headed for the door. If he and she had begun to talk, then both would probably have missed their transport. He knew so little of Chopper. Enough to realise the real possibility of manipulating him towards an end, but for a worthwhile cause . . . He would make amends, would see to it that Accounts paid him off well.

Agathe was gone and the door to his cubicle was closed, and the light next door switched off. He was back in the darkness and the quiet . . . Accounts were never generous in payments but he would do the best he could for Chopper before cutting him adrift.

The last night in his life as Kenny Harris.

The final evening that he would respond to the name of 'Chopper'.

By the next night, he'd have forsaken the role of paratrooper veteran, and one-time member of the Flying Squad and doing 'pavements' with them.

A few hours and all gone.

And he did not know, had not yet settled on it, what identity he would wear when the dusk next fell. Would be a quiet name, one that came off a mass-production belt: Jezza, Baz, or Ed – not one that was memorable, just as the clothes he'd have on his back would be from sweat shops and not attracting attention. Same for her. Julie was already asleep, stripped off, in her bed. He had come on tiptoe down the corridor, carrying his shoes, had undressed, emptied his pockets of car keys, loose change, a handkerchief that needed changing, and the periwinkle shell.

He was going back to his own room. It had been a poor loving session. Why? Both of them too tired, too tense. Needed the deal in place, the sign-off, and them drifting into the shadows and then flicking the ignition in a car and making distance, burning the rubber. He had put on his T-shirt, pants, and trousers, and was refilling his pockets and something dropped on the carpet. Could not see what it was. Reluctant to switch a light on . . . moved his left foot a couple of inches – and felt the give as his weight settled on it, and heard it fracture . . . Just an old shell from a beach, found among the pebbles, and gone. He crouched, let his fingers run over the carpet. Sharp little shards pricked his fingers . . . felt that a part of his life had been lost. The fact that he had destroyed it himself, through clumsiness, carelessness, hurt him hard.

He left the remnants of the shell on the carpet, and padded to the door.

Some light came through the curtains from the street and landed on the pillow. He thought her face was an angel's, but an angel who was pissed off, bothered, not at ease. Her breathing was heavy and a deep frown had settled on her forehead. Just a thought: would it have been better for her if he had not been able to run through his pain and had never caught up with her, and she had jogged away into the distance, into the haze of the heat, and he had never tried the implausible chat-up line? Dreamed up by Sunray, and beyond possibility that he had ever been kissed like Julie had done it to him, with her tongue down in his tonsils. Better for her? Better for him they had never met?

He went down the corridor, past her minder's door – and he was an oaf, stupid and ignorant – and took the lift to his own floor. And hoped, before he needed to work out who he was, to catch some sleep.

There had never been a girlfriend who had mattered to him. In his entire teenage and adult life, Walter Genge had missed out.

No woman had ever decided that he was a catch to be prized, worth giving him a good hump in the hope he would take the hint and put a ring on her finger, and promise all those bits about 'for ever' and 'until death do us part'. Not one. Not even one of the women who hung around the group that was run by Lachy Wilson because it oozed power and excitement, also restaurants and fizz. Others in his team had it chucked at them, like they were pop stars, but not Wally. That maudlin Victorian poetry had been part of the therapy of doing without – that, and occasional visits to a cat house, a brothel owned by the Wilson clan and where he could go and get the business done and be able to tell Lachy Wilson, first hand, how the place was doing. Trouble was that around Dorking and Horsham and Leatherhead and Guildford there were few such opportunities.

He sat on the bed, half-dressed. He had come in search of comfort. He had not found it.

Tears ran on his cheeks.

She was quite a kindly woman, not in the flush of youth but not old. She had checked her watch, was prepared to give him another fifteen minutes of inaction, had produced a condom but not found anything suitable to put it on – and in return for the quarter of an hour of licence, Wally Genge had paid up, even given her a small gratuity. He had gone to the first door in Schipperstraat, and had barely bothered to look through the plate-glass window behind which the talent paraded. She was not glamorous. Probably a housewife contributing to the family kitty.

He was also there because he needed to lose the matter churning in his mind, if only for thirty minutes. It hurt him so bad that he needed an escape. She rubbed his tense shoulders, but without enthusiasm. He studied the pattern of the wallpaper through misted and unfocused eyes . . . In rooms on either side, through thin partitions came the sounds of energetic effort from client and hostess, but that did not help him. He had become, he believed, an essential part of Lachy Wilson's family. He was relied on, was trusted, and in return offered a total and complete loyalty; his reward was a sense of security and of belonging, and he had never been criticised or threatened. He had two rooms in a wing of the house, plenty of space, had a cake baked for him each birthday and they all turned out for its cutting and toasted him. And he mowed the grass and touched up the paintwork and did the basic plumbing and electrical maintenance, and he minded Julie who was the heir to the family . . . and worshipped her. Had never had reason to complain about the treatment he was given by the family . . . and loved the young Julie.

His loyalties stretched to breaking point, he saw the woman glance again at her wristwatch, and only very few minutes left, and he'd had no break from the agonies inflicted on him . . . So, he wiped his eyes and finished dressing and sensed the relief of the woman that he was not intending to overstay that very limited welcome and she would not have to call on security to get rid of him.

The people carrier was parked where those inside had a decent view of the hotel's main entrance, and also of a side door used by staff.

The smell inside the vehicle was strong, the air thick with nicotine fumes.

They had sent Rajah to their hotel and he had cleared out their baggage, paid the bills, and brought the load back.

Plunket had decided that they should camp there for the night. Be there until it happened.

Plunket had asked, 'Tell me, Jacques, why are you still with us? Why has there not been a change of shift? Not that I'm complaining, we have nothing but praise for you. You are looking after us, are half our ears, half our eyes, and you drive us, and you sleep less than we do. How does that happen?'

Jacques had answered, 'Because of who I am, what I am.'

'This investigation matters to us. We think it could lead to a huge arrest. Mega headlines. Something that damages a Class A importation, a fight against corruption in office. To us, it's big . . . not to you. We go back to London tomorrow, maybe the day after, but soon. For you, it is just chauffeuring round three foreigners, too ill-educated to speak your language. For us you have given up your bed and your home, and your family – why?'

'Perhaps there is no replacement available.'

'Doesn't wash with me. Isn't your team leader, your superior, logging your hours?'

'I doubt they have missed me. I have not been promoted to that level of importance where people are concerned for me. Do they know I am working with you? It will be on file, but not acknowledged. It is what happens to men and women of minimal significance. It is the way it is. If I am truthful, I enjoy your company – even if I am a plonker and a wanker.'

Which had silenced them and then the laughter broke out, led by Plunket himself, who sensed the surprise of his colleagues. They were supposed to be, good surveillance tradecraft, quiet as a graveyard, had broken a rule set in stone. But the street was empty and the traffic was negligible. Laughing out loud, when the sound would carry, was not following protocol, but the liaison's droll humour deserved it. Good guy, and they thought it the best of luck that he had been allocated to meet them

And Jacques had said, 'Now, if you will excuse me . . .'

He had his Five-seven out of the holster, detached the magazine, and removed the twenty rounds from it and tipped them out onto his lap. Rajah would help him, offered his hand. Each cartridge case was cleaned with Rajah's handkerchief, and then slotted back until the magazine was again filled, and out of his jacket pocket a second magazine appeared, and the same procedure was followed . . . They had adopted him, like he was newly recruited, and accepted. The weapon was armed and the safety checked, and returned to his holster.

More fags were lit.

Nowhere else they should be, and the discomfort was immaterial, and the minutes crawled but the waiting in the vehicle was necessary – and the potential reward was beyond the limits of a dream.

Julie swore.

She had been awake and had felt the far side of the bed and realised the sheets were cold and the pillow empty.

They had been crap earlier that night. She knew it, but did not know if it was her fault or his, or was down to what might have been called 'circumstances', in the sort of language a defence lawyer might use. Waking, worrying, brought on a need for the bathroom. She went there . . . came out. Went to the unit and was rummaging there, and could not rightly remember for what. Was barefoot. And shivered, and stumbled, and had to stamp down a foot to prevent a lurch that might have felled her. And the pain went sharp and high.

So, Julie swore again.

She found the switch, flooded the room with light. She saw the blood oozing from her foot, saw the tiny pieces of shell.

Julie knew about the tradition that tied the Flying Squad to a periwinkle shell. Had thought it pathetic but had not said so. Her father had no eccentricities on that scale. Had his chickens, his dogs, his empire, but had not kept a fragile shell in his pocket. Her mother had her favourite jewellery, but hardly wore it. When she was a kid, Julie had had soft toys but had binned them on her tenth birthday. She had no need of such a valueless trinket as a small salt-scrubbed shell carried onto a beach and left there when the tide had gone out . . . but the carpet in her room was not pebbles, and she was not wearing strong footwear – was a bedroom in an Antwerp hotel – and this was the day. Her bloody foot bloody well hurt.

Had he been there, she might have snarled at him, 'You could have picked it up. So childish anyway, carting it round, and you are no longer part of it. Like a kid that has a photo of his mum on his phone. You must have known you'd smashed it, that the pieces were on the carpet and that I'd be padding around and thinking of getting dressed, and thinking of packing, and thinking of the day ahead, a fucking big day. How long would it have taken you to collect the pieces in the palm of your hand and dump them in the bin – ten seconds, twenty? Too busy were you? And I'm bleeding, and you're not here, and this is not just – if you didn't know it – an ordinary day in my life. Where the fuck are you? What the fuck are you doing?'

Hell of a long time since tears had last rolled on her cheeks. Julie Wilson had not cried when news had come through of her brother's death, certainly not when her other older brother had been sent down . . . It was the biggest day of her life, and time was running fast, like sand in an hourglass, and there was still a chance to tell him – who had the beautiful smile – to go screw himself and duck off down the road and not turn back. Her foot hurt. He was not there to shout at. Not there to hold her and whisper silly things in her ear.

Religion had never mattered to Walter Genge.

The gates were open, Saint Paulus. Near to the 'red light' area of the city and adjacent to the docks, it was also the seamen's place of worship. Had he possessed a guide book, or used his phone, he would have seen that Gothic and Baroque were the styles of architecture, that fine internal carvings had been created by celebrated craftsmen such as Artus Quellinus the Elder and Jan Claudius de Cock, and that the paintings on display were by Rubens and van Dyck. He supposed that by going into the grounds of the church he was hoping to find guidance.

With so much of value on the walls and in the confessionals it was predictable that the massive doors would be locked, He would not be able to drop to his knees, cover his eyes, imagine a Christ figure hanging above him, and beg for his help.

Wally Genge pushed at the door but it did not shift. There were statues outside but he did not know that they represented a Calvary, that they created an understanding of his personal anguish. It was late. The best of the trade on Schipperstraat would now have been done. Traffic had dropped off. Revellers had finished attempting to drink dry the tavern beyond the church boundary. If he reported what he knew to Lachy Wilson, woke him, told him what he knew, he was certain of the answer that would be given him, the instruction . . . If he did *not* report what he knew to Lachy Wilson, and so protected the young Julie, then he betrayed the trust of the family.

They were like the scales in the old-fashioned shops he could remember when he was a child, where sugar or flour or sweets were measured out and weighed. Sometimes the family obligations dragged down one arm, and then it would be jerked up because of his adoration of the girl he was charged to mind.

To make the call and disturb the house as they slept behind the barriers of wire and bolts and cameras, or not to make the call?

The train Jonas caught was near empty.

A miserable experience, but interesting to him. He thought he exposed himself to a layer of society he had no knowledge of: a few restaurant workers, drunks – some occasionally bellowing at their own reflection in the carriage windows and some slumped over their phone screens and struggling to make sense of what they saw – but one man called him 'sir', and another bumped into him while negotiating the aisle and addressed him as 'guvnor', and another asked him for money for a sandwich and called him 'mate'.

When the train pulled in at Raynes Park, he was the only passenger in the compartment. He went through the barriers. Saw no staff. The new council policy was to switch off some of the street lights after midnight, part of an economy drive. He walked briskly but not with any sense of fear. A cat shrieked at him and dived for cover. Music was playing loudly somewhere which was an affront. At volume, a couple argued . . . All rather interesting to

Jonas. It was possible that he spent too many of his waking hours concerning himself with the protection of those wrapped in a conventional culture: he was as much a servant, he reflected, of these night dwellers, would rather have enjoyed a conversation with one or more: might have been down by Ewell West if he had done . . . and chuckled, did it quite noisily.

He reached home, his fortress. The caravan was parked, and the car would have a full tank, and the caravan's water would have been topped up and the gas cylinder plugged in, and Vera would have repacked his bag and hers and stowed them, and the cat's cage and food. The light over the front door was subdued: *Waste not, want not*, Vera would have said. Olaf greeted him.

He called up the stairs, "Safe home, dear, all is well. We should be off and on the road by late morning. Everything wrapped up by then. Just going to sit down for a bit."

The lorry that pulled a trailer on which was fastened a shipping container trundled along the highway that carried directions to the Antwerp docks. It had no need to hurry as the time lost because of the puncture was now made up, and they cruised towards a rendezvous out by the city's municipal cemetery at Schoonselhof.

On the same highway, also on schedule, but a handful of kilometres further back, was the BharatBenz 4828R, powered by the 7200cc engine, and capable of pulling a load of 32,500 kilograms – of which 1,000 kilos had an especial importance to a driver and his colleague. On this last leg, Dragan drove and Mehmet navigated, and the conversation was relaxed, that of two old friends, who trusted each other, who had made the journey from the desert-scape of the Afghan border with the Islamic Republic of Iran, and had come through cities and seen off thieves and officialdom, and had left casualties behind them, and had needed to scrub their windscreen. Arrangements were in place for the lorry to be offloaded of its legal cargo and the vehicle to 'disappear' under fresh layers of paint and new logos on the trailer. They would both spend a night in another Belgian city and then head for their homes and their families, their bank accounts well rewarded. Another couple of hours, not more.

There was no witness in the garden around the church of St Paul.

The silence among the Calvary statues was broken only when perching crows were disturbed or when police sirens wailed in the distance.

He had no choice. Wally Genge dialled the necessary number.

He knew the system in the bedroom because he had wired it. The phone was on Lachy's bedside table. A light would flash. Unlikely that Vic would be woken. He could picture it . . . Lachy waking but slowly because he slept heavily, reaching for the phone and in a foul mood because business was not supposed to be done on the phone, any phone.

A fair chance it would be a wrong number and some poor sod about to get an earful and not knowing who had picked up – and him talking, and Wally Genge needing to trip his message off his tongue and keep it coherent, and expecting that he would face examination, of course he would. Having to stand up for himself, get the message across . . . always said that big men, truly big men who understood power and its burdens, did not go after the 'messenger'. Who told them the truth, the big men, who told it to them? The loyal bastards or the idiots? Thought how it would be. Heard the purring of the phone in his ear.

He waited for the phone to be picked up.

The drunk saw him, came tottering towards him.

And waited some more.

The drunk reached out to hug him, like they were old friends.

The phone was answered.

Wally Genge kicked the drunk in the crotch, and kicked him again and felt a soft flabbiness, and the guy crumpled and fell and jack-knifed, and was sick . . . Easy for Wally Genge to be brutal, and the call mattered to him, and the guy was heaving, and Wally wiped off what had landed on his trousers, and his foot hurt.

"Yeah . . . ?"

"Wally here, Lachy. It's Wally."

"Know what time it is?"

"Know very well, Lachy."

"Has to be something important?"

"I think it is."

"On this line, Wally?"

"Don't know how else, Lachy, and don't have the time to do something smart."

"Get this wrong, Wally, and I'll fucking skin you."

"Don't reckon I've got it wrong, Lachy."

"Got what wrong?"

The drunk was still throwing up, but not able to get much more out of his mouth, and also was squealing but softer . . . He heard Vic's voice, would be questioning. Heard the answer: it was the Prof calling in, middle of the goddamn night, and waffling and mumbling and in a state, and . . .

"It's about, Julie, Lachy."

Imagined the gulp in Lachy Wilson's throat, and Vic would by now have her head against her husband's and the phone wedged between their ears and her stiffening and a light now on, and both of them wide awake . . . had to get it right, or he was fucking cat's food.

"What about, Julie?"

"She's got a guy in tow."

"What guy? What are you saying?"

"Too easy, Lachy."

"Just say it, Wally, and be careful what you say about our Julie. Are you pissed? Better not be . . ."

"Am not. There is a guy here. He was on the Leipzig flight. We didn't come here, into Antwerp, together, her and me. She went off and I travelled alone. Said she wanted to go shopping. The guy dropped her off at the hotel here. Same guy is still with her. Was with her yesterday out at the place where we do the meet."

"She know you've seen her?"

"Does not."

"So, she has a guy – she's a good-looking girl, she—"

"That would be nice, Lachy . . . don't fucking eat me. He's a cop."

"What? Say that again."

"He's a cop – you hearing me, Lachy?"

"Certain? Like you've seen his warrant card?"

"Just that I know." He ploughed on, had to – had started so could not waver. "Was at a cemetery yesterday, military one. It was the way he stood facing the graves, RAF, I think, stood like a cop would. To attention."

"You got a drift of what you're saying, Wally?"

"I have."

"And the consequences . . . You know the consequences of what you're saying?"

"I do."

"You saying our Julie is shagging a cop."

"I *am* saying that . . . and sand on their shoes when they arrived here, and there are beaches up in the north on the Baltic."

Wally heard Vic's voice, saying that they had a property up there, a block with an apartment that was always available, like a bolt-hole. Lachy said, "You're not fucking me about, Wally?"

"I am not. He's a cop. What my nose says."

"You happy to live with them, the consequences?"

"Hard to believe me, of course. You are her fucking father, Lachy. I ask you, what's my record? What have I got wrong? When has my nose told a lie?"

"Going to call you back, Wally."

"Certain of it. Because of my nose for cops. Because of the way he stood in front of the graves. It is the biggest thing I have ever done for you, Lachy, telling you this. He knew which flight she was on out of Luton. She treats me like shit but I put up with it. But my first loyalty is to you . . . He's a cop, and screwing your Julie. What am I to do?"

The connection ended. He was trembling, didn't feel the cold, just the numbness of a betrayal.

He kicked the drunk again. Had no argument with him, but kicked him once more and hard.

He went away from the church and on to a silent street, and

began to walk back towards the hotel. He knew what their answer would be when they called him.

Jacques asked, "If this were in the UK how many people would be involved in the stake-out?"

Rajah answered, "Perhaps thirty – vehicle, bikes, foot surveillance."

Dawson chipped in, "And more to look after catering, and stand in for comfort breaks, and log the overtime."

But Plunket said, "Don't believe any of that. None of it. Start calling that number and what you get is a leak. What appeals to me is that we may fart a lot, and smoke too much, which means that we're hungry, thirsty, but we'll have no leakage."

Jacques said, liked to be dry, "Then if there is no new shift, we get to change our clothing and cut the quality of the aroma."

He described how it would be. His own clothing came from a plastic bag under his feet. He suggested that Miss Dawson should get the men's stuff from the bags in the boot. The lady showed neither shyness nor concern. Knickers off and tights, and wriggling into replacements. The guys matched him and changed their shirts and their pants. and their socks. Jacques collected the discarded items and took them to a rubbish bin and pushed them down. He had to take off his shoulder holster and in it was the Five-seven, and strapped to it was the spare magazine. Rajah had taken it while he changed.

Jacques was tucking in his shirt tails. "Is the risk of what you call a leak so great? Does it dominate your work?"

Plunket replied, "We work on the principle that pretty much everyone has a price."

Jacques said, "I have never been approached. This tells me I am not important enough to know anything that matters. That describes adequately who I am, and my footprint."

He held out his hand. The holster was passed back to him and he fitted the harness, fastened it, extended his hand again and the weapon was placed in his palm. A blunt question: had he ever used it? He had not, had never actually indicated he might nor drawn it from the holster. Was he a good shot? Was at the edge of adequacy, was at *la ligne de demarcation*, and needed to shoot well at his next test or risked having his firearms permission withdrawn and then all that would be open to him was checking parking tickets on the Meir, or filtering traffic when the lights broke down, and he confided that he would have felt naked or worse without a weapon. And he shrugged . . . like there was nothing he could do to prevent the weapon being withdrawn . . .

Rajah said, "I fancy we have Mr Genge, horrid little snake, and back from a night on the tiles. Does not look a happy boy."

The one they had identified as Walter Genge was on the other side of the road, heading towards the main entrance of the hotel. The diamond stores' windows were empty and dark, the fast food places were shuttered. He went slowly past them, then straightened, took his phone out of his pocket and clamped it to his ear.

"That you, Prof?"

"It's me, Lachy."

"Not changed your tune since what you called me about?"

Question asked easily, like it was not a big deal how the answer came.

"It's what I said, the same. She's bonking a cop. When I've seen them together he treats her like his bit of totty, not the girl who's your daughter."

"I'm asking you, Prof, a last time – you've no doubt?"

Lachy sat at the desk in his snug, Vic pacing behind him. His coffee was not yet tasted. They had talked for an hour. Need not have done . . . He had asked his wife, Julie's mother, whether she had ever doubted the Prof's nose. She had replied, blunt, that she had never questioned his judgement. They had talked some more, not that it was necessary.

"Haven't. Am certain."

"We've made up our minds. Anything you want to say, Prof?"

"I'd not have believed it, Lachy, if I hadn't seen it. I love that girl, took good care of her . . . Them, the Yard, they would have wanted to get me on their side, or Softboy, or your money man or the legal guy – any of the people you've worked with – put the screws on us. Would have been happy to have lined up Gregor in his cell except that he's an idiot and left too long on the shelf, but they went after her, little Julie, which was genius and turned her . . . Don't think it's an accident. Some bright bastard knew where to go and put the bait out, dangled it in front of her. He's a good-looking boy, a proper stud. They went for your soft underbelly, Lachy, and they scored. Enough?"

"Enough . . . You got a snake curled up round your wrist, and it has a sac full of venom. You cut its fucking head off as soon as you can. She authorises the shipment, then you do it. Except it's two snakes. So you get to be busy, Prof . . . you've told me enough . . ."

In his ear Lachy heard Wally Genge's breathing. He felt calm, and the rhythm of Vic's walking up and down behind him was almost soothing. The house had its own noises in the night. Too early for Mrs Plumb to be up, and the boys sleeping, and the creaking of window-frames and the sounds of shifting beams, and the wind on the glass.

"Enough talk. Take her down, Prof. Take her down and the boy. She has to sign it off. Right after she's done that. You got it?"

"Got it, Lachy."

"What have I told you to do?"

"You have told me, Lachy, to get it signed off, then take her down. You mean kill her, kill Julie, kill your girl, because of what I've told you? Yes, kill her. And the boy."

"Well done, Prof. See you when you're back."

He put the phone on the desk.

Lachy said, "Don't go sentimental on me, old girl."

"Why would I?"

"We should go back to bed, get some sleep. A busy couple of days coming up."

Past two on that church clock over to the west. Jonas stood on the kitchen step, the door closed behind him, and watched Olaf prowling the cut-back herbaceous bed. About at the limit of his kitchen abilities, he had made himself a mug of cocoa, which Vera said was good for his Vitamin D deficiency that the medical checks at work had shown up, and the caffeine she claimed would have a positive effect on his moods. Nothing wrong with them that he could recognise . . . No rain now, but a frost gathering strength on the grass and making crackling sounds in the plastic guttering above him. He assessed that Olaf would take advantage of being let out at that time, the small hours when death was supposed to come visiting, and would look to make a snatch before coming back inside and settling on the bed. Jonas was restless, not at ease with himself. In a quiet voice, soft enough, he hoped, not to disturb the Derbyshires' sleep next door, he addressed the cat.

"I used to think, Olaf, that I was simply boring, but I'm modifying that. *Boring* perhaps, but also conventional. Yes? Or ordinary. And out of conventional and ordinary, comes *efficient*, and what that means is – something I've long been aware of – that I am a functionary. I make the trains run on time and to their destination. Trouble is, I know where the trains are tasked to go, and I know who they are carrying. After the ceasefire and end of World War Two, the victors hanged the losers if they'd organised those timetables . . . Always useful, Olaf, to be on the winning team – which for you is me and Vera."

His dressing-gown was good quality, 100 per cent wool. A present from his wife more than thirty years before.

"It is, I assure you, necessary to be both efficient and ordinary if one is to play the game that I'm part of. It is an unpleasant game, sufficiently unpleasant to be best practised by unpleasant men. It is not one for decent people . . . Are you about to catch some small creature, Olaf, or not? Is your blood lust count not too high? Shall we go to bed? Difficult, I agree, to step aside when matters are not yet concluded. Unpleasant. Yes, that sort of work, but someone has to do it."

He stood there a few minutes longer, gave the cat a last opportunity for a kill, and the night sky was attractive. He wondered whether the same sky, pricked with stars, was seen by the couple, the young people – been dirty work on his part, bringing them together. Necessary, but unpleasant. There was a squeal of fear and pain, a tiny creature's cry. 'About time, Olaf,' he murmured. 'I was concerned you were losing your appetite.'

15

"I've a favour to ask." Jonas had gone out to on the landing. Had disturbed neither Vera nor the cat.

"Do you ever, Jonas, not have a favour to ask? Spit it out."

He spoke with Detective Chief Inspector 'Chalky' White. Supposed that the man had a given name, but he was Chalky to all who knew him.

"Hoping I didn't wake you."

"I'm up early today, what with the short notice, the planning I have to do, but not that early. Getting all stressed out, are you? End of the road for whatever daft code name you've called it, and scratching your backside to pass the time."

"Actually, it's *Humble Pie*. Thought it appropriate."

"And the favour?"

The detail had been swirling in Jonas's head from the time he had come upstairs, having bolted and locked the kitchen door. It involved the length of the caravan that he would be towing and the length of the car he would be driving, and a little rider that the space into which he would need to fit should not be too finite, give him a bit of room for manoeuvre, and might he need to walk and how far would that be – and would Chalky's people look out for him? It surprised Jonas that he was given such courtesy, accepted that the gratitude towards him stemmed from the notes he had passed in St John's Gardens to that senior policeman, and assumed also that his instructions would be carried out in full.

"What time should I be there?"

"As long as you don't get in the way . . . I'll call you on that. When I have taken another half hour's sleep, then swilled some coffee in my gut, then shit, showered, and shaved, dressed, gone to work, then got the calculator out and done the sums. If that would be okay for you, Jonas, to allow that – then I will take the opportunity to call you. You are an old bugger, Jonas, always worth a good laugh."

"I have my uses."

"Not flattering you, but the best laugh. I've not shared this yet but when I brief on where we're going and why then the applause will lift the roof."

"It is twenty-five miles and timed at forty minutes."

"You'll be told. Now piss off and let me go back to bed."

Jonas returned to bed. It was nearly a year ago that he had been loaded onto an executive jet, the sole passenger, and had been flown across Europe, then been collected at a central European airport and driven to meet up with a collection of Albanian special forces, desperadoes all of them. Had confronted a crime baron who held in custody one of those young men whom Jonas found so malleable to his needs, had been put face-down in a ditch that doubled as an open sewer when gunfire had started up. Had been a hero, had been pictured astride the bonnet of an armoured car as if he were the mascot of a football team . . . had done so damn well. *Except.* Except that the young man he had rescued, and had put into acute danger, had gone away to the far north croft on a remote peninsula, and had broken off contact, and a girl with him who Jonas had found both likeable and efficient. Had severed any contact. Likely would be the same again, repeat performance.

So easy to get wretchedly fond of them. So simple to put concern for their safety ahead of getting a job done.

He would make an effort. Would take the boy to a pub. Would demand of both Effie Bellingham and the AssDepDG that they show up as well. Three-line whip, that sort of thing. Bring her down from the Highlands and have Harry drive him in and make him stand at the bar, arm in a sling and all. Would even reach into his inner pocket and fish out his wallet. When he was back from the Isle of Purbeck, the pretty section of the Dorset coast.

He doubted he would sleep again.

Jonas lay on his back, and a new spider had taken up space on the ceiling's central lampshade and was hard at work spinning. Saw that face, and that smile – yes, owed him a drink when the job was done.

His trainers in one hand, his bag in the other, Chopper came to her door.

Put the bag and his shoes on the corridor carpet.

He tapped lightly at her door. She might have been up and might have been dressing, or might be still lingering in the last minutes of sleep before the alarm destroyed it.

No answer from inside.

He knew the minder's room was the next one down the corridor, but was beyond caring. It was about a lesson learned when he had been a paratrooper.

He spoke urgently, like he was desperate for a response.

"Julie, it's me. Of course it's me. I was foul, you probably were too. But me first. Nervy, frightened even. I was out of order and you probably were too … Sort of what they call last-chance saloon, because we don't have the time to bicker and flounce around, score points and leave the nood to fester. We are both on a cliff edge, Julie. We'll go forward, hand in hand, arm in arm, and reckon when we go over we will find something to hang on to, and survive together, or we back off and funk the chance, and step back, which means we go our own ways and the chance is lost … It was my mistake not clearing up the broken shell, leaving it. My mistake."

Whether at the barracks or out in grim weather on the Brecons, or in the heat of an Afghan summer, in the culture of the Regiment's foot soldiers best practice was: if in the wrong, get on and admit it. Get the bloody thing over. Don't let it wriggle, stay alive, and hurt and hurt again. Been in the wrong, don't ship the blame, hold your hand up.

"We won't have, either of us, this chance again. We take it now, or it never happens. You are trapped in your life, me in mine. We are coming from two worlds that will not tolerate contact between us. They will fight to prevent it, fight to keep us apart. We have one chance, and that is now. Julie, we shall live our own lives, and do our own thing and laugh together, bleed together, love together. It is how we are. You know where I will be, and you come looking for me. I am asking you to do that. Come looking for me.'

Had never in his life made such a speech. He listened but heard nothing. He slid into his trainers, allowed the laces to trail and lifted his bag. The door opened and Chopper had his back to it and headed for the lifts, and did not know whether he had said the right thing, or said enough.

Julie was not mentioned by either parent over their breakfast. There was work to be done.

Before dawn, there would be a meeting in a layby off the A25, nearer for him than for Yitzak Cohn, and the final detail of the huge sum of money to be transferred would be confirmed as soon as the daughter, a walking dead, sent the signal that the deal was in place, and ownership guaranteed when it cleared. Another meeting, in a different layby with the lawyer, would show the necessary guarantees for the purchase of property on the Costa and on the now fancied Brazilian resorts on the Atlantic, apartment blocks on the Montenegrin coast that were at a good price because the Russians were anxious to flog them, cheap and quick, for worthwhile currency. Important to have the purchases ready to go when the monies began to surge back to Lachy as the shipment went out onto the market. He would walk the dogs round the boundary and he would feed the chickens . . . and Mrs Plumb would take the kids to school.

Had thought, two and a half years before, that a shipment coming ashore to the UK, same route of Antwerp to Felixstowe, same lorry team, and same overland journey, but a twenty-five per cent hike in local price and also profit margin, would be the last. Part boredom, part the restless energy that he had possessed all his adult life, had driven him back to the market place. Plus the death of the idiot Hamish and the prosecution of Gregor, the dumb fool – and the emptiness of his life. He had no need to prove his brilliance as a maestro businessman but achieving that pinnacle spot always gave satisfaction.

The matter of Softboy was also on the day's agenda, but after he had been driven by his muscleman to the East Anglian port and seen the discreet unloading of a part of the shipping container's cargo, along with the rubbish shipped for the Foreign, Commonwealth and Development Office. Not certain yet about Softboy's future, but would be by the end of the day.

Coffee was made for him, and he thanked Mrs Plumb for bringing it. And the darkness still hung heavy outside the windows. A long day for him and Vic, but a shorter one for his daughter who was no longer the future, was not worth being talked about at her parents' early breakfast.

She left her room, went along the corridor and down the stairs to the lobby, empty but for the girls at Reception, and quiet. Nothing on her bill, and the account settled. Took a seat, and waited. She was dressed smartly, jacket, white blouse, and trousers and flat shoes and understated stud earrings

Julie Wilson thought about their future and where it might take them. She did not think about the present which involved a tonne weight of uncut heroin paste. She did not think about its quality, its value which was put at $100 million, or who would use it and what it would do to them. Her business was the future, tomorrow and the day after.

'If you are failing to plan you are planning to fail' was a statement believed in by Walter Genge. He had no idea where the phrase came from, but followed its message faithfully.

The dining area, also used for residents' breakfasts, was on the mezzanine floor.

He left his bag by the door.

He had heard a great deal that morning. The boy at her door, pleading for her to follow him, some of which the Prof did not catch, but he caught enough. Her shower starting. Her leaving her room. She would be waiting for him in the lobby . . . was tied to him, he believed, until the meeting at the end of the tram line, where the woodland started and the parkland in which the cemetery was set. There had been no call from the big house in Surrey that would have killed the task he had been given earlier. No call, no message. Now he had to think how he was to carry out the order.

No shops open.

Total darkness in the dining area, and no staff on duty.

He liked to feel confident in his ability to perform, and had considered how to leave loose ends well knotted.

On his keyring was a jiggler and a bobby pin, all that he might have needed. Last used when Mrs Plumb had locked herself out of the back door, but he remembered the skills required. Among his many talents was an ability to pick locks. At around the time that he had been signed up to Lachy Wilson's payroll he had managed a fair living by unfastening doors, windows, whatever impediment was in his way, and taking what he thought was of value from inside . . . On only two occasions had occupants challenged him, and each had been beaten with sudden brutality and had wisely decided against following police and prosecutor advice and giving evidence that might have led to a culprit's identification. All a long time ago. He had no record of extreme violence since, not personally, but had helped on many occasions to lure others to a place where they were unprotected, where they would be maimed, or killed and later buried. Had not done it himself, but had conspired . . . It would be a first time for him.

Easy to open the dining-room door.

Simple to use a pencil torch to slip between the pre-laid tables.

No challenge in opening the door into the kitchen.

The torch threw a narrow light onto the back of the kitchen where he saw wide drawers which he guessed, correctly, held a selection of the chefs' utensils and knives. He would only need one, but it was the nature of the Prof that he took two. Each was six or seven inches long, with a serrated blade and a pointed tip; they each had protective shields and fitted comfortably into his trouser belt and would be hidden by his anorak.

Of scant importance to Wally Genge, the Prof, that his phone stayed obstinately silent, refused to ring out. The instruction given him was not reversed. As a lad, first time in an adult gaol, he had met an old man, drifting through an interminable sentence, who had talked of hangings in Pentonville HMP, and the night before the trap door fell, many had waited for a telephone call from the office of the government's Attorney General, as well they might listen for the clamour of its bell. A condemned huddled on a bed, or wasting time playing card games with the officers minding him, and the executioner in a guest house near the prison gates, and the governor sitting in his office . . . In all the cells off the landings men would wile away the darkness hours and believe they might hear the sounds of the bell, if it rang. Right up to the hour, 8.00 am, all of them would wait. Most often the call was not made, that prisoner had told him, and the trap slammed down as the high clock chimed above the Administration block. Irrelevant that he hoped it would ring and he would not have call for what he had stolen from the hotel kitchen. He was loyal to the family . . .

He left as silently as he had entered, and refastened the two locks. He almost tripped and had to steady himself when he saw Julie sitting in the lobby, and the thought crossed his mind: what would it be like to stab her with that type of knife, that length of blade and its serrated edges? How many times would he do it? Just the once and a twist, or multiple times, what the papers called a 'frenzy', and then he wondered how much mess on his clothes her blood would leave.

"Hi, Julie," he said, and tried, feebly, to smile.

"Hi, Prof," she answered and seemed to mimic him. Then criticism, "I've been waiting for you."

"Sorry, Julie, sorry."

"So, can we shift?"

"Of course we can, Julie."

He went to open the outer door for her. She put him, the hired help, in his place. Would stick it in, as far as it bloody went. Would wipe that supercilious grin off her face. Would want to see, close up, the shock on her face set in before the pain . . . if he did not get a call. He reached out to take her bag, but she looked at him haughtily and moved it out of his reach. She set the pace, he followed, and they walked out to the car. A refuse lorry was emptying the pavement bins, and another was hosing and brushing the street, and nobody around, like they were the only ones needing to get to work that morning. She looked good, must have soaked up what the bastard had been telling her through her door. He remembered how she had looked up to him when she was a teenager and he collected her from school, and her running towards him and him holding open the passenger door, and other parents staring at him and knowing who she was and wondering who he was, not catching his eye because they were frightened of him.

He carried with him the responsibility of an order from Lachy Wilson, and it was unthinkable that he would disobey. She chucked her bag in the boot, opened the passenger door and slumped inside.

"Come on, Prof," she said, as he climbed into the driver's seat. "Not a morning to be late because you overslept."

He knew that once he started, the first stab, it would become a frenzy.

"When word gets out, where we've been, what we've done, our colleagues are going to wet themselves," Rajah said.

"Other people have tried to line up on Lachy Wilson, then seen it all crumble and the case fail. Good detectives – not all of them corrupt, but too many who are," Dawson said.

Plunket said, "They'll have to set up a special unit at the Yard because this is going to run and run. Once the cuffs go on Lachy, he will be looking to do a deal. I say at the Yard, but it will be off somewhere in south London, a place the Met doesn't know about and the detectives doing the trawl will be from other forces. It will run and run."

The Belgian listened to their quiet, victory roll of talk. He drove, eyes on the road. He was exhausted. They followed the vehicle with the German plates. Not easy, and Plunket acknowledged it, because the road was empty and the city of Antwerp

– cocaine capital, diamond centre, home of the Rubens production line – was not yet awake. They had no criticism of their driver and thought themselves blessed that he had been assigned them. Did not go too close, and did not hang back so far that they could have lost their target vehicle. It was good to talk because it kept them awake. The heater was on and Rajah smoked continuously and the air was thick. One thing stood out for all three of them.

"He's not using tradecraft," from Plunket.

A smirk from Dawson. "Well the file, such as it is, says Kenny Harris is parachute regiment and Flying Squad. Walking out of aeroplanes when it's two thousand feet to the ground is hardly a bright way to behave, and the Squad are Neanderthals – should have been put out to grass light years ago. Neither is a good place for the acquisition of counter-surveillance skills."

Rajah said, "Makes me think that he does not realise our effectiveness, has never considered it."

They headed into the suburbs. Saw the shutters going up at a Turkish café and all of them thinking that they would have killed for a mug of coffee and a pastry, or even a Golden Arches sign – the life-saver for the night-time watchers huddled in a people carrier.

"I wonder how they met . . . Reckon they targeted him?"

"Can't see what he brings them. He's hardly on the inside track."

"Perhaps Miss Wilson wanted somebody she could wave her stuff at . . . Once his usefulness is done with they'll give him the heave. She might have been the encouragement, perhaps had a requirement that needed . . . you know. He'll be out on his neck as soon as she realises how tedious he is."

They talked some more and smoked some more and spoke as if they were alone and private, had forgotten that they had a driver who listened, whose face was expressionless.

Dawson said, "And giving up so much . . . good job, good pension, all down the drain. Could get fifteen years and driving straight into it, like he's half blind or just blinkered."

Rajah said, "Be bad for him inside, unless Wilson puts the word out for him, provides a degree of protection . . . but the Wilson influence will be dropping off fast by the time he's locked away."

"Just about there, guys," Plunket announced.

The driver slowed and they could see their target park his car away from the tram shelter, near the closed school gates. He did not do anything remotely sensible like go and get himself a coffee from a pavement stall, but crossed the main road and turned into the park, and they lost sight of him.

Plunket said, "Won't be long, guys. I reckon an hour and then we're all neatly tucked up . . . Please, keep your eyes and ears open."

She asked him if it were the same old story.

Jonas answered her, "Vera, you are teasing and going into the No Comment area."

She said, that she was merely wondering if it still registered around the Montagues and Capulets, the lovers from opposite sides of the fence, a high one, and likely topped with barbed wire, and flanked by minefields.

"That is Off Limits, and you well know the domestic rules."

Of course she did. It was an affliction carried by many men and women working for the Service who were quizzed as soon as they reached home. *Had a good day, dear / darling / miserable sod?* And the response was *No comment / Off-limits* because employment at Thames House permitted no chatter over the supper table or lying in bed about what had happened that day. Put a strain on things unless the partner had that dry sense of humour possessed by Vera. A twinkle in her eyes which he recognised as a sign of danger. She said she was just postulating that things had not worked out well for the Montague and Capulet brats, actually turned out rather poorly for the starstruck youngsters.

"That is as maybe, and that is just a story. There is no Romeo and no Juliet, no balcony, no nurse, and no poison. When the lid comes off the box, after about another seventy-five years, and the story of what I have been doing is opened to the public, then you will be able to read of this job and make a judgement. So, please, be patient."

She repeated that it had ended badly. She hoped neither of his young people was in touch with an apothecary in some back street of wherever they were, and that he was comfortable with what he had fashioned. Then she struck. So, if everything was good, and sunshine bathing the uplands, when would they be leaving with the caravan for the journey to the Dorset coast? The glint was in her eye. What was the further hold-up down to?

"Just something I need to know."

What did he need to know?

"Some bits and pieces."

About his work? Not for the first time, and she doubted it would be the last, she threw back at him, like she had chucked a plate at his head, the question that so vexed her . . . Was there no one else in that great mausoleum of a building where he worked who could fulfil the role of her husband? Was the place so emptied of talent that no other officer was capable of stepping in and minding the shop when her husband was holidaying on the Isle of Purbeck? She would have seen him wince.

"It's a matter of keeping things shipshape . . ." Jonas said hesitantly. He could not tell the lie yet. It needed keeping for a better moment . . . Nor could he reveal that the single greatest pleasure that he took from work was being there at the final curtain, seeing it for himself, and many times ending up in Accident and Emergency because that addiction was so powerful. Even the risk of having his throat cut, being decapitated, drowned in the sewage-filled waters of the Thames, or a shoulder dislocated could keep him away. "Soon, yes, quite soon, we'll be off. Not long."

He picked up Olaf, tucked him under his arm, had the phone in his hand and went out through the kitchen into the garden. It was his usual escape route when under pressure, too cold for Vera to follow. He waited for his phone to ring.

A man arrived by taxi. Money handed to the driver and the passenger out and raking the area with sharp eyes. Checked for surveillance and looked for the transport he would take over, and saw neither so settled himself inside the gloom of the shelter by the tram stop.

Chopper watched.

There had been Helmand mornings when the darkness had covered the frosted ground and the platoon had been out, walking along drainage ditches dug at the side of the roads and looking in the faint light for the movement of bad boys. Then they would stop to dig out a hole in the verge and plant the 'improvised' device, that was in fact professionally made, and then sneak away playing out the command cable for a hundred metres. Waiting for the moment when an armoured car would come rolling down the road and would press the detonator. It was the job of a bullish company commander to send out platoons and attempt an ambush, and it had not yet worked but was a favoured tactic. Longing for a fag, forbidden. Dying for a piss, doing it in your pants because standing up would be a near court martial offence. Feeling the cold gnaw at his bones, and watching.

He saw Julie twisting her arm to see her wristwatch, clocking the time and wondering where the rendezvous vehicles were. Saw the guy who was always a pace behind her, never in front, his eyes on her back. Chopper lay on his stomach in the undergrowth close to the gates of the cemetery, and the ground was damp and chilly, and kept needing to wriggle his toes to keep his circulation moving. She and her minder stood on a grass verge about a hundred yards away. He had to keep the blood moving or his first strides would be stumbled, feeble. Would have to sprint if the need came. Was uncertain what might trigger it, but needed to be ready . . . and there was the people carrier, and three guys in it and a woman. Not regular surveillance folk, and they had a window down from which cigarette smoke came. A lorry turning off the main road that led to the port, and the fags stubbed out and the window closed. He had not seen the faces other than a glimpse of the woman's when she had lit up the last time. He did not know how to place them . . . If he had to run and his legs were cramped up then he would not be in time for whatever . . . did not know.

A lorry parked up on a wide grass verge across the main road from the cemetery entrance and out of the range of the lights from the tram stop. Attached to it was a trailer on which a shipping container was secured. The driver dropped down from his cab, walked round his load, checking all the time for cameras and for any light glinting from the lenses of cameras or binoculars. He was happy to have parked on the frozen grass because at that time of day the chances of a municipal jobsworth bearding him were minimal. When he reached the rear of the container, he used a key on his ring to unfasten the padlock and open one side of the door. With his torch he shone a quick beam into his cargo of diplomats' personal possessions and checked that the gap between the boxes was still clear and could be used, and fast, as a corridor through which a tonne weight of additional cargo could be shifted. And was caught for a moment in the bright glare of headlights on a Mercedes-powered lorry, as its wheels came close, churning the grass and spitting away clods of frozen earth.

It was a practised drill. No requirement for either Dragan or Mehmet to go over it one more time. They killed the engine and went to work. Always a restless energy from both of them when an assignment was in its final moments and a long journey – some 4,500 miles – completed.

Both saw the man sitting on the bench inside the tram shelter. His head ducked in acknowledgement of an identical gesture from Dragan. A car, headlights not dipped, came down the highway that led to the port, and the pair caught a momentary glimpse of a young woman getting out, and a man stumbling after her on the frost-covered concrete. She was known to them and a guttural confirmation from Mehmet.

"She's on time. Ready and wanting to go."

"Decent-looking kid."

"I tell you, friend, that is meat too rich for you to digest."

And humour, and all surprisingly calm, but they could follow a procedure laid down more than a decade before – a procedure that was proven and secure. And action . . . Dragan set about clearing the cab and Mehmet opened a flap in the canvas covering the back of the trailer. The Serb needed a clear head to remember all that was theirs in the spaces under and behind the cab seats. Firearms, ammunition, canisters for flash and bang and for gas and smoke, fake identification documents . . . All went into a black plastic bag, heavy-duty. The girl and her escort were walking towards them, a good stride, a swing of her hips, authority on display.

"Is that a certainty, that I would get stomach ache?"

"And something worse, I promise. She is the old man's future."

"It is free to dream."

Mehmet pulled himself up and inside and groped his way down the aisle they had made between the Turkish furniture that would be on sale in Antwerp by the next afternoon. Went as far as the back bulkhead and started to feel around for the trigger point that would release the grimy piece of plywood that secured the hidden compartment. Had it open, and began to heave along the narrow corridor, grunting and panting, and banging against table legs and chair backs, the cargo on which fortunes would be made, on which lives would be lost . . . not Mehmet's concern.

A crisp voice, controlled, disciplined, quiet. "You have kept a good schedule. I congratulate you."

He would only have needed ten or fifteen minutes – then would go back to his wife and his village, happy . . . He went on shifting the bales of the stuff, one at a time, sliding them along the smooth worn surface of the trailer's flooring. He would need help because the weight of the stuff was killing him. The bags would be transferred from the trailer to the container and hidden there. The girl had to satisfy herself again that the cargo was genuine as she had done in Leipzig, then would call her father in the UK. And he would authorise the payment of the outstanding sum, big bucks, to be transferred into whatever cloud of ether it was headed off to. All about the 'nature of light' or the 'structure of matter', as Mehmet understood it. And received, the Turk did not understand how, by the backer of the deal in the Gulf. Receipt would be confirmed, almost simultaneous, and a deal done and closed. The way people operated, a guarantee given because a man's word was behind it, and beyond manipulation: all about trust which was a code understood by Mehmet. The parties would go their separate ways, and the guy sitting in the tram shelter would take over the Mercedes lorry and the furniture load, and the plastic sack of weapons. The documents would be held by him and Dragan for safekeeping, maybe for the next time. All going well, as expected. And the planning was good and was familiar.

The girl monitored what he did. Each time he dragged another sack of the prize cargo to the end of the trailer, and straightened, and gasped, he caught her eye. He did not consider the consequences of such a repeated action. She caught his eye but gave him nothing in return, and the bastard who was with her, heavy and unfit, seemed strangely detached from what played out. He did not look around, did not probe into the darkness away from the one lit area of the tram stop across the main road. Could not see a young man who watched him, nor a people carrier parked in an area used by the residents of the apartments on the far side of the tram stop and its shed. Almost done, he told her. The driver of the lorry that would pull the trailer with the shipping container stayed in his cab, would drive only when told to, stayed out of sight.

The girl had her phone in her hand. All about trust, Mehmet would have said, and he passed her a short-bladed penknife, and a centimetre-long incision was made in one package, and when the blade was withdrawn it held a smear of glutinous paste – with a value knocking on gold bullion of similar purity. She ran her tongue along the blade, grimaced, nodded. Only one packet checked but in this world trust was paramount, and the retribution to be brought down for breaking that faith would be exceptional and painful.

Dragan was dragging the stuff from the back of the trailer to the carefully constructed corridor on the shipping container. Speed was now of importance – there was a ribbon of light on the horizon and the promise of a fine winter's day.

Close to completion, and all was well. Mehmet managed a grin under a load seeming to break his back and Dragan's smile was wide. Who did not smile, did not laugh? The miserable bastard who was supposed to mind the girl, a pitiful creature . . . The other driver was now out of his cab, impatient for the loading to be completed, and for his own day's work to start at the check-in area of the container port.

Was Julie satisfied?

A shrug, a nod . . . attitude and poise, and in charge.

The container door was closed and padlocked.

Julie tapped the keypad on her phone.

Jacques asked, "You need some more?"

Plunket answered, "We don't have an eyeball on the guy. On his vehicle but not him. He went off into the trees. We have the girl, and if we had the phone then it would be enough, I reckon. But we don't have the phone, so it is *nearly* enough."

Rajah said, "The details on the container, and on the lorry, and Peggy's picture. Not much gap between *nearly* and *enough*. Everything else is bonus time."

Dawson held her camera, and had draped a grey cloth with a loose weave over the lens, sufficient to mask the brightness of the lens from passing headlights. She said, "Missing the boy which is a shame, but we have good previous on him. Have the girl well stitched. Good images. She will have called her dad, and doesn't matter what code she used. Encryption won't help her. A very nice morning, boss, and well done, Jacques. Our hero."

General laughter, and she belted his shoulder which was the joshing way that they behaved in police units, all comrades together, but her aim was not great and she whacked her fist into the butt of his pistol where it protruded out of the holster, and then had to wring the fist because of the pain, and more laughter. Jacques laughed, and could not remember when, if ever, his efforts had been appreciated at this level. He had never actually witnessed serious organised crime taking place. A transfer from one vehicle to another, and so many bags, and such a weight, and of so much value – and involving only a couple of men in one vehicle, and only one from another with a 'Removals, Since 2005, Worldwide' logo, and a slip of a girl and an older man with her who padded close to her back.

"Suggest, boss," said Dawson, "we hang about a bit longer. See what flight lover boy and lover girl are on, and feed the container details into the system, and the haulage people and get the holiday snaps blown up and printed, and maybe do the lifts in a couple of days?"

"Sounds right," Plunket said.

"And coffee soon," from Rajah. "Because this is about played out."

"Yes?"

"Chalky here, Jonas."

"And?"

"I was called direct, no name given, but I've the mobile number—"

"I know the way a telephone works."

"Steady, Jonas. It's Chalky and I've known you more years than my neck's got wrinkles."

"So . . . ?"

"It's up and running, transfer done. All signed off."

"When?"

"With the lights and the hullabaloo we'll get there in an hour. Leaving in two minutes, all loaded up. I'll skin you, Jonas, if you are there before one hour and twenty from now."

"Done."

"And don't bloody get in the way."

"Would I ever?"

"Don't break the speed limit."

Olaf was waiting by the kitchen door. Jonas grinned, picked the cat up, and carried it inside. He locked the back door behind him and went through to the hall. Vera was waiting there, the flap to the cat basket open.

"Well?"

"Anything else you want to do inside, my dear? It is a bit early, what with roadworks and all those incumbent delays, and I think it will have cleared a bit if we hold off another thirty-five minutes, then we should have a smoother run."

She stood her full height, which made her at least two and a half inches taller than Jonas, and glared at him. "Jonas, are you about to deceive me? And then do something that is not entirely sensible? I would appreciate a truthful answer."

"Absolutely not."

"Cross your heart?"

"And hope not to die . . . Just a scenic route, very pretty countryside, and a good holiday which we all need. Everything utterly sensible."

He went into the kitchen, filled the kettle, took mugs out and a teabag, and then found there was no milk in the fridge. So he switched off the kettle and replaced the teabag in the jar, and put the mugs away in the cupboard. Vera had already trapped Olaf in the cage, the animal howling piteously, and was sitting on the stairs while Jonas stayed in the kitchen, hunched at the table, as if he needed to be out of sight, and hopefully out of mind.

Could have been worse, he thought. And certainly could have been worse for Chopper. He was pleased to have shrugged off all of the Montague and Capulet nonsense. He would go when he thought it right. More precisely, he would arrive when the parking space outside those high gates was ready for him. He recalled a charge along narrow Albanian tracks in an armoured personnel carrier towards a bandit village, with a three-legged dog on his lap and idolising him . . . and slid that image into the convoy of unmarked cars, sirens bellowing, lights blinding, and hammering south towards an outstandingly attractive rural corner. The sun was just starting to appear in the east, but not lifting the chill – and Jonas shivered.

16

A rasp in her voice, Vera called, "Jonas, I am waiting. Olaf is waiting."

"Yes, dear. Coming, dear."

Reluctantly, Jonas stood up. He pushed the chair back under the table. He looked around him and realised there was nothing left for him to usefully fiddle with and lose a few more minutes. He would have to drive slower because the instructions given him on an arrival time had been specific.

"Hurry up, Jonas . . . Are you being deliberately awkward?"

"Just a quick comfort stop. Better now than later."

He did that, flushed, came out into the hall. He wore the same clothes to go on holiday, pulling his caravan, to the Isle of Purbeck, that he wore when he went to the office. Brogues buffed up, flannel trousers, a Tattersall shirt, a jacket of Harris tweed, and the tie that Vera had given him last Christmas. A change of scarf and gloves, and had his raincoat folded on his arm and his trilby on his head . . . He should have heard by now, should have been told. Should have heard it from Chopper himself, and not via a third party, that all was well, and *Humble Pie* winding down and the boy coming home. And would have told him that he, Jonas, was away in the country for a few days and would be in touch on his return and time then for a short debrief; yes, the boy could wait around until Jonas was back, then – maybe – take a bit of leave before going back to wherever he was heading.

Vera, Olaf protesting in his cage, went ahead of him. He locked the front door, not that there was anything inside that would have excited a thief. He went to the car and climbed in. Vera had put Olaf in the caravan and fastened the cage and settled beside Jonas.

Derbyshire was on his own forecourt. Jonas smiled at him and lowered his window. Time for some small talk, the weather, where they were going. Nothing about Jonas's integral part in disrupting an importation of a hundred million's street value of high-quality heroin paste. Jonas believed he had a reputation in the street of being what the AssDepDG at Thames House called a grumpy old fucker, was proud of it, and could see that his neighbour was confused to be spoken to with such apparent sincerity. After the weather, Derbyshire had started explaining the detail of a sales conference for the south-west that would be held on the outskirts of Bristol and the marketing plan for the future.

Jonas glanced at his wristwatch. No more time needed killing.

"Right, can't hang about all day. Keep an eye on the house. Have to be on our way."

He backed the caravan into the street. A delivery van hooted. Traffic stopped for him, then more space was needed, reversed a few extra yards to give himself more room. The wheels tumbled off the kerb. His phone was on his lap and the route playing out on the screen but not where Vera could see it.

At the top of the street he took a left, not the predictable right.

"What's this about, Jonas?"

"What I said, dear, a scenic route in the countryside. Have to try something different. Can't always be lodged in a rut, dear, can we?"

If his instructions had changed, Wally Genge would have been told.

'Prof, we were thinking of it, what we said. Change of heart – she's our girl at the end of the day. Needs sorting out, but it'll be inside the family. Bring her home . . . But he had not had the call.

The goods had been transferred from the lorry trailer to the shipping container. The light of the day was starting to emerge. The frost crackled on the grass, streetlights beyond the tram shelter were losing their lustre, traffic was building. In front of him, Julie Wilson – condemned by her own family, and the job of executioner given to Wally Genge – looked around her. How many days since she had last bothered to give him a gracious word, say anything that showed her appreciation of what he did for her? He could justify what he did as his hand went beneath his anorak and found the handle of a knife. Gripped it, and thought the chance had come, needed taking. Would have been better if the guy had also been there and maybe he would have done him over first. But the guy sniffing at the Wilson girl was a big bastard and likely a handful of trouble, and more suitable for Softboy to take a run at. He could manage Julie, the heir, who had fucked up and he could not understand why – after all he had done for her, and after all the love he had lavished on her.

A choke in his throat, tears starting to well.

He went towards her. She had her back to him and was scanning the line of trees beside the cemetery gates . . . and the Prof understood what she was doing and why. Would be where her guy was: he would emerge from the gloom and they would steal away. Julie and the Prof were due to fly out of Antwerp that afternoon. Likely the two of them, the boy and Julie, would be screwing in a hotel room until it was time to leave for the airport. An anger blinded him, his adoration for her was trashed, everything he had done for her was comprehensively binned. Good that he thought in that way, and the tears had come on harder, and he gripped the handle of the kitchen knife.

He saw the drivers of the lorry that had made the journey from Afghanistan, making their farewells, one of them holding a heavy plastic bag. Saw the driver of the shipping container. Saw a man push himself up from the bench in the tram shelter and start to walk towards them. All relaxed and calm, and all reeking of success and confidence . . . and he would fucking show them because that was the demand that Lachy Wilson had made of him.

She was still gazing at the trees as the first shafts of sunlight hit the grass and made pretty lines of colour between the shadows. The Prof was not in the mood for poetry; he was a hitman, was paid for it, and did as he was told.

She turned. Perhaps she could hear the sound of his breathing, the tread of his feet on the frozen blades of grass. She saw it was

him, and shrugged. Only three or four strides until he was close
enough, and she was staring at him, and perhaps the low sunlight
had caught the moisture on his cheeks.

She was the girl he had indulged. The girl whom he had loved
as an uncle loves a niece. The girl to whom he had read until she
fell asleep. The girl who had confided in him when she had started
at a new school, what she liked, what she hated.

He lunged at her, surprised himself. Lachy would have gone
straight up to her, then grabbed. Softboy would have gone for her, no
hesitation, and might have allowed her to see the knife because she
would have frozen at the sight of it. His feet became tangled, but his
weight threw him forward. The Prof did not do killing. Could drive a
car, unpick a lock, mend a fuse, get life back into the plumbing, but
had not done killing . . . But it had to be done, done there, done now,
one job given to him. He grabbed at her, caught a fistful of hair and
had the blade out and the arm holding it was poised to thrust – and
she was yelling and scratching at him. The nails on her fingers were
as sharp as fucking razors and an arm was round her throat and
above it was bare flesh, where the knife needed to be.

He slashed at her. She writhed like a cat.

He slashed again at her throat, then went for an upward stab
into her stomach and chest – and the tears came worse.

Chopper thought himself too late.

He was running, but not fast. His legs were leaden, his breath
heavy.

Had seen her looking for him, running her eye over the woodland beside the road that led from the edge of the park and away
towards the cemetery and that corner of it where the quarried
Portland stones stood proud, like where his mate little Lofty might
have been. Lofty who lugged the loaded belts for the GPMG, all
the weight of the ammunition needed by the machine gun . . . and
that was the dream in his head when he saw the shape of Genge
and of Julie merged together, and would not have known the crisis
level but for the peeping sun hitting the blade, and for her little
stifled scream.

He lumbered out of the trees. He had no weapon. Only a key ring. But there had been fights in the pub-lands of Colchester when a ring of keys was considered more than adequate. And fights on the touchline of inter-unit football, where the officers turned away from their baying encouragement for him, Chopper, to 'kick the shit out of them, good lad', where boots and fists did all that was needed. And he was a killer. There were graves round villages, baked-mud compounds in the Helmand province, that were testimony that he could kill and feel nothing and then go have a beer if the officer said they'd done well enough to break out the six-packs.

He ran towards her and pain gripped his ankle where the old wound was. Ran and could not gain speed or surprise.

Heard her scream, and saw the blade.

Chopper threw himself forward, and landed short, was scrabbling against the grass, trying to heave himself closer.

Happening at a speed like nothing else she had known. She felt the knife, the shock. She was yelling, howling, and Chopper was shouting and little intermittent grunts came from the Prof. She could not understand how the man had put together the courage needed to come after her, was using this idiotic little knife. The kids who did killings used big-blade machetes, great long knives that they shoved into their trousers, the tip of the blade about level with their knees . . . But the prof had stabbed her, and inside the shock area, and inside the pain factor, was the wetness of her blood. And Chopper was not there.

Could smell the Prof's breath. Saw his arm coming up, which might be where it all ended, and did not know why Chopper was not there, did not save her.

Took the deepest breath, as if she were drowning. A last breath that might keep her alive a few more seconds. The Prof's breath was like an animal's, like her father's dogs.'

Peggy Dawson asked, "Does anyone know what the fuck is happening?"

Rajah said, "No idea – out of nowhere."

Plunket shook his head. "All I know is that someone with more clout than me said, 'Recollections may vary'. If we had to write it down, there would be three versions, all different."

Dawson: "Bloody hell, not my cup of tea."

Rajah: "I don't have the training for intervention stuff."

Plunket: "Well beyond my job description."

Through the windscreen of the people carrier, they could see a stretch of open grass, the sun had broken through and showed the writhing shapes on the ground, and every few seconds a car or a van or a lorry came down the main road, going at speed, and their headlights caught the bodies but no one stopped.

The struggle was coming to an end, the movements were slacker.

In the distance, the man from the train shelter reached the lorries. The guy holding a black bin bag was reaching inside it, and the guy with him was shining a phone torch down into the bag to help him.

Jacques shifted in his seat, a set look on his face, and jutted his jaw. He opened his door and was groping for his holster.

Plunket: "He wants to be a hero, that's his decision."

Dawson: "Count me out."

Rajah: "Not for me."

The Belgian deliberately closed the driver's door behind him. The team from the Anti-Corruption Unit would have agreed that he wore an expression that reflected his sense of duty, that suited what his action would be. The team would have also concluded that the expertise that their new best friend, Jacques, possessed was way different from that of a calm, cold-blooded marksman – like a non-swimmer who went into a riptide to save the family dog and ended up being washed ashore, while the dog had paddled back to the beach, shook itself, and went off to look for its tea.

They heard an explosion.

"This is getting worse."

"Boss, are we serving any useful purpose being here?"

Plunket said, "Have to stay. He's got the fucking ignition key."

A dense grey smoke was rising from where the two men and the woman had been struggling on the grass. A smoke grenade had been thrown by the man with the black plastic bag. And then another, louder, thunderclap which was a flash and bang canister that lit the thick smoke, and then another one.

Jacques aimed his pistol and fired his first shot.

"What target has he got?"

"Nothing to aim at."

"It's a clusterfuck" – Plunket's opinion.

Jacques felt calm, which surprised him.

He kept shooting and believed each bullet was fired in the manner of the instructors' teaching.

Sometimes he could see the target through the smoke from the grenades, and sometimes he could not.

It was the first time that he had drawn his weapon in any situation other than in the indoor ranges where the police were sent when their certificates needed renewing. There was a junior officer in Liège, and at a conference in Brussels – every spare policeman called in from the regions for a vexatious EU conference with security concerns – who had been pointed out to Jacques. The whispered explanation for his celebrity status was that he had, nine years before, shot dead two bank robbers and critically wounded a third. The officer from Liège walked with a swagger and obviously took pride in his moment of fame . . . but must have been stupid because he had not been promoted. Jacques had never met or seen any other officer who had opened fire and killed. He kept on firing into the heap of entwined bodies, but was not sure why.

Fired again and again, until his trigger finger went slack, and there was no further kick and the aim stayed down and did not lift with the recoil. He saw the shapes lurch and twitch and could not distinguish which was the girl and which was her boy, and which was the older man who had set out to kill with a kitchen knife.

Jacques realised that each time he had fired, a sense of

unnatural excitement coursed in him – better than when a big pike was on his line.

Realised the magazine was exhausted, began to extract the used magazine and reach into his pocket for the spare one, and was about to reload, and . . . lights blinded him.

From inside the people carrier came little whistles of astonishment.

Emerging from the smoke was the minder, Genge, crawling like a stubborn but crippled animal. With great effort he edged towards Jacques who did those fast hand movements that changed a magazine. The lorries were spitting fumes out of their exhausts and were beginning to manoeuvre clear of each other, and threw out massive light in front of their cabs.

They were, all three of them, police officers who regarded themselves as hardened. Not to Beirut or Gaza standards, or those of the eastern Ukraine front lines, but able to absorb the 'difficult times' in any inner London housing estate, and would have seen close up the ravages of a street stabbing or the immediate results of a Class A overdosing. This overshadowed everything they had known. The minder, Genge, had almost reached the feet of the Belgian police officer, was perhaps a yard short, and the pistol was cocked, and Jacques might have been on one of his training courses because he was seen to take aim, methodically and in his own time, and from inside the vehicle the barrel looked as if it pointed directly at the top of Genge's skull.

"I don't believe it."

"What should we do?"

Plunket said, "We don't have a dog in this fight – we do nothing."

A shot was fired. The pistol kicked.

"That is murder."

"Extraordinary. Quite unjustified. Cold-blooded."

Plunket said, "I saw nothing. Cannot corroborate anything you might think you saw. Nothing that I could be sure of, did not have an eyeline."

"Too right."

"And me. Saw nothing."

Plunket said, "I regard him as a very steady officer, a credit to his force."

Jacques bent, scrabbled in the grass, picked up his cartridge cases, and walked back towards the people carrier.

Mehmet said, "I reckon it's time to move."

Dragan said, "Reckon it past that time."

The Mercedes lorry, pulling a trailer laden with Turkish furniture for an aspiring-middle-class market in western Europe, drove past them and the massive wheels cut deep ruts in the frosted grass.

A wave from the ground.

The lorry braked, skidded a couple of metres, stopped. The driver's door opened.

Mehmet called out, "We have no need again for these."

Dragan echoed him, "Better they are not with us."

The black plastic bag, carrying the weight of gas and flash and bang and smoke canisters and a loaded pistol and a Kalashnikov assault rifle, two magazines taped together and slotted, was heaved up and sunshine glittered on it in the moment before a hand took it inside. The driver's door slammed shut and the lorry lurched onto the road and headed off to the north and soon the SatNav would be showing the route to Brussels. The second lorry, pulling the trailer on which a shipping container was lodged, followed the first one onto the highway, but then veered off in the opposite direction and joined a thickening queue of heavy goods vehicles.

A light wind was up and further thinned the pall of smoke.

Jonas read the message that had come up on his phone screen, which then reverted to the map.

One of his talents was an ability to show no sign of anxiety or stress. Just a momentary pursing of his lips.

Vera said, "It's not a route I know, Jonas."

He was sharp. "Perhaps because the last time you came along it you were either asleep with me driving, or concentrating on the traffic if you were driving yourself."

A bit savage, but the message from Chalky White, Flying Squad, had disturbed him.

Grumpy old fucker (appropriate?). Had expected further confirmation of onward shipment. Your boy gone quiet. Relying on previous message re deal terms activated. Not satisfactory but will have to do. Chalky.

They went through Cobham, where footballers from the better south London teams were reputed to live . . . The only footballer he cared about was Chopper Harris who should have been in close touch, like an air traffic controller guiding the team in. He felt peevish, as if the day was blighted, and made a remark about how pretty the road was, and Vera snorted as they drove past a park of storage warehouses.

Both lapsed into silence.

He reflected that *the best-laid plans of mice and men oft' go awry*, which seemed a suitable response, and Robert Burns had realised it, and written of a mouse who had dug a hole in a field as a secure residence until the farmer ploughed over it . . . The AssDepDG would have characterised the moment with acute vulgarity or obscenity. He assumed that Vera would have reckoned that the matter of a Montague and a Capulet joined in romance and walking away from their own families was a fraught idea and in danger of a greater catastrophe than his mouse faced. Better that he and she stayed quiet.

He drove on. Then suddenly had to veer onto a hard shoulder. Came to a juddering halt. His mirrors were filled with the sharp lights of three police wagons, and their numberplates confirmed them as from the Metropolitan area, but an unmarked car led them with lights flashing behind the radiator grille, and a front passenger waved to him – quite an impertinent gesture – and only when the convoy was well past did Jonas nudge back onto the road. He assumed the sirens would have been throttled by the time they approached that well-heeled Surrey village where the watercress beds were and through which the Tillingbourne meandered and where a man of power, brutality, and wealth lived – and who believed himself 'too big to be brought down'. Jonas drove steadily.

Vera eyed him with a steely gaze. She would have doubted anything happened by accident or by coincidence.

And Jonas would have agreed.

The children were starting to arrive at the school, pride of place in the Antwerp suburb of Hoboken. Mothers, fathers, grandparents, neighbours were dropping them at the just-opened outer gate, and all were oblivious to what had happened beyond the terminus for the tram line, and across the main highway to the city centre and also to the Schoonselhof municipal cemetery. Soon, the children would be whooping and yelling in their play area, and the wintry sun was rising and would soon clear the treetops. Ignorance ruled. What might have alerted them was a little pyre of dark smoke, but the wind was sufficient to disperse it. Traffic thickened. The day started. Staff came to the school, and coffees were served in the canteen, and footballs were kicked round the play area and kids' cycles manoeuvred between them – and a crime scene discovery team was on the move. Dog walkers would soon be heading towards the woodland around the cemetery.

Walter Genge had been addressed as the Prof, and had been treated with a degree of respect by those who knew he was on Lachy Wilson's payroll. Would he be mourned? Not at all. He lay on his side and the angle at which he had fallen determined that the majority of his head, what was still in place, was visible. The wound caused by a point-blank shot from a 5.7x28mm cartridge was mostly hidden. A nearby patch of grass had been flattened, and marks of the struggle remained, along with a short kitchen knife with a serrated edge. And not a squeak of Rossetti out of him. Nothing about *Remember me when I am gone away, Gone far away into the silent land.* He was ignored as the dawn shifted towards the day. Any casual walker within twenty feet of him would have seen only his crumpled coat, and within ten feet would have assumed that one more citizen needed to sleep off an excess of alcohol or cocaine, or both.

A big lorry, carrying furniture, was now in the middle lane of a highway that was signed to Brussels, the A1 route. Phone calls had been made and at a service station shortly to be reached, the driver would be met, a plastic bag handed down from the cab, and all left clean inside.

Another lorry, hauling a shipping container, was approaching the gates of the port where its papers – all in order – would be shown, and very soon a cargo would be unloaded and hoisted high to await transfer to a boat scheduled to leave for Felixstowe on the east coast of England.

After a tram ride into the city centre, and a brisk walk up the hill to the railway station, Mehmet and Dragan caught a train to Amsterdam. An eighty-five-minute journey and two an hour, an excellent service. A crowded carriage and they were unremarkable and unnoticed – and would go their different ways in Amsterdam . . . might meet again soon, and might not.

"He blew the beggar's head off. Seems pretty relaxed about it," Rajah said.

"I talked once to a Federation guy and he'd dealt with a cop who killed while on duty and reckoned the shock bashed him sideways and he was kept away from the investigation people for at least forty-eight hours, protected from incrimination because he could easily talk himself into facing a murder rap," Dawson said.

"Looks like he expects their king to come along and pin a medal on his chest."

"But, it's all wrong, isn't it?"

The two of them were out of Jacques's earshot. His pistol was now holstered, and the site sanitised . . . except that it was empty.

Plunket was ahead of them, hunched down where the frosted grass was flattened. Using a pencil to push aside individual blades of grass, he was searching diligently but already the wind was at work. He turned, looked up.

"Not what we *say* we saw, but what we *actually* saw . . . they're not here – fucking obvious. Our chum was emptying a magazine – twenty shots – into smoke. He hit Genge because the holes are obvious in his torso, but there aren't enough of them. Where are lover boy and lover girl? The three were all wrestling on the ground, and the blood is here on the grass. Where are they? I didn't see them go. Didn't see them carted off when the lorries pulled out. Didn't see any strangers come in off the street and with a mission to do some house-keeping, tidy it all up. But they have to be dead or at least injured and critical. Tell you what I think . . . wild animals, if they're shot they creep off to hide, get into the undergrowth, hunker down, stay there till their last breath. Go where their enemies don't find them. Make themselves scarce until the Big Reaper comes calling, and cannot be long if not already arrived . . . Just a thought. Smoke was thick from those bloody bombs but we should have seen something. Saw nothing . . . Look at the place."

The three of them stared at the ground. Around them was a prosperous middle-class suburb of a sophisticated European city. A school bell was ringing and kids would be drifting inside to their classrooms. The grass was pressed down as it would have been when two men and a woman were on top of each other, making almost a small pyramid, and a full twenty-bullet magazine had been fired, and blood enough to keep a transfusion unit going – and only Genge still there. A tram was sounding its klaxon for pedestrians to get off its tracks, and was pulling away.

Plunket said, "I don't really see there is much mileage for us here."

"Quite right, boss, nothing that'll help us down the road." The relief was writ large on Peggy Dawson's face.

"Too right, boss," said Rajah. "Hang on here and we'll be enmeshed. Questions and more questions, and authorisation, and legality and what was our mission . . . I reckon it's off to the airport, double damn fast, and someone does the tickets and someone gives our best friend Jacques a big box of chocs for his missus, and we're on our way. Just so as we understand each other – what did we see?"

"Nothing." Dawson lit a fag.

"Saw fuck all of nothing," Plunket said.

They walked back to the people carrier, and gestured for Jacques to follow them, which he did. He was smiling – like his day had started well – and they had nothing appropriate to say to him.

"Very scenic, Jonas. Good of you to bring me. And sensible."

He muttered something about firing up her Kindle, or getting stuck into her crossword book.

She told him they were both inside the caravan.

Not the best moment for a domestic. There was indeed a space closed off with cones and an area of a rural verge to go with it. In front and behind were police wagons. He had a feeling that the space allocated him would be challenging for him to park in, and there were beads of sweat already forming on the back of his neck.

A uniform walked up to Vera's door. She wound down the window. He asked, "Is he Merrick?"

"That's him. Are you about to cart him off?"

"This space is for him."

"Very generous."

They indicated where he was to park – on the far side at the grass and mud at the side of the road – and Jonas saw a ditch. Not very deep, only about a foot, but if the caravan wheels went into it, or the Rover's tyres, then they would probably need a tow rope to extract them.

"Nice to see an old job like this one, ma'am. Rover SD1 – my dad used to have one. Amazing how it's lasted, and you've kept the bodywork well. Suppose this is one of the last run, 1984, wasn't it, when they packed it in? You might like to get out, ma'am, while he's doing the business."

But he was her husband. People said she was a candidate for a birth among the angels because she stayed with him, tolerated him. She sat tight. Had forgotten all the paraphernalia of deceit, and understood that this was part of the Verona connection. Kept her belt fastened. Reached across and squeezed his arm, her gesture of support. So, the vehicle was forty years old, technically a classic, needed an enthusiastic mechanic, a motoring geek, to keep it on the road, and it worked . . . He was her husband and she'd not give fuel to any uniform with a sneer on his face.

"Come on, Jonas, do it."

He said, "Sorry, dear, but had to be here. This is the home of the Capulet girl. I expect they've a tidy little balcony above the front door."

He started to reverse, then go forward, then reverse some more, then forward again, and all the time she had her hand, for reassurance, on his arm. He made a damn good effort of it. Looked wrung through when he had finished, turned off the engine, and had a decent-sized audience. She pecked his cheek, as if she was proud of him, almost. The uniform, stonily now, told him that Detective Chief Inspector White was up at the house with the rest of the glamour guys, and he was to walk up the drive. Might have to get a move on if he didn't want to miss the rubber-necking moment. Jonas's phone pinged.

He climbed out of the car, careful that he didn't fall into the ditch. The uniform had the door open for Vera but she declined to get out.

Of course he could manage the parking, but as a general had said it had been a *damned serious business*, at the least, more likely *the nearest run thing you ever saw*. Would have liked to sit down, but the opportunity was denied him.

He read what Chalky had sent him. *All a bit of a mystery. Shooting in Antwerp, a foreigner killed by local police, name of Genge, Walter – British passport holder. Confusing reports. Gunfire and grenades, and the body found by dog walkers. Believed to be more casualties but no confirmation of identities or whereabouts.*

He faced an ornate pair of wrought-iron gates, expensive but without class, and turned to her. "That business about the Montague boy and the Capulet girl. It was just a story. We have to cling to that – just a story."

17

When he was level with them, Jonas could see that the wide gates were askew. They had been wrenched apart – probably by a chain hitched up to a tow bar, nothing as time-consuming as a powered oxyacetylene jet – and they were sufficiently bent to make them difficult to move fully open. He doubted it mattered or that the aesthetics of the place were important.

Just inside the gates, set back from them, was a lodge. Jonas thought it ugly, inappropriate for the rather pretty scenery now confronting him. A man was sitting by the open front door. Wore a white police-issue paper over-garment, used when the arrested person's own clothes were bagged up for forensics. He was hand-cuffed, his expression mixed heartache with crumpled resignation, and he was muttering inaudibly. Jonas recognised him as the one they called Softboy. Two officers stood over him. Both wore trainers and jeans, hoodies over their upper bodies, and police baseball caps, and both already looked bored.

One whistled for Jonas Merrick's attention. "You looking for DCI White?"

Jonas nodded.

"Find him up at the house. Quite a way, you be all right?"

He shrugged. Have to be. "And this is Softboy?"

"The very man. Keeps moaning about not having written a letter to a solicitor – and that seems to give him grief. Straight on, sir, and I can't promise they'll wait for you."

He lengthened his stride. Jonas Merrick had never been on a military parade ground, had never worn his King's Gallantry Medal and the bar awarded him for a second time. But he did an apology for a march, his chest protruding and his arms swinging.

Thought he might replicate it when he was back in London and heading over Lambeth Bridge on the way to his place of work. Adjacent to the lodge was a kennel area but with German Shepherds, not spaniels, and they lay on their stomachs, heads between their front paws, eyes narrowed and ears down, like their authority had been taken from them, put under lock and key.

The sun was almost up, would soon clear the trees. They were oaks and made an attractive avenue. There was enough frost on the ground to have frozen over the minor dips and uneven surfaces on which the previous days' rain had puddled. Where the boundary was angled he could see the loosely coiled bundles of razor wire, and the posts, twelve feet high, lights mounted on top. Not quite a ploughed strip, not likely to be anti-personnel mines as on the old DDR frontier, or modern Russia's, or that behind which the fat man of North Korea sheltered, but formidable – and more so if those dogs were given free rein to run. Jonas chuckled. Himself, the predator in this case, he inhabited a three-bedroom semi-detached house, mock Tudor façade, narrow concreted area at the front where the caravan was parked most of the year, and a hundred feet of garden at the rear which was sufficient as a killing zone for Olaf. His quarry, who he believed he had now trapped – where many had failed, which gave acute pleasure – lived behind these defences because the threat to his wellbeing, and his family's, was great. There was a copse ahead and the drive snaked round it. On either side of the drive was post and rail fencing, in good condition and not leaning, but no livestock. Jonas supposed that having a local farmer graze the fields would have introduced a threat to the security of the owners, more trouble than it was worth. He wondered if he was supposed to feel a twinge of sympathy for any man needing to live behind barricades that were necessary to keep out those with hatred in their hearts . . .

He had reached the copse. A mix of oak and beech, and more post and rail surrounding it. The drive swung round . . . and he faced the house.

Police wagons were parked messily, no effort made to get them in a line. He saw more by walking than he had noted when he had come in the van, supposedly Surrey constabulary and Scenes of Crime, and had worn the same garment in which Softboy was now encased. Effie Bellingham had driven, he had been beside her and had noticed very little because his attention had been directed towards people, not scenery, possible wildlife, probable bird species. Typical of the Squad, and typical of his good friend who was the DCI on the job – typical of Chalky White to have the battle wagons come roaring up the drive and the guys pile out. Likely that some of the attack force would have had handguns drawn and more would have had tasers ready, and a couple would have battering rams in their hands. All down to him . . . just a little job that had been put into the path of Jonas, something for him to do, and a result gained. At what cost?

The cost of it was something that he had tried to put out of his mind.

Shut it away, because this was a moment of triumph, one that he would have been loath to give up. Put it on a back burner and would reflect later on his boy: a decent enough lad.

He saw feathers. White and brown, small red flecks among them. Then saw a claw, a chicken's, severed at the ankle. The trail of feathers formed a path from the rear of the house and disappeared into a shrub at the side. A wind was coming with greater strength and lifted more feathers, tugging them from the undergrowth and they flew like kites on a string. More of Chalky's people were here, similarly dressed to the men down at the lodge. He approached the haphazardly parked wagons.

"Are you Chalky White's visitor?"

"I am."

"Guv'nor said one would show up."

"It seemed the right place to be."

"Don't mind me asking, are you a big part of this circus?"

"Just on the edge, far from central. What's with the feathers?"

"Always one evening, isn't there? My family used to keep chickens in Shropshire. Always one evening when the weather was foul, or someone forgot, and the birds weren't shut up safely. The bloody fox comes. Suppose it comes every night and takes a look.

They'd let their guard down last night and the birds weren't put away properly. Most are dead, one's been taken, the ones left are in shock and might as well be gone . . . Him inside, he's more shook up by his birds, what's happened to them, than his own future – which is pretty bleak. You want me to tell the DCI you're here – what did you say your name was?"

"I didn't – I expect he has enough on his plate, don't bother him."

Jonas smiled, the wintry one.

The kids came first, in school uniforms, the housekeeper woman with them.

He supposed it was next to impossible to separate the actions of parents from the influencing stains it would put on the minds of teenage children. Obviously an attempt to portray the situation as something of a blip, soon to be sorted out, nothing too much out of the ordinary. They had not shed tears but were close to it, chins wobbling, and a defiance writ loud. Trying to be brave, but realising that it was different that morning from having the Surrey police coming inside and taking their shoes off and having refreshments brought to them. Not knowing why they were there, because this was the Flying Squad on an away-day excursion from London and who did not expose their socks and brought their own tea and had their own biscuits, and dressed shambolically – and also had brought handcuffs. Jonas knew the housekeeper was Mrs Plumb, had briefly considered her as worth taking in and working over as the possible source, but had seen her those months before and had ditched the thought. In amongst the wagons was a small car, and the boys marched towards it, and one spat and one showed a finger and both trailed satchels. He wondered what they knew of their sister, which could not be less than Jonas did.

And the boys' mother came out of the house. No cuffs on her. Hardly about to do a runner. She looked around and went to the little car . . . did the parental bit, and gave them each a kiss on the cheek, and both flinched as if that did not fit their image of resist-ance, damaged the theatre. They were in the car, and Mrs Plumb extricated it from among the wagons, and drove off, and Victoria Wilson watched them all the way.

No one had ever accused Vic Wilson of stupidity.

She saw Jonas and her memory ground through the gears. Saw him in a raincoat and wearing spectacles, and with a trilby on his head.

No one would have called Vic Wilson slow to react to augmented danger.

She was a policeman's daughter. Mrs Plumb had been instructed to take the boys to school, to stay in Dorking until it was time to collect them and then she should drive them to her parents. Their bags had already been put in the car. All arranged, done with a minimum of drama, fifteen minutes earlier.

Vic saw Jonas and stared at him for a moment, and worked through her memory and scratched for the link . . . and remembered a woman with a camera that was metal and reinforced, and who hardly used it, and remembered her daughter coming out of her room and appearing on the landing, half dressed – correction: quarter dressed. Remembered the man behind the girl who carried a tripod, and had little to do, and neither had accepted the teas or coffees offered them.

Remembered what she had seen, and what she saw now.

Not stupid and not slow. It was the Flying Squad that had come into her home. Not a polite ring of the door bell, and a request for the front door to be opened, but the window beside it smashed, and alarms sounding and men and women coming inside and scampering for the stairs and around the house, and doors thrown open – and Lachy and herself at the kitchen table and him white with pain because the fox had been at the chickens, his pride and his joy, and him eating nothing and drinking nothing, and looking like he was broken . . . Vic was not stupid and not slow, and recognised him, and knew that a unit like the Flying Squad would not have allowed a second-rater close to the house at this time. Not possible. She turned, gave no indication of what she now believed as certainty, went inside – would smile and cajole, would use her reservoir of charm, would get permission to speak ever so briefly, and quietly, to her husband.

Revenge was best served cold, but if that version could not be served, then was best delivered any way possible.

It was a problem that rarely confronted Jonas Merrick, so was not one that he acknowledged. He did not regard his appearance as anything out of the ordinary. No other passenger on the early train up to town from Raynes Park in the morning, or coming back in the afternoon, was dressed as he was. No other pedestrian crossing Lambeth Bridge was clutching a trilby, while a Harris tweed jacket flapped in the wind and his brogues stamped on the pavement . . . no other individual standing outside the front door of the Wilson home was so easy to identify. Chalky White was brought out and stood on the step and gave Jonas a thumbs up.

What was he there for?

Jonas could have mumbled something about a gambler's obsession, about an addict's compulsion. He *needed* to be there, and the string of times when he had felt the same requirements and had put himself in a line of fire, were ignored. Not relevant, forgotten . . . and on this day, in a morning of occasional sunshine and scudding clouds, was half of the total complement that made up the Flying Squad, respected for athleticism, street-level arrest capability, tough guys and girls, all present and correct and therefore rendering him about as safe, tucked up securely, as he was ever likely to be.

Spent the hours of his working week hunched close to his screen in a makeshift office space in the Post Room, or in a cubicle off a room where surveillance people gathered for briefings. Shut away, ignored. Until those rare times that he came down from a mountain peak and delivered. He needed to see the truth and all that vanity medicine of 'making a difference', the achievement of what he did, but not up in lights. Be up there with it, shoulder to shoulder, eye to eye. Just to know it was *real*.

Was there and had to be there, and being there was worth the lie to Vera . . . in a few more minutes he would have had his 'fix', been lifted by it, would be driven down to the gates, then would get his Rover and his caravan off the verge and would head off towards the Isle of Purbeck, a camp site near Langton Matravers, and cliff walks and ploughman lunches. And then perhaps even some covert praise when he returned to London … though it irked him that the AssDepDG was still on sick leave and that Effie Bellingham had walked out on him.

He almost missed the moment, had been indulging himself.

Chalky had emerged, caught Jonas's eye, winked fractionally – just between the two of them – and came down the steps and stood to one side.

"Bit parky today. What we call a Pearl Harbor, don't you know?"

Jonas had no idea what he meant so put on an evasive grimace.

Their prisoner followed. Lachy Wilson was handcuffed, arms behind his back. Detective Sergeant Paddy Dickens had a hold of his right arm. Wore the white suit which stripped dignity from him. He paused on the bottom step, was allowed to, turned slowly and gazed up at his home. Was unlikely to be seeing much of it in the next few years, indeed for many years. A central extravagant portico but no balcony capping it, two wings leading off the main lobby, sash windows on the ground floor and conventional ones on the upper levels. A little Virginia creeper that was new and had so far failed to flourish, a rose garden that needed a hoe or a fork taken to it. A window at the side where the glass was scattered and where the sunlight caught the pieces by his feet. He looked away from his house and two more feathers were blown towards him, and … Inevitable that he would see this stranger, what Jonas believed himself to be. Paddy Dickens gave him a yank. Chalky in front and Dickens and Lachy Wilson behind.

There would be a room upstairs that belonged to Julie – and her parents did not know where she was and nor did Jonas Merrick. And another room in a Camden Town block where Agathe – Scotland Yard night cleaner with privileged access – lived and she did not know where Chopper was and nor did Jonas.

They came towards him and behind them was a queue of guys and girls, none of them in uniform and all with caps on and most with armbands, and some had handguns showing, Glocks. Jonas was thinking of the girl and of his boy, and them seeming more important than this moment when Lachy Wilson was paraded past him. He had brought the man down, had done it with his own brand of guile. Should have been one of his proudest moments, and the moment was of emptiness, and his mind echoed because of the void – did not know where the girl and his boy were. A shooting reported . . . He had grimaced in his ignorance and barely noticed that the big man – brought down by Jonas Merrick – was level with him.

Lachy swung on his toes, a fast swivel, a short man with power in his shoulders. All done fast enough to break the loose grip that Dickens had on his arm. Too fast for Jonas to react – and the face was up against his. Then the neck bent back, and Dickens was scrambling to get a hold of him, and Chalky White had the look on his face that said it was not a training run, was *actually happening*, and it was. Jonas stood as if his feet were in setting concrete.

Jonas saw the veins throb in the man's forehead, and heard Victoria shout, 'Do the bastard, Lachy. Do him proper.' Wilson's forehead landed straight on Jonas's nose. Caught it four-square, and it gave, as did Jonas's legs. His spectacles spun off his face, and his eyes were wet, and his lips, and he was tasting the blood that seeped into his mouth, and more came down his nasal passages and dribbled into his throat. And Dickens had a hold on Lachy Wilson and dragged him off, but the man had a grin, faint as a wafer. And Victoria said, 'Well done, Lachy, great hit,' and Jonas wobbled, and could barely see as the gangster was hustled off, and after him came the wife and she was crowing pleasure . . . Had lost their empire, lost their money, lost their daughter, lost their chickens, and this was the moment that mattered to them most.

Jonas was escorted to a garden bench. A glass of water was brought him.

A medic came. Jonas was told that he had to go to A&E, the Royal Surrey in Guildford. His nose was broken, his spectacles would need Sellotape to fasten them, his shirt would require a double dose of washing, and he heard an officer remark that he'd bled like a stuck pig. For a broken nose, the medic said, a doctor might try a splint to straighten it, or do nasal packing, and suggested a bag of frozen peas be applied. He was given a lift down to his car and the caravan. A uniform would drive him to the Royal Surrey. Vera had a number on her phone which found Harry, who drove for the AssDepDG and had a knowledge of Jonas's previous mishaps, and would take a train to Guildford.

Vera said, "They might do worse than put you down . . . Are you claiming that getting beaten up by a manacled man was anything other than pure and selfish indulgence? And staggering incompetence?" He could not answer her because it hurt too much to talk.

The uniform, who was now Vera's best pal, brought tea and a chocolate biscuit, but Jonas could not drink and could not eat. He saw Victoria – handcuffed now – put into a car, and then Softboy, still moaning, shoved behind the grille at the back of a wagon.

The caravan door was open and Olaf in his cage was getting fresh air and sustenance and a police dog snarled at him, and the cat scowled back, stood his corner, as Jonas believed he had stood his. He checked his phone and had no message from Chopper.

He should have felt a pride, but could not find it.

Driven towards London in a police wagon, guns front and behind, and a motorcycle escort, quite the VIP, Lachy Wilson was addressed by a cheekily confident uniform who was handcuffed to him.

"Not much of a future for you, Mr Wilson, because – from what I hear – they'll bang you up and then chuck away the key."

Lachy did not answer but smiled softly, almost kindly, and closed his eyes as if he needed sleep and perhaps to dream of his prized chickens, and the future of a fox, and who would put the poison down and where, and how much it would hurt the vermin before it passed.

At the same time a flight from London Heathrow to Barbados, with the full passenger list aboard, was – without explanation

– held on the apron, and two plainclothes came on board and walked into Business Class, and one spoke to a passenger belted up and ready for take-off.

"Mr Lyons, Mr Henry Lyons . . . Grateful if you could come with us, sir."

His wife was left on board. Flushed crimson with embarrassment, every eye on him, the lawyer was escorted off and taken into a bare room in the airside section of the terminal. Sitting there, with an El Al tag on his hand-baggage and the address of a Tel Aviv hotel was a man he disliked intensely.

Yitzak Cohn said to him, "Another one you've fucked up, Lyons, like everything you touch."

Lyons answered him, "It was because of her, the daughter – the heir to the empire. Should have been drowned at birth . . . but we should be friends. Don't they always say, *Better to hang together than hang separately?*"

"Except, I'll wager Lachy won't be beside us on the gallows. No chance."

A month later (March '26)

Jonas was as reluctant to be there as any matelot on a man of war about to be put over the side and keel-hauled. He stood, bristling, close to the door of the Deputy Director General's office on the fifth floor. He had been escorted up from the basement by his mentor.

The AssDepDG stood beside him and carried a grin of sheer amusement. He still wore his arm in a medical sling and looked thinner and more drawn than before the 'incident' at the hockey match, and flexed his fingers as if to show that he had taken the physiotherapist's demands seriously.

Brian, number two at Thames House and with ambitions, laboured at his laptop as if it were necessary for a man of stature to keep visitors waiting and demonstrate the scale of his workload. He looked up and saw them, and let a glimpse of surprise cross his face.

Brian said, "Just wanted you to know, Jonas, that I am a generous man where praise is due. May not always concur with the methods you employ. Find some of them quite dubious, and better that I don't ferret too far into the tactics you use. But credit where credit is deserved. I was fêted yesterday at Scotland Yard. Quite a gushing welcome, and a very steady drip of gratitude, over a very good buffet and fine wines. Seems you engineered something, Jonas, which they were incapable of achieving. They are in debt to us and we should always call in what we are owed, and I'll be working on that. It will be many years before those pompous clowns try to lord it over us in the Service. This is not a blank cheque for you, Jonas, to break every rule of legitimacy and legality. Far from it, but just this once it has proved acceptable. Well done, Jonas – and I must say I think your nose is looking a tad straighter than I expected. I believe I have emphasised it enough – I don't wish to be bogged down in detail, best I avoid that. I'm grateful, Jonas. Thank you."

He turned on his heel. The DDG would barely have had time to power up the laptop again before Jonas was out of the door.

Good to see the AssDepDG back again, but still nurturing some sick leave, and seeming a bit of a husk compared with what he had been. A question asked as they waited for a lift to come.

"You heard any more about them, the young lovers? Your facilitators?"

The lift came. The button was pressed. Jonas said, "Nothing confirmed. There was a rumour that both were found dead from gunshot wounds in the woodland by the Hoboken suburb. Buried in graves already dug and waiting to be filled. Sort of clandestine because no one wanted the responsibility of taking ownership . . . It was a rumour. Suppose nobody really wanted them . . . A sort of Romeo and Juliet finale. Just a rumour."

Two months later (April '26)

Those who knew Jonas Merrick could always get a one-on-one with him before 08:30 and around 17:00 if they positioned them-selves on Lambeth Bridge and looked out for the jaunty trilby approaching and the spectacles held together with tape, awaiting the new pair, and that regular stride that was more of a struggle each season, and a bent nose, easy to spot.

Chalky White was there. A bright spring morning, a fresh breeze, and a query.

"Hoped I'd meet you, Jonas. Just a little problem, a loose end. How do we remember Chopper Harris? Good guy or an incompetent? Principled enough to bring down Lachy Wilson? Or a freebooter only interested in himself? Was he one of our stars and worth a place on a Roll of Honour, or rather disreputable? Alive or dead, confirmed or not confirmed? And the girl, alive or dead? Help me, Jonas."

He said it was just a rumour, and without proven detail, and the only path to confirmation of its accuracy was to dig up more than a hundred graves in that busy cemetery and exhume all those bodies and take a look at them, run the rule over them, DNA tests. Failing that, sleeping dogs, et cetera, best left alone. He had smiled sweetly and had walked on. Not a day went by without him thinking of Chopper, and wishing he had met the girl, had that chance, and bought him that beer, and . . . Had headed off briskly, and the pain still in his nose to remind him of *Humble Pie*, which had been a good show.

Four months later (June '26)

Going into the café and ordering his cappuccino and Danish pastry, Jonas was annoyed to see two men and a woman eyeing him from the table nearest the door. It was the woman who came forward, said her name was Dawson, Peggy Dawson, and flashed a warrant card at him, and an Asian guy held up another, and the third of them said his name was Plunket. Would he, please, sit with them? A polite request, not a bully's demand.

He sat, oozed suspicion. Was told they were Anti-Corruption Unit, informed them that he had faced the kangaroo crowd in his own building. "We were told where we might find you, not knowing your name or needing to. Wanted to brief you, then to ask one, only one, question. Here goes with the brief: sixteen weeks back, a tonne weight of pure heroin was intercepted at the gates of the Antwerp port and local authorities were happy to claim it, good for their interception statistics, but this has severely damaged the prosecution of Lachlan Wilson, a major organised crime gang leader, long hunted and finally captured and evidence presented against him to Prosecution . . . and a plea bargain was completed a couple of days ago. He will now face minor charges and in return agree to identify, with details, all of the tainted detectives who have protected him for decades. For this squad of the ACU it represents a haul like no other since Operation Countryman half a century ago. We have heard, only heard on the grapevine, that you, sir, now kind enough to sit with us, had known of Kenneth Harris, known as Chopper. We were present in Antwerp when the mayhem took place at a cargo switch. This former Flying Squad officer, and the Wilson daughter, disappeared, but only after a smoke grenade had been detonated and a full handgun magazine was discharged at close range to them. The query: did you, sir, know anything of what had happened to this officer?"

Jonas preened.

In the doorway of the café was his protection – word must have spread that he – the guv'nor, the boss, the legend – had been intercepted by strangers, cops. Kev and Leroy from the armed police detachment guarding Thames House loomed heavy and intimidating in the doorway.

Jonas said, "Had a very vague knowledge of him. Rumours I heard said he was buried, clandestine stuff, and the girl, in the Schoonselhof cemetery . . . But also heard, a very faint whisper, that both were severely wounded and were taken to a clinic run by Roman Catholic nuns somewhere outside Garmisch-Partenkirchen, in Bavaria. And treated there for life-changing injuries. But just rumours. You will, of course, excuse me. I am just a lowly analyst and have hours to complete on my daily shift. Sorry I cannot be of more help."

He was gone, taking his coffee and his pastry. It was a smooth exit because, once he was through the door, the two officers with draped H&K machine pistols and webbing and canisters and vests filled the space and seemed to prevent the visitors from following for the length of time needed for Jonas to be off the pavement, gone . . . A clinic? It had been just a whisper.

Eight months later (October '26)

Another morning, and the trek across the bridge done, and his coffee pleasant and his pastry a treat, and autumn coming fast. The gardener had work to do because a sharp wind loosened the leaves that a frost overnight had further turned. Jonas was in no hurry to be away from St John's where the grass was thin and the stones had evaded a summer scrub to remove lichen. He was pleased to see the gardener, and the reason he lingered was that his screen, up in his cubicle off Aggie Burns's territory, carried little that interested him. She still lit a candle for him, and kept the two frames on her wall – Jonas perched on the armoured car with the triple-legged dog on his lap and celebrating an Albanian triumph, and the blood-stained gilet, provided by Aggie, that should have been worn by a pot-hole officer in Liverpool, where a marksman had saved his life.

Had nothing to hurry back for, and work was not offered him. As if he were placed on a diet – damn near starved. The gardener raked, and shovelled up the leaves and branches and dirt and filled his wheelbarrow, and the songbirds hopped close to Jonas's brogues in search of crumbs, and his coffee was finished. He had news, news after a fashion, and wanted to share it. He would have preferred to have had work that used up a similar energy to what the gardener used, but it had not been dumped on his lap – only this latest news.

"Can you shift your feet, sir."

An instruction, not a question, and Jonas did as he was asked. The birds bounced away a matter of inches but stayed close. He valued the gardener, thought him likely to be the wisest man he knew in terms of morality and advice . . . Did not know his name, nothing except that he was a veteran and suffered from post-traumatic stress disorder, nowadays half the world and their dog seemed to claim it, but this chap had served in Iraq, had killed for his country and also in southern Spain on a Five mission which had further restrained his recovery – had been used, as many were.

"I spoke once to you of an *irregular*."

"Did indeed, sir – keep your feet back, please." Not a leaf left there, and not a crumb.

"A young man with that attitude, an irregular's, which was why I chose him."

"I'm sure you knew what you were doing, sir – and hopefully, he knew why you picked him." The gardener was about to back off, take away his wheelbarrow.

Jonas said, "I think I told you that the assignment seemed to end in a short sharp gun battle, but apparently people – does not matter who they were – carpeted the scene with smoke canisters, blotted out what could be seen. A great number of shots were fired."

"That's what you told me . . . I have a shift to finish, sir."

"And when the smoke cleared there was no sign of him, nor of a girl that mattered to him."

"Well, as you said, he was an irregular, and they tend to be survivors. Did I tell you that, sir?"

"You might have. May I share with you what I've learned? He was quite a naughty boy, not exactly on the straight and narrow."

"What you wanted to recruit, sir. It's a busy time in the garden, sir, autumn and the leaves coming, and bushes needing cutting back. Keep it brief, please, sir."

So, Jonas rather gabbled through what he knew. "There is a little part of eastern Europe where frontiers come together, Romania and Moldova and Ukraine and Poland, and almost up into Germany, and a Romanian newspaper, *Adevarul* – which means Truth, a good title – reported that a *gangsta strain* was at work and flitting between nations while knocking off cash supplies and loads of high-value goods. That is foreign gangster in the local tongue."

"Good while it lasts, sir. What an 'irregular' might see as a useful career move."

"Then the *Wall Street Journal*, fairly reluctant to go sensational, reported the presence of both a gangster *extranjero* and a gangster *extranjera*, male and female, operating as a couple out of the southern area of Paraguay, close to Brazil and Argentina, not far from Uruguay and Bolivia. What they can thieve they do so. They run rings round the local law enforcement, and hop over frontiers. Have weapons, and a bolthole, steal with a certain ruthlessness anything worth taking. Can be violent. Being hunted by a task force, but not yet cornered. And the *Buenos Aires Times* has run a similar report."

"It will not finish well. The boy will try hard not to be taken. Again, sir, shift your feet."

"They have never been identified, let alone photographed, but the reports are doing the rounds . . . Better than being dumped in an unmarked grave or suffering a vegetable existence in a hospital bed, and better than what happened to the Montague lad and the Capulet girl."

"If you say so, sir. Best you believe what you want to believe. I'll be getting on then."

The wheelbarrow squealed as it was pushed away, and new beds of leaves were searched out, and the songbirds scratched for the final crumbs.

Jonas sat for several more minutes. A few leaves landed on his shoulders and lodged on his trilby.

Yes, good advice, excellent advice. Believe what you want to believe.

Before he pushed himself up and made ready to go back to the Post Room, he murmured a few words to himself, to the trees.

"Could all be just another story. If not . . . fly far, dear boy, and fly high, but not too near the sun."

Dear Reader,

We'd love your attention for one more page to tell you about the crisis in children's reading, and what we can all do.

Studies have shown that reading for fun is the **single biggest predictor of a child's future life chances** – more than family circumstance, parents' educational background or income. It improves academic results, mental health, wealth, communication skills, ambition and happiness.[1]

The number of children reading for fun is in rapid decline. Young people have a lot of competition for their time. In 2024, 1 in 10 children and young people in the UK aged 5 to 18 did not own a single book at home.[2]

Hachette works extensively with schools, libraries and literacy charities, but here are some ways we can all raise more readers:

- Reading to children for just 10 minutes a day makes a difference
- Don't give up if children aren't regular readers – there will be books for them!
- Visit bookshops and libraries to get recommendations
- Encourage them to listen to audiobooks
- Support school libraries
- Give books as gifts

There's a lot more information about how to encourage children to read on our website: **www.RaisingReaders.co.uk**

Thank you for reading.

---

[1] OECD, '21st-Century Readers: Developing Literacy Skills in a Digital World', 2021, https://www.oecd.org/en/publications/21st-century-readers_a83d84cb-en.html

[2] National Literacy Trust, 'Book Ownership in 2024', November 2024, https://literacytrust.org.uk/research-services/research-reports/book-ownership-in-2024